P9-DNT-504

forever peace

JOE HALDEMAN

ACE BOOKS, NEW YORK

THE BERKLEY PUBLISHING GROUP
Published by the Penguin Group
Penguin Group (USA) Inc.
375 Hudson Street, New York, New York 10014, USA
Penguin Group (Canada), 90 Eglinton Avenue East, Suite 700, Toronto, Ontario M4P 2Y3, Canada
(a division of Pearson Penguin Canada Inc.)
Penguin Books Ltd., 80 Strand, London WC2R 0RL, England
Penguin Group Ireland, 25 St. Stephen's Green, Dublin 2, Ireland (a division of Penguin Books Ltd.)
Penguin Group (Australia), 250 Camberwell Road, Camberwell, Victoria 3124, Australia
(a division of Pearson Australia Group Pty. Ltd.)
Penguin Books India Pvt. Ltd., 11 Community Centre, Panchsheel Park, New Delhi—110 017, India
Penguin Group (NZ), 67 Apollo Drive, Rosedale, North Shore 0632, New Zealand
(a division of Pearson New Zealand Ltd.)
Penguin Books (South Africa) (Pty.) Ltd., 24 Sturdee Avenue, Rosebank, Johannesburg 2196,
South Africa

Penguin Books Ltd., Registered Offices: 80 Strand, London WC2R 0RL, England

This is a work of fiction. Names, characters, places, and incidents either are the product of the author's imagination or are used fictitiously, and any resemblance to actual persons, living or dead, business establishments, events, or locales is entirely coincidental. The publisher does not have any control over and does not assume any responsibility for author or third-party websites or their content.

FOREVER PEACE

An Ace Book / published by arrangement with the author

PRINTING HISTORY
Ace hardcover edition / October 1997
Ace mass-market edition / October 1998

ISBN: 978-0-441-00566-6

Visit our website at www.penguin.com

ACE
Ace Books are published by The Berkley Publishing Group,
a division of Penguin Group (USA) Inc.,
375 Hudson Street, New York, New York 10014.
ACE and the "A" design are trademarks of Penguin Group (USA) Inc.

PRINTED IN THE UNITED STATES OF AMERICA

25   24   23   22   21

Ace Books by Joe Haldeman

WORLDS APART
DEALING IN FUTURES
FOREVER PEACE
FOREVER FREE
THE COMING
GUARDIAN
CAMOUFLAGE
OLD TWENTIETH
A SEPARATE WAR AND OTHER STORIES
THE ACCIDENTAL TIME MACHINE
MARSBOUND
STARBOUND
EARTHBOUND

Ace Books edited by Joe Haldeman

BODY ARMOR: 2000
NEBULA AWARDS STORIES SEVENTEEN
SPACE FIGHTERS

Ace Books by Joe Haldeman and Jack C. Haldeman II

THERE IS NO DARKNESS

This novel is for two editors: John W. Campbell, who rejected a story because he thought it was absurd to write about American women who fight and die in combat, and Ben Bova, who didn't.

"Man was born into barbarism, when killing his fellow man was a normal condition of existence. He became endowed with a conscience. And he has now reached the day when violence toward another human being must become as abhorrent as eating another's flesh."

—MARTIN LUTHER KING, JR.

Caveat lector: This book is not a continuation of my 1975 novel *The Forever War*. From the author's point of view it is a kind of sequel, though, examining some of that novel's problems from an angle that didn't exist twenty years ago.

forever peace

it was not quite completely dark, thin blue moonlight threading down through the canopy of leaves. And it was never completely quiet.

A thick twig popped, the noise muffled under a heavy mass. A male howler monkey came out of his drowse and looked down. Something moved down there, black on black. He filled his lungs to challenge it.

There was a sound like a piece of newspaper being torn. The monkey's midsection disappeared in a dark spray of blood and shredded organs. The body fell heavily through the branches in two halves.

Would you lay off the goddamn monkeys? Shut up! *This place is an ecological preserve.* My watch, shut up. Target practice.

Black on black it paused, then slipped through the jungle like a heavy silent reptile. A man could be standing two yards away and not see it. In infrared it wasn't there. Radar would slither off its skin.

It smelled human flesh and stopped. The prey maybe thirty meters upwind, a male, rank with old sweat, garlic on his breath. Smell of gun oil and smokeless powder residue. It tested the direction of the wind and back-tracked, circled around. The man would be watching the path. So come in from the woods.

It grabbed the man's neck from behind and pulled his head off like an old blossom. The body shuddered and gurgled and crapped. It eased the body down to the ground and set the head between its legs.

Nice touch. Thanks.

It picked up the man's rifle and bent the barrel into a right angle. It lay the weapon down quietly and stood silent for several minutes.

Then three other shadows came from the woods, and they all converged on a small wooden hut. The walls were beaten-down aluminum cans nailed to planks; the roof was cheap glued plastic.

It pulled the door off and an irrelevant alarm sounded as it switched on a headlight brighter than the sun. Six people on cots, recoiling.

"—Do not resist," it boomed in Spanish. "—You are prisoners of war and will be treated according to the terms of the Geneva Convention."

"Mierda." A man scooped up a shaped charge and threw it at the light. The tearing-paper sound was softer than the sound of the man's body bursting. A split second later, it swatted the bomb like an insect and the explosion blew down the front wall of the building and flattened all the occupants with concussion.

The black figure considered its left hand. Only the thumb and first finger worked, and the wrist made a noise when it rotated.

Good reflexes. Oh, shut up.

The other three shapes turned on sunlights and pulled off the building's roof and knocked down the remaining walls.

The people inside looked dead, bloody and still. The machines began to check them, though, and a young woman suddenly rolled over and raised the laser rifle she'd been concealing. She aimed it at the one with the broken hand and did manage to raise a puff of smoke from its chest before she was shredded.

The one checking the bodies hadn't even looked up. "No good," it said. "All dead. No tunnels. No exotic weapons I can find."

"Well, we got some stuff for Unit Eight." They turned off their lights and sped off simultaneously, in four different directions.

The one with the bad hand moved about a quarter-mile and stopped to inspect the damage with a dim infrared light. It beat the hand against its side a few times. Still, only the two digits worked.

Wonderful. We'll have to bring it in.

So what would you have done?

Who's complaining? I'll spend part of my ten in base camp.

The four of them took four different routes to the top of a treeless hill. They stood in a row for a few seconds, arms upraised, and a cargo helicopter came in at treetop level and snatched them away.

Who got the second kill there? thought the one with the broken hand.

A voice appeared in all four heads. "Berryman initiated the response. But Hogarth commenced firing before the victim was unambiguously dead. So by the rules, they share the kill."

The helicopter with the four soldierboys dangling slipped down the hill and screamed through the night at treetop level, in total darkness, east toward friendly Panama.

i didn't like scoville having the soldierboy before me. You have to monitor the previous mechanic for twenty-four hours before you take it over, to warm up and become sensitive to how the soldierboy might have changed since your last shift. Like losing the use of three fingers.

When you're in the warm-up seat you're just watching; you're not jacked into the rest of the platoon, which would be hopelessly confusing. We go in strict rotation, so the other nine soldierboys in the platoon also have replacements breathing over their mechanics' shoulders.

You hear about emergencies, where the replacement has to suddenly take over from the mechanic. It's easy to believe. The last day would be the worst even without the added stress of being watched. If you're going to crack or have a heart attack or stroke, it's usually on the tenth day.

Mechanics aren't in any physical danger, deep inside the Operations bunker in Portobello. But our death and disability rate is higher than the regular infantry. It's not bullets that get us, though; it's our own brains and veins.

It would be rough for me or any of my mechanics to replace people in Scoville's platoon, though. They're a hunter/killer group, and we're "harassment and interdiction," H & I; sometimes loaned to Psychops. We don't often kill. We aren't selected for that aptitude.

All ten of our soldierboys came into the garage within a couple of minutes. The mechanics jacked out and the exoskeleton shells eased open. Scoville's people climbed out like little old men and women, even though their bodies had been exercised constantly and adjusted for fatigue poisons. You still couldn't help feeling as if you'd been sitting in the same place for nine days.

I jacked out. My connection with Scoville was a light one, not at all like the near-telepathy that links the ten mechanics in the platoon. Still, it was disorienting to have my own brain to myself.

We were in a large white room with ten of the mechanic shells and ten warm-up seats, like fancy barber chairs. Behind them, the wall was a huge backlit map

of Costa Rica, showing with lights of various colors
where soldierboy and flyboy units were working. The
other walls were covered with monitors and digital read-
outs with jargon labels. People in white fatigues walked
around checking the numbers.

Scoville stretched and yawned and walked over to me.

"Sorry you thought that last bit of violence was unnecessary. I felt the situation called for direct action."
God, Scoville and his academic airs. Doctorate in Lei-
sure Arts.

"You usually do. If you'd warned them from outside,
they would've had time to assess the situation. Surrender."

"Yes indeed. As they did in Ascensión."

"That was one time." We'd lost ten soldierboys and
a flyboy to a nuclear booby trap.

"Well, the second time won't be on my watch. Six
fewer pedros in the world." He shrugged. "I'll go light
a candle."

"Ten minutes to calibration," a loudspeaker said.
Hardly enough time for the shell to cool down. I followed Scoville into the locker room. He went to one end
to get into his civvies; I went to the other end to join
my platoon.

Sara was already mostly undressed. "Julian. You
want to do me?"

Yes, like most of our males and one female, I *did,* as
she well knew, but that's not what she meant. She took
off her wig and handed me the razor. She had three
weeks' worth of fine blond stubble. I gently shaved off
the area surrounding the input at the base of her skull.

"That last one was pretty brutal," she said. "Scoville
needed the body count, I guess."

"It occurred to him. He's eleven short of making E-
8. Good thing they didn't come across an orphanage."

"He'd be bucking for captain," she said.

I finished her and she checked mine, rubbing her

thumb around the jack. "Smooth," she said. I keep my head shaved off duty, though it's unfashionable for black men on campus. I don't mind long bushy hair, but I don't like it well enough to run around all day wearing a hot wig.

Louis came over. "Hi, Julian. Give me a buzz, Sara." She reached up—he was six feet four and Sara was small—and he winced when she turned on the razor.

"Let me see that," I said. His skin was slightly inflamed on one side of the implant. "Lou, that's going to be trouble. You should've shaved before the warm-up."

"Maybe. You gotta choose." Once you were in the cage you were there for nine days. Mechanics with fast-growing hair and sensitive skin, like Sara and Lou, usually shaved once, between warm-up and the shift. "It's not the first time," he said. "I'll get some cream from the medics."

Bravo platoon got along pretty well. That was partly a matter of chance, since we were selected out of the pool of appropriate draftees by body size and shape, to fit the platoon's cages and the aptitude profile for H & I. Five of us were survivors of the original draft pick: Candi and Mel as well as Lou, Sara, and me. We've been doing this for four years, working ten days on and twenty off. It seems like a lot longer.

Candi is a grief counselor in real life; the rest of us are academics of some stripe. Lou and I are science, Sara is American politics, and Mel is a cook. "Food science," so called, but a hell of a cook. We get together a few times a year for a banquet at his place in St. Louis.

We went together back to the cage area. "Okay, listen up," the loudspeaker said. "We have damage on Units One and Seven, so we won't calibrate the left hand and right leg at this time."

"So we need the cocksuckers?" Lou asked.

"No, the drains will not be installed. If you can hold it for forty-five minutes."

"I'll certainly try, sir."

"We'll do the partial calibration and then you're free for ninety minutes, maybe two hours, while we set up the new hand and leg modules for Julian and Candi's machines. Then we'll finish the calibration and hook up the orthotics, and you're off to the staging area."

"Be still my heart," Sara murmured.

We lay down in the cages, working arms and legs into stiff sleeves, and the techs jacked us in. For the calibration we were tuned down to about ten percent of a combat jack, so I didn't hear actual words from anybody but Lou—a "hello there" that was like a faint shout from a mile away. I focused my mind and shouted back.

The calibration was almost automatic for those of us who'd been doing it for years, but we did have to stop and back up twice for Ralph, a neo who'd joined us two cycles ago when Richard stroked out. It was just a matter of all ten of us squeezing one muscle group at a time, until the red thermometer matched the blue thermometer on the heads-up. But until you're used to it, you tend to squeeze too hard and overshoot.

After an hour they opened the cage and unjacked us. We could kill ninety minutes in the lounge. It was hardly worth wasting time getting dressed, but we did. It was a gesture. We were about to live in each other's bodies for nine days, and enough was enough.

Familiarity breeds, as they say. Some mechanics become lovers, and sometimes it works. I tried it with Carolyn, who died three years ago, but we could never bridge the gap between being combat-jacked and being civilians. We tried to work it out with a relator, but the relator had never been jacked, so we might as well have been talking Sanskrit.

I don't know that it would be "love" with Sara, but it's academic. She's not really attracted to me, and of course can't hide her feelings, or lack of same. In a physical way we're closer than any civilian pair could be, since in full combat jack we are this one creature with twenty arms and legs, with ten brains, with five vaginas and five penises.

Some people call the feeling godlike, and I think there have been gods who were constructed along similar lines. The one I grew up with was an old white-bearded Caucasian gent without even one vagina.

We'd already studied the order of battle, of course, and our specific orders for the nine days. We were going to continue in Scoville's area, but doing H & I, making things difficult in the cloud forest of Costa Rica. It was not a particularly dangerous assignment, but it was distasteful, like bullying, since the rebels didn't have anything remotely like soldierboys.

Ralph expressed his discomfort. We had sat down at the dining table with tea and coffee.

"This overkill gets to me," he said. "That pair in the tree last time."

"Ugly," Sara said.

"Ah, the bastards killed themselves," Mel said. He sipped the coffee and scowled at it. "We probably wouldn't have noticed them if they hadn't opened up on us."

"It bothers you that they were children?" I asked Ralph.

"Well, yeah. Doesn't it you?" He rubbed the stubble on his chin. "Little girls."

"Little girls with machine guns," Karen said, and Claude nodded emphatically. They'd come in together about a year ago, and were lovers.

"I've been thinking about that, too," I said. "What if we'd known they were little girls?" They'd been about ten years old, hiding in a tree house.

"Before or after they started shooting?" Mel asked.

"Even after," Candi said. "How much damage can they do with a machine gun?"

"They damaged *me* pretty effectively!" Mel said. He'd lost one eye and the olfactory receptors. "They knew exactly what to aim for."

"It wasn't a big deal," Candi said. "You got field replacements."

"Felt like a big deal to me."

"I know. I was there." You don't exactly feel pain when a sensor goes out. It's something as strong as pain, but there's no word for it.

"I don't think we would've had to kill them if they were out in the open," Claude said. "If we could see they were just kids and lightly armed. But hell, for all we knew they were FOs who could call in a tac nuke."

"In Costa Rica?" Candi said.

"It happens," Karen said. It had happened once in three years. Nobody knew where the rebels had gotten the nuke. It had cost them two towns, the one the sol- dierboys were in when they were vaporized, and the one we took apart in retaliation.

"Yeah, yeah," Candi said, and I could hear in those two words all she wasn't saying: that a nuke on our position would just destroy ten machines. When Mel flamed the tree house he roasted two little girls, probably too young to know what they were doing.

There was always an undercurrent in Candi's mind, when we were jacked. She was a good mechanic, but you had to wonder why she hadn't been given some other assignment. She was too empathetic, sure to crack before her term was up.

But maybe she was in the platoon to act as our col- lective conscience. Nobody at our level knew why any- body was chosen to be a mechanic, and we only had a vague idea why we were assigned to the platoon we got. We seemed to cover a wide range of aggressiveness, from Candi to Mel. We didn't have anybody like Scoville, though. Nobody who got that dark pleasure out of killing. Scoville's platoon always saw more action than mine, too; no coincidence. Hunter/killers—they're definitely more congenial with mayhem. So when the Great Computer in the Sky decides who gets what mission, Scoville's platoon gets the kills and ours gets reconnaissance.

Mel and Claude, especially, grumbled about that. A confirmed kill was an automatic point toward promotion, in pay grade if not in rank, whereas you couldn't count on the PPR—Periodic Performance Review—for a dime. Scoville's people got the kills, so they averaged about twenty-five percent higher pay than my people. But what could you spend it on? Save it up and buy our way out of the army?

"So we're gonna do trucks," Mel said. "Cars and trucks."

"That's the word," I said. "Maybe a tank if you hold your mouth right." Satellites had picked up some IR traces that probably meant the rebels were being resupplied by small stealthed trucks, probably robotic or remote. One of those outbursts of technology that kept the war from being a totally one-sided massacre.

I suppose if the war went on long enough, the enemy might have soldierboys, too. Then we could have the ultimate in something: ten-million-dollar machines reducing each other to junk while their operators sat hundreds of miles away, concentrating in air-conditioned caves.

People had written about that, warfare based on attrition of wealth rather than loss of life. But it's always been easier to make new lives than new wealth. And economic battles have long-established venues, some political and some not, as often among allies as not.

Well, what does a physicist know about it? My science has rules and laws that seem to correspond to reality. Economics describes reality after the fact, but isn't

too good at predicting. Nobody predicted the nanoforges.

The loudspeaker told us to saddle up. Nine days of
truck-stalking.

all ten people in Julian Class's platoon had the
same basic weapon—the soldierboy, or Remote Infantry
Combat Unit: a huge suit of armor with a ghost in it.
For all the weight of its armor, more than half of the
RICU's mass was ammunition. It could fire accurate
sniper rounds to the horizon, two ounces of depleted
uranium, or at close range it could hose a stream of
supersonic flechettes. It had high explosive and incen-
diary rockets with eyes, a fully automatic grenade
launcher, and a high-powered laser. Special units could
be fitted with chemical, biological, or nuclear weapons,
but those were only used for reprisal in kind.

(Fewer than a dozen nuclear weapons, small ones, had
been used in twelve years of war. A large one had destroyed Atlanta, and although the Ngumi denied responsibility, the Alliance responded by giving twenty-four
hours notice, and then leveling Mandellaville and Sao
Paulo. Ngumi contended that the Alliance had cynically
sacrificed one nonstrategic city so it could have an excuse to destroy two important ones. Julian suspected
they might be right.)

There were air and naval units, too, inevitably called
flyboys and sailorboys, even though most flyboys were
piloted by females.

All of Julian's platoon had the same armor and weapons, but some had specialized functions. Julian, being
platoon leader, communicated directly and (in theory)
constantly with the company coordinator, and through
her to the brigade command. In the field, he received
constant input in the form of encrypted signals from fly-

over satellites as well as the command station in geo-
synchronous orbit. Every order came from two sources
simultaneously, with different encryption and a different transmission lag, so it would be almost impossible
for the enemy to slip in a bogus command.

Ralph had a "horizontal" link similar to Julian's
"vertical" one. As platoon liaison, he was in touch with
his opposite number in each of the other nine platoons
that made up Bravo. They were "lightly jacked"—the
communication wasn't as intimate as he had with other
members of the platoon, but it was more than just a radio
link. He could advise Julian as to the other platoons'
actions and even feelings, morale, in a quick and direct
way. It was rare for all the platoons to be engaged in a
single action, but when they were, the situation was chaotic and confusing. The platoon liaisons then were as
important as the vertical command links.

One soldierboy platoon could do as much damage as
a brigade of regular infantry. They did it quicker and
more dramatically, like huge invincible robots moving
in silent concert.

They didn't use actual armed robots, for several reasons. One was that they could be captured and used
against you; if the enemy could capture a soldierboy
they would just have an expensive piece of junk. None
had ever been captured intact, though; they self-destruct
impressively.

Another problem with robots was autonomy: the machine has to be able to function on its own if communications are cut off. The image, as well as the reality,
of a heavily armed machine making spot combat decisions was not something any army wanted to deal with.
(Soldierboys had limited autonomy, in case their mechanics died or passed out. They stopped firing and went
for shelter while a new mechanic was warmed up and
jacked.)

The soldierboys were arguably more effective psychological weapons than robots would be. They were like all-powerful knights, heroes. And they represented a technology that was out of the enemy's grasp.

The enemy did use armed robots, like, as it turned out, the two tanks that were guarding the convoy of trucks that Julian's platoon was sent to destroy. Neither of the tanks caused any trouble. In both cases they were destroyed as soon as they revealed their position by firing. Twenty-four robot trucks were destroyed, too, after their cargos had been examined: ammunition and medical supplies.

After the last truck had been reduced to shiny slag, the platoon still had four days left on its shift, so they were flown back to the Portobello base camp, to do picket duty. That could be pretty dangerous, since the base camp was hit by rockets a couple of times a year, but most of the time it was no challenge. Not boring, though—the mechanics were protecting their own lives, for a change.

sometimes it took me a couple of days to wind down and be ready to be a civilian again. There were plenty of joints in Portobello willing to help ease the transition. I usually did my unwinding back in Houston, though. It was easy for rebels to slip across the border and pass as Panamanians, and if you got tagged as a mechanic you were a prime target. Of course there were plenty of other Americans and Europeans in Portobello, but it's possible that mechanics stood out: pale and twitchy, collars pulled up to hide the skull jacks, or wigs.

We lost one that way last month. Arly went into town for a meal and a movie. Some thugs pulled off her wig, and she was hauled into an alley and beaten to a pulp and raped. She didn't die but she didn't recover, either. They had pounded the back of her head against a wall until the skull fractured and the jack came out. They shoved the jack into her vagina and left her for dead.

So the platoon was one short this month. (The neo Personnel delivered couldn't fit Arly's cage, which was not surprising.) We may be short two next month: Samantha, who is Arly's best friend, and a little bit more, was hardly there this week. Brooding, distracted, slow. If we'd been in actual combat she might have snapped out of it; both of them were pretty good soldiers—better than me, in terms of actually liking the work—but picket duty gave her too much time to meditate, and the truck assignment before that was a silly exercise a flyboy could have done on her way back from something else.

We all tried to give Samantha support while we were jacked, but it was awkward. Of course she and Arly couldn't hide their physical attraction for one another, but they were both conventional enough to be embarrassed about it (they had boyfriends on the outside), and had encouraged kidding as a way of keeping the complex relationship manageable. There was no banter now, of course.

Samantha had spent the past three weeks visiting Arly every day at the convalescent center, where the bones of her face were growing back, but that was a constant frustration, since the nature of her injuries meant they couldn't be jacked, couldn't be close. Never. And it was Samantha's nature to want revenge, but that was impossible now. The five rebels involved had been apprehended immediately, slid through the legal system, and were hanged a week later in the public square.

I'd seen it on the cube. They weren't hanged so much as slowly strangled. This in a country that hadn't used capital punishment in generations, before the war.

Maybe after the war we'll be civilized again. That's the way it has always happened in the past.

julian usually went straight home to Houston, but not when his ten days were up on a Friday. That was the day of the week when he had to be the most social, and he needed at least a day of preparation for that. Every day you spent jacked, you felt closer to the other nine mechanics. There was a terrible sense of separation when you unjacked, and hanging around with the others didn't help. What you needed was a day or so of isolation, in the woods or in a crowd.

Julian was not the outdoor type, and he usually just buried himself in the university library for a day. But not if it was Friday.

He could fly anywhere for free, so on impulse he went up to Cambridge, Massachusetts, where he'd done his undergraduate work. It was a bad choice, dirty slush everywhere and thin sleet falling in a constant sting, but he grimly persisted in his quest to visit every bar he could remember. They were full of inexplicably young and callow people.

Harvard was still Harvard; the dome still leaked. People made a point of not staring at a black man in uniform.

He walked a mile through the sleet to his favorite pub, the ancient Plough and Stars, but it was padlocked, with a card saying BAHAMA! taped inside the window. So he squished back to the Square on frozen feet, promising simultaneously to get drunk and not lose his temper.

There was a bar named after John Harvard, where they brewed nine kinds of beer on the premises. He had a pint of each one, methodically checking them off on the blotter, and flowed into a cab that decanted him at the airport. After six hours of off-and-on slumber, he flew his hangover back to Houston Sunday morning, following the sunrise across the country.

Back at his apartment he made a pot of coffee and attacked the accumulated mail and memos. Most of it was throwaway junk. Interesting letter from his father, vacationing in Montana with his new wife, not Julian's favorite person. His mother had called twice about a money problem, but then called again to say never mind. Both brothers called about the hanging; they followed Julian's "career" closely enough to realize that the woman who'd been attacked was in his platoon.

His actual career had generated the usual soft sifting pink snowfall of irrelevant interdepartmental memos, which he did have to at least scan. He studied the minutes of the monthly faculty meeting, just in case something real had been discussed. He always missed it, since he was on duty from the tenth to the nineteenth of every month. The only way that might have hurt his career would be jealousy from other faculty members.

And then there was a hand-delivered envelope, a small square under the memos, addressed "J." He saw a corner of it and pulled it out, pink slips fluttering, and ripped open the flap, over which a red flame had been rubber-stamped: it was from Blaze, who Julian was allowed to call by her real name, Amelia. She was his coworker, ex-adviser, confidante, and sexual companion. He didn't say "lover" in his mind, yet, because that was awkward, Amelia being fifteen years older than him. Younger than his father's new wife.

The note had some chat about the Jupiter Project, the particle-physics experiment they were engaged in, including a bit of scandalous gossip about their boss, which did not alone explain the sealed envelope. "Whatever time you get back," she wrote, "come straight over. Wake me up or pull me out of the lab. I need my little boy in the worst way. You want to come over and find out what the worst way is?"

Actually, what he'd had in mind was sleeping for a few hours. But he could do that afterward. He stacked the mail into three piles and dropped one pile into the recycler. He started to call her but then put the phone down unpunched. He dressed for the morning cool and went downstairs for his bicycle.

The campus was deserted and beautiful, redbuds and azaleas in bloom under the hard blue Texas sky. He pedaled slowly, relaxing back into real life, or comfortable illusion. The more time he spent jacked, the harder it was to accept this peaceful, monocular view of life as the real one. Rather than the beast with twenty arms; the god with ten hearts.

At least he wasn't menstruating anymore.

He let himself into her place with his thumbprint. Amelia was actually up at nine this Sunday morning, in the shower. He decided against surprising her there. Showers were dangerous places—he had slipped in one once, experimenting with a fellow clumsy teenager, and had wound up with a cut chin and bruises and a decidedly unerotic attitude toward the location (and the girl, for that matter).

So he just sat up in her bed, quietly reading the newspaper, and waited for the water to stop. She sang bits of tunes, happy, and switched the shower from fine spray to coarse pulse and back. Julian could visualize her there and almost changed his mind. But he stayed on the bed, fully clothed, pretending to read.

She came out toweling and started slightly when she saw Julian; then recovered: "Help! There's a strange man in my bed!"

"I thought you liked strange men."

"Only one." She laughed and eased alongside him, hot and damp.

all of us mechanics talk about sex. Being jacked automatically accomplishes two things that normal people pursue through sex, and sometimes love: emotional union with another and the penetration, so to speak, of

the physical mysteries of the opposite sex. These things
are automatic and instantaneous, jacked, as soon as they
turn on the power. When you unjack, it's a mystery you
all have in common, and you talk about that as much as
anything.

Amelia's the only civilian I've talked about it with at
any length. She's intensely curious about it, and would
take the chance if it were possible. But she would lose
her position, and maybe a lot more.

Eight or nine percent of the people who go through
the installation either die on the operating table or,
worse, come out of it with their brains not working at
all. Even those of us who come out successfully jacked
face an increase in the frequency of cerebrovascular incidents, including fatal stroke. For mechanics in soldierboys, the increase is tenfold.

So Amelia could get jacked—she has the money and
could just slip down to Mexico City or Guadalajara and
have it done at one of the clinics there—but she would
automatically lose her position: tenure, retirement,
everything. Most job contracts had a "jack" clause; all
academic ones did. People like me were exempt because
we didn't do it voluntarily, and it was against the law
to discriminate against people in National Service. Amelia's too old to be drafted.

When we make love I sometimes have felt her stroking the cold metal disk at the base of my skull, as if she
were trying to get in. I don't think she's aware of doing
it.

Amelia and I had been close for many years; even
when she was my Ph.D. adviser, we had a social life
together. But it didn't become physical until after Carolyn died.

Carolyn and I were first jacked at the same time;
joined the platoon on the same day. It was an instant
emotional connection, even though we had almost nothing in common. We were both black Southerners (Ame-

lia's pale Boston Irish) and in graduate school. But she was no intellectual; her MFA was going to be in Creative Viewing. I never watched the cube and she wouldn't know a differential equation if it had reared up and bit her on the butt. So we had no rapport at that level, but that wasn't important.

We'd been physically attracted to each other during training, the shoe stuff you go through before they put you in a soldierboy, and had managed to sneak a few minutes of privacy, three times, for hasty sex, desperately passionate. Even for normal people, that would have been an intense beginning. But then when we were jacked it was something way beyond anything either of us had ever experienced. It was as if life were a big simple puzzle, and we suddenly had a piece dropped in that nobody else could see.

But we couldn't put it together when we weren't jacked. We had a lot of sex, a lot of talks, went to relators and counselors—but it was like we were one thing in the cage and quite another, or two others, outside.

I talked to Amelia about it at the time, not only because we were friends, but because we were on the same project and she could see my work was starting to suffer. I couldn't get Carolyn off my mind, in a very literal way.

It was never resolved. Carolyn died in a sudden brain blowout when we weren't doing anything particularly stressful, just waiting for a pickup after an uneventful mission.

I had to be hospitalized for a week; in a way, it was even worse than just losing someone you loved. It was like that plus losing a limb, losing part of your brain.

Amelia held my hand that week, and we were holding each other soon enough.

I don't usually fall asleep right after making love, but this time I did, after the weekend of dissipation and the sleepless hours on the plane—you'd think a person who spent a third of his life as part of a machine would be comfortable traveling inside another one, but no. I have to stay awake to keep the damned thing in the air.

The smell of onions woke me up. Brunch, lunch, whatever. Amelia has a thing about potatoes; her Irish blood, I suppose. She was frying up a pan with onions and garlic. Not my favorite wake-up call, but for her it was lunch. She told me she'd gotten up at three to log on and work out a decay sequence that turned out to be nothing. So her reward for working on Sunday was a shower, a somewhat awake lover, and fried potatoes.

I located my shirt but couldn't find my pants, and settled on one of her nightgowns, not too pretty. We were the same size.

I found my blue toothbrush in her bathroom and used her weird clove-flavored toothpaste. Decided against a shower because my stomach was growling. It wasn't grits and gravy, but it wasn't poison.

"Good morning, bright eyes." No wonder I couldn't find my pants. She was wearing them.

"Have you gone completely strange?" I said.

"Just an experiment." She stepped over and held me by both shoulders. "You look stunning. Absolutely gorgeous."

"What experiment? See what I would wear?"

"See *whether*." She stepped out of my jeans and handed them over, and walked back to her potatoes wearing only a T-shirt. "I mean, really. Your generation is so prudish."

"Oh, are we?" I slipped off the gown and came up behind her. "Come on. I'll show you prudish."

"That doesn't count." She half-turned and kissed me. "The experiment was about clothes, not sex. Sit down before one of us gets burned."

I sat down at the dinette and looked at her back. She stirred the food slowly. "I'm not sure why I did that, really. Impulse. Couldn't sleep but didn't want to wake you up, going through the closet. I stepped on your jeans getting out of bed and I just put them on.''

"Don't explain. I want it to be a big perverse mystery.''

"If you want coffee you know where it is." She had a pot of tea brewed. I almost asked for a cup. But to keep the morning from being too full of mystery, I stuck with coffee.

"So Macro's getting a divorce?" Dr. "Mac" Roman was dean of research and titular head of our project, though he wasn't involved in the day-to-day work.

"Deep dark secret. He hasn't told anybody. My friend Nel passed it on." Nel Nye was a schoolmate who worked for the city.

"And they were such a lovely couple together." She laughed one "ha," stabbing at the potatoes with the spatula. "Was it another woman, man, robot?"

"They don't put that on the form. They're splitting this week, though, and I have to meet with him tomorrow before we go to Budget. He'll be even more distracted than usual." She divided the potatoes between two plates and brought them over. "So you were out blowing up trucks?"

"Actually, I was lying in a cage, twitching." She dismissed that with a wave. "There wasn't much to it. No drivers or passengers. Two saps.''

"Sapients?"

" 'Sapient defense units,' yeah, but that puts a pretty low threshold on sapience. They're just guns on tracks with AI routines that give them a certain degree of autonomy. Pretty effective against ground troops and conventional artillery and air support. Don't know what they were doing in our AO.''

"Is that a blood type?" she said over her teacup.

"Sorry. 'Area of operations.' I mean, one flyboy could have taken them out in a single treetop pass.''

"So why didn't they use a flyboy? Rather than risk

damaging your expensive armored carcass.''

"Oh, they said they wanted the cargo analyzed, which was bullshit. The only stuff besides food and ammo were some solar cells and replacement boards for field mainframes. So we know they use Mitsubishi. But if they buy anything from a Rimcorp firm, we automatically get copies of the invoices. So I'm sure that was no big surprise.''

"So why'd they send you?''

"Nobody said officially, but I got a thread on my vertical jack that they were feeling out Sam, Samantha.''

"She's the one who, her friend?''

"Got beaten up and raped, yeah. She didn't do too well.''

"Who would?''

"I don't know. Sam's pretty tough. But she wasn't even half there.''

"That would go rough on her? If she got a psychiatric discharge.''

"They don't like to give them, unless there's actual brain damage. They'd either 'find' that or put her through an Article 12.'' I got up to find some catsup for my potatoes. "That might not be as bad as rumor has it. Nobody in our company has gone through it.''

"I thought there was a congressional investigation of that. Somebody with important parents died.''

"Yeah, there was talk. I don't know that it got any further than talk. Article 12 has to be a wall you can't climb. Otherwise half the mechanics in the army would try for a psych discharge.''

"They don't want to make it that easy.''

"So I used to think. Now I think part of it is keeping a balanced force. If you made an Article 12 easy, you'd lose everyone bothered by killing. The soldierboys would wind up a berserker corps.''

"That's a pretty picture.''

"You should see what it looks like from inside. I told you about Scoville."

"A few times."

"Imagine him times twenty thousand." People like Scoville are completely disassociated from killing, especially with the soldierboys. You find them in regular armies, too, though—people for whom enemy soldiers aren't human, just counters in a game. They're ideal for some missions and disastrous for others.

I had to admit the potatoes were pretty good. I'd been living on bar food for a couple of days, cheese and fried meats, with corn chips for a vegetable.

"Oh . . . you didn't get on the cube this time." She had her cube monitor the war channels and keep any sequences where my unit appeared. "So I was pretty sure you were having a safe, boring time."

"So shall we find something exciting to do?"

"You go find something." She picked up the plates and carried them to the sink. "I have to go back to the lab for half a day."

"Something I could help you with?"

"Wouldn't speed it up. It's just some data formatting for a Jupiter Project update." She sorted the plates into the dishwasher. "Why don't you catch up on your sleep and we'll do something tonight."

That sounded good to me. I switched the phone over, in case somebody wanted to bother me on Sunday morning, and returned to her rumpled bed.

the jupiter project was the largest particle accelerator ever built, by several orders of magnitude.

Particle accelerators cost money—the faster the particle, the more it costs—and the history of particle physics is at least partly a history of how important really fast particles have been to various sponsoring governments.

Of course, the whole idea of money had changed with the nanoforges. And that changed the pursuit of "Big Science."

The Jupiter Project was the result of several years' arguing and wheedling, which resulted in the Alliance sponsoring a flight to Jupiter. The Jupiter probe dropped a programmed nanoforge into its dense atmosphere, and deposited another one on the surface of Io. The two machines worked in concert, the Jupiter one sucking up deuterium for warm fusion and beaming the power to the one on Io, which manufactured elements for a particle accelerator that would ring the planet in Io's orbit and concentrate power from Jupiter's gargantuan magnetic field.

Prior to the Jupiter Project, the biggest "supercollider" had been the Johnson Ring that circled several hundred miles beneath Texas wasteland. This one would be ten thousand times as long and a hundred thousand times as powerful.

The nanoforge actually built other nanoforges, but ones that could only be used for the purpose of making the elements of the orbiting particle accelerator. So the thing did grow at an exponential rate, the busy machines chewing up the blasted surface of Io and spitting it out into space, forming a ring of uniform elements.

What used to cost money now cost time. The researchers on Earth waited while ten, a hundred, a thousand elements were chucked into orbit. After six years there were five thousand of them, enough to start firing up the huge machine.

Time was involved in another way, a theoretical measure. It had to do with the beginning of the universe— the beginning of time. One instant after the Diaspora (once called the Big Bang), the universe was a small cloud of highly energetic particles swarming outward at close to the speed of light. An instant later, they were a different swarm, and so on out to a whole second, ten seconds, and so on. The more energy you pumped into a particle accelerator, the closer you could come to duplicating the conditions that obtained soon after the Diaspora, the beginning of time.

For more than a century there had been a back-and-forth dialogue between the particle physicists and the cosmologists. The cosmologists would scribble their equations, trying to figure out which particles were flitting around at what time in the universe's development, and their results would suggest an experiment. So the physicists would fire up their accelerators and either verify the cosmologists' equations or send them back to the blackboard.

The reverse process also happens. One thing most of us agree on is that the universe exists (people who deny that usually follow some trade other than science), so if some theoretical particle interaction would lead ultimately to the nonexistence of the universe, then you can save a lot of electricity by not trying to demonstrate it.

Thus it went, back and forth, up to the time of the Jupiter Project. The Johnson Ring had been able to take us back to conditions that were obtained when the universe was one tenth of a second old. By that time, it was about four times the size the Earth is now, having expanded from a dimensionless point at a great rate of speed.

The Jupiter Project, if it worked, would take us back to a time when the universe was smaller than a pea, and filled with exotic particles that no longer exist. But it would be the biggest machine ever built, by several orders of magnitude, and it was being built by automatic robots with no direct supervision. When the Jupiter group sent an order out to Io, it would get there fifteen to twenty-four minutes later, and of course the response would be delayed by an equal length of time. A lot can happen in forty-eight minutes; twice, the Project had to be halted and reprogrammed—but you couldn't really "halt" it, not all at once, because the submachines that were making the parts that would go into orbit just kept on going for forty-eight minutes plus however long it took to figure out how to reprogram them.

Over the Jupiter Program director's desk, there was a picture from a movie over a century old: Mickey Mouse as the Sorcerer's Apprentice, staring dumbfounded at the endless line of brainless brooms marching through the door.

i slept a couple of hours and woke up suddenly, in a panic sweat. I couldn't remember what I'd been dreaming about, but it left me with a fading sense of vertigo, falling. It had happened a few times before, the first day or two off duty.

Some people wound up never getting any deep sleep unless they were jacked. Sleeping that way gave you total blackness, total lack of sensation or thought. Practicing up for death. But relaxing.

I lay there staring into the watery light for another half hour and decided to stop trying. Went into the kitchen and buzzed up some coffee. Really ought to work, but I wouldn't have any papers until Tuesday, and Research could wait until tomorrow morning's meeting.

Catch up on the world. I'd resolutely stayed away from it in Cambridge. I turned on Amelia's desk and decrypted a thread to my news module.

It humors me and puts the light stuff first. I read through twenty pages of comics and the three columns I knew to be safely immune from politics. One of them did a broad satire about Central America anyhow.

Central and South America took up most of the world news section, unsurprisingly. The African front was quiet, still stunned a year after our nuking of Mandela-ville. Perhaps regrouping and calculating which of our cities would be next.

Our little sortie wasn't even mentioned. Two platoons of soldierboys took the towns of Piedra Sola and Igatimi, in Uruguay and Paraguay; supposedly rebel strongholds. We did it with their governments' foreknowledge and permission, of course—and there were no civilian casualties, equally of course. Once they're dead they're rebels. *"La muerte es el gran convertidor,"* they say—"Death is the great converter." That must be literally true as well as a sarcasm about our body counts. We've killed a quarter-million in the Americas and God knows how many in Africa. If I lived in either place I'd be a "rebel."

There was a business-as-usual running report about the Geneva talks. The enemy is so fragmented they will never come together on terms, and I'm sure at least some of the rebel leaders are plants, puppets ordered to keep the thing good and confused.

They did actually come to agreement over nuclear weapons: neither side would use them except in retaliation, starting now, though Ngumi still won't take responsibility for Atlanta. What we really need is an agreement on agreements: "If we promise something, we won't break the promise for at least thirty days." Neither side would agree to that.

I turned off the machine and checked Amelia's refrigerator. No beer. Well, that was my responsibility. Some fresh air wouldn't hurt, anyhow, so I locked up and pedaled toward the campus gate.

The shoe sergeant in charge of security looked at my ID and made me wait while he phoned for verification. The two privates with him leaned on their weapons and smirked. Some shoes have a thing about mechanics, since we don't "actually" fight. Forget that we have to stay in longer and have a higher death rate. Forget that we keep them from having to do the really dangerous jobs.

Of course, that's exactly it for some of them: we also stand in the way of their being heroes. "It takes all kinds of people to make a world," my mother always says. Fewer kinds to make an army.

He finally admitted I was who I was. "You carrying?" he asked as he filled out the pass.

"No," I said. "Not in the daytime."

"Your funeral." He folded the pass precisely in two and handed it over. Actually, I *was* armed, with a putty-knife and a little Beretta belt-buckle laser. It might be his own funeral someday, if he couldn't tell whether or not a man was armed. I saluted the privates with one erect finger between the eyes, traditional draftee greeting, and went out into the zoo.

There were about a dozen whores lounging around the gate, one of them a jill, her head shaved. She was old enough to be an ex-mechanic. You always wondered.

Of course, she noticed me. "Hey, Jack!" She stepped onto the path and I stopped the bike. "I got something you can ride."

"Maybe later," I said. "You're lookin' good." Actually, she wasn't. Her face and posture showed a lot of stress; the telltale pink in her eyes tagged her as a cherrybomb user.

"Half price for you, honey." I shook my head. She grabbed on to my handlebars. "Quarter price. Been so long since I done it jacked."

"I couldn't do it jacked." Something made me honest, or partly so. "Not with a stranger."

"So how long would I be a stranger?" She couldn't hide the note of pleading.

"Sorry." I pushed off onto the grass. If I didn't get away fast, she'd be offering to pay *me*.

The other hookers had watched the exchange with various attitudes: curiosity, pity, contempt. As if they weren't all addicts of one kind or another, themselves. Nobody had to fuck for a living in the Universal Welfare State. Nobody had to do anything but stay out of trouble. It works so well.

They had legalized prostitution in Florida for a few years, when I was growing up. But it went the way of the big casinos before I was old enough to be interested.

Hooking's a crime in Texas, but I think you have to be a real nuisance before they lock you up. The two cops who watched the jill proposition me didn't put the cuffs on her. Maybe later, if they had the money.

Jills usually get plenty of work. They know what it feels like to be male.

I pedaled past the college-town stores, with their academic prices, into town. South Houston was not exactly savory, but I was armed. Besides, I figured that bad guys kept late hours, and would still be in bed. One wasn't.

I leaned the bike up against the rack outside of the liquor store and was fiddling with the cranky lock, which was supposed to take my card.

"Hey boy," a deep bass voice said behind me. "You got ten dollars for me? Maybe twenny?"

I turned around slowly. He was a head taller than me, maybe forty, lean, muscle suit. Shiny boots up to his knees and the tightly braided ponytail of an Ender: God would use that to haul him up to heaven. Soon, he hoped.

"I thought you guys didn't need money."

"I need some. I need it now."

"So what's your habit?" I put my right hand on my hip. Not natural or comfortable, but close to the putty-knife. "Maybe I got some."

"You don't got what I need. Got to buy what I need." He drew a long knife with a slender wavy blade from his boot.

"Put it away. I got ten." The silly dagger was no

match for a puttyknife, but I didn't want to perform a dissection out here on the sidewalk.

"Oh, you got ten. Maybe you got fifty." He took a step toward me.

I pulled out the puttyknife and turned it on. It hummed and glowed. "You just lost ten. How much more you want to lose?"

He stared at the vibrating blade. The shimmering mist on the top third was as hot as the surface of the sun. "You in the army. You a mechanic."

"I'm either a mechanic or I killed one and took his knife. Either way, you want to fuck with me?"

"Mechanics ain't so tough. I was in the army."

"You know all about it, then." He took a half-step to the right, I think a feint. I didn't move. "You don't want to wait for your Rapture? You want to die right now?"

He looked at me for a long second. There was nothing in his eyes. "Oh, fuck you anyhow." He put the knife back in his boot, turned, and walked away without looking back.

I turned off the puttyknife and blew on it. When it was cool enough, I put it back and went into the liquor store.

The clerk had a chrome Remington airspray. "Fuckin' Endie. I would've got him."

"Thanks," I said. He would've gotten *me* too, with an airspray. "You got six Dixies?"

"Sure." He opened the case behind him. "Ration card?"

"Army," I said. I didn't bother with the ID.

"Figured." He rummaged. "You know they got a law I got to let the fuckin' Endies in the store? They never buy anything."

"Why should they?" I said. "World's going up in smoke tomorrow, maybe the next day."

"Right. Meanwhile they steal y' blind. All I got's cans."

"Whatever." I was starting to shake a little. Between the Ender and this trigger-happy clerk I'd probably come closer to dying than I ever would in Portobello.

He put the six-pack in front of me. "You don't want to sell that knife?"

"No, I need it all the time. Open fan mail with it."

That was the wrong thing to say. "Got to say I don't recognize you. I follow the Fourth and Sixteenth, mainly."

"I'm Ninth. Not nearly as exciting."

"Interdiction," he said, nodding. The Fourth and Sixteenth are hunter/killer platoons, so they have a considerable following. Warboys, we call their fans.

He was a little excited, even though I was just Interdiction. And Psychops. "You didn't catch the Fourth last Wednesday, did you?"

"Hey, I don't even follow my own outfit. I was in the cage then, anyhow."

He stopped for a moment with my card in his hand, struck dumb by the concept that a person could live nine days in a row inside a soldierboy and then not jump straight to the cube and follow the war.

Some do, of course. I met Scoville when he was out of the cage once, here in Houston for a warboy "assembly." There's one every week somewhere in Texas— they haul in enough booze and bum and squeak to keep them cross-eyed for a long weekend, and pay a couple of mechanics to come in and tell them what it's really *really* like. To be locked inside a cage and watch yourself murder people by remote control. They replay tapes of great battles and argue over fine points of strategy.

The only one I've ever gone to had a "warrior day," where all of the attendees—all except us outsiders— dressed up as warriors from the past. That was kind of scary. I assumed the tommy guns and flintlocks didn't function; even criminals were reluctant to risk that. But the swords and spears and bows looked real enough, and they were in the hands of people who had amply demonstrated, to me at least, that they shouldn't be trusted with a sharp stick.

"You were going to kill that guy?" the clerk said conversationally.

"No reason to. They always back off." As if I knew.

"But suppose he didn't."

"It wouldn't be a problem," I heard myself saying. "Take his knife hand off at the wrist. Call 9-1-1. Maybe they'd glue it back on upside down." Actually, they'd probably take their time responding. Give him a chance to beat the Rapture by bleeding to death.

He nodded. "We had two guys last month outside the store, they did the handkerchief thing, some girl." That was where two men bite down on opposite corners of a handkerchief, and have at each other with knives or razors. The one who lets go of the handkerchief loses. "One guy was dead before they got here. The other lost an ear; they didn't bother to look for it." He gestured. "I kept it in the freezer for awhile."

"You're the one who called the cops?"

"Oh yeah," he said. "Soon as it was over." Good citizen.

I strapped the beer onto the rear carrier and pedaled back toward the gate.

Things are getting worse. I hate to sound like my old man. But things really were better when I was a boy. There weren't Enders on every corner. People didn't duel. People didn't stand around and watch other people duel. And then police picked up the ears afterward.

not all enders had ponytails and obvious attitudes.

There were two in Julian's physics department, a secretary and Mac Roman himself.

People wondered how such a mediocre scientist had come out of nowhere and brown-nosed his way into a position of academic power. What they didn't appreciate was the intellectual effort it took to successfully pretend to believe in the ordered, agnostic view of the universe that physics mandated. It was all part of God's plan, though. Like the carefully falsified documents that had put him in the position of being minimally qualified for the chairmanship. Two other Enders were on the Board of Regents, able to push his case.

Macro (like one of those Regents) was a member of a militant and supersecret sect within a sect: the Hammer of God. Like all Enders, they believed God was about to bring about the destruction of humankind.

Unlike most of them, the Hammer of God felt called upon to help.

on the way back to campus I took a wrong turn and, circling back, passed a downscale jack joint I'd never seen. They had feelies of group sex, downhill skiing, a car crash. Done there; been that. Not to mention all the combat ones.

Actually, I'd never done the car crash. I wonder if the actor died. Sometimes Enders did that, even though jacking's supposed to be a sin. Sometimes people do it to be famous for a few minutes. I've never jacked into one of those, but Ralph has his favorites, so when I'm jacked with Ralph I get it secondhand. Guess I'll never understand fame.

There was a new sergeant at the gate to the university, so we went through the delaying song and dance again.

I pedaled aimlessly through the campus for an hour. It was pretty deserted, Sunday afternoon of a long weekend. I went into the physics building to see whether any students had slipped papers under my door, and one had—an *early* problem set, wonder of wonders. And a note saying he'd have to miss class because his sister had a coming-out party in Monaco. Poor kid.

Amelia's office was one floor above mine, but I didn't bother her. I really ought to work out the answers to the problem set, get ahead of the game. No, I ought to go back to Amelia's and waste the rest of the day.

I did go back to Amelia's, but in a spirit of scientific inquiry. She had a new appliance they called the "anti-microwave;" you put something in it and set the temperature you want, and it cools it down. Of course the appliance has nothing to do with microwaves.

It worked well on a can of beer. When I opened the door, wisps of vapor came out. The beer was forty degrees, but the ambient temperature inside the machine must have been a lot lower. Just to see what would happen, I put a slice of cheese in it and set it to the lowest temperature, minus forty. When it came out I dropped it on the floor, and it shattered. I think I found all the pieces.

Amelia had a little alcove behind the fireplace that she called "the library." There was just room for an antique futon and a small table. The three walls that defined the space were glassed-in shelves, full of hundreds of old books. I'd been in there with her, but not to read.

I set the beer down and looked at the titles. Mostly novels and poetry. Unlike a lot of jacks and jills, I still read for pleasure, but I like to read things that are supposed to be true.

My first couple of years of college, I majored in history with a minor in physics, but then switched around. I used to think it was the degrees in physics that got me drafted. But most mechanics have the usual compulsory-ed degrees—gym, current events, communication skills.

You don't have to be that smart to lie in the cage and twitch.

Anyhow, I like to read history, and Amelia's library was lean in that subject. A few popular illustrated texts. Mostly twenty-first century, which I planned to read about when it was over.

I remembered she wanted me to read the Civil War novel *The Red Badge of Courage,* so I took it down and settled in. Two hours and two beers.

The differences between their fighting and ours were as profound as the difference between a bad accident and a bad dream.

Their armies were equally matched in weaponry; they both had a diffuse, confused command structure that essentially resulted in one huge mob being thrown against another, to flail away with primitive guns and knives and clubs until one mob ran away.

The confused protagonist, Henry, was too deeply involved to see this simple truth, but he reported it accurately.

I wonder what poor Henry would think about our kind of war. I wonder whether his era even knew the most accurate metaphor: exterminator. And I wondered what simple truth my involvement kept me from seeing.

julian didn't know that the author of *The Red Badge of Courage* had had the advantage of not having been a part of the war he wrote about. It's harder to see a pattern when you're part of it.

That war had been relatively straightforward in terms of economic and ideological issues; Julian's was not. The enemy Ngumi comprised a loose alliance of dozens of "rebel" forces, fifty-four this year. In all enemy countries there was a legitimate government that cooperated with the Alliance, but it was no secret that few

of those governments were supported by a majority of
their constituents.

It was partly an economic war, the "haves" with their
automation-driven economies versus the "have-nots,"
who were not born into automatic prosperity. It was
partly a race war, the blacks and browns and some yellows versus the whites and some other yellows. Julian
was uncomfortable on some level about that, but he
didn't feel much of a bond with Africa. Too long ago,
too far away, and they were too crazy.

And of course it was an ideological war for some—
the defenders of democracy versus the rebel strong-arm
charismatic leaders. Or the capitalist land-grabbers versus the protectors of the people, take your pick.

But it was not a war that was going to have a con-
clusive endgame, like Appomattox or Hiroshima. Either
the slow erosion of the Alliance would make it collapse
into chaos, or the Ngumi would be swatted down hard
enough in all locations that they would become a col-
lection of local crime problems rather than a somewhat
unified military one.

The roots of it went back to the twentieth century and
even beyond; many of the Ngumi traced their political
parentage back to when white men first brought sailing
ships and gunpowder to their lands. The Alliance dismissed that as so much jingoistic rhetoric, but there was
logic to it.

The situation was complicated by the fact that in some
countries the rebels were strongly linked to organized
crime, as had happened in the Drug Wars that simmered
early in the century. In some, there was nothing left *but*
crime, organized or disorganized, but universal, from
border to border. In some of those places, Alliance
forces were the only vestige of law—often underappre-
ciated, when there was no legal commerce and the population's choice was between a well-stocked black
market and essentials-only charity from the Alliance.

Julian's Costa Rica was anomalous. The country had managed to stay out of the war early on, maintaining the neutrality that had kept it out of the twentieth century's cataclysms. But its geographic location between Panama, the only Alliance stronghold in Central America, and Nicaragua, the hemisphere's most powerful Ngumi nation, finally dragged it into the war. At first, most of the patriotic rebels spoke with a suspicious Nicaraguan accent. But then there was a charismatic leader and an assassination—both engineered by Ngumi, the Alliance claimed—and before long the forests and fields were filled with young men, and some women, ready to risk their lives to protect their land against the cynical capitalists and their puppets. Against the huge bulletproof giants who stalked the jungle quiet as cats; who could level a town in minutes.

Julian considered himself a political realist. He didn't swallow the facile propaganda of his own side, but the other side was just plain doomed; their leaders should be making deals with the Alliance rather than annoying it. When they nuked Atlanta they hammered the last nail into their coffin.

If indeed Ngumi had done it. No rebel group claimed responsibility, and Nairobi said it was close to being able to prove that the bomb had come from the Alliance nuclear archives: they had sacrificed five million American lives to pave the way for total war, total annihilation.

But Julian wondered about the nature of the proof, that they could be "close" to it and not be able to say anything specific. He didn't rule out the possibility that there were people on his own side insane enough to blow up one of their own cities. But he did wonder how such a thing could be kept secret for long. A lot of people would have to be involved.

Of course that could be dealt with. People who would murder five million strangers could sacrifice a few dozen friends, a few hundred coconspirators.

And so it went around and around, as it had in everybody's thoughts in the months since Atlanta, Sao Paulo, and Mandelaville. Would some actual proof emerge? Would another city be snuffed out tomorrow; and then another one, in retaliation?

It was a good time for those who owned rural real estate. People who could move were finding country life appealing.

the first few days I'm back are usually nice and intense. The homecoming mood energizes our love life, and all the time I'm not with her I'm deeply immersed in the Jupiter Project, catching up. But a lot depends on the day of the week I come back, because Friday is always a singularity. Friday is the night of the Saturday Night Special.

That's the name of a restaurant up in the Hidalgo part of town, more expensive than I would normally patronize, and more pretentious: the theme of the place is the romanticized California Gang Era—grease, graffiti, and grime, safely distant from the table linen. As far as I'm concerned, those people were no different from today's whackers and slicers—if anything, worse, since they didn't have to worry about the federal death penalty for using guns. The waiters come around in leather jackets and meticulously grease-stained T-shirts, black jeans, and high boots. They say the wine list is the best in Houston.

I'm the youngest of the Saturday Night Special crowd by at least ten years; the only one who's not a full-time intellectual. I'm ''Blaze's boy''; I don't know which of them knew or suspected I literally *was* her boy. I came as her friend and coworker, and everybody seemed to accept that.

My primary value to the group was the novelty of

being a mechanic. That was doubly interesting to them, because a senior member of the group, Marty Larrin, was one of the designers of the cyberlink that made jacking, and thus soldierboys, possible.

Marty had been responsible for designing the system's security. Once a jack was installed, it was failsafed at a molecular level, literally impossible to modify, even for the original manufacturers; even for researchers like Marty. The nanocircuitry inside would scramble itself within a fraction of a second if any part of the complex device was tampered with. Then it would take another round of invasive surgery, with a one-in-ten chance of death or uselessness, to take the scrambled jack out and install a new one.

Marty was about sixty, the front half of his head shaved bald in a generation-old style, the rest of his white hair long except for the shaved circle around his jack. He was conventionally handsome, still; regular leading-man features, and it was obvious from the way he treated Amelia that they had a past. I once asked her how long ago that had been, the only such question I've ever asked her. She thought for a moment and said, "I guess you were out of grade school."

The population of the Saturday Night Special crowd varies from week to week. Marty is almost always there, along with his traditional antagonist, Franklin Asher, a mathematician with a chair in the philosophy department. Their jocular sniping goes back to when they were graduate students together; Amelia's known him nearly as long as Marty.

Belda Magyar is usually there, an odd duck but obviously one of the inner circle. She sits and listens with a stern, disapproving look, nursing a single glass of wine. Once or twice a night she makes a hilarious remark, without changing expression. She's the oldest, over ninety, a professor emeritus in the art department. She claims to remember having met Richard Nixon, when she was very small. He was big and scary, and gave her a book of matches, no doubt a White House souvenir, which her mother took away.

I liked Reza Pak, a shy chemist in his early forties, the only one besides Amelia with whom I socialized outside the club. We met occasionally to shoot pool or play tennis. He never mentioned Amelia and I never mentioned the boyfriend who always drove up to fetch him, exactly on time.

Reza, who also lived on campus, usually gave me and Amelia a ride to the club, but this Friday he was already uptown, so we called a cab. (Like most people, Amelia doesn't own a car and I've never even driven, except in Basic Training, and then only jacked with someone who knew how.) We could bike to Hidalgo in daylight, but coming back after dark would be suicide.

It started raining at sundown anyhow, and by the time we got to the club it was a full-fledged thunderstorm, with tornado watch. The club had an awning, but the rain was almost horizontal; we got drenched between the cab and the door.

Reza and Belda were already there, at our usual table in the grease section. We talked them into moving to the Club Room, where a phony-but-warm fireplace crackled.

Another semi-regular, Ray Booker, came in while we were relocating, also drenched. Ray was an engineer who worked with Marty Larrin on soldierboy technology, and a serious 'grass musician who played banjo all over the state, summers.

"Julian, you should of seen the Tenth today." Ray had a little warboy streak in him. "Delayed replay of an amphibious assault on Punta Patuca. We came, we saw, we kicked butt." He handed his wet overcoat and hat to the wheelie that had followed him in. "Almost no casualties."

"What's 'almost'?" Amelia said.

"Well, they ran into a shatterfield." He sat down heavily. "Three units lost both legs. But we got them evac'ed before the scavengers could get to them. One psych, a girl on her second or third mission."

"Wait," I said. "They used a shatterfield inside a city?"

"They sure as hell did. Brought down a whole block of slums, urban renewal. Of course they said we did it."

"How many dead?"

"Must be hundreds." Ray shook his head. "That's what got the girl, maybe. She was in the middle of it, immoblilized with both her legs off. Fought the rescue crew; wanted them to evac the civilians. They had to turn her off to get her out of there."

He asked the table for a scotch and soda and the rest of us put our orders in. No greasy waiters in this section. "Maybe she'll be okay. One of those things you have to learn to live with."

"We didn't do it," Reza said.

"Why would we? No military advantage, bad press. Shatterfield's a terror weapon, in a city."

"I'm surprised anyone survived," I said.

"Nobody on the ground; they were all instant chorizo. But those were four- and five-story buildings. People in the upper stories just had to survive the collapse.

"The Tenth set up a knockout perimeter with UN markers and called it a no-fire zone, collateral casualty, once we had all our soldierboys out. Dropped in a Red Cross med crawler and moved on.

"The shatterfield was their only real 'tech touch. The rest of it was old-fashioned, cut-off-and-concentrate tactics, which doesn't work on a group as well integrated as the Tenth. Good platoon coordination. Julian, you would have appreciated it. From the air it was like choreography."

"Maybe I'll check it out." I wouldn't; never did, unless I knew somebody in the fight.

"Any time," Ray said. "I've got two crystals of it, one jacked through Emily Vail, the company coordinator. The other's the commercial feed." They didn't show battles while they were happening, of course, since the enemy could jack in. The commercial feed was edited both for maximum drama and minimum disclosure. Normal people couldn't get individual mechanics' unedited feeds; lots of warboys would cheerfully kill for one. Ray had top-secret clearance and an unfiltered jack. If a civilian or a spy got ahold of Emily Vail's crystal, they would see and feel a lot that wasn't on the commercial version, but selected perceptions and thoughts would be filtered out unless you had a jack like Ray's.

A live waiter in a clean tuxedo brought our drinks. I was splitting a jug of house red with Reza.

Ray raised a glass. "To peace," he said, actually without irony. "Welcome back, Julian." Amelia touched my knee with hers under the table.

The wine was pretty good, just astringent enough to make you consider a slightly more expensive one. "Easy week this time," I said, and Ray nodded. He always checked on me.

A couple of others showed up, and we broke down into the usual interlocking small conversational groups. Amelia moved over to sit with Belda and another man from fine arts, to talk about books. We usually did separate when it seemed natural.

I stayed with Reza and Ray; when Marty came in he gave Amelia a peck and joined the three of us. There was no love lost between him and Belda.

Marty was really soaked, his long white hair in lanky strings. "Had to park down the block," he said, dropping his sodden coat on the wheelie.

"Thought you were working late," Ray said.

"This isn't late?" He ordered coffee and a sandwich. "I'm going back later, and so are you. Have a couple more scotches."

"What is it?" He pushed his scotch away a symbolic inch.

"Let's not talk shop. We have all night. But it's that girl you said you saw on the Vail crystal."

"The one who cracked?" I asked.

"Mm-hm. Why don't *you* crack, Julian? Get a discharge. We enjoy your company."

"Your platoon, too," Ray joked. "Nice bunch."

"How could she fit into your cross-linking studies?" I asked. "She must hardly have been linking at all."

"New deal we started while you were gone," Ray said. "We got a contract to study empathy failures. People who crack out of sympathy for the enemy."

"You may *get* Julian," Reza said. "He just loves them pedros."

"It doesn't correlate much with politics," Marty said. "And it's usually people in their first year or two. More often female than male. He's not a good candidate." The coffee came and he picked up the cup and blew on it. "So how about this weather? Clear and cool, they said."

"Love them Knicks," I said.

Reza nodded. "The square root of minus one." There was going to be no more talk of empathy failures that night.

julian didn't know how selective the draft really was, finding people for specific mechanics' slots. There were a few hunter/killer platoons, but they tended to be hard to control, on a couple of levels. As platoons, they followed orders poorly, and they didn't integrate well "horizontally," with other platoons in the company. The individual mechanics in a hunter/killer platoon tended not to link strongly with one another.

None of this was surprising. They were made up of the same kind of people earlier armies chose for "wet work.'' You expected them to be independent and somewhat wild.

As Julian had observed, most platoons had at least one person who seemed like a really unlikely choice. In his outfit it was Candi, horrified by the war and unwilling to harm the enemy. They were called stabilizers.

Julian suspected she acted as a kind of conscience for the platoon, but it would be more accurate to call her a governor, like the governor on an engine. Platoons that didn't have one member like Candi had a tendency to run out of control, go "berserker." It happened sometimes with the hunter/killer ones, whose stabilizers couldn't be *too* pacifistic, and it was tactically a disaster. War is, according to von Clausewitz, the controlled use of force to bring about political ends. Uncontrolled force is as likely to harm as to help.

(There was a mythos, a commonsense observation, that the berserker episodes had a good effect in the long run, because they made the Ngumi more afraid of the soldierboys. Actually, the opposite was true, according to the people who studied the enemy's psychology. The soldierboys were most fearsome when they acted like actual machines, controlled from a distance. When they got angry or went crazy—acting like men in robot suits—they seemed beatable.)

More than half of the stablilizers did crack before their term was up. In most cases it was not a sudden process, but was preceded by a period of inattention and indecision. Marty and Ray would be reviewing the performance of stabilizers prior to their failure, to see whether there was some invariable indicator that would warn commanders that it was time for a replacement or modification.

The unbreakable jack fail-safe supposedly was to keep people from harming themselves or others, though everybody knew it was just to maintain the government monopoly. Like a lot of things that everybody knows, it wasn't true. It wasn't quite true that you couldn't modify a jack in place, either, but the changes were limited to memory—usually when a soldier saw something the army wanted him or her to forget. Only two of the Saturday Night Special group knew about that.

Sometimes they erased a soldier's memory of an event for security reasons; less often, for humane ones.

Almost all of Marty's work now was with the military, which made him uncomfortable. When he had started in the field, thirty years before, jacks were crude, expensive, and rare, used for medical and scientific research.

Most people still worked for a living then. A decade later, at least in the "first world," most jobs having to do with production and distribution of goods were obsolete or quaint. Nanotechnology had given us the nanoforge: ask it for a house, and then put it near a supply of sand and water. Come back tomorrow with your moving van. Ask it for a car, a book, a nail file. Before long, of course, you didn't have to ask it; it knew what people wanted, and how many people there were.

Of course, it could also make other nanoforges. But not for just anybody. Only for the government. You couldn't just roll up your sleeves and build yourself one, either, since the government also owned the secret of warm fusion, and without the abundant free power that came from that process, the nanoforge couldn't exist.

Its development had cost thousands of lives and put a huge crater in North Dakota, but by the time Julian was in school, the government was in a position where it could give everybody any material thing. Of course, it wouldn't give you everything you *wanted;* alcohol and other drugs were strictly controlled, as were dangerous things like guns and cars. But if you were a good citizen, you could live a life of comfort and security without lifting a finger to work, unless you wanted to. Except for the three years you were drafted.

Most people spent those three years working in uniform a few hours a day in Resource Management, which was dedicated to making sure the nanoforges had access to all the elements they needed. About five percent of the draftees put on blue uniforms and became caregivers, people whose tests said they would be good working with the sick and elderly. Another five percent put on green uniforms and became soldiers. A small fraction of those tested out fast and smart, and became mechanics.

People in National Service were allowed to reenlist, and a large number did. Some of them didn't want to face a lifetime of total freedom, perhaps uselessness. Some liked the perquisites that went along with the uniform: money for hobbies or habits, a kind of prestige, the comfort of having other people tell you what to do, the ration card that gave you unlimited alcohol, off duty.

Some people even liked being allowed to carry a gun.

The soldiers who weren't involved in soldierboys, waterboys, or flyboys—the people mechanics called "shoes"—got all of those perquisites, but always faced a certain probability of being ordered to go out and sit on a piece of disputed real estate. They usually didn't have to fight, since the soldierboys were better at it and couldn't be killed, but there was no doubt that the shoes fulfilled a valuable military function: they were hostages. Maybe even lures, staked goats for the Ngumi long-range weapons. It didn't make them love the mechanics, as often as they owed their lives to them. If a soldierboy got blown to bits, the mechanic just put on a fresh one. Or so they thought. They didn't know how it felt.

i liked sleeping in the soldierboy. Some people thought it was creepy, so complete a knockout it was like death. Half the platoon stands guard while the other half is shut down for two hours. You fall asleep like a light being turned out and wake up just as suddenly, disoriented but as rested as you would have been after eight hours of normal sleep. If you get the full two hours, that is.

We had taken refuge in a burned-out schoolhouse in an abandoned village. I was on the second sleep shift, so I first spent two hours sitting at a broken window, smelling jungle and old ashes, patient in the unchanging darkness. From my point of view, of course, it was neither dark nor unchanging. Starlight flooded the scene like monochromatic daylight, and once each ten seconds I switched to infrared for a moment. The infrared helped me track a large black cat that stalked up on us, gliding through the twisted remains of the playground equipment. It was an ocelot or something, aware of motion in the schoolhouse and looking for a meal. When it got within ten meters it froze for a long period, scenting nothing, or maybe machine lubricant, and then was away in a sudden flash.

Nothing else happened. After two hours, the first shift woke up. We gave them a couple of minutes to get their bearings and then passed on the "sit-rep," situation report: negative.

I fell asleep and instantly awoke to a blaze of pain. My sensors brought in nothing but blinding light, a roar of white noise, searing heat—and complete isolation! All of my platoon was disconnected or destroyed.

I knew it wasn't real; knew I was safe in a cage in Portobello. But it still hurt like a third-degree burn over every square centimeter of naked flesh, eyeballs fried in their sockets, one dying inhalation of molten lead, enema of same: complete feedback overload.

It seemed to last for a long time—long enough for me to think this was actually it; the enemy had cracked Portobello or nuked it, and it was actually me dying, not my machine. Actually, we were switched off after 3.03 seconds. It would have been quicker, but the mechanic

in Delta platoon who was our horizontal liaison—our
link to the company commander if I died—was disoriented by the sudden intensity of it, even secondhand.

Later satellite analysis showed two aircraft catapulted
from five kilometers away. They were stealthed and,
with no propellant, left no heat signature. One pilot
ejected just before the plane hit the schoolhouse. The
other plane was either automatically guided or its pilot
came in with it—kamikaze or ejection failure.

Both planes were full of incendiaries. About one hundredth of a second after Candi sensed something was
wrong, all our soldierboys were trying to cope with a
flood of molten metal.

They know we have to sleep, and know how we do
it. So they contrive things like this setup: a camouflaged
catapult, zeroed on a building we would sooner or later
use, its two-pilot crew waiting for months or years.

They couldn't have just boobytrapped the building,
because we would have sensed that amount of incendi-
ary or other explosive.

In Portobello, three of us went into cardiac arrest;
Ralph died. They used air-cushion stretchers to move us
to the hospital wing, but it still hurt to move; just to
breathe.

Physical treatment wouldn't touch where that pain
was, the phantom pain that was the nervous system's
memory of violent death. Imaginary pain had to be
fought through the imagination.

They jacked me into a Caribbean island fantasy,
swimming warm waters with lovely black women. Lots
of virtual fruit-and-rum drinks, and then virtual sex, virtual sleep.

When I woke up still in pain, they tried the opposite
scenario—a ski resort, thin dry cool air. Fast slopes, fast
women, the same sequence of virtual voluptuousness.
Then canoeing in a calm mountain lake. Then a hospital
bed in Portobello.

The doctor was a short guy, darker than me. "Are you awake, sergeant?"

I felt the back of my head. "Evidently." I sat up and clutched at the mattress until the dizziness subsided. "How are Candi and Karen?"

"They'll be all right. Do you recall . . ."

"Ralph died. Yes." I dimly remembered when they had stopped working on him, and brought the other two out of the cardiac unit. "What day is it?"

"Wednesday." The shift had started Monday. "How do you feel? You're free to go as soon as you feel up to it."

"Medical leave?" He nodded. "The skin pain is gone. I still feel strange. But I've never spent two days jacked into fantasies before." I put my feet on the cold tile floor and stood up. I walked shakily across the room to a closet and found a dress uniform there, and a bag with my civvies.

"Guess I'll hang around awhile, check on my platoon. Then go home or wherever."

"All right. I'm Dr. Tull, in RICU Recovery, if you have any problems." He shook hands and left. Do you salute doctors?

I decided to wear the uniform and dressed slowly and sat there for awhile, sipping ice water. I'd lost soldier-boys twice before, but both times it was just a twist of disorientation and then switch-off. I'd heard about these total feedback situations, and knew of one instance when a whole platoon had died before they could be turned off. Supposedly, that couldn't happen anymore.

How would it affect our performance? Scoville's platoon went through it last year. We all had to spend a cycle training with the replacement soldierboys, but they seemed unaffected, other than being impatient with not fighting. Theirs was only a fraction of a second, though, not three seconds of burning alive.

I went down to see Candi and Karen. They'd been

out of jack therapy for half a day, and were pale and weak but otherwise all right. They showed me the pair of red marks between their breasts where they'd been jolted back to life.

Everyone but them and Mel had checked out and gone home. While I waited for Mel I went down to Ops and replayed the attack.

I didn't replay the three seconds, of course; only the minute leading up to them. All the people on guard heard a faint "pop" that was the enemy pilot ejecting. Then Candi, out of the corner of her eye, saw one plane for a hundredth of a second, as it cleared the trees that bordered the parking lot and dove in. She started to swing, to target it with her laser, and then the record ended.

When Mel came out, we had a couple of beers and a plate of tamales at the airport. He went off to California, and I went back to the hospital for a few hours. I bribed a tech to jack me with Candi and Karen for five minutes—not strictly against regulations; in a way, we were still on duty—which was long enough for us to reassure each other that we would be all right, and to share grief about Ralph. It was especially hard on Candi. I took on some of the fear and pain they had about their hearts. Nobody likes to face the possibility of a replacement, having a machine at the center of your life. They were likely candidates now.

When we unjacked, Candi held my hand very hard, actually just the forefinger, staring at me. "You hide your secrets better than anyone else," she whispered.

"I don't want to talk about it."

"I know you don't."

"Talk about what?" Karen said.

Candi shook her head. "Thanks," I said, and she released my finger.

I backed out of the small room. "Be . . . ," Candi

said, and didn't complete the sentence. Maybe that *was* the sentence.

She had seen how profoundly I hadn't wanted to wake up.

I called Amelia from the airport and said I'd be home in a few hours, and would explain later. It would be after midnight, but she said to come straight over to her place. That was a relief. Our relationship didn't have any restrictions, but I always hoped she slept alone, waiting, the ten days I was away.

Of course she knew something was seriously wrong. When I got off the plane, she was there, and had a cab waiting outside.

The machine's programming was stuck in a rush-hour pattern, so it took us twenty minutes to get home, via surface roads I never see except on bicycle. I was able to tell Amelia the basic story while we drove through the maze that avoided nonexistent traffic. When we got to the campus the guard looked at my uniform and waved us through, wonder of wonders.

I let her talk me into some reheated stir-fry. I wasn't really hungry, but knew she liked to feed me.

"It's hard for me to visualize," she said, rummaging for bowls and chopsticks while the stuff warmed. "Of course it is. I'm just talking." She stood behind me and massaged my neck. "Tell me you're going to be all right."

"I *am* all right."

"Oh, bullshit." She dug in. "You're stiff as a board. You're not halfway back from . . . wherever that was."

She had nuked some sake. I poured a second cup. "Maybe. I . . . they let me go back and jack with Candi and Karen in the cardiac recovery unit. Candi's in a pretty bad way."

"Afraid of getting her heart pulled?"

"That's more Karen's problem. Candi's going round and round about Ralph. She can't handle losing him."

She reached over me and poured herself a cup. "Isn't she a grief counselor? Out of uniform."

"Yeah, well, why does somebody take that up? She lost her father when she was twelve, an accident while she was in the car. That's never buried very deep. He's there in the background with every man she, she's close to."

"Loves? Like you?"

"Not love. It's automatic. We've been through this."

She crossed the kitchen to stir the pot, her back to me. "Maybe we should go through it again. Maybe every six months or so."

I almost blew up at her, but held back. We were both tired and rattled. "It's not at all like Carolyn. You just have to trust me. Candi's more like a sister—"

"Oh sure."

"Not like *my* sister, okay." I hadn't heard from her in more than a year. "I'm close to her, intimate, and I guess you could call it a kind of love. But it's not like you and me."

She nodded and measured the stuff into bowls. "I'm sorry. You go through hell there and get more hell here."

"Hell and stir-fry." I took the bowl. "Time of the month?"

She put her own bowl down a little hard. "That's another goddamned thing. Sharing their periods. That's more than 'intimate.' It's just plain strange."

"Well, count your blessings. You've got a couple of years' peace." The women in a platoon synchronize periods pretty quickly, and the men are of course affected. It's a problem with the thirty-day rotation cycle: the first half of last year I came home every month crabby with PMS, proof that the brain is mightier than the gland.

"What was he like, Ralph? You never said much about him."

"It was only his third cycle," I said. "Still a neo. Never saw any real combat."

"Just enough to kill him."

"Yeah. He was a nervous guy, maybe oversensitive. Two months ago, when we were parallel-jacked, Scoville's platoon was worse than usual, and he was bouncing around for days. We all had to hang on to him, keep him putting one foot in front of the other. Candi was best at that, of course."

She played with her food. "So you didn't know all that intimate stuff about him."

"Intimate, yeah, but not as deep as the others. He wet the bed until puberty, had terrible childhood guilt over killing a turtle. Spent all his money on jacksex with the jills that hang around Portobello. Never had real sex until he was married, and didn't stay married long. Before he got jacked he used to masturbate compulsively to tapes of oral sex. Is that intimate?"

"What was his favorite food?"

"Crab cakes. The way his mother made them."

"Favorite book?"

"He didn't read much, not at all for pleasure. He liked *Treasure Island* in school. Wrote a report about Jim in eleventh grade and then recycled it in college."

"He was likeable?"

"Nice enough guy. We never did anything social—I mean nobody did, with him. He'd get out of the cage and run to the bars, with a hard-on for the jills."

"Candi didn't, none of the women wanted to . . . help him out that way?"

"God, no. Why would you?"

"That's what I don't understand. Why *wouldn't* you? I mean, all the women knew he went off with these jills."

"That's what he wanted to do. I don't think he was unhappy on that score." I pushed the bowl away and poured some sake. "Besides, it's an invasion of privacy on a cosmic scale: when Carolyn and I were together, every time we went back to the platoon we had eight people who knew everything we had done, from both sides, as soon as we jacked. They knew how Carolyn felt about what I did, and vice versa, and all the feedback states that that kind of knowledge generates. You don't start that sort of thing casually."

She persisted. "I still don't see why not. You're all used to everybody knowing everything. You know each other's *insides,* for Christ's sake! A little friendly sex wouldn't be that earthshaking."

I knew my anger was unreasonable, that it didn't really come from her questions. "Well, how would you like to have the whole Friday night gang in the bedroom with us? Feeling everything you felt?"

She smiled. "I wouldn't mind. Is that a difference between men and women or between you and me?"

"I think it's a difference between you and merely sane people." My smile might not have been totally convincing. "It's actually not the physical sensations. The details vary, but men pretty much feel like men and women feel like women. Sharing that isn't a big deal after the initial novelty. It's how the rest of you feels that's personal. And embarrassing."

She took our bowls to the sink. "You wouldn't be able to tell that from the ads." Her voice dropped. " 'Feel how it feels to *her.*' "

"Well, you know. People who pay to have a jack installed often do it out of sexual curiosity. Or something deeper; they feel trapped in the wrong kind of body but don't want to do the swap-op." I shuddered. "Understandably."

"People do it all the time," she said, teasing, knowing how I felt. "It's less dangerous than jacking, and reversible."

"Oh, reversible. You get somebody else's dick."

"Men and their dicks. It's mostly your own tissue."

"Used to be inseparable." Karen had been male until she turned eighteen, and was able to file with National Health for a swap. She took a few tests and they agreed she'd be better off outside-in.

The first one's free. If she wanted to go back to being a male, she'd have to pay. Two of the jills that Ralph liked were ex-males trying to earn enough to buy their dicks back. What a wonderful world.

people outside of national Service did have legitimate ways to earn money, though not many of them were paid as much as prostitutes. Academics made small stipends, larger ones for people who did "hands-on" teaching, only a token for people who just did research. Marty was the head of his department and was a world-renowned authority on brain/machine and brain/brain interfacing—but he made less money than a teaching assistant like Julian. He made less money than the greaseball kids who served drinks at the Saturday Night Special. And like most people in his position, Marty took a perverse pride in being broke all the time—he was too *busy* to make money. And he rarely needed the things you could buy with it, anyhow.

You could buy objects with money, like handcrafts and original art, or services; masseur, butler, prostitute. But most people spent money on rationed things—things the government allowed you to have, but didn't allow you *enough* of.

Everyone had three entertainment credits a day, for instance. One credit would get you a movie, a roller-coaster ride, one hour of hands-on driving on a sports car track, or entry into a place like the Saturday Night Special.

Once inside, you could sit all night for free, unless you wanted something to eat or drink. Restaurant meals ranged from one to thirty credits, mostly depending on how much labor went into them, but the menu also had dollar amounts, in case you had used up all your entertainment and had money.

Plain money wouldn't buy alcohol, though, unless you were in uniform. You were rationed one ounce of alcohol per day, and it made no difference to the government whether you parceled it out to yourself as two small glasses of wine each night or as a once-a-month binge with two bottles of vodka.

It made abstainers and people in uniform sought-after companions in some wobbly circles—and, perhaps predictably, did nothing to reduce the number of alcoholics. People who had to have it would either find it or make it.

Illegal services were available for money, and in fact were the most active part of the dollar economy. Penny-ante activities like home-brewing or freelance prostitution were either ignored or taken care of with small regular bribes. But there were big operators who moved a lot of cash for hard drugs and services like murder.

Some medical services, like jack installation, cosmetic surgery, and sex-change operations, were theoretically available through National Health, but not many people qualified. Before the war, Nicaragua and Costa Rica had been the places to go to buy "black medicine." Now it was Mexico, though a lot of the doctors had Nicaraguan or Costa Rican accents.

black medicine came up at the next Friday night gathering. Ray was on a little vacation in Mexico. It was no secret he'd gone there to have a few dozen pounds of fat removed.

"I suppose the medical advantages outweigh the risk," Marty said.

"You had to approve the leave?" Julian asked.

"Pro forma," Marty said. "Pity he couldn't put it against sick leave. I don't think he's ever used a day of it."

"Well, it's vanity," Belda said in a quavering voice. "Male vanity. I liked him fine, fat."

"He didn't want to get in bed with *you,* darling," Marty said.

"His loss." The old woman patted her hair.

The waiter was a surly handsome young man who looked as if he'd stepped out of a movie poster. "Last call."

"It's only eleven," Marty said.

"So maybe you get one more."

"Same all around?" Julian said. Everyone said yes except Belda, who checked her watch and bustled out.

It was getting toward the end of the month, so they put all the drinks on Julian's tab, to conserve ration points, and paid him under the table. He offered to let them do it all the time, but it was technically against the law, so most of the people usually demurred. Except Reza, who had never spent a dime in the club except in payoffs to Julian.

"I wonder how fat you have to be to go to National Health," Reza said.

"You have to need a forklift to get around," Julian said. "Your mass has to alter the orbits of nearby planets."

"He did apply," Marty said. "He didn't have high enough blood pressure or cholesterol."

"You're worried about him," Amelia said.

"Of course I am, Blaze. Personal feelings aside, if something happened to him I'd be stopped dead on three different projects. The new one especially, the empathy failures. He's pretty much taken that over."

"How's that coming along?" Julian asked. Marty

raised a palm and shook his head. "Sorry. Didn't mean to—"

"Oh, well, you might as well know one thing—we've been studying one of your people. You'll know all about it next time you jack with her."

Reza got up to go to the bathroom, so it was just the three of them: Julian, Amelia, and Marty.

"I'm very happy for you both," Marty said, in a distant tone, as if he were talking about the weather.

Amelia just stared. "You . . . you have access to my string," Julian said.

"Not directly, and not for the purpose of invading your privacy. We've been studying one of your people. So naturally I know a lot about you, secondhand, and so does Ray. Of course we will keep your secret for as long as you wish it to remain a secret."

"Nice of you to tell us," Amelia said.

"I don't mean to embarrass you. But of course Julian would know the next time he jacks with her. I was glad to finally get you alone."

"Who was it?"

"Private Defollette."

"Candi. Well, that makes sense."

"She's the one who was so hurt about the death last month?" Amelia said.

Julian nodded. "You expect her to crack?"

"We don't expect anything. We're simply interviewing one person per platoon."

"Chosen at random," Julian said.

Marty laughed and raised an eyebrow. "We were talking about liposuction?"

i didn't expect a lot of action the next week, since we'd have to break in a new set of soldierboys and start with a new mechanic as well. Almost two new ones, since Rose, Arly's replacement, had no experience other than last month's disaster.

The new mechanic was not a neo. For some reason they broke up India platoon to use as replacements. So we all sort of knew the new man, Park, because of the diffuse platoon-level link through Ralph, and Richard before him.

I didn't much like Park. India had been a hunter/killer platoon. He'd killed more people than all the rest of us put together, and unabashedly enjoyed it. He collected crystals of his kills and replayed them off duty.

We trained in the new soldierboys three hours on, one off, destroying the fake town "Pedropolis," built for that purpose on the Portobello base.

When I had time, I linked up to Carolyn, the company coordinator, and asked what was going on—why did I wind up with a man like Park? He'd never really fit in.

Carolyn's reply was sour and hot with confusion and anger. The order to "decompose" India platoon had come from somewhere above the brigade level, and it was causing organizational problems everywhere. The India mechanics were a bunch of mavericks. They hadn't gotten along all that well even with each other.

She assumed it was a deliberate experiment. As far as she knew, nothing like it had been done before; the only time she'd heard of a platoon being broken up, it was because four of them had died at once, and the other six couldn't work together anymore, with the shared grief. India, on the other hand, was one of the most successful platoons they had, in terms of kills. It didn't really make sense to split them up.

I was the lucky one, to have Park, she said. He had been the horizontal liaison, and so had been directly linked to mechanics outside his platoon for the past three years. His cohorts, except for the platoon leader, had only had each other, and they were a fun bunch. They made Scoville look like a pedro lover.

Park liked to kill nonhuman things, too. During the training exercise he occasionally popped a songbird out of the air with his laser, not an easy task. Samantha and Rose both objected when he zapped a stray dog. He sardonically defended his action by pointing out that it didn't belong in the AO, and could have been rigged up as a spy or boobytrap. But we all were linked, and had felt how he felt when he targeted the enemy mutt: it was simple obscene glee. He'd cranked up to maximum magnification to watch the dog explode.

The last three days combined perimeter guard with training, and I had visions of Park using kids as target practice. Children often watch the soldierboys from a safe distance, and no doubt some of them report to Dad, who reports to Costa Rica. But most of them are just kids fascinated by machines, fascinated by war. I probably went through a stage like that. My memories before eleven or twelve are vague almost to nonexistence, a by-product of the jack installation that affects about a third of us. Who needs a childhood when the present is so much fun?

We had more than enough excitement for anybody the last night. Three rockets came in simultaneously, two of them from the sea and one, a decoy, coming in at treetop level, launched from the balcony of a high-rise on the edge of town.

The two that came in from the sea were in our sector. There were automatic defenses against this kind of attack, but we backed them up.

As soon as we heard the explosion—Alpha knocking out the rocket on the other side of the camp—we stifled the natural impulse to look and turned to watch in the opposite direction, facing directly out from the camp. The two rockets immediately appeared, stealthed but bright in IR. A flak wall sprayed up in front of them, and we targeted them with our heavy bullets about the time they hit that. Two crimson fireballs. They were still glowing impressively in the night sky when a pair of flyboys screamed out to sea in search of the launching platform.

Our reaction time had been fast enough, but we didn't set any records. Park, of course, got in the first shot, .02 of a second ahead of Claude, which made him smug. We all had people in the warm-up seats, it being the last day of our cycle and the first of theirs; I got a confused query from Park's second, through my second: *Is there something wrong with this guy?*

Just a real good soldier, I said, and knew my meaning was clear. My second, Wu, didn't have any more killer instinct than I did.

I left five soldierboys on perimeter and took the other five down to the beach to police up debris from the missiles. No surprises. They were Taiwanese RPB-4s. A note of protest would be sent, and the reply would lament the obvious theft.

But the rockets were just a diversion.

The actual attack was timed pretty well. It was less than one hour before the shift ended.

As far as we could reconstruct it, the plan was a combination of patience and sudden desperate force. The two rebels who did it had been working for the food service in Portobello for years. They rolled into the lounge adjacent to the locker room to set up the buffet most of us tore into after our shift. But they had scatterguns, two streetsweepers, taped under the food carts. There was a third person, never caught, who cut the fiber line that gave Command its physical picture of the lounge and locker room.

That gave them about thirty seconds of "somebody tripped over the cable," while the two pulled out their weapons and walked through the unlocked doors that connect the lounge to the locker room and the locker room to Operations. They stepped into Ops and started shooting.

The tapes show that they lived for 2.02 seconds after the door opened, during which time they got off seventy-eight 20-gauge buckshot blasts. They didn't hurt any of us in the cages, since that would take armor-piercing shells and more, but they killed all ten of the warm-up mechanics and two of the techs, who were behind supposedly bulletproof glass. The shoe guard, who dozes over us in his armored suit, woke up at the noise and toasted them. It was actually a close thing, as it turned out, because he took four direct hits. They didn't harm him, but if they'd hit the laser, he would have had to lumber down and attack them hand to hand. That might have given them time to crack the shells. They each had five shaped charges taped under their shirts.

All the weapons were Alliance issue; the fully automatic shotguns fired depleted uranium ammunition.

The propaganda machine would play up the suicide aspect of it—lunatic pedros who place no value on human life. As if they had just run amok and wiped out twelve young men and women. The reality was frightening, not only because of their success in infiltrating and attacking, but also in the bold and desperate dedication that it bespoke.

We hadn't just hired those two people off the street. Everyone who worked on the compound had to pass an exhaustive background check, and psychological testing that proved they were safe. How many other time bombs were walking around Portobello?

Candi and I were lucky, in a grim way, because both our seconds died instantly. Wu didn't even have time to turn around. He heard the door click open and then a shotgun blast took off the top of his head. Candi's second, Marla, died the same way. Some of them were pretty bad. Rose's second had time to stand up and turn half around, and was shot in the chest and abdomen. She lived long enough to drown in blood. Claude's was shot in the crotch as a reward for facing the enemy; he lived for a long couple of seconds jackknifed in pain before a second blast tore out his lower spine and kidneys.

It was a light jack, but still profoundly disturbing, especially for those of us whose seconds died in pain. We were all tranked automatically before they popped our cages and rolled us to Trauma. I got a glimpse of the carnage all around, the big white machines that were trying to hammer life back into the ones whose brains were intact. The next day we found out that none of those had been successful. Their bodies were too completely shredded.

So there was no next shift. Our soldierboys stood in frozen postures in their guard positions while shoe infantry, suddenly pressed into guard detail, swarmed around them. The natural assumption was that the attack on our seconds would be followed immediately by a ground attack on the base itself, before another platoon of soldierboys could be brought in. Maybe it would have happened if one or two of the rockets had found their mark. But all was quiet, this time, and Fox platoon, from the Zone, was in place in less than an hour.

They let us out of Trauma after a couple of hours, and at first said we weren't to tell anyone what happened. But of course the Ngumi weren't going to keep it quiet.

automatic cameras had recorded the carnage, and a copy of the scene fell into Ngumi hands. It was powerful propaganda, in a world that couldn't be shocked by death or violence. To the camera, Julian's ten comrades were not young men and women, naked under an unrelenting spray of lead. They were symbols of weakness, triumphant evidence of the Alliance's vulnerability in the face of Ngumi dedication.

The Alliance called it a freakish kamikaze attack by

two murderous fanatics. It was a situation that could never be duplicated. They didn't publicize the fact that all of the native staff in Portobello were fired the next week, replaced by American draftees.

This was hard on the economy of Portobello proper, as the base was its largest single source of income. Panama was a "most favored nation," but not a full Alliance Member, which in practical terms meant it had limited use of American nanoforges, but there weren't any of the machines within its boundaries.

There were about two dozen small countries in a similar unstable situation. Two nanoforges in Houston were reserved for Panama. The Panama Import/Export Board decided what they were to be used for. Houston supplied them with a "wish book," a list of how long it took to make something, and what raw materials had to be supplied by the Canal Zone. Houston could supply air and water and dirt. If something required an ounce of platinum or a speck of dysprosium, Panama would have to dig it up somewhere or somehow.

The machine had limits. You could give it a bucket of coal and it could return a perfect copy of the Hope Diamond, which would make a dandy paperweight. Of course, if you wanted a fancy gold crown, you'd have to supply the gold. If you wanted an atomic bomb, you'd have to give it a couple of kilograms of plutonium. But fission bombs were not in the wish book; nor were soldierboys or any other products of advanced military technology. Planes and tanks were okay, and among the most popular items.

This is the way things worked: the day after the Portobello base was emptied of native workers, the Panama Import/Export Board presented the Alliance with a detailed analysis of the impact of the loss of income. (It was obvious that someone had foreseen the eventuality.) After a couple of days' haggling, the Alliance agreed to increase their nanoforge allotment from forty-eight hours per day to fifty-four, along with a onetime settlement of a half-billion dollars' credit in rare materials. So if the prime minister wanted a Rolls-Royce with a solid gold chassis, he could have it. But it wouldn't be bulletproof.

The Alliance did not officially care how client nations came up with their requests for the machines' largesse. In Panama there was at least a pretense of democracy, the Import/Export Board being advised by elected representatives, *compradores,* one from each province and territory. So there were occasional well-publicized imports that benefited only the poor.

Like the United States, technically, they had a semi-socialist electrocash economy. The government supposedly took care of basic needs, and citizens worked for money for luxuries, which were paid for either by electronic credit transfer or cash.

But in the United States, luxuries were just that: entertainments or refinements. In the Canal Zone they were things like medicine and meat, more often bought with cash than with plastic.

There was a lot of resentment, of their own government and Tio Rico to the north, which gave rise to an ironic pattern common to most client states: incidents like the Portobello massacre ensured that Panama would not have its own nanoforges for a long time, but the unrest that led to the massacre was directly traceable to its lack of the magic box.

we got no peace the first week after the massacre. The huge publicity machine that fueled the warboy mania, and was usually concerned with more interesting platoons, turned its energies on us; the general media wouldn't leave us alone, either. In a culture that lived on news, it was the story of the year: bases like Portobello were attacked all the time, but this was the first time the mechanics' inner sanctum had been violated. That the mechanics who were killed had not been in charge of the machines was a detail repeatedly stressed by the government and downplayed by the press.

They even interviewed some of my UT students to see how I was "taking it," and of course they were quick to defend me by saying it was business as usual in the classroom. Which of course demonstrated how unfeeling I was, or how strong and resilient, or how traumatized, depending on the reporter.

Actually, it may have demonstrated all of the above, or maybe just that a particle-physics practicum is not a place where you discuss personal feelings.

When they tried to bring a camera into my classroom, I called a shoe and had them evicted. It was the first time in my academic career that being a sergeant meant more than being an instructor, however junior.

Likewise, I was able to commandeer two shoes to keep the reporters at a distance when I went out. But for almost a week they did have at least one camera watching me, which kept me away from Amelia. Of course, she could just walk into my apartment building as if she were visiting someone else, but the possibility that someone would make a connection—or happen to see her walking into my own apartment—was too great to risk. There were still some people in Texas who would be unhappy about a white woman who had a black man, fifteen years younger, for a lover. There might even be some people in the university who would be unhappy about it.

The newsies seemed to have lost interest by Friday, but Amelia and I went to the club separately, and I brought along my shoes to stand guard outside.

We overlapped trips to the bathroom, and managed a quick embrace unobserved. Otherwise, most of my apparent attention went to Marty and Franklin.

Marty confirmed what I had suspected. "The autopsy

showed that your second's jack was disconnected by the same blast that killed him. So there's no reason for it to have felt any different to you than just being unplugged."

"At first, I didn't even realize he was gone," I said, not for the first time. "The input from the rest of my platoon was so strong and chaotic. The ones whose seconds were hurt but still alive."

"But it wouldn't be as bad for them as being fully jacked to someone who died," Franklin said. "Most of you have gone through that."

"I don't know. When somebody dies in the cage, it's a heart attack or stroke. Not being ripped open by buckshot. A light jack may only feed back, say, ten percent of that sensation, but it's a lot of pain. When Carolyn died . . ." I had to clear my throat. "With Carolyn it was just a sudden headache, and she was gone. Just like coming unjacked."

"I'm sorry," Franklin said, and filled both our glasses. The wine was a duped Lafite Rothschild '28, the wine of the century, so far.

"Thanks. It's years now." I sipped the wine, good but presumably beyond my powers of discrimination. "The bad part, *a* bad part, was that it didn't occur to me that she'd died. Nor to anybody else in the platoon. We were just standing on a hill, waiting for a snatch. Thought it was a comm failure."

"They knew at the company level," Marty said.

"Of course they did. And of course they wouldn't tell us, risk our screwing up the snatch. But when we popped, her cage was empty. I found a medic and she said they'd done a brain scan and there wasn't enough to save; they'd taken her down to autopsy already. Marty, I've told you this more than once before. Sorry."

Marty shook his head in commiseration. "No closure. No leave-taking."

"They should've popped you all, once you were in

place," Franklin said. "They can snatch cold 'boys as easily as warm ones. Then you would've at least known, before they took her away."

"I don't know." My memory of the whole thing is cloudy. They knew we were lovers, of course, and had me tranked before I was popped. A lot of the counseling was just drug therapy with conversation, and after a while I wasn't taking the drugs anymore and I had Amelia there in place of Carolyn. In some ways.

I felt a sudden pang of frustration and longing, partly for Amelia after this stupid week of isolation, partly for the unattainable past. There would never be another Carolyn, and not just because she was dead. That part of me was dead, too.

The talk moved on to safer areas, a movie everybody but Franklin had hated. I pretended to follow it. Meanwhile, my mind went round and round the suicide track.

It never seems to surface while I'm jacked. Maybe the army knows all about it, and has a way of suppressing it; I know I'm suppressing it myself. Even Candi only had a hint.

But I can't keep this up for five more years, all the killing and dying. And the war's not going to end.

When I feel this way I don't feel sad. It's not loss, but escape—it's not whether, but when and how.

I guess after I lose Amelia is the "when." The only "how" that appeals to me is to do it while jacked. Maybe take a couple of generals with me. I can save the actual planning for the moment. But I do know where the generals live in Portobello, Building 31, and with all my years jacked it's nothing to slide a comm thread to the soldierboys who guard the building. There are ways I can divert them for a fraction of a second. Try not to kill any shoes on my way in.

"Yoo-hoo. Julian? Anybody home?" It was Reza, from the other table.

"Sorry. Thinking."

"Well, come over here and think. We have a physics question that Blaze can't answer."

I picked up my drink and moved over. "Not particle, then."

"No, it's simpler than that. Why does water emptying out of a tub go one direction in the Northern Hemisphere and the other in the Southern?"

I looked at Amelia and she nodded seriously. She knew the answer, and Reza probably did, too. They were rescuing me from the war talk.

"That's easy. Water molecules are magnetized. They always point north or south."

"Nonsense," Belda said. "Even I would know it if water were magnetized."

"The truth is that it's an old wives' tale. You'll excuse the expression."

"I'm an old widow," Belda said.

"Water goes one way or the other depending on the size and shape of the tub, and peculiarities of the surface near the outlet. People go through life believing the hemisphere thing without noticing that some of the basins in their own house go the wrong way."

"I must go home and check," Belda said. She drained her glass and unfolded slowly out of the chair. "You children be good." She went to say good-bye to the others.

Reza smiled at her back. "She thought you looked lonely there."

"Sad," Amelia said. "I did, too. Such a horrible experience, and here we are bringing it up all over."

"It's not something they covered in training. I mean, in a way they do. You get jacked to strings recorded while people died, first in a light jack and then deeper."

"Some jackfreaks do it for fun," Reza said.

"Yeah, well, they can have *my* job."

"I've seen that billboard." Amelia hugged herself.

"Strings of people dying in racing accidents. Executions."

"The under-the-counter ones are worse." Ralph had tried a couple, so I'd felt them secondhand. "Our backups who died, their strings are probably on the market by now."

"The government can't—"

"Oh, the government loves it," Reza broke in. "They probably have some recruitment division that makes sure the stores are full of snuff strings."

"I don't know," I said. "Army's not wild about people who are already jacked."

"Ralph was," Amelia said.

"He had other virtues. They'd rather have you associate the specialness of being jacked with being in the army."

"Sounds really special," Reza said. "Somebody dies and you feel his pain? I'd rather—"

"You don't understand, Rez. You get larger in a way, when somebody dies. You share it and"—the memory of Carolyn suddenly hit me hard—"well, it makes your own death less earthshaking. Someday you'll buy it. Big deal."

"You live on? I mean, they live on, in you?"

"Some do, some don't. You've met people you'd never want to carry around in your head. Those guys die the day they die."

"But you'll have Carolyn forever," Amelia said.

I paused a little too long. "Of course. And after I die, the people who've been jacked to me will remember her too, and pass her down."

"I wish you wouldn't talk like that," Amelia said. Rez, who had known for years that we were together, nodded. "It's like a boil you keep picking at, like you were getting ready to die all the time."

I almost lost it. I literally counted to ten. Rez opened his mouth but I interrupted. "Would you rather I just watched people die, *felt* them die, and came home asking 'What's for dinner?' '' I dropped to a whisper. "How would you feel about me if that didn't hurt me?"

"I'm sorry."

"Don't. I'm sorry you lost a baby. But that's not what you are. We go through these things, and then we more or less absorb them, and we become whatever we are becoming."

"Julian," Reza said in a warning tone, "perhaps you ought to save this for later?"

"That's a good idea," Amelia said, rising. "I have to go on home anyhow." She signaled the wheelie and it went for her coat and bag.

"Share a cab?" I asked.

"It's not necessary," she said in a neutral tone. "End of the month." She could use leftover entertainment points for a cab ride.

Other people didn't have points left over, so I bought a lot of wine and beer and whiskey, and drank more than my share. Reza did, too; his car wouldn't let him drive. He came along with me and my two bodyguard shoes.

I had them drop me at the campus gate, and walked the two kilometers to Amelia's through a cool mist of rain. No sign of any newsies.

All the lights were out; it was almost two. I let myself in through the back and belatedly thought I should have buzzed. What if she wasn't alone?

I turned on the kitchen light and harvested cheese and grape juice from the refrigerator. She heard me moving around and shuffled in, rubbing her eyes. "No reporters?" I asked.

"They're all under the bed."

She stood behind me and put her hands on my shoulders. "Give them something to write about?" I turned around in the chair and buried my face between her breasts. Her skin had a warm, sleepy smell.

"I'm sorry about earlier."

"You've been through too much. Come on." I let her lead me into the bedroom and she undressed me like a child. I was still a little drunk, but she had ways of getting around that, mostly patience, but other things, too.

I slept like a creature stunned and woke to an empty house. She'd left a note on the microwave that she had a sequence scheduled at 8:45 and would see me at the lunch group meeting. It was after ten.

A Saturday meeting; science never sleeps. I found some clean clothes in "my" drawer and took a quick shower.

the day before i went back to Portobello, I had an appointment with the Luxury Allocation Board in Dallas, the people who handle special requests for the nanoforge. I took the Triangle monorail, and so got a glimpse of Fort Worth streaming by. I'd never gotten off there.

It was a half hour to Dallas, but then another hour crawling through traffic out to the LAB, which took up a huge piece of land outside the city limits. They had sixteen nanoforges, and hundreds of tanks and vats and bins that held the raw materials and the various nanos that put them together in millions of ways. I didn't have time to walk around, but had taken a guided tour of the place with Reza and his friend, the year before. That's when I got the idea to get something special for Amelia. We didn't do birthdays or religious holidays, but next week was the second anniversary of the first time we were intimate. (I don't keep a diary, but could trace the date down through lab reports; we both missed the next day's sequence.)

The evaluator assigned to my request was a sour-faced

man, about fifty. He read the form with a fixed glum expression. "You don't want this piece of jewelry for yourself. This is for some woman, some lover?"

"Yes, of course."

"I'll have to have her name, then."

I hesitated. "She's not exactly my—"

"I don't care about your relationship. I just have to know who will eventually own this object. If I should approve it."

I wasn't enthusiastic about having our relationship officially documented. Of course anyone who tapped me with a deep jack would know about it, so it was only as secret as anything in my life was secret.

"It's for Amelia Blaze Harding," I said. "A coworker."

He wrote that down. "She also lives at the university?"

"That's right."

"Same address?"

"No. I'm not sure what her address is."

"We'll find it." He smiled like a man who had sucked on a lemon and tried to smile. "I see no reason to disapprove your request." A printer in his desk hissed and a piece of paper flipped up in front of me.

"That will be fifty-three utility credits," he said. "If you sign here, the finished piece should be available at Unit Six within half an hour."

I signed. More than a month's worth of credits for a handful of sand transformed was one way to think of it. Or fifty-three worthless government counters for a thing of beauty that would have been literally beyond price a generation ago.

I went out into the corridor and followed a purple line that led to Units 1 through 8. That split, and I followed a red line to Units 5 through 8. Door after door concealing people who sat at desks slowly doing work that machines could have done better and faster. But machines had no use for extra utility and entertainment credits.

I went through a revolving door into a pleasant rotunda built around a rock garden. A thin silvery stream fell and washed through it, splashing among exotic tropical plants that grew out of a gravel of rubies, diamonds, emeralds, and dozens of glittering stones with no common names.

I checked at the Unit 6 counter and it said I still had a half-hour wait. There was a cafe, though, with tables ringed around half the rock garden. I produced my military ID and got a cold beer. At the table where I sat, somebody had left a folded-up copy of the Mexican magazine *¡Sexo!*, so I spent the half hour improving my language skills.

A card on the table explained that the gems were specimens rejected for esthetic or structural flaws. They were nevertheless well out of reach.

The desk announced my name and I went over and picked up a small white package. I unwrapped it carefully.

It was exactly what I had ordered, but seemed more dramatic than its picture. A gold chain necklace supporting a dark green nightstone inside a halo of small rubies. Nightstones had only been around for a few months. This one looked like a small egg of onyx that somehow had a green light imbedded. As you turned it, the green changed shape, square to diamond to cross.

It would look good on her delicate skin, the red and green echoing her hair and eyes. I hoped it wouldn't be too exotic for her to wear.

On the train ride back, I showed it to a woman who sat next to me. She said it was pretty, but in her opinion was too dark for a black woman's skin. I told her I'd have to think about that.

I left it on Amelia's dresser, along with a note reminding her it was two years, and went on to Portobello.

julian was born in a university town, and grew up surrounded by white people who weren't overtly racist. There were race riots in places like Detroit and Miami, but people treated them as urban problems, far removed from their comfortable reality. That was close to the truth.

But the Ngumi War was changing white America's feelings about race—or, cynics maintained, allowing them to express their true feelings. Only about half the enemy were black, but most of the leaders who appeared on the news were from that half. And they were shown crying out for white blood.

The irony wasn't lost on Julian, that he was an active part of a process that was turning American whites against blacks. But that kind of white person was alien to his personal world, his daily life; the woman on the train literally came from a foreign land. The people in his university life were mostly white but color-blind, and the people he jacked with might have started out otherwise, but didn't stay racist: you couldn't think black people were inferior if you lived inside black skin, ten days every month.

our first assignment had a lot of potential to turn ugly. We had to "remand for questioning"—kidnap—a woman who was suspected of being a rebel leader. She was also the mayor of San Ignacio, a small town high in the cloud forest.

The town was so small that any two of us could have destroyed it in minutes. We circled it in a silent flyboy, studying the infrared signature and comparing that to maps and low-orbit pictures. The town was lightly defended, apparently; ambushes set on the main road where it entered and left the town. Of course there could be automated defenses that didn't betray themselves with body heat. But it wasn't that rich a town.

"Let's try to do this quietly," I said. "Drop into the coffee plantation about *here*." I pointed mentally to a spot almost two kilometers downhill from the town. "Candi and I'll work up through the plantation to the rear of Señora Madero's house. See whether we can make the snatch without raising any fuss."

"Julian, you ought to take at least two more," Claude said. "The place is gonna be wired and 'trapped."

I gave him a nonverbal rebuttal: You know I considered that. "Just you be ready to charge up if something happens. We start making noise, I want all ten of you to run up the hill in a tight formation and circle Candi and me. We'll keep Madero protected. Lay down smoke and we head straight down the valley *here* and then up this little rise for a cargo snatch." I felt the flyboy relay that information laterally and, in a second, confirm that we could have a warm-body snatch in place.

"Now," I said, and all twelve of us were falling fast through the cold night air. We spaced ourselves fifty meters apart and after a minute the black chutes whispered out and we drifted invisibly down into the acres of low coffee trees—bushes, actually; a person of even normal height would have a hard time hiding out there. It was a calculated risk. If we'd landed closer to town, in the actual forest, we would have made a lot of noise.

It was easy to aim between the neat rows. I sank up to my knees in the soft wet soil. The chutes detached and folded and rolled themselves into tight cylinders that quietly fused into solid bricks. They'd probably wind up as part of a wall or fence.

Everybody moved silently to the tree line and took cover, while Candi and I worked uphill, weaving quietly between trees, avoiding brush.

"Dog," she said, and we froze. From where I was, slightly behind her, I couldn't see it, but through her sensors smelled the fur and breath and then saw the IR blob. It woke up and I heard the beginning of a growl that ended with the "thap" of a tranquilizer dart. It was a human dose; I hoped it wouldn't kill the dog.

Just past the dog was the neatly trimmed lawn behind Madero's house. There was a light on in the kitchen— worse luck. The house had been dark when we jumped.

Candi and I could just hear two voices through the closed window. The conversation was too fast and too heavily accented for either of us to follow, but the tone was clear—Señora Madero and some man were anxious, whispering urgently.

Expecting company, Candi thought.

Now, I thought. In four steps, Candi was at the window and I was at the back door. She smashed the window with one hand and fired two darts with the other. I pulled the door off its hinges and stepped into a storm of gunfire.

Two people with assault rifles. I tranked them both and stepped toward the kitchen. An alarm whooped three times before I could track down the relay clicking and rip it out of the wall.

Two people, three people running down the stairs. *Smoke and VA,* I thought to myself and Candi, and dropped two grenades in the hall. Using vomiting agent was a little tricky, since our snatch was unconscious; we couldn't let her inhale it and possibly choke on her own puke. But we had to work fast anyhow.

Two people were slumped over the kitchen table. There was a circuit-breaker box on the wall; I smashed it and everything went dark, though for Candi and me it was bright red figures in a dark red kitchen.

I picked up Madero and her companion and started back for the hall. But along with the sounds of gagging and retching I heard the greased-metal "snick-chk" of a weapon being armed, and the snap of a safety switch. I flashed an image to Candi and she stuck one arm through the window and swept half the wall down. The roof sagged with a creak and then a splintering crash, but by then I was in the backyard with my two guests. I dropped the man and cradled Madero like a baby.

"Wait for the others," I vocalized unnecessarily. We could hear townsfolk running down the gravel road toward the house, but our people were moving faster.

Ten black giants exploded out of the forest behind us. *Smoke there there there,* I thought. *Lights on.* White smoke welled up in a semicircle around us and became an opaque blinding wall with our sunlights. I turned my back on it, shielding Madero from the random chatter of gunfire and laser stab and sweep. *Everyone VA and split!* Eleven canisters of vomiting agent popped; I was already in the woods and running. Bullets hummed and rustled harmlessly overhead. As I ran I checked her pulse and respiration, normal under the circumstances, and checked the dart site on the back of her neck. The dart had fallen out and she'd already stopped bleeding.

Leave the note?

Candi thought, *Yes: on the table somewhere under the roof now.* We had a supposedly legal warrant for Señora Madero's detainment. That and a hundred pesos would get you a cup of coffee, if there was any left after export.

Out of the forest, I could run faster. It was exhilarating, bounding over the rows of low coffee bushes, even though in some corner of my mind I always knew I was lying inert a hundred miles away, inside an armored plastic shell. I could hear the others running just behind me and, as I moved up the hill toward the pickup, the faint hiss and snap of the approaching chopper and flyboys.

When it's just us soldierboys they snatch us at speed; we hold up our arms and grab the bail as it sails by. For a warm-body snatch, though, they have to actually land the helicopter, which is why she had two flyboys as escorts.

I got to the top of the hill and broadcasted a bleep, which the helicopter returned. The rest of the platoon came loping up in twos and threes. It occurred to me that I should have called for two choppers; do a regular snatch on the other eleven. It was dangerous for all of us to stand out in the open for any length of time, with the helicopter noise attracting attention.

As if in answer to my concern, a mortar round hit fifty meters to my left, orange flash and muted thump. I linked with the flyboy in the chopper and sensed a short argument she had with Command. Someone wanted us to drop the body and do a regular snatch. As the flyboy came over the horizon, another mortar round hit, maybe ten meters behind me, and we got the modified order: line up for a regular snatch and she would come in as slowly as practical.

We got together in file with our left arms up, and I had one second to wonder whether I should hold Madero tightly or loosely. I opted for tight, and most of the others agreed, which might have been wrong.

The bail snatched us with an impulse shock of fifteen or twenty gees. Nothing to a soldierboy but, we found out later, it cracked four of the woman's ribs. She woke up with a shriek as two mortar rounds hit close enough to hole the chopper and damage Claude and Karen. Madero wasn't hit by the shrapnel, but she found herself dozens of meters off the ground and rising fast, and she struggled hard, beating at me and screaming, writhing around. All I could do was hold her more tightly, but my arm had her pinned just below the breasts, and I was afraid to press her too hard.

Suddenly she went slack, fainting or dead. I couldn't check her pulse or respiration, hands full, but there was not much I could have done in any case, other than not drop her.

After a few minutes we landed on a bald hill, and I confirmed that she was still breathing. I carried her in-

side the helicopter and strapped her into a stretcher that
was clamped to the wall. Command asked whether there
were any handcuffs, which I thought was kind of amusing; but then she elaborated: this woman was a true be-
liever. If she woke up and found herself in an enemy
helicopter, she would jump out or otherwise do away
with herself.

The rebels told each other horror stories about what
we did to prisoners to make them talk. It was all nonsense. Why bother to torture someone when all you have
to do is put her under, drill a hole in her skull, and jack
her? That way she can't lie.

Of course, international law is not clear on the practice. The Ngumi call it a violation of basic human rights;
we call it humane questioning. The fact that one of ten
winds up dead or brain-dead makes the morality of it
pretty clear to me. But then we only do it to prisoners
who refuse to cooperate.

I found a roll of duct tape and bound her wrists together and then taped loops around her chest and knees,
fixing her to the stretcher.

She woke up while I was doing her knees. "You are
monsters," she said in clear English.

"We come by it naturally, Señora. Born of man and
woman."

"A monster and a philosopher."

The helicopter roared into life and we sprang off the
hill. I had a fraction of a second's warning, and so was
able to brace myself. It was unexpected but logical: what
difference did it make whether I was inside the vehicle
or hanging on outside?

After a minute we settled into a quieter, steady progress. "Can I get you some water?"

"Please. And a painkiller."

There was a toilet aft, with a drinking water tap and
tiny paper cups. I brought her two and held them to her
lips.

"No painkillers until we land, I'm afraid." I could knock her out with another trank, but that would complicate her medical situation. "Where do you hurt?"

"Chest. Chest and neck. Could you take this damned tape off? I'm not going anywhere."

I cleared it with Command and a foot-long razor-keen bayonet snicked into my hand. She shrank away, as much as her bonds would allow. "Just a knife." I cut the tape around her chest and knees and helped her to a sitting position. I queried the flyboy and she confirmed that the woman was apparently unarmed, so I freed her hands and feet.

"May I use that toilet?"

"Sure." When she stood up she doubled over in pain, clutching her side.

"Here." I couldn't stand upright in the seven-foot-high cargo area, either, so we shuffled aft, a bent-over giant helping a bent-over dwarf. I helped her with her belt and trousers.

"Please," she said. "Be a gentleman."

I turned my back on her but of course could still see her. "I can't be a gentleman," I said. "I'm five women and five men, working together."

"So that's true? You make women fight?"

"You don't fight, Señora?"

"I protect my land and my people." If I hadn't been looking at her I would have misinterpreted the strong emotion in her voice. I saw her hand flick into a breast pocket and caught her wrist just before her hand made it to her mouth.

I forced her fingers open and took a small white pill. It had an odor of bitter almonds, low-tech.

"That wouldn't do any good," I said. "We'd just revive you and you'd be sick."

"You kill people and, when it pleases you, you bring them back from the dead. But you are not monsters."

I put the pill in a pocket on my leg and watched her

carefully. "If we were monsters we would bring them back to life, extract our information, and kill them again."

"You don't do that."

"We have more than eight thousand of your people in prison, awaiting repatriation after the war. It would be easier to kill them, wouldn't it?"

"Concentration camps." She stood and pulled up her trousers, and sat back down.

"A loaded term. There are camps where the Costa Rican prisoners of war are concentrated. With UN and Red Cross observers, making sure they're not mistreated. As you'll see with your own eyes." I don't often defend Alliance policies. But it was interesting to watch a fanatic at work.

"I should live that long."

"If you want to, you will. I don't know how many more pills you have." I linked through the flyboy to Command and brought a speech analyzer on line.

"That was the only one," she said, as I'd expected, and the analyzer said she was telling the truth. I relaxed slightly. "So I'll be one of your prisoners of war."

"Presumably. Unless this has all been a case of mistaken identity."

"I've never fired a weapon. I've never killed anybody."

"Neither has my commander. She has degrees in military theory and cybernetic communication, but she's never been a soldier."

"But she has actually killed people. Lots of us."

"And you helped plan the assault on Portobello. By that logic, you killed friends of mine."

"No I didn't," she said. Quick, intense, lying.

"You killed them while I was intimately connected to their minds. Some of them died very horribly."

"No. No."

"Don't bother to lie to me. I can bring people back

from the dead, remember? I could have destroyed your village with one thought. And I can tell when you're lying.''

She was silent for a moment, considering that. She must have known about voice analyzers. "I am the mayor of San Ignacio. There will be repercussions.''

"Not legal ones. We have a warrant for your detention, signed by the governor of your province.''

She made a spitting sound. "Pepe Ano." His name was Pellipianocio, Italian, but her Spanish converted it to "Joe Asshole.''

"I take it he's not popular with the rebels. But he was one of you.''

"He inherited a coffee plantation from his uncle and was such a bad farmer he couldn't make a radish grow. You bought his land, you bought him.''

She thought that was the truth, and it probably was. "We didn't coerce him," I said, guessing. I didn't know much about the town's or province's history. "Didn't he come to us? Declare himself—''

"Oh, really. Like a hungry dog would come to anybody who put out food. You can't pretend to think that he represents us.''

"As a matter of fact, Señora, we were not consulted. Are your soldiers consulted before being given orders?''

"We . . . I don't know anything about such matters.'' That one set the bells off. As she knew, their soldiers *were* in on the decision-making process. That cut down on their efficiency but did give some logic to calling themselves the Democratic Army of the People.

The helicopter suddenly lurched left and right, accelerating up. I put out a hand and kept her from falling.

"Missile," I said, in touch with the flyboy.

"A pity it missed.''

"You're the only living creature aboard this craft, Señora. The rest of us are safe in Portobello.''

At that she smiled. "Not so safe, I think. Wasn't that the point of this little kidnapping?"

the woman was one of the lucky ninety percent who survived jacking intact, and she did give Alliance questioners the names of three other *tenientes* who had been in on the Portobello massacre. For her own part in it she was sentenced to death, but the sentence was commuted to life imprisonment. She was sent to the large POW camp in the Canal Zone, the jack in the back of her skull guaranteeing that she wouldn't be part of any conspiracy there.

Unsurprisingly, during the four hours it had taken to get her to Portobello and install the jack, the three other *tenientes* and their families had dissolved into the bush, driven underground—perhaps to return. Their fingerprints and retinal patterns tagged them as rebels, but there was no real guarantee that the ones on file were authentic. They had had years to effect substitution. Any one of them might show up at the entrance to the camp at Portobello with a job application.

Of course, the Alliance had fired every Hispanic employee at the Portobello camp, and could do the same everywhere else in the city, even the country. But that might be counterproductive in the long run. The Alliance provided one out of three jobs in Panama. Putting those people out of work would probably add one more country to the Ngumi ranks.

Marx and others thought and taught that war was fundamentally economic in nature. No one in the nineteenth century, though, could have foreseen the world of the twenty-first, where half the world had to work for its rice or bread and the other half just lined up in front of generous machines.

the platoon returned to the town just before dawn, with warrants for the three rebel leaders. They entered the houses in groups of three, simultaneously crashing inside in clouds of smoke and vile gas, lowering real estate values but finding no one. There was no effective resistance, and they sped away in ten separate directions.

They rendezvoused at a place about twenty kilometers downhill, a feed store and cantina. The cantina had been closed for hours, but one customer remained, collapsed under one of the outside tables, snoring. They didn't wake him up.

The rest of the mission was an exercise in malice dreamed up by some half-awake genius who was annoyed at not taking any more prisoners that night. They were to go back up the hill and systematically destroy the crops that belonged to the three escaped rebels.

Two of them were coffee planters, so Julian ordered his people to uproot the bushes and leave them in place; presumably they could be replanted the next day.

The third man's "crop" was the town's only hardware store. If Julian had asked, they probably would have been ordered to torch it. So he didn't ask; he and three others just broke down the doors and threw all of the merchandise out on the street. Let the town decide whether they would respect the man's belongings.

Most of the town was tired of dealing with the soldierboys by now, and had gotten the message that the machines weren't going to kill anyone unless provoked. Still, two ambitious snipers came in with lasers and had to be shot, but the soldierboys were able to use tranquilizing darts.

Park, the platoon's new homicidal addition, gave Julian some trouble there. He argued against using the darts—which technically was insubordination under fire, a court-martial offense—and then when he did take aim with the dart, he aimed for the sniper's eye, which would have been fatal. Julian monitored that just in time to send a mental shout, "Cease fire!" and reassign the sniper to Claude, who tranked him in the shoulder.

So as a show of force, the mission was reasonably successful, though Julian wondered what the sense of it was. The townspeople would probably see it as bullying vandalism. Maybe he *should* have torched the store and sterilized the two farmers' lands. But he hoped the restrained approach would work better: with his laser he wrote a scorched message on the whitewashed wall of the hardware store, translated by Psychops into formal Spanish: "—By rights, twelve of you should perish for the twelve of us you killed. Let there not be a next time."

when i came home Tuesday night there was a note under my door:

Darling,

The gift is beautiful. I went to a concert last night just so I could dress up and show it off. Two people asked who it was from, and I was enigmatic: a friend.

Well, friend, I've made a big decision, I suppose in part a present to you. I've gone down to Guadalajara to have a jack installed.

I didn't want to wait and discuss it with you because I don't want you to share the responsibility, if something should go wrong. My mind was actually made up by a news item, which I've put on your queue as "law.jack."

Basically, a man in Austin got jacked and fired from his administrative job, then challenged the antijack clause under Texas job discrimination laws. The court ruled in his favor, so at least for the time being, it's professionally safe for me to go ahead and do it.

I know all about the physical danger, and I also know how unseemly it is for a woman of my years and position to take that risk because of what amounts to jealousy: I can't compete with your memory of Carolyn and I can't share your life the way Candi and the others do—the women you swear you don't love.

No arguments this way. I'll be back on Monday or Tuesday. Do we have a date?

Love,
Amelia

I read it over twice and then ran for the phone. There was no answer at her place. So I played back the other messages, and got the one I most feared:

"Señor Class, your name and number were given to us by Amelia Harding as a person to be reached in case of emergency. We are also contacting a Professor Hayes.

"Profesora Harding came here to the *Clínica de cirugía restorativa y aumentativa de Guadalajara* to have a *puente mental*, what you call a jack, installed. The operation did not go well, and she is completely paralyzed. She can breathe without help, and responds to visual and auditory stimuli, but cannot speak.

"We want to discuss various options with you. Señora Harding listed your name in lieu of next of kin. My name is Rodrigo Spencer, chief of *la división quirúrgica para instalación y extracción de implantas craniales*— Surgical Unit for Installation and Removal of Cranial Implants." He gave his number and the address.

That message was Sunday night. The next was from Hayes, Monday, saying he'd checked my schedule and wouldn't do anything until I got home. I took time for a quick shave and called him at home.

It was only ten, but he answered no-face. When he

heard it was me, he turned on the screen, rubbing his face. I'd obviously gotten him out of bed.

"Julian. Sorry . . . I've been on an odd schedule because we're testing for the big jump. The engineers had me up till three last night.

"Okay, look, about Blaze. It's no secret that you two are keeping company. I understand why she wants to be discreet, and appreciate it, but that's not a factor between you and me." His smile had real pain in it. "Okay?"

"Sure. I figured . . ."

"So what about Guadalajara?"

"I, I'm still a little in shock. I'll go downtown and get the first train; two hours, four, depending on connections . . . no, I'll call the base first and see if I can get a flight."

"Once you get down there?"

"I'll have to talk to people. I have a jack but don't know much about the installation—I mean, I was drafted; nobody gave me a choice. See whether I can talk to her."

"Son, they said she can't talk. She's paralyzed."

"I know, I know. But that's just motor function. If we can jack, we can talk. Find out what she wants."

"Okay." He shook his head. "Okay. But tell her what I want. I want her back in the shop *today*. Yesterday. Macro is going to have her head on a platter." He was trying to sound angry. "Damn fool stunt, just like Blaze. You call me from Mexico."

"Will do." He nodded and cut off.

I called the base and there weren't any direct flights scheduled. I could go back to Portobello and hitch up to Mexico City in the morning. *Gracias, pero no gracias.* I punched up the train schedule and called a cab.

It was only three hours to Guadalajara, but a bad three hours. I got to the hospital about one-thirty but of course couldn't get past the front desk. Not until seven; even then, I wouldn't be able to see Amelia until Dr. Spencer came in, maybe eight, maybe nine.

I got a mediocuarto—half-room—at a motel across the street, just a futon and a lamp. Couldn't sleep, so I found an all-night place and got a bottle of tequila *almendrada* and a news magazine. I sipped about half the bottle, laboriously picking my way through the magazine article by article. My everyday Spanish is all right but it's hard for me to follow a complicated written argument, since I never studied the language in school. There was a long article about the pros and cons of a euthanasia lottery for the elderly, which was scary enough even when you only got half the words.

In the war news there was a paragraph about our kidnapping venture, which was described as a peacekeeping police action ambushed by rebels. I don't guess they sell too many copies in Costa Rica. Or they probably just print a different version.

It was an amusing magazine, with ads that would have been illegal pornography in some of the United States. Six-image manifolds that move with stroboscopic jerkiness if you shake the page. Like most male readers, I suppose, I came up with an interesting way to shake the page, which finally helped me get to sleep.

I went over to the waiting room at seven and read less interesting magazines for an hour and a half, when Dr. Spencer finally showed up. He was tall and blond and spoke English with a Mexican accent thick as guacamole.

"Into my office, first, come." He took me by the arm and steered me down the hall. His office was a plain windowless room with a desk and two chairs; one of the chairs was occupied.

"Marty!"

He nodded. "Hayes called me, after he talked to you. Blaze had said something about me."

"An honor to have you here, Dr. Larrin." Spencer sat down behind the desk.

I sat on the other hard chair. "So what are our options?"

"Directed nanosurgery," Spencer said. "There are no other options."

"But there is," Marty said, "technically."

"Not legally."

"We could get around that."

"Would somebody tell me what you're talking about?"

"Mexican law is less liberal than American," Marty said, "in matters of self-determination."

"In your country," Spencer said, "she would have the option of remaining a vegetable."

"Well put, Dr. Spencer. Another way of putting it is that she would have the option of not risking her life and sanity."

"I'm missing something," I said.

"You shouldn't be. She's *jacked,* Julian! She can live a very full life without moving a muscle."

"Which is obscene."

"It's an option. The nanosurgery is risky."

"Not so. Not so risky. *Más o menos* the same as the jack. We have ninety-two percent recovery."

"You mean ninety-two percent survival," Marty said. "What percent total recovery?"

He shrugged, twice. "These numbers. They don't mean anything. She's healthy and relatively young. The operation will not kill her."

"She's a brilliant physicist. If she comes out with brain damage, that's the same as no recovery."

"Which is explained to her before the installation of the jack." He held up a document five or six pages long. "Before she signs the release."

"Why don't you jack her and ask her?" I said.

"It is not simple," Spencer said. "The first moment

she is jacked, is new, new neural pathways are formed. The network grows . . ." He gestured with one hand. "It grows more than fast."

"It grows at an exponential rate," Marty said. "The longer she's jacked, the more experiences she has, the harder it is to undo."

"And so this is why we do not ask her."

"In America you'd have to," Marty said. "Right of full disclosure."

"America is a very strange country. You don't mind my saying?"

"If I jacked with her," I said, "I could be in and out *muy pronto*. Dr. Larrin's had a jack longer, but it's not an everyday tool, the way it is with a mechanic." Spencer frowned at that. "A soldier."

"Yes . . . I suppose that's true." He leaned back and paused. "Still, it is against the law."

Marty gave him a look. "This law is never broken."

"I think you would say 'bent.' The law is bent, for foreigners." Marty made an unambiguous gesture with thumb and two fingers. "Well . . . not a bribe, as such. Some bureaucracy, and a tax. Do either of you have a . . ." He opened a desk drawer and said, *"Poder."*

The drawer answered, "Power of attorney."

"Do you have one of those with her?"

We looked at each other and shook our heads. "This was a surprise to both of us."

"She was not well advised. This is something she should have done. Is either of you her fiancé?"

"You could say that," I said.

"Bueno, okay." He picked a card out of a drawer and passed it over. "Go to this office after nine o'clock and this woman will issue you a temporary *designación de responsabilidad*." He repeated it into the drawer. "State of Jalisco Temporary Assignment of Legal Responsibility," it translated.

"Wait," I said. "This allows a person's fiancé to authorize a life-threatening surgical procedure?"

He shrugged. "Brother, sister, too. Uncle, aunt, nephew. Only when the person cannot decide for himself, herself. People wind up in Profesora Harding's situation every day. Several people every day, counting Mexico City and Acapulco."

It made sense; elective surgery must be one of the biggest sources of foreign income for Guadalajara, maybe for all of Mexico. I turned the card over; the English side said, "Accommodations to the Mexican Legal System."

"How much is this going to cost?"

"Maybe ten thousand pesos." Five hundred dollars.

"I can pay for it," Marty said.

"No, let me do it. I'm the fiancé." I also make three times his salary.

"Whoever," Spencer said. "You come back with the piece of paper and me, I set up the jack. But have your mind ready. Find the answer and then unplug. That will be safer and easier all around."

But what would I do if she asked me to stay?

It took almost as long to find the lawyer as it had to get to Guadalajara from Texas. They had moved.

Their new digs were not impressive, a table and a moth-eaten couch, but they did have all the paperwork. I wound up with a limited power of attorney that gave me authority for medical decisions. It was a little scary, how easy the process was.

When I came back, I was directed to Surgery B, a small white room. Dr. Spencer had Amelia prepped for both jacking and surgery, lying on a gurney with a drip in each arm. A thin cable led from the back of her head to a gray box on a table. Another jack was coiled on top of it. Marty was dozing in a chair by the door. He woke up when I came in.

"Where's the doctor?" I said.

"*Aquí.*" He was right behind me. "You have the paper?'' I handed it to him; he glanced at it, folded it, and put it in his pocket.

He touched Amelia on the shoulder, and then put the back of his hand on her cheek, then her forehead, an oddly maternal gesture.

''For you, you know . . . this is not going to be easy.''

''Easy? I spend a third of my life—''

''Jacked, *sí*. But not with someone who's never done it before. Not with someone you love.'' He pointed. ''Bring that chair here and sit.''

While I was doing that, he rummaged through a couple of drawers. ''Roll up your sleeve.''

I did that and he buzzed off a little patch of hair with a razor, then unwrapped a 'derm and slapped it on.

''What's that, a trank?''

''Not exactly. It does trank, tranquilize, in a way. It softens the blow, the shock of first contact.''

''But I've done first contact a dozen times.''

''Yes, but only while your army had control over your . . . what? System of circulation. You were drugged then, and now you will be drugged as well.''

It hit me like a soft slap. He heard my sudden intake of breath.

''*¿Listo?*''

''Go ahead.'' He uncoiled the cable and slipped the jack into my socket with a metallic click. Nothing happened. Then he turned on a switch.

Amelia suddenly turned to look at me and I had the familiar double-vision sensation, seeing myself while I looked at her. Of course it wasn't familiar to her, and I was seized with secondhand confusion and panic. *It gets easy dear hold on!* I tried to show her how to separate the two pictures, a mental twist really no harder than defocusing your eyes. After a moment she got it, calmed, and tried to make words.

You don't have to verbalize, I *felt* at her. Just think what you want to say.

She asked me to touch my face and run my hand slowly down my chest to my lap, my genitals.

"Ninety seconds," the doctor said. *"Tenga prisa."*

I basked in the wonder of discovery. It wasn't like the difference between blindness and sight, exactly, but it was as if all your life you'd been wearing thick tinted glasses, one lens opaque, and suddenly they were gone. A world full of brilliance, depth and color.

I'm afraid you get used to it, I felt. It becomes just another way of seeing. Of *being,* she answered.

In one burst of gestalt I told her what her options were, and of the danger of staying jacked too long. After a silence, she answered in individual words. I transferred her questions to Dr. Spencer, speaking with robotic slowness.

"If I have the jack removed, and the brain damage is such that I can't work, can I have the jack reinstalled?"

"If somebody pays for it, yes. Though your perceptions would be diminished."

"I'll pay for it."

"Which one are you?"

"Julian."

The pause seemed very long. She spoke through me: "I'll do it, then. But on one condition. First we make love this way. Have sex. Jacked."

"Absolutely not. Every second you talk is increasing the risk. If you do that you might never return to normal."

I saw him reaching for the switch and grabbed his wrist. "One second." I stood and kissed Amelia, one hand on her breast. There was a momentary storm of shared joy and then she disappeared as I heard the switch click, and I was kissing an inert simulacrum, tears mingling. I sat back down like a sack falling. He unplugged us and didn't say anything, but gave me a stern look and shook his head.

Part of that surge of emotion had been "Whatever the

risk, this is worth it," but whether that came from her or me or both of us together, I couldn't say.

A man and a woman dressed in green pushed a cart of equipment into the room. "You two have to go now. Come back in ten, twelve hours."

"I'd like to scrub and watch," Marty said.

"Very well." In Spanish, he asked the woman to find Marty a gown and show him to the *limpiador*.

I went down to the lobby and out. The sky was reddish-orange with pollution; I used the last of my Mexican money to buy a mask from a vending machine.

I figured I would walk until I found a moneychanger and a city map. I'd never been to Guadalajara before and didn't even know which direction downtown was. In a city twice the size of New York, it probably didn't make much difference. I walked away from the sun.

This hospital area was thick with beggars who claimed they needed money for medicine or treatment; who thrust their sick children at you or showed sores or stumps. Some of the men were aggressive. I snarled back in bad Spanish and was glad I'd bribed the border guard ten dollars to let me bring the puttyknife through.

The children looked wan, hopeless. I didn't know as much about Mexico as I should, living just north of it, but I was certain they had some form of socialized medicine. Not for everyone, obviously. Like the bounty from the nanoforges we graciously allocated to them, I supposed: the people in the front of the line didn't get there by lot.

Some of the beggars pointedly ignored me or even whispered racial epithets in a language they thought I didn't understand. Things had changed so much. We'd visited Mexico when I was in grade school, and my father, who had grown up in the South, gloried in the color blindness here. Being treated like any other gringo. We blame the Ngumi for Mexico's *prejuicio,* but it's partly America's fault. And example.

I came to an eight-lane divided avenue, clogged with slow traffic, and turned right. Not even one beggar per block here. After a mile or so of dusty and loud low-income housing, I came to a good-sized parking island over an underground mall. I went through a security check, which cost another five dollars for the knife, and took the slidewalk down to the main level.

There were three change booths, offering slightly different rates of exchange, all with different commission arrangements. I did the arithmetic in my head and was not surprised to find that, for everyday amounts, the one with the least favorable exchange rate actually gave the best deal.

Starving, I found a ceviche shop and had a bowl of octopus, little ones with inch-long legs, along with a couple of tortillas and a pot of tea. Then I went off in search of diversion.

There were a half-dozen jack shops in a row, offering slightly different adventures from their American counterparts. Be gored by a bull—*no gracias*. Perform or receive a sex-change operation, either way. Die in childbirth. Relive the agony of Christ. There was a line for that one; must have been a holy day. Maybe every day's a holy day here.

There were also the usual girly-boy attractions, and with them one that offered an accelerated-time tour of "your own" digestive tract! Restrain me.

A confusing variety of shops and market stalls, like Portobello multiplied a hundred times. The everyday things that an American had delivered automatically had to be bought here—and not for a fixed price, either.

That part was familiar from walking around Portobello. Housewives, a few men, came to the *mercado* every morning to haggle over the day's supplies. Still plenty here at two in the afternoon. To an outsider, it looks as if half the stalls are scenes of pretty violent argument, voices raised, arms waving. But it's really just part of the social routine, for vendor and customer alike. "What do you mean, ten pesos for these worthless beans? Last week they were five pesos and excellent quality!" "Your memory is fading, old woman. Last week they were eight pesos and so shriveled I couldn't give them away! These are beans among beans!" "I could give you six pesos. I need beans for supper, and my mother knows how to soften them with soda." "Your mother? Send your mother down here and she'll pay me nine pesos," and so on. It was a way to pass the time; the real battle would be between seven and eight pesos.

The fish market was diverting. There was a much greater variety than you found in Texas stores—large cod and salmon that originally came from the cold north Atlantic and Pacific, exotic brightly colored reef fish, wriggling live eels, and tanks of huge Japanese shrimp— all of them produced in town, cloned and force-grown in vats. The few native fresh fish—whitebait from Lake Chapala, mostly—cost ten times as much as the most exotic.

I bought a small plate of those—minnows, sun-dried and marinated, served with lime and hot chile—which would have marked me as a tourist even if I weren't black and dressed like an American.

Counted my pesos and started looking for a gift for Amelia. I'd already done jewelry, to help get us into this mess, and she wouldn't wear ethnic clothing.

A horrible practical whisper told me to wait until after the operation. But I decided that buying the gift was more for me than for her, anyhow. A commercial kind of substitute for prayer.

There was a huge stall of old books, the paper kind and also the earlier versions of view-books—most of them, with formats and power supplies decades out of date, were for collectors of electronic curiosities, not readers.

They did have two shelves of books in English, most of them novels. She'd probably like one, but it posed a dilemma: if a book was well-known enough for me to recognize the title, then she probably already had it, or at least had read it.

I killed about an hour deciding, reading the first few pages of every book there I hadn't heard of. I finally returned to *The Long Good-bye,* by Raymond Chandler, which was good reading and also had a leather binding, embossed "Midnite Mystery Club."

I sat by a fountain and read for awhile. An engrossing book, a time trip not only for what it was about and the way it was written, but also the physicality of it—the heavy yellowed paper, the feel and musty smell of the leather. The skin of an animal dead more than a century, if it was real leather.

The marble steps weren't all that comfortable, though—my legs fell asleep from butt to knees—so I wandered awhile more. There were more expensive shops on the second floor down, but they included a set of jack booths that cost almost nothing, sponsored by travel agencies and various countries. For twenty pesos, I spent thirty minutes in France.

That was a strange experience. The spoken cues were all in rapid Mexican Spanish, hard for me to follow, but of course the unspoken ones were the same as ever. I walked around Montmartre for awhile, then lounged on a slow barge drifting through the Bordeau region, and finally sat at an inn in Burgundy, feasting on rich cheeses and complex wines. When it was over, I was starving again.

Of course there was a French restaurant right across from the booth, but I didn't even have to look at the menu to know it was beyond me. I retreated back upstairs and found a place with lots of small tables and music that wasn't too loud, and wolfed down a plate of taquitos varios. Then I washed up and finished reading the book there, nursing a beer and a cup of coffee.

When I finished the book it was only eight, still two hours before I could check on Amelia. I didn't want to go hang around the clinic, but the mall was getting oppressively loud as it moved from evening into night-time mode. A half-dozen mariachi bands competing for attention along with the blare and rumble of modern music from the night clubs. Some very alluring women sitting in the windows of an escort service, three of them wearing PM buttons, which meant they were jacked. That would be a great way to spend the next two hours—jacksex and guilt.

I wound up wandering through the residential neighborhood, reasonably confident because of the puttyknife, even though the area was rundown and a bit menacing.

I picked up a bouquet of flowers at the hospital store, half price because they were closing, and went up to the waiting room to wait. Marty was there, jacked into a portable work terminal. He glanced up when I came in, subvocalized something into a throat pickup, and unjacked.

"It looks pretty good," he said, "better than I would have expected. Of course we won't know for sure until she's awake, but her multiphase EEGs look good, look normal for her."

His tone was anxious. I set the flowers and book down on a low plastic table scattered with paper magazines. "How long till she comes out of it?"

He looked at his watch. "Half an hour. Twelve."

"Doctor around?"

"Spencer? No, he went home right after the procedure. I've got his number if . . . just in case."

I sat down too close to him. "Marty. What aren't you telling me?"

"What do you want to know?" His gaze was steady but there was still something in his voice. "You want to see a tape of the disconnection? I can promise you'll puke.''

''I just want to know what you're not telling me.''

He shrugged and looked away. ''I'm not sure how much you know. From the most basic, up . . . she won't die. She will walk and talk. Will she be the woman you loved? I don't know. The EEGs don't tell us whether she can do arithmetic, let alone algebra, calculus, whatever it is you people do.''

''Jesus.''

''But look. Yesterday at this time she was on the edge of dying. If she'd been in a little worse shape, the phone call you got would've been whether or not to turn off the respirator.''

I nodded; a nurse at Reception had used the same words. ''She might not even know who I am.''

''And she might be exactly the same woman.''

''With a hole in her head because of me.''

''Well, a useless jack, not a hole. We put it back in after the disconnection, to minimize mechanical stress on the surrounding brain tissue.''

''But it's not hooked up. We couldn't—''

''Sorry.''

An unshaven nurse came in, slumped with fatigue. ''Señor Class?'' I put up a hand. ''The patient in 201, she asks for you.''

I started down the corridor. ''Don't stay. She needs sleep.''

''Okay.'' Her door was open. There were two other beds in the room, but they were empty. She was wearing a cap of gauze, eyes closed, sheet pulled up to her shoulders. No tubes or wires, which surprised me. A monitor over her bed displayed the jagged stalactites of her heartbeat.

She opened her eyes. ''Julian.'' She twisted a hand out from under the sheet and grabbed mine. We kissed gently.

"I'm sorry it didn't work," she said. "But I'll never be sorry for trying. Never."

I couldn't say anything. I just rubbed her hand between both of mine.

"I think I'm . . . unimpaired. Ask me a question, a science question."

"Uh . . . what's Avagadro's Number?"

"Oh, ask a chemist. It's the number of molecules in a mole. You want the number of molecules in an armadillo, that's Armadillo's Number."

Well, if she could make bad jokes, she was partway back to normal. "What's the duration of a delta resonance spike? Pions exciting protons."

"About ten to the minus twenty-third. Give me a hard one?"

"You say that to all the guys?" She smiled weakly. "Look, you get some sleep. I'll be outside."

"I'll be all right. You go on back to Houston."

"No."

"One day, then. What is it, Tuesday?"

"Wednesday."

"You have to be back tomorrow night to cover the seminar for me. Senior seminar."

"We'll talk in the morning." There were plenty of people better qualified.

"Promise me?"

"I promise I'll take care of it." At least with a phone call. "You get some sleep now."

Marty and I went down to the machine cantina in the basement. He had a cup of strong Bustelo—stay awake for the 1:30 train—and I had a beer. It turned out to be nonalcoholic, specially brewed for hospitals and schools. I told him about "Armadillo's Number" and all.

"She seems to be all there." He tasted his coffee and put another double sugar in it. "Sometimes people lose bits of memory, that they don't miss for awhile. Of course it's not all loss."

"No." One kiss, one touch. "She has the memory of being jacked for what, three minutes?"

"And there might be something more," he said cautiously. He took two data strings out of his shirt pocket and set them on the table. "These are complete copies of her records here. I'm not supposed to have them; they cost more than the operation itself."

"I could help pay—"

"No, it's grant money. The point is, her operation failed for a reason. Not a lack of skill or care on Spencer's part, necessarily, but a reason."

"Something that could be reversed?"

He shook his head and then shrugged. "It's happened."

"You mean it could be reinstalled? I've never heard of that."

"Because it's so rarely done. Usually not worth the risk. They'll try it if, after the extraction, the patient is still in a vegetative state. It's a chance to re-establish contact with the world.

"In Blaze's case it would be too dangerous, at the present state of the art. And it is as much art as science. But it keeps evolving, and maybe someday, if we find out what went wrong . . ." He sipped at his coffee. "Probably won't happen, not in the next twenty years. Almost all of the research funding is military, and it's not an area they're deeply interested in. If a mechanic's installation fails, they just draft somebody else."

I tasted the beer again and decided it wasn't going to improve. "She's totally disconnected now? If we jacked, she wouldn't feel anything?"

"You could try it. There's still a connection with a few minor ganglia. A few neurons here and there—when we replace the metal core of the jack, some of them re-establish contact."

"Be worth a try."

"Don't expect anything. People in her condition can

go to a jack shop and rent a really extreme one, like a deathtrip, but all they get is a mild hallucinating buzz; nothing concrete. If they just jack with a person, no go-between, there's no real effect. Maybe a placebo effect, if they expect something to happen.''

"Do us a favor," I said. "Don't tell her that."

compromising, julian took the train up to Houston, staying just long enough to cover Amelia's particle seminar—the students weren't wild about having a young postdoc unexpectedly substitute for Dr. Blaze— and then caught a midnight train back to Guadalajara.

As it turned out, Amelia was released the next day, traveling by ambulance to a care facility on campus. The clinic didn't want a patient who was just resting under observation to take up a valuable bed on Friday; most of their high-ticket customers checked in that day.

Julian was allowed to ride with her, which was mostly a matter of watching her sleep. When the sedative wore off, about an hour from Houston, they talked primarily about work; Julian managed to avoid lying to her about what might happen if they jacked in her almost-connected state. He knew she would read all about it soon enough and then they'd have to deal with their hopes and disappointments. He didn't want her to build up some transcendental scenario based on that one beautiful instant. The best that could happen would be a lot less than that, and there would probably be no effect at all.

The care center was shiny on the outside and shabby on the inside. Amelia got the only bed left in a four-bed "suite," inhabited by women twice her age, long-term or permanent residents. Julian helped her settle in, and when it became obvious that he wasn't just working for her, two of the old ladies were ostentatiously horrified at the difference in color and age. The third was blind.

Well, they were out in the open now. That was one good thing that had come from the mess, for their personal lives if not their professional ones.

Amelia hadn't read the Chandler book, and was delighted. It seemed unlikely that she would spend much time in conversation.

Julian was headed for conversation that night, of course, Friday. He decided to show up at the club at least an hour late, so Marty could tell the others about the operations and reveal the sordid truth about him and Amelia. If indeed it was actually secret to anybody there. Straitlaced Hayes knew and had never given a hint.

There was plenty to occupy him before the Saturday Night Special, since he hadn't even checked his mail after reading the note under his door, when he returned from Portobello. An assistant to Hayes had written up a summary of the runs he and Amelia had missed; that would take a few hours' study. Then there were notes of concern, mostly from people he would see that night. It was the sort of news that traveled fast.

Just to make life interesting, there was a note from his father saying he'd like to drop by on his way home from Hawaii, so Julian could get to know "Suze," his new wife, better. Unsurprisingly, there was also a phone message from Julian's mother, wondering where he was, and would he mind if she came down to escape the last of the bad weather? Sure, Mom, you and Suze will get along just fine; think of how much you have in common.

In this case, the easiest course was the truth. He punched up his mother and said she could come down if she wanted, but that his father and Suze were going to be here at the same time. After she calmed down from that, he gave her a quick summary of the past four days' excitement.

Her image on the phone took on an odd appearance as he talked. She'd grown up with sound-only, and had never mastered the neutral expression that most people automatically assumed.

"So you're pretty serious about this old woman."

"Old white woman, Momma." Julian laughed at her indignation. "And I've been telling you for a year and a half how serious we were."

"White, purple, green; doesn't make any difference to me. Son, she's only ten years younger than I am."

"Twelve."

"Oh, thank God, *twelve*! Don't you see how foolish you look now to the people around you?"

"I'm just glad it's not a secret anymore. And if we look foolish to some people, well, that's their problem, not ours."

She looked away from the screen. "It's me that's the fool, and a hypocrite, too. Mother's got to worry."

"If you'd come down once and meet her, you'd stop worrying."

"I should. Okay. You call me when your father and his playmate have gone on up to Akron—"

"Columbus, Mom."

"Wherever. You call me and we'll work out a time."

He watched her image fade and shook his head. She'd been saying that for more than a year; something always came up. She had a busy life, admittedly, still teaching full-time at a junior college in Pittsburgh. But that obviously wasn't it. She really didn't want to lose her little boy at all, and to lose him to a woman old enough to be her sister was grotesque.

He'd talked to Amelia about their going up to Pittsburgh, but she said she didn't want to force the issue. There was something less simple at work with her, as well.

The two women had opposite attitudes toward his being a mechanic, too. Amelia was plainly worried sick all the time he was in Portobello—much worse now, since the massacre—but his mother treated it as a kind of brainless second job that he had to do, even though it got in the way of his actual work. She never seemed to have any curiosity about what went on down there. Amelia followed his unit's actions with the single-minded intensity of a warboy. (She'd never admitted this, which Julian supposed was to spare him anxiety, but she often slipped and asked questions about things that nobody could have found out if they simply followed the news.)

It suddenly, belatedly, occurred to Julian that Hayes, and probably everybody else in the department, knew or suspected there was something going on because of the way Amelia acted when he was away. They worked hard at (but also had fun) playing the role of "just friends" when they came together at work. Maybe their audience knew the script.

All part of the past now. He was impatient to get to the club and see how people had reacted to the news. But he still had a couple of hours if he was going to give Marty ample time to set them up. He didn't really feel like working, even answering mail, so he flopped down on the couch and asked the cube to search.

The cube had a built-in learning routine that analyzed every selection he made, and from the content of what he liked, constructed a preference profile that it used to search through the eighteen hundred available channels. One problem with that was that you couldn't communicate with the routine; its only input was your choices. The first year or so after he was drafted, Julian had obsessively watched century-old movies, perhaps to escape into a world where people and events were simply good or bad. So now when the thing searched, it dutifully came up with lots of Jimmy Stewart and John Wayne, and Julian had found through objective observation that it did no good to yell at it.

Humphrey Bogart at Rick's. Reset. Jimmy Stewart headed for Washington. Reset. A tour of the lunar south pole, through the eyes of the robot landers. He'd seen most of it a couple of years before, but it was interesting enough to see again. It also helped deprogram the machine.

everyone looked up when I walked into the room, but I suppose they would do that under any circumstances. Perhaps they kept looking a little longer than usual.

There was an empty chair at a table with Marty, Reza, and Franklin.

"You get her safely ensconced?" Marty asked.

I nodded. "She'll be out of that place as soon as they let her walk. The three women she's sharing the room with are straight out of *Hamlet*."

"*Macbeth*," Reza corrected me, "if you mean crones. Or are they sweet young lunatics about to commit suicide?"

"Crones. She seems okay. The ride up from Guadalajara wasn't bad, just long." The sullen waiter in the artfully stained T-shirt slouched over. "Coffee," I said, then caught Reza's look of mock horror. "And a pitcher of Rioja." It was getting on toward the end of the month again. The guy started to ask for my ration card, then recognized me and slumped away.

"Hope you re-enlist," Reza said. He took my number and punched in the price of the whole pitcher.

"When Portobello freezes over."

"Did they say when she'd be released?" Marty asked.

"No. Neurologist sees her in the morning. She'll call me."

"Better have her call Hayes, too. I told him everything was going to be all right, but he's nervous."

"*He's* nervous."

"He's known her longer than you have," Franklin said quietly. So had he and Marty.

"So did you see any Guadalajara?" Reza asked. "Fleshpots?"

"No. Just wandered around a little. Didn't get into the old city or out to T-town, what do they call it?"

"Tlaquepaque," Reza said. "I spent an eventful week there one day."

"How long have you and Blaze been together?" Franklin asked. "If you don't mind my asking."

"Together" probably wasn't the word he was searching for. "We've been close for three years. Friends a couple of years before that."

"Blaze was his adviser," Marty said.

"Doctoral?"

"Post-doc," I said.

"That's right," Franklin said with a small smile. "You came from Harvard." Only an Eli could say that with a trace of pity, Julian mused.

"Now you're supposed to ask me whether my intentions are honorable. The answer is we have no intentions. Not until I get out of service."

"And how long is that?"

"Unless the war ends, about five years."

"Blaze will be fifty."

"Fifty-two, actually. I'll be thirty-seven. Maybe that bothers you more than it does us."

"No," he said. "It might bother Marty."

Marty gave him a hard look. "What have you been drinking?"

"The usual." Franklin displayed the bottom of his empty teacup. "How long has it been?"

"I only want the best for both of you," Marty said to me. "You know that."

"Eight years, nine?"

"Good God, Franklin. Were you a terrier in a former life?" Marty shook his head as if to clear it. "That was over long before Julian joined the department.''

The waiter sidled over with the wine and three glasses. Sensing tension, he poured as slowly as was practical. We all watched him in silence.

"So," Reza said, "how 'bout them Oilers?"

the "neurologist" who came to see Amelia the next morning was too young to have an advanced degree in anything. He had a goatee and bad skin. For half an hour, he asked her the same simple questions over and over.

"When and where were you born?"

"August 12, 1996. Sturbridge, Massachusetts."

"What was your mother's name?"

"Jane O'Banian Harding."

"Where did you go to grade school?"

"Nathan Hale Elementary, Roxbury."

He paused. "Last time you said Breezewood. In Sturbridge."

She took a deep breath and let it out. "We moved to Roxbury in '04. Maybe '05."

"Ah. And high school?"

"Still O'Bryant. John D. O'Bryant School of Mathematics and Science."

"That's in Sturbridge?"

"No, Roxbury! I went to middle school in Roxbury, too. You haven't—"

"What was your mother's maiden name?"

"O'Banian."

He made a long note in his notebook. "All right. Stand up."

"What?"

"Get out of bed, please. Stand up."

Amelia sat up and cautiously put her feet on the floor.

She took a couple of shaky steps and reached back to hold the gown closed.

"Are you dizzy?"

"A little. Of course."

"Raise your arms, please." She did, and the back of the gown fell open.

"Nice bottom, sweetheart," croaked the old lady in the bed next to her.

"Now I want you to close your eyes and slowly bring your fingertips together." She tried and missed; she opened her eyes and saw that she had missed by more than an inch.

"Try it again," he said. This time the two fingers grazed.

He wrote a couple of words in the notebook. "All right. You're free to go now."

"What?"

"You're released. Take your ration card to the checkout desk on your way out."

"But . . . don't I get to see a *doctor*?"

He reddened. "You don't think I'm a doctor?"

"No. Are you?"

"I'm qualified to release you. You're released." He turned and walked away.

"What about my clothes? Where are my *clothes*?" He shrugged and disappeared out the door.

"Try the cabinet there, sweetheart." Amelia checked all the cabinets, moving with creaky slowness. There were neat stacks of linen and gowns, but no trace of the leather suitcase she'd taken to Guadalajara.

"Likely somebody took 'em," another old lady said. "Likely that black boy."

Of course, she suddenly remembered: she'd asked Julian to take it home. It was valuable, handmade, and there was no place here where it would have been secure.

What other little things had she forgotten? The John D. O'Bryant School of Mathematics and Science was on

New Dudley. Her office at the lab was 12-344. What was Julian's phone number? Eight.

She retrieved her toiletry kit from the bathroom and got the miniphone out of it. It had a toothpaste smear on the punch-plate. She cleaned it with a corner of her sheet and sat on the bed and punched #-08.

"Mr. Class is in class," the phone said. "Is this an emergency?"

"No. Message." She paused. "Darling, bring me something to wear. I've been released." She set the phone down and reached back and felt the cool metal disk at the base of her skull. She wiped away sudden tears and muttered "Shit."

A big square female nurse rolled in a gurney with a shriveled little Chinese woman on it. "What's the story here?" she said. "This bed is supposed to be vacant."

Amelia started laughing. She put her kit and the Chandler book under her arm and held her gown closed with the other hand and walked out into the corridor.

it took me a while to track Amelia down. Her room was full of querulous old women who either clammed up or gave me false information. Of course she was at Accounts Receivable. She didn't have to pay anything for the medical attention or room, but her two inedible meals had been catered, since she hadn't requested otherwise.

That may have been the last straw. When I brought in her clothes she just shrugged off the pale blue hospital gown. She didn't have anything on underneath. There were eight or ten people in the waiting room.

I was thunderstruck. My dignified Amelia?

The receptionist was a young man with ringlets. He stood up. "Wait! You . . . you can't do that!"

"Watch me." She put on the blouse first, and took

her time buttoning it. "I was kicked out of my room. I don't have anyplace to—"

"Amelia—" She ignored me.

"Go to the ladies' room! Right now!"

"Thank you, no." She tried to stand on one foot and put a sock on, but teetered and almost fell over. I gave her an arm. The audience was respectfully quiet.

"I'm going to call a guard."

"No you're not." She strode over to him, in socks but still bare from ankles to waist. She was an inch or two taller and stared down at him. He stared down, too, looking as if he'd never had a triangle of pubic hair touch his desktop before. "I'll make a scene," she said quietly. "Believe me."

He sat down, his mouth working but no words coming out. She stepped into her pants and slippers, picked up the gown and threw it into the 'cycler.

"Julian, I don't like this place." She offered her arm. "Let's go bother someone else." The room was quiet until we were well out into the corridor, and then there was a sudden explosion of chatter. Amelia stared straight ahead and smiled.

"Bad day?"

"Bad place." She frowned. "Did I just do what I think I did?"

I looked around and whispered, "This is Texas. Don't you know it's against the law to show your ass to a black man?"

"I'm always forgetting that." She smiled nervously and hugged my arm. "I'll write you every day from prison."

There was a cab waiting. We got in fast and Amelia gave it my address. "That's where my bag is, right?"

"Yeah . . . but I could bring it over." My place was a mess. "I'm not exactly ready for polite company."

"I'm not exactly company." She rubbed her eyes. "Certainly not polite."

In fact, the place had been a mess when I went to Portobello two weeks earlier, and I hadn't had time to do anything but add to it. We entered a one-room disaster area, ten meters by five of chaos: stacks of papers and readers on every horizontal surface, including the bed; a pile of clothes in one corner aesthetically balanced by a pile of dishes in the sink. I'd forgotten to turn off the coffeepot when I'd gone to school, so a bitter smell of burnt coffee added to the general mustiness.

She laughed. "You know, this is even worse than I expected?" She'd only been here twice and both times I'd been forewarned.

"I know. I need a woman around the place."

"No. You need about a gallon of gasoline and a match." She looked around and shook her head. "Look, we're out in the open. Let's just move in together."

I was still trying to cope with the striptease. "Uh . . . there's really not enough room. . . ."

"Not *here*." She laughed. "My place. And we can file for a two-bedroom."

I cleared off a chair and steered her to it. She sat down warily.

"Look. You know how much I'd like to move in with you. It's not as if we hadn't talked about it."

"So? Let's do it."

"No . . . let's not make *any* decisions now. Not for a couple of days."

She looked past me, out the window over the sink. "I, you think I'm crazy."

"Impulsive." I sat down on the floor and stroked her arm.

"It is strange for me, isn't it?" She closed her eyes and kneaded her forehead. "Maybe I'm still medicated."

I hoped that was it. "I'm sure that's all it is. You need a couple of days' more rest."

"What if they botched the operation?"

"They didn't. You wouldn't be walking and talking."

She patted my hand, still looking abstracted. "Yeah, sure. You have some juice or something?"

I found some white grape juice in the refrigerator and poured us each a small glass. I heard a zipper and turned around, but it was only her leather suitcase.

I brought her drink over. She was staring intently, slowly picking through the contents of the suitcase. "Think something might be missing?"

She took the drink and set it down. "Oh, no. Or maybe. Mainly I'm just checking my memory. I do remember packing. The trip down. Talking to Dr., um, Spencer." She backed up two steps, felt behind her, and sat down slowly on the bed.

"Then the blur—you know, I was sort of awake when they operated. I could see lots of lights. My chin and face were in a padded frame."

I sat down with her. "I remember that from my own installation. And the drill sound."

"And the smell. You know you're smelling your own skull being sawed open. But you don't care."

"Drugs," I said.

"That's part of it. Also looking forward to it." Well, not in my case. "I could hear them talking, the doctor and some woman."

"What about?"

"It was Spanish. They were talking about her boyfriend and . . . shoes or something. Then everything went black. I guess it went white, then black."

"I wonder if that was before or after they put the jack in."

"It was after, definitely after. They call it a bridge, right?"

"From French, yeah: *pont mental.*"

"I heard him say that—*ahora, el puente*—and then they pressed really hard. I could feel it on my chin, on the cushion."

"You remember a lot more than I did."

"That was about it, though. The boyfriend and the shoes and then *click*. The next thing I knew, I was lying in bed, unable to move or speak."

"That must have been terrifying."

She frowned, remembering. "Not really. It was like an enormous . . . lassitude, numbness. As if I could move my arms and legs, or speak, if I really had to. But the effort would have been tremendous. That was probably mood drugs, too, to keep me from panicking.

"They kept moving my arms and legs around and shouting nonsense at me. It was probably English, and I just couldn't decipher their accents, in my condition."

She gestured and I handed her the grape juice. She sipped. "If I remember this right . . . I was really, really annoyed that they wouldn't just go away and let me lie in peace. But I didn't say anything, because I wouldn't give them the satisfaction of hearing me complain. It's an odd thing to remember. I was really being infantile."

"They didn't try the jack?"

She got a faraway look. "No . . . Dr. Spencer told me about that later. In my condition it was better to wait and have the first time be with someone I knew. Seconds count, he explained that to you?"

I nodded. "Exponential increase in the number of neural connections."

"So I lay in a darkened room then, for a long time; lost track of time, I suppose. Then all the things that happened before we . . . we jacked, I thought it was a dream. Everything was suddenly flooded with light and a couple of people lifted me and bit me on the wrists— the IVs—and then we were floating from room to room."

"Riding a gurney."

She nodded. "It really felt like levitation, though—I remember thinking, '*I'm dreaming*,' and resolving to enjoy it. An image of Marty floated by, asleep in a chair, and I accepted that as part of the dream. Then you and Dr. Spencer appeared—okay, you were in the dream, too.

"Then it was all suddenly real." She rocked back and forth, remembering the instant we jacked. "No, not *real*. Intense. Confusing."

"I remember," I said. "The double vision, seeing yourself. You didn't recognize yourself at first."

"And you told me most people don't. I mean you told me in one word, somehow, or no words. Then it all snapped into focus, and we were . . ." She nodded rhythmically, biting her lower lip. "We were all the same. We were one . . . thing."

She took my right hand in both of hers. "And then we had to talk to the doctor. And he said we couldn't, he wouldn't let us . . ." She lifted my hand to her breast, the way it had been that last moment, and leaned forward. But she didn't kiss me. She put her chin on my shoulder and whispered, voice cracking: "We'll never have that again?"

I automatically tried to feed her a gestalt, the way you do jacked, about how she might be able to try again in a few years, about Marty having her data, about the partial re-establishment of neuron connection so we might try, we might try; and a fraction of a second later I realized *no, we weren't connected; she can only hear something if I say it.*

"Most people never even have it once."

"Maybe they're better off," she said, muffled, and sobbed quietly. Her hand moved up to squeeze my neck and caress the jack.

I had to say something. "Look . . . it's possible you haven't lost it all. There might be a small fraction of the ability still there."

"What do you mean?" I explained about some of the neurons homing back into the jack's receptor areas. "How much might be there?"

"I don't have the faintest idea. I'd never even heard of it until a couple of days ago." Though I knew with sudden certainty that some of the jills must be that way, unable to make a really deep connection. Ralph had brought back memories of some who had hardly seemed jacked at all.

"We have to try. Where could we . . . could you bring the equipment back from Portobello?"

"No, I'd never get it off the base." And be court-martialed, if I tried.

"Hmm . . . Maybe we could find a way to sneak into the hospital—"

I laughed. "You don't have to sneak anywhere. Just buy time at one of the jack joints."

"But I don't want that. I want to do it with you."

"That's what I mean! They have double unis—two-person universes. Two people jack in and go someplace together." That's where the jills took their customers. You can screw on the streets of Paris, floating in outer space, riding a canoe down rapids. Ralph had brought us back the weirdest memories.

"Let's go do it."

"Look, you're still beat from the hospital. Why not get a day or two rest and then—"

"No!" She stood up. "For all we know, the connections might be fading while we sit here and talk about it." She picked up the phone off the table and punched two numbers; she knew my cab code. "Outside?"

I got up and followed her to the door, afraid I'd made a big mistake. "Look, don't expect the world."

"Oh, I don't expect anything. Just have to try it, find out." For someone who didn't expect anything, she was awfully eager.

It was infectious. While we waited for the cab, I went from thinking *Well, at least we'll find out one way or the other* to being sure that there would be at least something there. Marty had said there would be a placebo effect, if nothing more.

I couldn't give the cab a specific address, since I'd only been there once. But I asked whether it knew where the block of jack joints was, just outside the university, and it said yes.

We could have biked there, but it was the neighborhood where that guy had pulled a knife on me—it had started pretty low and gone downhill—and I figured it might be dark by the time we finished our experiment.

It was a good thing the cab turned off the meter while we went through security. The shoe in charge saw our destination and jerked us around for ten minutes, I supposed to watch Amelia's discomfort. Or try to get some sort of rise out of me. I wouldn't give him the satisfaction.

We had the cab let us off on the near end of the block, so we could walk the length of it and check the menus in each joint. The price was important; payday was two days away for both of us. I made three times as much as she did, but the Mexican excursion had brought me down to less than a hundred bucks. And Amelia was flat.

There were more jills than pedestrians. Some of them offered to join us in a three-way. I hadn't known that was possible. It sounded more confusing than alluring, even under good conditions. And being more intimately linked to the jill than to Amelia would be a disaster.

The place with the best double uni deal was also one of the nicest, or the least sleazy. It was called Your World, and instead of car crashes and executions, it offered a menu of explorations—like the French tour I'd taken in Mexico, but more exotic.

I suggested the underwater tour of the Great Barrier Reef.

"I'm not a good swimmer," Amelia said. "Would that make a difference?"

"Me neither; don't worry. It's like being a fish." I'd done this one. "You don't even think about swimming."

It was a dollar a minute, cash, or two minutes for three dollars, plastic. Ten minutes up front. I paid cash; keep the plastic for emergencies.

A stern-looking fat lady, black with a springy forest of white hair, led us to the booth. It was a small cubicle just over a meter high, with a padded blue mat on the floor, two jack cables hanging from the low ceiling.

"Time start' when the first one plug in. You-all want to take your clothes off first, I s'pose. Place been sterilized. You-all have a good time, now."

She turned abruptly and bustled away. "She thinks you're a jill," I said.

"I could use a second income." We entered the place on our hands and knees and when I shut the door the air conditioner started to whir. Then a white-noise generator added a steady hiss.

"Does the light make a difference?"

"It goes off automatically." We helped each other undress and she lay down the right way, on her stomach facing the door.

She was rigid and trembling slightly. "Relax," I said, kneading her shoulders.

"I'm afraid nothing will happen."

"If nothing happens, we'll try it again." I remembered what Marty had said—she really should start off with something like jumping off a cliff. Well, I could tell her that later.

"Here." I slid over a diamond-shaped pillow that supports your face on the chin, cheekbones, and forehead. "This'll help your neck relax." I stroked her back for a minute, and when she seemed looser, I moved the jack interface into place over the metal socket in her head. There was a faint click and the light went out.

Of course after thousands of hours, I didn't need the

pillow; I could jack standing up or hanging upside down. I groped for the cable and stretched out so we were touching, arm and hip. Then I jacked in.

The water was warm as blood and it tasted good, salt and seaweed, on my lips, as I breathed it in. I was in less than two meters of water, bright coral formations all around, tiny fish with brilliant colors ignoring me until I came close enough to be a danger. A small green moray eel, face like a cartoon villain, stared at me from a hole in the coral.

Volition is strange when you're jacked like this. I "decided" to go off to the left, although there was nothing obvious there, just a plain of white sand. Actually, the person who had recorded the trip had a good reason to check it out, but the customer wasn't in contact with him or her at that level; nothing but the sensorium, amplified.

Sunlight refracting through the ripples on the surface made a pleasant shimmering pattern on the sand, but that wasn't why we had come here. I hovered over two eye-stalks that poked out of the sand, twitching, agitated. Suddenly the sand exploded underneath me, and to the left and right, and a tiger-striped manta ray flew out from where it had been hiding, under a few centimeters of sand. It was huge, easily three meters wide. I shot forward and grabbed a wing, before it had time to gather speed.

One powerful flap of the wings and we surged forward; another, and we were going faster than any merely human swimmer, the water churning smoothly down my body . . .

And hers. Amelia was there, definitely but faintly, like a shadow inside me. The turbulence from the fast water made my genitals flutter, but part of me didn't have that; for that part of me the water flowed smoothly tickling between her legs.

Intellectually, I knew that they'd had to merge two

strings to create this, and wondered how hard it had been to find a large manta for both the man and the woman or how they'd gotten around it. But mainly I focused on that particular dual sensation and tried to make contact with Amelia through it.

I couldn't, quite. No words, no specificity; just a vague "isn't this thrilling" gestalt that I felt reflected with a different twist, Amelia's personality. There was also a faint different excitement that must have been her realization that we were in contact.

The sand surface fell away in an underwater cliff and the manta dived, the water suddenly cool and the pressure increasing. We lost our grip and went tumbling alone in the dark water.

As we slid slowly upward I felt little butterfly flutterings that I knew were Amelia's hands on me, back in the cubical, and as I became erect it was wetness that wasn't the imaginary ocean around me, and then the ghostly clasp of her legs and a faint pulsing up and down.

It wasn't like Carolyn, where I was her and she was me. It was more like a compelling sexual dream that possessed you while you were half awake.

The water above was like beaten silver, and three sharks scudded there as we floated up. There was a little shiver of fear, though I knew they were harmless, since the string wasn't rated D or I; death or injury. I tried to project to Amelia not to be scared, but I didn't feel any fear from her. She was preoccupied. Her physical presence grew stronger in me, and she wasn't exactly swimming.

Her orgasm was faint but long, radiating and pulsating in that strange-but-familiar way that I hadn't felt in the three years since I lost Carolyn. The ghosts of her arms and legs rocked me left and right as we rose up toward the sharks.

It was one large nurse shark and two dogfish, no danger. But as we passed them I felt myself go soft and slip out of her. It wasn't going to work, not this time, not for both of us.

Her hands on me were like feathers, coaxing, pleasant but not enough. There was a sudden faint loss of something, dimensionality, that meant she had come unjacked, and then she was using her mouth, cool and then warm, but it still wouldn't work. Most of me was still in the reef.

I felt for the cable and unjacked myself. The lights went on and I immediately started to respond to Amelia's ministrations. I slipped my arms around her slipperiness and rested my head on her hip and didn't think about Carolyn, and worked a couple of fingers between her legs from behind, and in a minute we both came at once.

We were allowed about five seconds' rest, and then the lady was pounding on the cubicle door, saying we had to get out or pay rent; she had to clean it up for the next customers.

"The meter stops running when we both unjack, I guess," Amelia said. She nuzzled me. "I could pay a dollar a minute for this, though. You want to tell her that?"

"Nah." I reached for our clothes. "Let's go home and do it for free."

"Your place or mine?"

"Home," I said. "Your place."

julian and amelia spent the next day moving and cleaning house. Since it was Sunday, they couldn't get any paperwork done, but they didn't expect any problems. There was a waiting list for singles who qualified for Julian's efficiency, and Amelia's place was rated for two, or even two adults and a child.

(A child was something that was never going to happen. Twenty-four years before, after a miscarriage, Amelia had opted for voluntary sterilization, which gave her a monthly cash-and-coupon bonus until age fifty. And Julian's view of the world was so sufficiently dark that he wasn't eager to bring a new person into it.)

When they had everything boxed, and Julian's apartment clean enough to satisfy the landlord, they called Reza for his car. He scolded Julian for not calling him earlier so he could have helped, and Julian said, honestly, that it hadn't occurred to him.

Amelia listened to the conversation with interest, and a week later would point out that there had been a good reason for them to do it alone, a kind of sacramental labor—or something even more elemental, nest-building. But what she said when Julian hung up was, "It'll take him ten minutes to get here," and hurried him to the couch, one last quick time in this place.

It only took two trips to move all the boxes. On the second trip Reza and Julian were alone, and when Reza offered to help unpack, Julian said well, you know, maybe Blaze wants to go to bed.

In fact, she did. They collapsed exhausted and slept until dawn.

once or twice a year, they don't bring the soldierboys in between shifts; they just immobilize us one by one and have the mechanic's second move straight from barber chair to cage, a "hot transfer." It usually meant something interesting was going on, since we don't normally work the same AO as Scoville's hunter/killer platoon.

But Scoville had been grouchy because nothing had happened. They'd gone to three different ambush sites in nine days with nothing but bugs and birds showing up. It was obviously a make-work assignment, marking time.

He crawled out of the cage and it sealed shut for its ninety-second cleaning cycle. "Have fun," Scoville said. "Bring something to read."

"Oh, I think they'll come up with some little chore for us to do." He nodded morosely and hobbled away. They wouldn't do a hot transfer if there was a choice. So it was something important that the hunter/killers weren't supposed to know about.

The cage popped and I wiggled into it, quickly setting the muscle sensors and plugging in the orthotics and blood shunt. Then I closed the shell and jacked.

It was always disorienting for a moment, but a lot more so with a hot transfer, since being platoon leader, I went first, and was suddenly jacked with a bunch of relative strangers. I did know Scoville's platoon vaguely, since I spent one day a month lightly jacked with him. But I didn't know all the intimate details of their lives, and really didn't care to know. I was plopped in the middle of this convoluted soap opera, an interloper who suddenly knew all the family secrets.

Two by two, they were replaced by my own men and women. I tried to concentrate on the problem at hand, which was to keep guard on the pairs of soldierboys as they spent their couple of minutes of immobile vulnerability, which was easy. I also tried to open a vertical link to the company commander and find out what was really going on. What were we going to do that was so secret Scoville was kept in the dark?

There was no answer until all of my people were in place. Then it came in a gestalt trickle while I automatically scanned the morning jungle for signs of trouble: there was a spy in Scoville's platoon. Not a willing spy, but somebody whose jack was tapped, real time.

It might even have been Scoville himself, so he couldn't be told. Brigade had set up an elaborate manipulation, where each member of the platoon was misinformed as to the location of their ambush. When an enemy force showed up in the middle of nowhere, they'd know which one was the leak.

I had a lot more questions than the company commander had answers. How could they control all the feedback states? If nine of the people thought they were at point A and one thought they were at point B, wouldn't there be conspicuous confusion? How could the enemy tap a jack in the first place? What was going to happen to the mechanic who was affected?

That last one, she could answer. They would examine him and take out his jack, and he would serve out the rest of his term as a tech or a shoe, depending. Depending on whether he could count to twenty without taking off his shoes and socks, I supposed. Army neurosurgeons made a lot less than Dr. Spencer.

I cut off the thread to the commander, which didn't mean she couldn't eavesdrop on me if she wanted to. There were some large implications here, and you didn't need a degree in cybercomm to see them. All of Scoville's platoon had spent the last nine days in an elaborate and tightly maintained virtual-reality fiction. Everything each one saw and felt was monitored by Command, and fed back instantly in an altered state. That state included nine other tailor-made fictions for the rest of the platoon. A total of a hundred discrete fictions, constantly created and maintained nonstop.

The jungle around me was no more or less real than the coral reef I'd visited with Amelia. What if it bore no relation to where my soldierboy actually was?

Every mechanic has entertained the fantasy that there is no war at all; that the whole thing is a cybernetic construction that the governments maintain for reasons of their own. You can turn on the cube when you get home, and watch yourself in action, replaying the news—but that could be faked even more easily than the input/feedback state that connects soldierboy to mechanic. Had anybody actually *been* to Costa Rica, any mechanic? No one in the military could legally visit Ngumi territory.

Of course, that was nothing but a fantasy. The piles of shattered bodies in the control room had been real. They couldn't have faked the nuclear flattening of three cities.

It was just a place to retreat from your own responsibility for the carnage. I suddenly felt pretty good, and realized my blood chemistry was being adjusted. I tried to hold on to the thought: how could you, how could you justify . . . well, they actually *did* ask for it. It was sad that so many Ngumi had to die for their leaders' lunacy. But that's not the thought; that's not the thought . . .

"Julian," the company commander thought down, "move your platoon northwest three kilometers for a pickup. As you approach the PZ, you want to home in on a twenty-four megahertz beeper."

I rogered. "Where we headed?"

"Town. We're going to join up with Fox and Charlie for a daytime thing. Details on the way."

We had ninety minutes to get to the pickup zone, and the jungle wasn't thick, so we just spread out in echelon, maintaining about twenty meters between each soldierboy, and picked our way northwest.

My uneasiness faded in the mundane business of keeping everybody in line and moving. I realized that my train of thought had been interrupted, but wasn't sure whether it was anything important. No way to write a note to myself, I realized for about the hundredth time. And things sort of fade when you get out of the cage.

Karen saw something and I froze everybody. After a moment she said false alarm; just a howler monkey and its baby. "Out of the branches?" I asked, and got a nod back. I projected uneasiness to everybody, as if that were necessary, and had us split into two groups and move in file, two hundred meters apart. Very quietly.

"Animal behavior" is an interesting term. When an animal misbehaves, it's for a reason. Howler monkeys are more vulnerable on the ground.

Park sighted a sniper. "Got a pedro at ten o'clock, range a hundred ten meters, in a tree blind about ten meters up. Permission to fire."

"Not granted. Everyone stop and look around." Claude and Sara got the same one, but there weren't any others obvious.

I put all three images together. "She's asleep." I got the gender from Park's olfactory receptors. The IR pattern gave me almost nothing, but her breathing was regular and sonorous.

"Let's drop back about a hundred meters and circle around her." I got a confirm from the company commander and an angry "?" from Park.

I expected others—people don't just wander out into the woods and climb a tree; she was protecting something.

"Possible she knew we were coming?" Karen asked.

I paused . . . Why else would she be here? "If so, she's pretty calm about it, to be able to sleep. No, it's a coincidence. She's guarding something. We don't have time to look for it, though."

"We have your coordinates," the commander said. "Flyboy coming in, in about two minutes. You want to be elsewhere."

I gave the platoon the order to move out fast. We didn't make too much noise, but enough: the sniper woke up and fired a burst at Lou, who was bringing up the rear on the left flank.

It was a pretty sophisticated antisoldierboy weapon, explosive rounds with depleted-uranium punchers, probably. Two or three rounds hit Lou about waist-level and blew out his leg control. As he fell over backward, another one blew off his right arm.

He hit the ground with a jarring crash, and for a moment everything was still, the high leaves over him rustling in the morning breeze. Another round exploded into the ground next to his head, showering his eyes with dirt. He shook his head to clear them.

"Lou, we can't do a pickup. Get out of there except for eyes and ears."

"Thanks, Julian." Lou jacked out, and the warning-signal pains from his back and arm stopped. He was just a camera pointed at the sky.

We were most of a kilometer away when the flyboy screamed overhead. I linked to her through Command and got a strange double view: from above the forest canopy, a spreading blossom of napalm shot through with glittering streaking sparkles, hundreds of thousands of flechettes. On the ground, a sudden sheet of fire overhead that dripped down through the branches, loud splintering crackle as the flechettes tore through the forest. Sonic boom and then silence.

Then a man screaming and another one talking to him in low tones, and one shot that ended the screaming. A man ran by, close but out of sight, and threw a grenade at the soldierboy. It bounced off the chest and exploded harmlessly.

The napalm dripped and flames from the underbrush licked up toward it. Monkeys screamed at the fire. Lou's eyes flickered twice and went out. As we moved away from the inferno, two more flyboys came in low and dropped fire retardant. It was an ecological preserve, after all, and the napalm had done all we wanted it to.

As we approached the PZ, Command said they'd calculated a body count of four—our sniper and both of the men plus one for whoever else might have been there—and gave three of them to the flyboy and split one among us. Park didn't like that at all, since there wouldn't have been a sortie if he hadn't spotted the sniper, and she would've been an easy kill if I hadn't ordered otherwise. I advised him to hold that in; he was on the verge of a public tantrum that would leak up to command and force an Article 15—pro forma company-level punishment for petty insubordination.

As I shot that warning to him, I had to think how much easier it must be to be a shoe. You can hate your sergeant and smile at him at the same time.

The PZ was obvious without the radio beacon, the denuded dome of a hill that had been cleaned up recently with a controlled burn-and-blast.

As we picked our way up the muddy ashes of the hillside, two flyboys came in and hovered protectively. Not a normal fast snatch.

The cargo helicopter came in and landed, or at least hovered a foot off the ground while the rear door slammed down to form an unsteady ramp. We scrambled aboard to join twenty other soldierboys.

My opposite number in Fox platoon was Barboo Seaves; we'd worked together before. I had a double-weak link to her, through Command and through Rose, who had replaced Ralph as horizontal liaison. By way of greeting, Barboo projected a multisensory image of carne asada, a meal we'd shared at the airport a few months ago.

"Anybody tell you anything?" I asked.

"I am but a mushroom." That military joke was old when my father heard it: *They keep me in the dark and feed me bullshit.*

The chopper was rising and tilting as soon as the last soldierboy dove in off the ramp. We all sort of crashed around, getting acquainted.

I didn't really know Charlie platoon's leader, David Grant. Half of his platoon had been replaced in the past year—two stroked out and the others "Temporarily reassigned for psychological adjustment." David had only been in command for two cycles. I hello'ed him, but at first he was busy with his platoon, trying to calm down a couple of neos who were afraid we were going into a kill situation.

With luck, we wouldn't be. When the door slammed shut I got an outline of the general order, which was basically a parade, or show of force, in an urban area that was due for a reminder that we See All, Know All. It was the el Norte section of Liberia, which, oddly enough, had both guerrilla activity and a high concentration of Anglos. They were a mixture of older Americans who had retired to Costa Rica and the children and grandchildren of earlier retirees. The pedros thought that the presence of a lot of gringos would protect them. We were supposed to demonstrate otherwise.

But if the enemy stayed out of sight, there wouldn't be any problems. Our orders were to use force "only reactively."

So we were to be both bait and hook. It didn't look like a good situation. The rebels in Guanacaste province had been faring badly and needed their own demonstration. I supposed Command had taken that into account.

We picked up some riot control accessories—extra gas grenades and a couple of tanglefoot projectors. They spray out a skein of sticky string that makes it impossible to walk; after ten minutes, it suddenly evaporates. We were also issued extra concussion grenades, though I'm not sure they're a good idea with civilians. Blow out somebody's eardrums and expect him to be grateful you didn't do worse? None of the riot control weapons are pleasant, but that's the only one that does permanent damage. Unless you're staggering around blinded by tear gas and get run over by a truck. Or breathe VA and choke on vomit.

We came in over the city at treetop level, lower than many of the buildings, helicopter and two flyboys in tight slow formation, loud as three banshees. I suppose that was good psychology, show we're not afraid and at the same time rattle their windows. But again I wondered whether we weren't set out as tempting bait. If somebody fired at us, I had no doubt the sky could be full of flyboys in a few seconds. The enemy must have figured that out, too.

Once on the ground and out of the chopper, the twenty-nine soldierboys could easily destroy the city themselves, without air support. Part of our show was going to be a "public service" demonstration: a block of tenements to be razed. We could save the city a lot of construction, or deconstruction, expense. Just walk in and pull things down.

We set down gently on the town square, flyboys hovering, and disembarked into a parade formation, ten by three, minus one. Only a scattering of people were there to watch us, which surprised no one. A few curious children and defiant teenagers and old people who live in the park. Only a few police; most of the force, it turned out, was waiting down by our demonstration area.

The buildings surrounding the square were late colonial architecture, graceful in the shadow of the glass-and-metal geometries that hovered over them. The blind reflective windows of those modern buildings could conceal a city full of watchers, maybe snipers. As we marched off in robotic lockstep I was more than ever aware of the fact that I was a safe puppeteer a couple of hundred miles away—if rifles did appear in each window and started firing, no actual people would be killed. Until we retaliated.

We broke step into a carefully random rolling gait as we crossed an old bridge, so as not to be embarrassed by shaking it apart and falling into the noisome trickle below, and then went back to the slam-slam-slam that was supposed to be so intimidating. I did see a dog run away. If any humans were being terrorized along our route, they were doing it indoors.

Past the postmodern anonymity of downtown, we went through a few blocks of a residential neighborhood, presumably upper-class dwellings, all hidden behind tall whitewashed walls. Watchdogs howled at our echoing steps, and in several places we were tracked by surveillance cameras.

Then we got into the barrios. I always felt a kind of referred sympathy for the people who lived in these circumstances, here and in Texas, so similar to the American black ghettos that I had avoided by accident of birth. I also knew that there were sometimes compensations, family and neighborhood bonds that I never experienced. But I could never be sentimental enough to consider that a reasonable trade-off for my longer life expectancy; higher life expectations.

I turned down my olfactory receptors a notch. Smell of standing sewage and urine starting to steam in the morning sun. There was also the good smell of corn baking, and good strong peppers, and somewhere a chicken roasting slowly, maybe a celebration. A chicken was not an everyday menu item here.

You could hear the crowd several blocks before we got to the demonstration site. We were met by two dozen mounted police—mounted on horses—who formed a protective V, or U, around us.

It made you wonder who was demonstrating what. Nobody pretended that the party in power represented the actual will of the people. It was a police state, and there was no question whose side we were on. I suppose it didn't hurt to reinforce that every now and then.

There must have been two thousand people milling around the demolition site. It was obvious we were moving into a pretty complicated political situation. There were signs and banners proclaiming ACTUAL PEOPLE LIVE HERE and ROBOT PUPPETS OF RICH LANDOWNERS, and so forth—more signs in English than in Spanish, for the cameras. But there were a lot of Anglos in the crowd, too, retirees showing support for the locals. Anglos who *were* locals.

I asked Barboo and David to halt their platoons in place for a minute, and sent a query up to Command. "We're being used here, and it looks like a potentially bad situation."

"That's why you were issued all the extra riot gear," she said. "This crowd's been gathering since yesterday."

"But this isn't our *job*," I said. "It's like using a sledgehammer to swat a fly."

"There are reasons," she said, "and you have orders. Just be careful."

I relayed that to the others. "Be careful?" David said. "Of us hurting them or of them hurting us?"

"Just try not to step on anybody," Barboo said.

"I'd go further," I said. "Don't injure or kill anybody to save the machines."

Barboo agreed. "That's a corner the rebels may try to back us into. Stay in control of the situation."

Command was listening. "Don't be too conservative. This *is* a show of force."

It started out well. A young Ender who'd been standing on a box, haranguing, suddenly jumped off and ran over to stand in the way of our progress. One of the mounted police touched him on the bare back with a cattle prod, which knocked him down and threw him into a trembling seizure at David's feet. David stopped dead and the soldierboy behind him, distracted by something, ran into him with a crash. It would have been perfect if David had fallen over and crushed the helpless fanatic, but at least we were spared that. Some of the crowd laughed and jeered, not a bad response under the circumstances, and they spirited the unconscious man away.

That might protect him for a day, but I'm sure the police knew his name, address, and blood type.

"Straighten up the ranks and files," Barboo said. "Let's keep moving and get this over with."

The block we were supposed to demolish was identified with a girdle of orange spray paint. Hard to miss, anyhow, since a solid square of police and sawhorses kept the crowd a neat hundred meters away on all four sides.

We didn't want to use explosives more powerful than the two-inch grenades; with the rockets, for instance, individual fragments of brick could go a lot farther than a hundred meters, with the force of a bullet. But I queried for a calculation and got permission to use the grenades to weaken the buildings' foundations.

They were six-story concrete slab constructions with crumbling brick facades. Less than fifty years old, but the work had been done with inferior concrete—too much sand in the mixture—and one building had already collapsed, killing dozens.

So it didn't sound like a big deal to bring them down. Grenades to jar things loose at the foundation, then put a soldierboy at each corner to push and pull, putting torsion on the framework structure, and jump back as it falls—or don't jump back; demonstrate our invulnerability by standing there unaffected by the rain of concrete and steel.

The first one went perfectly—a textbook demonstration, if there were a textbook on bizarre demolition techniques. The crowd was very quiet.

The second building was recalcitrant; the front facade fell away, but the steel frame wouldn't twist enough to snap. So we used lasers to cut through a few exposed I-beams, and then it came down with a satisfying crash.

The next building was a disaster. It came down as easily as the first, but it rained children.

More than two hundred children had been squeezed into one room on the sixth floor, bound and gagged and drugged. It turned out that they were from a suburban private school. A guerrilla team had come in at eight in the morning, killed all the teachers, kidnapped all the children, and moved them into the condemned building in crates covered with UN markings, just an hour before we had gotten there.

None of the children survived falling sixty feet and being buried by rubble, of course. It was not the sort of political demonstration a rational mind might have conceived, since it demonstrated their brutality rather than ours—but it did speak directly to the mob, which collectively was no more rational.

When we saw all the children, of course we stopped everything and called for a massive medevac. We started clearing away rubble, numbly looking for survivors, and a local *brigada de urgencia* crew came in to help us.

Barboo and I organized our platoons into search parties, covering two thirds of the building's "footprint," and David's platoon should have done the other third, but the shock had them badly disorganized. Most of them had never seen anyone killed. The sight of all those children mangled, pulverized—concrete dust turning blood into mud and transforming the small bodies into anonymous white lumps—it unhinged them. Two of the soldierboys stood frozen, paralyzed because their mechanics had fainted. Most of the others were wandering aimlessly, ignoring David's orders, which were barely coherent, anyhow.

I was moving slowly, myself, stunned by the enormity of it. Dead soldiers on a battlefield are bad enough—one dead soldier is bad enough—but this was almost beyond belief. And the carnage had just started.

A big helicopter sounds aggressive no matter what its actual function is. When the medevac chopper came beating in, someone in the crowd started shooting at it. Just lead bullets that bounced off, we ascertained later, but the chopper's defenses automatically acquired the

target, a man shooting from behind a billboard, and fried
him.

It was a little too impressive, a large spalling laser
that made him explode like a dropped ripe fruit. The cry
''Murderers! Murderers!'' began, and in less than a minute the crowd broke through the police lines and attacked us.

Barboo and I had our people move quickly around the
perimeter, spraying tanglefoot, curling threads of neon
that quickly expanded to finger thickness, then to ropes.
It was effective at first, sticky as Superglue. It immobilized the front couple of ranks of people, bringing
them to their knees or flattening them. But that didn't
stop the ones behind them, who eagerly crowded over
their comrades' backs to get to us.

In seconds the mistake was apparent, as hundreds of
them, immobilized, were crushed under the weight of
the screaming mob that charged us. We popped VA and
CS gas everywhere, but it barely slowed them down.
More fell and were trampled.

A Molotov cocktail exploded on one of Barboo's platoon, turning him into a flaming symbol of staggering
helplessness—in reality, he was just blinded for a
moment—and then weapons came out all over, machine
guns chattering, two lasers lancing through the dust and
smoke. I watched a row of men and women fall in unison, swept down by a misaimed spray of their own machine gun fire, and relayed the order from Command,
''Shoot anyone with a weapon!''

The lasers were easy to spot, and went down first, but
people would pick them up again and keep firing. The
first man I ever killed, a boy actually, had scooped up
the laser and was firing offhand, standing up. I aimed
for his knees, but then somebody knocked him down
from behind. The bullet struck the center of his chest
and blew his heart out his back. On top of everything
else, that pushed me over the edge, into paralysis.

Park went over the edge, too; the other edge, berserk. A man got to him with a knife, and tried to climb up and poke out his eyes, as if that were possible. Park grabbed an ankle and swung the man like a doll, spattering his brains on a concrete slab, and tossed his twitching body into the mob. Then he waded into the crowd like an insane mechanical monster, kicking and punching people to death. That snapped me out of my shock. When he wouldn't respond to shouted orders, I asked Command to deactivate him. He killed more than a dozen before they complied, and his suddenly inert soldierboy went down under a pile of enraged people, pounding it with rocks.

It was a truly Dantean scene, bloody crushed bodies everywhere, thousands of people staggering or crouching, blinded, gagging and spewing as the gas swirled around them. Part of me, vertiginous with horror, wanted to leave the place by fainting, let the crowd have this machine. But my crew was in bad shape, too; I couldn't desert them.

The tanglefoot suddenly dissipated in a cloud of colored smoke, but it didn't make any difference. Everyone who had been immobilized by it was lying dead or crippled.

Command told us to clear out; go back to the square as quickly as possible. We could have done an extraction right there, while the crowd was subdued, but didn't want to take the chance of more helicopters and flyboys setting them off again. So we picked up four immobilized soldierboys and rushed off in victory.

On the way, I told Command that I was going to file a recommendation that Park be given a psychological discharge, at the very least. Of course, she could read my actual feelings: "You really want him tried for murder, for war crimes. That isn't possible."

Well, I knew that, but said that I wouldn't have him as part of my platoon anymore, even if my refusal meant administrative punishment. The rest of the platoon had had enough of him, too. Whatever the idea had been that prompted them to insert him into our family, today's action proved it wrong.

Command said that every factor would be taken into consideration, including my own confused emotional state. I was ordered to go directly to Counseling when we jacked out. Confused? How are you *supposed* to feel, when you precipitate mass murder?

But the mass death, I could rationalize away the blame for that. We had tried everything our training had given us to minimize loss. But the single death, the one I shot myself—I couldn't stop reliving that moment. The boy's determined look as he pointed and fired, pointed and fired; my own aiming circle dropping from his head to his knees, and then just as I pulled the trigger, his annoyed frown at being jostled. His knees hit the pavement just as my bullet ripped his heart out, and for an instant he still had that annoyed expression. Then he pitched forward, dead before his face hit the ground.

Something in me died then, too. Even through the belated stabilizing soup of mood drugs. I knew there was only one way to get rid of the memory.

julian was wrong on that score. One of the first things the counselor told him was "You know, it is possible to erase specific memories. We can make you forget killing that boy." Dr. Jefferson was a black man maybe twenty years older than Julian. He rubbed a fringe of gray beard. "But it's not simple or complete. There would be emotional associations we can't erase, because it's impossible to track down every neuron that was affected by the experience."

"I don't think I want to forget," Julian said. "It's part of what I am now, for better or worse."

"Not better, and you know it. If you were the type of person who could kill and walk away from it, the army would've put you in a hunter/killer platoon."

They were in a wood-paneled office in Portobello, bright native paintings and woven rugs on the walls. Julian obeyed an obscure impulse and reached over to feel the rough wool of a rug. "Even if I forget, he stays dead. It doesn't seem right."

"What do you mean by that?"

"I owe him my grief, my guilt. He was just a kid, caught up in the—"

"Julian, he had a gun and was firing all over the place. You probably *saved* lives by killing him."

"Not our lives. We were all safe, here."

"Civilians' lives. You don't do yourself any good by thinking of him as a helpless boy. He was heavily armed and out of control."

"I was heavily armed and *in* control. I aimed to disable him."

"The more reason for you not to blame yourself."

"Have you ever killed anybody?" Jefferson shook his head, one short jerk. "Then you don't know. It's like not being a virgin anymore. You can erase the memory of the event, okay, but that wouldn't make me a virgin again. Like you say, 'emotional associations.' Wouldn't I be even *more* fucked up? Not being able to trace those feelings back to their trigger?"

"All that I can say is that it's worked with other people."

"Ah ha. But not with everybody."

"No. It's not an exact science."

"Then I respectfully decline."

Jefferson leafed through the file on his desk. "You may not be allowed to decline."

"I can disobey an order. This isn't combat. A few months in the stockade wouldn't kill me."

"It's not that simple." He counted off on his fingers.

"One, a trip to the stockade *might* kill you. The shoe guards are selected for aggressiveness and they don't like mechanics.

"Two, a prison term would be disastrous to your professional life. Do you think the University of Texas has ever granted tenure to a black ex-con?

"Three, you may not have any choice, literally. You have clear-cut suicidal tendencies. So I can—"

"When did I ever say anything about suicide?"

"Probably never." The doctor took the top sheet from the file and handed it to Julian. "This is your overall personality profile. The dotted line is average for men

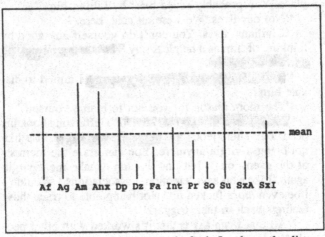

at your age when you were drafted. Look at the line above 'Su.' "

"This is based on some written test I took five years ago?"

"No, it integrates a number of factors. Army tests, but also various clinical observations and evaluations made since you were a child."

"And on the basis of that, you can force me into a medical procedure, against my will?"

"No. On the basis of 'I'm a colonel and you're a sergeant.' "

Julian leaned forward. "You're a colonel who took the Hippocratic oath and I'm a sergeant with a doctorate in physics. Can we talk for just a minute like two men who've spent most of their lives in school?"

"Sorry. Go ahead."

"You're asking me to accede to a medical treatment that will drastically affect my memory. Am I supposed to believe that there's no chance that it will hurt my ability to do physics?"

Jefferson was silent for a moment. "The chance is there, but it's very small. And you sure won't be doing any physics if you kill yourself."

"Oh, for Christ's sake. I'm not going to kill myself."

"Right. Now what do you think a potential suicide would say?"

Julian tried not to raise his voice. "Do you hear yourself? You mean that if I said, 'Sure, I think I'll do it,' you'd pronounce me safe and let me go home?"

The psychiatrist smiled. "Okay, that's not a bad response. But you have to see that it could be a calculated one, from a potential suicide."

"Sure. Anything I say can be evidence of mental illness. If you're convinced that I'm ill."

He studied his own palm. "Look, Julian. You know I've jacked into the cube that recorded how you felt when you killed that boy. In a way, I've been there. I've been you."

"I know that."

He put Julian's file away and brought out a small white jar of pills. "This is a mild antidepressant. Let's try it for two weeks, a pill after breakfast and one after dinner. It won't affect your intellectual abilities."

"All right."

"And I want to see you"—he checked a desk calendar—"at ten o'clock on July ninth. I want to jack with

you and check your responses to this and that. It'll be a
two-way jack; I won't hold anything back from you.''

"And if you think I'm nuts, you'll send me to the
memory eraser.''

"We'll see. That's all I can say.''

Julian nodded and took the white jar and left.

i would lie to Amelia; say it was just a routine
checkup. I took one of the pills and it did help me fall
asleep, and sleep without dreams. So maybe I would
keep taking them if they didn't affect my mental acuity.

In the morning I felt less sad and conducted an internal debate regarding suicide, perhaps in preparation for
Dr. Jefferson's invasion. I couldn't lie to him, jacked.
But maybe I could bring about a temporary "cure." It
was easy to argue against the act—not only the effect
on Amelia and my parents and friends, but also the ultimate triviality of the gesture, as far as the army was
concerned. They would just find somebody else my size
and send the soldierboy out with a fresh brain. If I did
succeed in killing a few generals with my exit, they
would likewise just promote some colonels. There's
never any shortage of meat.

But I wondered whether all the logical arguments
against suicide would do anything to conceal the depth
of my own resolution. Even before the boy's death I
knew I was only going to live as long as I had Amelia.
We've stayed together longer than most people do.

And when I came home, she was gone. Gone to see
a friend in Washington, the note said. I called the base
and found I could fly out to Edwards as a supernumerary
if I could get my butt down there in ninety minutes. I
was in the air over the Mississippi before I realized I
hadn't called the lab to arrange for someone else to monitor the scheduled runs. Was that the pills? Probably not.

But there was no way to call from a military plane, so it was ten o'clock Texas time before I was able to phone the lab. Jean Gordie had covered for me, but that was pure luck; she'd come in to grade some papers, seen I wasn't in, and checked the run schedule. She was more than slightly pissed off, since I couldn't offer a really convincing excuse. Look, I had to take the first flight to Washington to decide whether or not to kill myself.

From Edwards I took the monorail into old Union Station. There was a map machine on the car that showed me I'd be only a couple of miles from her friend's address. I was tempted to walk over and knock on the door, but decided to be civilized and call. A man answered.

"I have to talk to Blaze."

He looked at the screen for a moment. "Oh, you're Julian. Just a moment."

Amelia came on, looking quizzical. "Julian? I said I'd be home tomorrow."

"We have to talk. I'm here in Washington."

"Come on over then. I was just about to fix lunch."

How domestic. "I'd rather . . . we have to talk alone."

She looked offscreen and then back, worried. "Where are you?"

"Union Station."

The man said something I couldn't quite overhear. "Pete says there's a bar on the second floor called the Roundhouse. I can meet you there in thirty or forty minutes."

"Go ahead and finish lunch," I said. "I can—"

"No. I'll be down as fast as I can."

"Thanks, darling." I thumbed off and looked into the mirror of the screen. Despite the night's sleep, I still looked pretty haggard. I should've shaved and changed out of my uniform.

I ducked into a men's room for a quick shave and comb and then walked down to the second floor. Union

Station was a transportation hub, but also a museum of
rail technology. I walked by some subways of the previous century, with their makeshift bulletproofing all pit-
ted and dented. Then a steam-powered locomotive from
the nineteenth that actually looked to be in better shape.

Amelia was waiting at the door to the bar. "I took a
cab," she explained as we embraced.

She steered me into the gloom and odd music of the
bar. "So who's this Pete? A friend, you said?"

"He's Peter *Blankenship*." I shook my head. The
name was vaguely familiar. "The *cosmologist*." A serving robot took our iced tea orders and said we had to
spend ten dollars to take the booth. I got a glass of whiskey.

"So you're old friends."

"No, we just met. I wanted to keep our meeting secret."

We took our drinks to an empty booth and sat down.
She looked intense. "Let me try to—"

"I killed somebody."

"What?"

"I killed a boy, a civilian. Shot him with my soldierboy."

"But how could you? I thought you weren't even supposed to kill soldiers."

"It was an accident."

"What, you stepped on him or something?"

"No, it was the laser—"

"You 'accidentally' shot him with a laser?"

"A bullet. I was aiming for his knees."

"An unarmed *civilian*?"

"He was armed—it was *him* with the laser! It was a
madhouse, a mob out of control. We were ordered to
shoot anyone with a weapon."

"But he couldn't have hurt *you*. Just your machine."

"He was shooting wildly," I lied; half-lied. "He
could have killed dozens himself."

"You couldn't have shot for the weapon he was using?"

"No, it was a heavy-duty Nipponex. They have Ablar, a bulletproof and antispalling coating. Look, I aimed for his *knees*, then somebody jostled him from behind. He pitched forward and the bullet hit him in the chest."

"So it was sort of an industrial accident. He shouldn't have been playing with the big boys' toys."

"If you want to put it that way."

"How would *you* put it? You pulled the trigger."

"This is crazy. You don't know about Liberia yesterday?"

"Africa? We've been too busy—"

"There's a Liberia in Costa Rica."

"I see. That's where the boy was."

"And a thousand others. Also past tense." I took a long drink of whiskey and coughed. "Some extremists killed a couple of hundred children, and made it look like we'd been responsible. That was horrible enough. Then a mob attacked us, and . . . and . . . the riot control measures backfired. They're supposed to be benign, but they caused the death of hundreds more, trampled. Then they started shooting, shooting their own people. So we, we . . ."

"Oh, my God. I'm sorry," she said, her voice trembling. "You need real support, and here I come all edgy with fatigue and preoccupied. You poor . . . have you been to a counselor?"

"Yeah. He was a big help." I plucked an ice cube from the tea and dropped it in the whiskey. "He said I'd get over it."

"Will you?"

"Sure. He gave me some pills."

"Well, be careful with the pills and the booze."

"Yes, doctor." I took a cool sip.

"Seriously. I'm worried."

"Yeah, me too." Worried, wearied. "So what are you and this Pete doing?"

"But you—"

"Let's just change the subject. What did he want you for?"

"Jupiter. He's challenging some basic cosmological assumptions."

"Then why you? Probably everyone from Macro on down knows more about cosmology—hell, *I* probably do."

"I'm sure you do. But that's *why* he chose me—everyone senior to me was in on the planning stages of the Project, and they have this consensus about . . . certain aspects of it."

"What aspects?"

"I can't tell you."

"Oh, come on."

She touched her tea but didn't drink it; looked into it. "Because you can't really *keep* a secret. All your platoon would know as soon as you jacked."

"They wouldn't know shit. Nobody else in that platoon can tell a Hamiltonian from a hamburger. Anything technical, they might pick up on my emotional reaction, but that's it. No technical details; they might as well be in Greek."

"Your emotional reaction is what I'm talking about. I can't say any more. Don't ask me."

"Okay. Okay." I took another drink of whiskey and pushed the order button. "Let's get something to eat." She asked it for a salmon sandwich and I got a hamburger and another whiskey, a double.

"So you're total strangers. Never met before."

"What is that supposed to mean?"

"Only what I asked."

"I met him maybe fifteen years ago, at a colloquium in Denver. If you must know, that's when I was living with Marty. He went to Denver and I tagged along."

"Ah." I finished the first whiskey.

"Julian. Don't be upset about that. There's nothing going on. He's old and fat and more neurotic than you."

"Thanks. So you'll be home, when?"

"I have to teach tomorrow. So I'll be home by morning. Then come back here Wednesday if we still have work to do."

"I see."

"Look, don't tell anyone, especially Macro, that I'm here."

"He'd be jealous?"

"What is this with jealousy? I told you there's nothing . . ." She slumped back. "It's just that Peter's been in fights with him, in *Physics Review Letters*. I may be in a position where I have to defend Peter against my own boss."

"Great career move."

"This is bigger than career. It's . . . well, I can't tell you."

"Because I'm so neurotic."

"No. That's not it. That's not it at all. I just—" Our order rolled up to the booth and she wrapped the sandwich in a napkin and stood. "Look, I'm under more pressure than you know. Will you be all right? I have to get back."

"Sure. I understand about work."

"This is more than just work. You'll forgive me later." She slid out of the booth and gave me a long kiss. Her eyes were wet with tears. "We have to talk more about that boy. And the rest of it. Meanwhile, take the pills; take it easy." I watched her hurry out.

The hamburger smelled good but it tasted like dead meat. I took a bite but couldn't swallow it. I transferred the mouthful to a napkin, discreetly, and drank up the double in three quick swallows. Then I buzzed for another, but the table said it couldn't serve me alcohol for another hour.

I took the tube to the airport and had drinks in two places, waiting for the flight back home. A drink on the plane and a sour nap in the cab.

When I got home I found a half-bottle of vodka and poured it over a large mug of ice cubes. I stirred it until the mug was good and frosty. Then I emptied out the bottle of pills and pushed them into seven piles of five each.

I was able to swallow six of the piles, one mouthful of icy vodka apiece. Before I swallowed the seventh, I realized I should write a note. I owed Amelia that much. But I tried to stand up to find some paper and my legs wouldn't obey; they were just lumps. I considered that for awhile and decided to just take the rest of the pills, but I could only make my arm swing like a pendulum. I couldn't focus on the pills, anyhow. I leaned back and it was peaceful, loose, like floating in space. It occurred to me that this was the last thing I would ever feel, and that was all right. It was a lot better than going after all those generals.

amelia smelled urine when she unlocked the door eight hours later. She ran from room to room and finally found him in the reading alcove, slumped sideways in her favorite chair, the last neat pile of five pills in front of him, along with the empty prescription vial and half a large glass of warm watered vodka.

Sobbing, she felt his neck for a pulse and thought maybe there was a slight thread. She slapped him twice, hysterically hard, and he didn't respond.

She called 9-1-1 and they said all units were out; it might be an hour. So she switched to the campus emergency room and described the situation and said she was bringing him in. Then she called a cab.

She heaved him out of the chair and tried to pick him

up under the arms, staggering back out of the alcove. She wasn't strong enough to carry him that way, though, and she wound up dragging him ignominiously by the feet through the apartment. Backing out through the door, she almost ran into a large male student, who helped her carry him to the cab and went along with her to the hospital, asking questions that she answered in monosyllables.

He wasn't necessary at that end, it turned out; there were two orderlies and a doctor waiting at the ER entrance. They swung him up onto a gurney and a doctor gave him two shots, one in the arm and one in the chest. When he got the chest one, Julian groaned and trembled, and his eyes opened but showed only whites. The doctor said that was a good response. It might be a day before they knew whether he would recover; she could wait here or go home.

She did both. She took a cab with the helpful student back to the apartment building, picked up the notes and papers for her next class, and returned to the hospital.

There was nobody else in the waiting room. She got a cup of coffee from the machine and sat at the end of a couch.

The papers were all graded. She looked at her lecture notes but couldn't concentrate on them. It would have been hard to go through the teaching routine even if she had come home to a normal Julian. If Peter was right, and she was sure he was, the Jupiter Project was over. It had to be shut down. Eleven years, most of her career as a particle physicist, down the drain.

And now *this*, this strangely reciprocal crisis. A few months ago he had sat this deathwatch for her, brain-deathwatch. But she had caused both of them. If she had been able to put the work with Peter aside—put her career aside—and give him the kind of loving support that he needed to work through his guilt and anguish, he wouldn't have wound up here.

Or maybe he would. But it wouldn't have been her fault.

A black man in a colonel's uniform sat down next to her. His lime cologne cut through the hospital smell. After a moment he said, "You're Amelia."

"People call me Blaze. Or Professor Harding."

He nodded and didn't offer his hand. "I'm Julian's counselor, Zamat Jefferson."

"I have news for you. The counseling didn't take."

He nodded the same way. "Well, I knew he was suicidal. I jacked with him. That's why I gave him those pills."

"What?" Amelia stared at him. "I don't understand."

"He could take the whole bottle at once and survive. Comatose, but breathing."

"So he's not in danger?"

The colonel put a pink laboratory form on the table between them, and smoothed it out with both hands. "Look where it says 'ALC.' The alcohol content of his blood was 0.35 percent. That's more than halfway to suicide by itself."

"You knew he drank. You were jacked with him."

"That's just it. He's not normally a heavy drinker. And the scenario he had for suicide . . . well, it didn't involve either alcohol or pills."

"Really? What was it?"

"I can't say. It involved breaking the law." He picked up the form and refolded it neatly. "One thing . . . one thing you might be able to help with."

"Help him or help the army?"

"Both. If he comes out of this, and I'm almost certain he will, he'll never be a mechanic again. You could help him get through that."

Amelia's face narrowed. "What do you mean? He hates being a soldier."

"Maybe so, but he doesn't hate being jacked with his

platoon. Quite the contrary; like most people, he's become more or less addicted to it, to the intimacy. Perhaps you can distract him from that loss.''

''With intimacy. Sex.''

''That.'' He folded the paper twice again, creasing it with his thumbnail. ''Amelia, Blaze, I'm not sure you know how much he loves you, depends on you.''

''Of course I do. The feeling's mutual.''

''Well, I've never been inside your head. From Julian's point of view, there's some imbalance, asymmetry.''

Amelia sat back in the couch. ''So what does he want of me?'' she said stiffly. ''He knows I only have so much time. Only have one *life*.''

''He knows you're married to your work. That what you do is more important than what you are.''

''That's harsh enough.'' They both flinched when someone in another room dropped a tray of instruments. ''But it's true of most of the people we know. The world's full of proles and slacks. If Julian were one of them, I would never have even met him.''

''That's not quite it. I'm in your class, too, obviously. Sitting around consuming would drive us crazy.'' He looked at the wall, reaching for words. ''I guess I'm asking that you take a part-time job, as therapist, in addition to being a full-time physicist. Until he's better.''

She stared at him in a way she sometimes stared at a student. ''Thank you for not pointing out that he's done the same thing for me.'' She stood up suddenly and crossed over to the coffee machine. ''Want a cup?''

''No, thank you.''

When she came back she hooked a chair around so that the table was between them. ''A week ago I would have dropped everything to be his therapist. I love him more than you, or he, seem to think, and of course I owe him, too.''

She paused and leaned forward. ''But the world has

gotten a lot more complicated in the last few days. Did you know he went to Washington?''

"No. Government business?"

"Not exactly. But that's where I was, working. He came to me with what I see now was obviously a cry for help."

"About killing the boy?"

"And all the other death, the tramplings. I was properly horrified, even before I saw the news. But I . . . I . . ." She started to take a drink of coffee but put it down and sobbed, a startling, racking sound. She knuckled away sudden tears.

"It's all right."

"It's *not* all right. But it's bigger than him or me. Bigger than whether we even live or die."

"What, wait. Slow down. Your work?"

"I've said too much. But yes."

"What is it, some sort of defense application?"

"You could say that. Yes."

He sat back and pressed on his beard, as if it were pasted on. "Defense. Blaze, Dr. Harding . . . I spend all day watching people lie to me. I'm not an expert in much, but I'm an expert in that."

"So?"

"So nothing. Your business is your business, and my interest in it begins and ends with how it affects my patient. I don't care if your job is saving the country, saving the world. All I ask is that when you're not working with that, you're working with him."

"I'll do that, of course."

"You do owe him."

"Dr. Jefferson. I have one Jewish mother already. I don't need one with a beard and a suit."

"Point well taken. I didn't mean to be insulting." He stood up. "I'm misdirecting my own sense of responsibility onto you. I should not have let him go after we jacked. If I'd admitted him, put him under observation, this wouldn't have happened."

Amelia took his offered hand. "Okay. You beat yourself up over this, and I'll beat myself up over it, and our patient will have to improve, by osmosis."

He smiled. "Take care. Take care of yourself. This kind of thing is a terrible strain."

This kind of thing! She watched him leave and heard the outer door close. She felt her face redden and fought the pressure of tears behind her eyes, then let it win.

when i'd started to die it felt like I was drifting through a corridor of white light. Then I wound up in a big room with Amelia and my parents and a dozen or so friends and relations. My father was the way I remember him from grade school, slim and beardless. Nan Li, the first girl I was ever serious about, was standing next to me with her hand in my pocket, stroking. Amelia had an absurd grin, watching us.

Nobody said anything. We just looked at each other. Then everything faded out and I woke up in the hospital with an oxygen mask over my face and the smell of vomit deep inside my nose. My jaw hurt, as if someone had punched me.

My arm felt like it belonged to someone else, but I managed to drag my hand up and pull the mask down. There was someone in the room, out of focus, and I asked for a Kleenex and she handed it to me. I tried to blow my nose but it triggered retching, and she held me up and put a metal bowl under my chin while I coughed and drooled most attractively. Then she handed me a glass of water and said to rinse, and I realized it was Amelia, not a nurse. I said something romantic like "oh, shit," and started to black out again, and she eased me back to the pillow and worked the mask over my face.

I heard her calling for a nurse and then I passed out.

It's strange how much detail you recall from some parts of an experience like this, and how little of others. They told me later that I slept a solid fifteen hours after the little puking ceremony. It felt more like fifteen seconds. I woke up as if from a slap, with Dr. Jefferson drawing a hypo gun away from my arm.

I wasn't wearing the oxygen mask anymore. "Don't try to sit up," Jefferson said. "Get your bearings."

"Okay." I was just able to focus on him. "First bearing, I'm not dead, right? I didn't take enough pills."

"Amelia found you and saved you."

"I'll have to thank her."

"By that, you mean you're going to try again?"

"How many people don't?"

"Plenty." He held out a glass of water with a plastic straw. "People attempt suicide for various reasons."

I drank a cold sip. "You don't think I was actually serious about it."

"I do. You're pretty competent at everything you do. You'd be dead if Amelia hadn't come home."

"I'll thank her," I repeated.

"She's sleeping now. She stayed with you for as long as she could keep her eyes open."

"Then you came."

"She called me. She didn't want you to wake up alone." He weighed the hypodermic gun in his hand. "I decided to help you along with a mild stimulant."

I nodded and sat up a little. "It feels pretty good, actually. Did it counteract the drug? The poison."

"No, you've already been treated for that. Do you want to talk about it?"

"No." I reached for the water and he helped me. "Not with you."

"With Amelia?"

"Not now." I drank and was able to replace the glass

by myself. "I guess first I want to jack with my platoon. They'd understand."

There was a long silence. "You're not going to be able to do that."

I didn't understand. "Of course I can. It's automatic."

"You're out, Julian. You can't be a mechanic anymore."

"Hold it. Do you think any of my platoon would be *surprised* by this? Do you think they're that dumb?"

"That's not the point. It's just that they can't be made to live through it! I'm trained for it, and I can't say I look forward to jacking with you. Do you want to kill your friends?"

"Kill them."

"Yes! Exactly. Don't you think it's possible you might push one of them into doing the same? Candi, for instance. She's close to clinical depression most of the time, anyhow."

I could see the sense in that, actually. "But after I'm cured?"

"No. You'll never be a mechanic again. You'll be reassigned to some—"

"A *shoe*? I'll be a *shoe*?"

"They wouldn't want you in the infantry. They'll take advantage of your education, and put you in a technical post somewhere."

"Portobello?"

"Probably not. You'd jack socially with members of your platoon, your ex-platoon." He shook his head slowly. "Can't you see? That wouldn't be good for you or for them."

"Oh, I see; I see. From your point of view, anyhow."

"I *am* the expert," he said carefully. "I don't want you to be hurt and I don't want to be court-martialed for negligence—which is what would happen if I let you go back to your platoon and some of them couldn't handle sharing your memories."

"We've shared the feelings of people while they died, sometimes in great pain."

"But they didn't come back from the dead. Come back and discuss how desirable it might be."

"I may be cured of that." Even as I said it, I knew how false it sounded.

"One day, I'm sure you will be." That didn't sound too convincing, either.

julian endured one more day of bed rest and then was transferred to an "observation unit," which was like a hotel room, except that it only locked from the outside, and was always locked. Dr. Jefferson came in every other day for a week, and a kindly young civilian therapist, Mona Pierce, talked to him daily. After a week (by then, Julian was convinced he *was* going to go insane) Jefferson jacked with him, and the next day, he was released.

The apartment was too neat. Julian went from room to room trying to figure out what was wrong, and then it hit him—Amelia must have hired someone to come in and clean. Neither of them had any instinct or talent in that direction. She must have found out when he was going to be released and squandered a few bucks on it. The bed was made with military precision—a dead give-away—and on it was a note with today's date inside a heart.

He made a pot of coffee (spilling both water and grounds but scrupulously cleaning them up) and sat down to the console. There was a lot of mail stacked up for him, most of it awkward. A letter from the army giving him one month's leave at reduced pay, followed by a posting right on campus, not a mile from where he lived. The title was "senior research assistant"; it was TDY, so he could live at home, "hours to be arranged."

If he was reading between the lines correctly, the army was pretty well through with him, but on principle wouldn't just discharge him. It would be a bad example, being able to get out of the army just by killing yourself.

Mona Pierce had been a good listener who asked the right questions. She didn't condemn Julian for what he did—was angry at the military for not seeing it and discharging him before the inevitable happened—and didn't really disapprove of suicide in an absolute way, giving Julian tacit permission to do it again. But not over the boy. A lot of factors caused the boy's death, but Julian had been present against his will, and his part in it had been reflexive and appropriate.

If the personal mail had been awkward to write, it was doubly awkward to answer. He wound up with two basic replies: One was a simple "Thanks for your concern; I'm okay now" brush-off, and the other was a more detailed explanation, for those who deserved it and wouldn't be too bothered by it. He was still working on that when Amelia came in, carrying a suitcase.

She hadn't been able to see him during the week he was incarcerated in the observation unit. He'd called as soon as he was released, but she wasn't at home. The office said she was out of town.

They embraced and said the obvious things. He poured her a cup of coffee without asking. "I've never seen you look so tired. Still going back and forth to Washington?"

She nodded and took the cup. "And Geneva and Tokyo. I had to talk with some people at CERN and Kyoto." She looked at her watch. "Midnight flight to Washington."

"Jesus. What is it that's worth killing yourself over?" She looked at him for a moment and they both laughed, an embarrassed giggle.

She pushed the coffee away. "Let's go set the alarm

for ten-thirty and get some rest. You feel up to going to
Washington?''

"Meet the mysterious Peter?"

"And do some math. I'm going to need all the help
I can get, convincing Macro."

"Of what? What's so damned . . ."

She slipped out of her dress and stood up. "First bed.
Then sleep. Then explanations."

while amelia and i sleepily dressed and threw together some clothes for the trip, she gave me a rough
outline of what to expect in Washington. I didn't stay
sleepy long.

If Amelia's conclusions about Peter Blankenship's
theory proved correct, the Jupiter Project had to be shut
down. It could literally destroy everything: the Earth, the
solar system; the universe itself, eventually. It would re-
create the Diaspora, the "big bang" that started everything.

Jupiter and its satellites would be consumed in a fraction of a second; Earth and the Sun would have a few
dozen minutes. Then the expanding bubble of particles
and energy would muscle its way out to consume every
star in the Galaxy, and then go on to the main course:
the rest of everything.

One aspect of cosmology that the Jupiter Project had
been designed to test was the "accelerated universe"
theory. It was almost a century old, and had survived in
spite of inelegance and a prevailing skepticism over its
"ad hoc"-ness, because in model after model, the theory seemed to be necessary in order to account for what
happened the tiniest fraction of a second after creation—
10^{-35} of a second.

Simply stated, during that tiny period, you either had
to temporarily increase the speed of light or make time

elastic. For various reasons, the elasticity of time had always been the more likely explanation.

All of this took place when the universe was very tiny, growing from the size of a BB to the size of a small pea.

In the cab to the airport and during the flight, Amelia slept while I skimmed the field equations and tried to attack her method, using pseudo-operator theory. Pseudo-operator theory was so new I'd never applied it to a practical problem; Amelia had only heard of it. I needed to talk to some people about applying it, and to do it right required a lot more computing power than my notebook could muster.

(But suppose I *did* demonstrate they were wrong, and the Jupiter Project went ahead, but it turned out to be me and my new technique that were in error. A guy who couldn't live with killing one person would wind up destroying all life, everywhere.)

The danger was that the Jupiter Project would focus furious energies into a volume much smaller than a BB. Peter and Amelia thought that this would re-create, in reverse, the environment that characterized the universe when it was that small, and, an infinitesimal fraction of a second later, precipitate a tiny accelerated universe, and then a new Diaspora. It was bizarre to realize that something that happened in an area the size of a paramecium could trigger the end of the world. Of the universe.

Of course the only way of really checking it would be to do the experiment. Sort of like loading a gun and testing it by putting the muzzle in your mouth and pulling the trigger.

I thought of that metaphor while I was setting up operator conditions, typing on the plane, but didn't pass it on to Amelia. It occurred to me that a man who had recently tried to kill himself might not be the ideal companion for this particular venture.

Because of course the universe does end when you die. From whatever cause.

Amelia was still asleep, her head against the window, when we landed in Washington, and the change in vibration didn't wake her. I touched her awake and took down both our bags. She let me carry hers without protest, evidence of how tired she was.

I bought a pack of speedies at the airport newsstand while she called to make sure Peter was up. As she suspected, he was up and speeding, so we put the patches behind our ears and were wide awake by the time we got to the tube. Great stuff if you don't overdo it. I asked, and she confirmed that Peter was living on it.

Well, if your mission is saving the universe, what's a little sleep deprivation? Amelia was taking a lot of it, too, but coming down (with sleepies) to sleep three or four hours a day. If you don't do that, sooner or later you'll crash like a meteorite. Peter needed a complete and ironclad argument ready before he could allow himself to sleep, and knew he would pay for it.

Amelia had told him I was "sick," but hadn't elaborated. I suggested we call it food poisoning. Alcohol is a sort of a food.

He never asked. His interest in people began and ended with their usefulness to "the Problem." My credentials were that I could be trusted to keep my mouth shut and had been studying this new corner of analysis.

He met us at the door and gave me a cold damp handshake while he stared at me with pinpoint speedie pupils. As he led us to the office he gestured at an untouched tray of cold cuts and cheese that looked old enough to give you *actual* food poisoning.

The office was a familiar-looking mess of papers and readers and books. He had a console with a large double screen. One screen was a fairly straightforward Hamiltonian analysis and the other was a matrix (actually one visible face of a hypermatrix) full of numbers. Anybody

familiar with cosmology could decode it; it was basically
a chart of various aspects of the proto-universe as it aged
from zero to ten thousand seconds old.

He gestured at that screen. "Identify . . . can you identify the first three rows?"

"Yes," I said, and paused long enough to gauge his
sense of humor: none. "The first row is the age of the
universe in powers of ten. The second row is the temperature. The third row is the radius. You've left out the
zero-th column."

"Which is trivial."

"As long as you know it's there. Peter . . . should I
call you—"

"Peter. Julian." He rubbed two or three days' worth
of stubble. "Blaze, let me freshen up before you tell me
about Kyoto. Julian, familiarize yourself with the matrix.
Touch to the left of the row if you have any questions
about the variable."

"Have you slept at all?" Amelia asked.

He looked at his watch. "When did you leave? Three
days ago? I slept a little then. Don't need it." He strode
out of the room.

"If he got one hour of sleep," I said, "he'd still be
down."

She shook her head. "It's understandable. Are you
ready for this? He's a real slave driver."

I showed her a pinch of dark skin. "It's in my heri-
tage."

My approach to the Problem was about as old as
physics, post-Aristotle. First, I would take his initial conditions and, ignoring his Hamiltonians, see whether
pseudo-operator theory came to the same conclusion. If
it did, then the next thing, probably the only thing, we
had to worry about was the initial conditions themselves.
There were no experimental data about conditions close
to the "accelerated universe" regime. We could check
some aspects of the Problem by instructing the Jupiter

accelerator to crank up energies closer and closer to the critical point. But how close to the edge of a cliff do you want to push a robot when it might be forty-eight minutes between command and response? Not too close.

The next two days were a sleepless marathon of mathematics. We took a half hour off when we heard explosions outside and went up to the roof to watch the Fourth of July fireworks over the Washington Monument.

Watching the crash-bang of it, smelling the powder, I realized it was kind of a dilute preview of coming attractions. We had a little more than nine weeks. The Jupiter Project, if it went on schedule, would produce the critical energy level on September 14.

I think we all made the connection. We watched the finale silently and went back to work.

Peter knew a little about pseudo-operator analysis, and I knew a little about microcosmology; we spent a lot of time making sure I was understanding the questions and he was understanding the answers. But at the end of two days, I was as convinced as he and Blaze were. The Jupiter Project had to die.

Or *we* all had to die. A terrible thought occurred to me while I was twanging on speedies and black coffee: I could kill both of them with two blows. Then I could destroy all the records and kill myself.

I would become Shiva, Destroyer of Worlds, to paraphrase a nuclear pioneer. With a simple act of violence, I could destroy the universe.

A good thing I was sane.

It wouldn't be difficult for the Project engineers to prevent the disaster; any random change of the position of a few elements of the ring would do it. The system had to line up just so in order to work: a circular collimation over a million kilometers in circumference that would last for less than a minute before gravity from Jupiter's moons pulled it apart forever. Of course that minute would be eons long compared to the tiny interval that was being simulated. And plenty of time for the accelerating surge to make one orbit and produce the supercharged speck that would end it all.

i was growing to like Peter, in spite of himself. He *was* a slave driver, but he drove himself harder than he did me or Amelia. He was temperamental and sarcastic and blew up about as regularly as Old Faithful. But I've never met anyone so absolutely dedicated to science. He was like a mad monk lost in his love of the divine.

Or so I thought.

Speedies or no, I'm still blessed and cursed with a soldier's body. In the soldierboy I was exercised constantly, to keep from cramping up; at the university I worked out every day, alternating an hour of running with an hour on the gym machines. So I could get along without sleep, but not without exercise. Every morning at dawn I'd excuse myself from the proceedings and go off to run.

I was systematically exploring downtown Washington during my morning jogs, taking the Metro down and going in a different direction each day. I'd seen most of the monuments (which might be more moving to someone who'd actually *chosen* to be a soldier) and ranged as far afield as the Washington Zoo and Alexandria, when I felt like doing a few extra miles.

Peter accepted the fact that I had to have the exercise to keep from cramping up. I also contended that it cleared my head, but he pointed out that *his* head was clear enough, and the only exercise he got was wrestling with cosmology.

That was not entirely true. On the fifth day I got almost all the way to the Metro station and realized I'd left my card behind. I jogged on back to the apartment and let myself in.

My street clothes were in the living room, by the fold-out bed that Amelia and I shared. I took the card out of my wallet and started back to the front door, but then heard a noise from the study. The door was partly open; I looked in.

Amelia was sitting on the edge of the table, naked from the waist down, her legs scissored around Peter's bald head. She was gripping the edge of the table so hard her knuckles were bone-white, her face to the ceiling in a rictus of orgasm.

I closed the door with a quiet click and ran out.

I ran as hard as I could for several hours, stopping a few times to buy water and choke it down. When I got to the border gate between D.C. and Maryland, I couldn't get through because I didn't have my interstate pass. So I stopped running and slid into a dive called the Border Bar, icy air sharp with tobacco smoke, legal in D.C. I drank down a liter of beer and then sipped another liter with a shot of whiskey.

The combination of speedies and alcohol is not entirely pleasant. Your mind goes off in all directions.

When we first started going together, we talked about fidelity and jealousy. There's a kind of generation problem: When I was in my teens and early twenties, there was a lot of sexual experimentation and swapping around, with the defendable basis that sex is biology and love is something else, and a couple could negotiate the two issues independently. Fifteen years earlier, when Amelia had been that age, attitudes were more conservative—no sex without love, and then monogamy afterward.

She agreed at the time to go along with my principles—or lack of same, her contemporaries might say—even though we both thought it was unlikely we would exercise our freedom.

So now she had, and for some reason it was devastating. Less than a year ago, I would have jumped at the opportunity of having sex with Sara, jacked or not. So what right did I have to feel injured because she had done exactly the same thing? She'd been living with Peter more closely than most married couples live, for quite a while, and she respected him enormously, and if he asked for sex, why not say yes?

I had a feeling it was she who had asked, though. She certainly had been enjoying it.

I finished the drinks and switched to iced coffee, which tasted like cold battery acid, even with three sugars.

Did she know that I'd seen? I had closed the door automatically, but they might not remember having left it slightly open. Sometimes the current from the airco cycling on and off would ease a door shut.

"You look lonely, soldier." I did my running in fatigue uniform, in case I wanted an unrationed beer. "You look sad." She was pretty, blond, maybe twenty.

"Thanks," I said, "but I'm all right."

She sat down on the stool next to me and showed me her ID, professional name Zoë, medical inspection only one day old. Only one customer had signed the book. "I'm not just a whore. I'm also a professional expert on men, and you're not 'all right.' You look like you're about to jump off a bridge."

"So let me."

"Huh-uh. Not enough men around to waste one." She lifted up the back of her wig. "Not enough jacked men, anyhow."

Her off-white shift was raw silk, hanging loosely on her graceful athletic body, revealing nothing and everything: *This merchandise is so good I don't have to advertise.*

"I've used up most of my entertainment points," I said. "Can't afford you."

"Hey, I'm not doing any business. Give you one for free. Got a dime for the jack?"

I did have ten dollars. "Yeah, but look. I've had too much to drink."

"No such thing, with me." She smiled, perfect hungry teeth. "Money-back guarantee. I'll refund your dime."

"You just want to do it jacked."

"And I like soldiers. Was one."

"Come on. You're not old enough."

"I'm older than I look. And I wasn't in for long."

"What happened?"

She tilted toward me so that I could see her breasts. "One way to find out," she whispered.

There was a jack joint two doors down. In a few minutes I was in the dark humid cube with this intimate stranger, memories and feelings crashing together and mingling. I felt our finger slide easily into our vagina, tasted the salt sweat and musk of our penis, sucking it rigid. Breasts radiating. We shifted around so we were two mouths working together. There was a slight distracting ache from two of her molars that needed work. She was terrified of dentists and all of her beautiful front teeth were plastic.

She had thought about suicide but never attempted it, and our sexual rhythm faltered while she relived my memory—but she understood! She had spent one day as a mechanic, assigned to a hunter/killer platoon by a clerical error. She watched two people die and had a nervous breakdown, her soldierboy paralyzed.

She knew nothing of science or mathematics, physical education major, and although she felt my end-of-the-world anxiety, she just linked it with the suicide attempt. For several minutes, we stopped the sex and just held on to each other, sharing sorrows at a level that's hard to describe, independent of actual memory, I suppose body chemistry talking to body chemistry.

There was a two-minute warning chime and we recoupled, hardly moving, slight internal contractions bringing us to a slow-flowing orgasm.

And then we were standing in the lemon heat of the afternoon sun, trying to figure out what to say.

She squeezed my hand. "You aren't going to do it again—kill yourself?"

"I don't think so."

"I know what you think. But you're still 'way too upset about him and her."

"You helped with that. Having you, being you."

"Oh." She handed me her card and I signed on the back.

"Even when you don't charge?" I said.

"Except for husbands," she said. "Your own, that is." Her brow furrowed. "I got a little ghost of something."

I felt a sudden new sweat break out. "Of what?"

"You jacked with her. Only once? Once and a . . . another time that, that wasn't really the real thing?"

"Yeah. She had a jack put in, but it didn't take."

"Oh. I'm sorry." She came close and plucked at my shirt. She looked up at me and whispered, "The stuff I was thinking about you being black, you know I'm not a racist or anything."

"I know." She was, in a way, but not malicious and not in a way she could control.

"The other two . . ."

"Don't worry about it." She'd had only two other black customers, jacked, full of anger and passion. "We come in all flavors."

"You're so cool, so thoughtful. Not cold. She ought to hang on to you."

"Can I give her your phone number? For a reference?"

She giggled. "Let her bring it up. Let her talk first."

"I'm not sure she knows I saw them."

"If she doesn't know, she will know. You got to give

her time to work out what she's gonna say."

"Okay. I'll wait."

"Promise?"

"I promise."

She stood up on tiptoe and kissed me on the cheek. "You need me, you know how to get me."

"Yeah." I repeated her number. "Hope you have a good day."

"Ah, men. Never get any real action before sundown." She waved with two fingers and walked away, the silk artfully revealing and concealing with every step, a flesh metronome. I had a sudden backflash and for a moment I was in her body again, warm with afterglow and hunting for more. A woman who enjoyed her work.

It was three o'clock; I'd been gone for six hours. Peter would throw a fit. I took the Metro back and got an armload of groceries at the station store.

Peter didn't say anything, and neither did Amelia. Either they knew that I'd seen them, and were embarrassed, or they'd been too busy to worry about my absence. Whichever, this week's bundle of data had come in from Jupiter, and that meant a few hours of painstaking sorting and redundancy checks.

I put away the groceries and told them chicken stew tonight. We alternated cooking—rather, Amelia and I alternated cooking; Pete always called out for pizza or Thai. He had some private source of money, and got around the rationing because he'd wangled a reserve commission in the Coast Guard. He even had a captain's uniform hanging in plastic in the front hall closet, but he didn't know whether it fit.

The new data gave me plenty to do, too; pseudo-operator analysis requires some careful planning before you actually start to grind numbers through it. I tried to put the disturbing events of the day behind me, and concentrate on physics. I was only partly successful. Whenever I glanced over at Amelia I had a flash of her face lost in ecstasy, and a pang of reactive defiance and guilt over Zoë.

At seven I put the chicken into a pot of water and dumped the frozen vegetables on top; sliced up an onion and added it with some garlic. Zapped it to a quick boil and then left it to simmer for forty-five minutes, while I put on headphones and listened to some of this new Ethiopian stuff. The enemy, but their music is more interesting than ours.

Our custom was to eat at eight and watch at least the first part of the *Harold Burley Hour,* a Washington news distillation for people who could read without moving their lips.

Costa Rica was quiet today; fighting in Lagos, Ecuador, Rangoon, Magreb. The Geneva peace talks continued their elaborate charade.

It had rained frogs in Texas. They actually had amateur footage of that. Then a zoologist explained how it was all just an illusion caused by sudden local flooding. Nah. Secret Ngumi weapon; they'll go hopping all over the country and then suddenly explode, releasing poison frog gas. I'm a scientist; I know these things.

There was a consumer "demonstration" in Mexico City, which would have been called a riot if it had happened in enemy territory. Someone had gotten hold of the three-hundred-page manifest that detailed what was actually created last month with their "most favored nation" nanoforges. To everyone's surprise, most of it had been used to make luxuries for the rich. That was not what the public record had said.

Closer to home, Amnesty International was trying to subpoena the strings recording the activities of a 12th Division hunter/killer platoon that had been accused of torture, in an operation in rural Bolivia. Of course it was all pro forma; the request was going to be held up by technicalities until the heat death of the universe. Or until the crystals could be destroyed and convincing fakes synthesized. Everybody, including Amnesty International, knew that there were "black" operations whose existence was not even recorded at the division level.

A potential terrorist had been stopped at the Brooklyn Bridge customs point and summarily executed. As usual, no details were available.

Disney revealed plans for a Disneyworld in low Earth orbit, first launch scheduled to go up in twelve months. Peter pointed out that that was significant because of the inside information it implied. The area around the half-completed Chimborazo spaceport had been "pacified" for more than a year. Disney wouldn't start building if they hadn't had a guarantee that there would be a way of getting customers up there. So we were going to have routine civilian spaceflight again.

Amelia and I had shared a bottle of wine with dinner. I declared that I wanted to get a few hours' sleep before I pasted a new patch, and Amelia said she'd join me.

I was lying under the covers, wide awake, when she finished in the bathroom and slid in next to me. She held herself still for a moment, not touching.

"I'm sorry you saw us," she said.

"Well, it's always been part of our arrangement. The freedom."

"I didn't say I was sorry I did it." She turned on her side, facing me in the darkness. "Though maybe I am. I said I was sorry you saw us."

That was reasonable. "Has it always been like this, then? Other men?"

"Do you really want me to answer that? You'll have to answer the same question."

"That's easy. One woman, one time, today."

She put her palm on my chest. "I'm sorry. Now I feel like a real shit." She stroked me with her thumb, over my heart. "It's only been Peter, and only since you . . .

you took the pills. I just, I don't know. I just couldn't stand it."

"You didn't tell him why."

"No, as I said. He just thought you were sick. He's not the kind of man to press for details."

"But he *is* the kind of man to press . . . for other things."

"Come on." She scrunched over so her body was long against my side. "Most unattached men constantly radiate their availability. He didn't have to *ask*. I think all I did was put a hand on his shoulder."

"And then surrender to the inevitable."

"I suppose. If you want me to ask for your forgiveness, I'm asking."

"No. Do you love him?"

"What? *Peter?* No."

"Case closed, then." I rolled over on my side to embrace her and then tipped her onto her back, pressing against her lightly. "Let's make some noise."

I was able to start, but not finish; I wilted inside of her. When I tried to continue with my hand, she said no, let's just sleep. I couldn't.

the case was not closed, of course. The encounter with Zoë kept coming back to him, resonating with all the complicated emotions he still felt for Carolyn, dead more than three years. Sex with Amelia was as different as a snack is from a feast. If he wanted a feast every day, there were thousands of jills in Portobello and Texas who would be more than willing. He wasn't that hungry.

And although he appreciated Amelia's directness, he wasn't sure he quite believed her. If she did feel some love for Peter, under the circumstances she could justify lying about it, to spare Julian's feelings. She certainly hadn't *looked* casual, his face buried in her womanhood.

But there was time for all that later. Julian finally fell asleep some seconds before the alarm went off. He groped around for the box of speedie patches and they both took a paste. By the time they were dressed, the cobwebs were melting away and Julian was one cup of coffee away from math.

After they ground the fresh data through the mill, Julian's modern method and Peter's tried-and-true, all three were convinced. Amelia had been writing up the results; they spent half a day cutting and fine-tuning it, and zapped it to the *Astrophysical Journal* for peer review.

"A lot of people will want our heads," Peter said. "I'm going to go away for about ten days, and not take a phone. Sleep for a week."

"Where to?" Amelia asked.

"Place down in the Virgin Islands. Want to come?"

"No, I'd feel out of place." They all laughed nervously. "We have to teach, anyhow."

There was a little discussion over that, optimistic on Peter's part and exasperated on Amelia's. She already had been missing one or two classes a week, so why not a few more? *Because* she had already missed so many, she insisted.

Julian and Amelia flew back to Texas thoroughly exhausted, still running on speedies since they didn't dare come down until the weekend. They went through the motions of teaching and grading, waiting for their world to fall apart. None of their colleagues was on the *Aph. J.* review board currently, and apparently no one was consulted.

Friday morning, Amelia got a terse note from Peter: "Peer review report due this afternoon. Optimistic."

Julian was downstairs. She buzzed him up and showed him the message. "I think we might want to make ourselves scarce," he said. "If Macro finds out about it before he leaves the office, he'll call us up. Just as soon wait till Monday.''

"Coward,'' she said. "Me, too. Why don't we go out to the Saturday Night Special early? We could kill some time at the gene zoo.''

The gene zoo was the Museum of Genetic Experimentation, a place that was regularly closed by animal rights groups and reopened by lawyers. Ostensibly, the privately owned museum was a showcase for groundbreaking technology in genetic manipulation. Actually, it was a freak show, one of the most popular entertainments in Texas.

It was only a ten-minute walk from the Saturday Night Special, but they hadn't been there since the last time it was reopened. There were lots of new exhibits.

Some of the preserved specimens were fascinating, but the real attraction was the live ones, the actual zoo. They had somehow managed to contrive a snake with twelve legs. But they couldn't teach it how to walk. It would step forward with all six pairs at once, and lurch in one rippling flop after another—not a conspicuous advance over slithering. Amelia pointed out that the legs' connection to the animal's nervous system must be the same as goes to a normal snake's ribs, which undulate together to make it move.

The value of a more mobile snake might be questionable, and the poor creature obviously was made just as a curiosity, but another new one did have a practical application, besides scaring children: a spider the size of a pillow that spun a thick strong web back and forth on a frame, like a living loom. The resulting cloth, or mat, had surgical applications.

There was a pygmy cow, less than a meter tall, that wasn't touted as having any practical purpose. Julian suggested that it could answer the dairy needs of people like them, who liked cream in their coffee, if you could figure out how to milk it. It didn't move like a cow, though; it waddled around with earnest curiosity, probably gene-jumped with a beagle.

to save credits and money, we went to the zoo snack machines for some bread and cheese. There was a covered area behind the place with picnic tables, new since the last time we'd been there. We got a table to ourselves in the afternoon heat.

"So how much do we say to the gang?" I said, slicing cheddar in crumbling chunks with a plastic knife. I had my puttyknife but it would make a raclette out of the stuff, or a bomb.

"About you? Or the Project?"

"You haven't been there since I was in the hospital?" She shook her head. "Let's not bring it up. I meant should we talk about Peter's findings; our findings."

"No reason not to. It'll be common knowledge tomorrow."

I stacked an uneven pile of cheese on a slab of dark bread and passed it to her on a napkin. "Rather talk about that than me."

"People will know. Marty, for sure."

"I'll talk to Marty. If I have a chance."

"I think maybe the end of the universe might upstage you, anyhow."

"It does put things into perspective."

The half-mile walk to the Saturday Night Special was hot and dusty, even with the sun setting; a chalky kind of dust. We were glad to step into the air-conditioning. Marty and Belda were there, sharing a plate of appetizers. "Julian. How are you?" Marty said with careful neutrality.

"All right now. Talk about it later?" He nodded. Belda said nothing, concentrating on dissecting a shrimp. "Anything new on the project with Ray? The empathy thing."

"Quite a bit of new data, actually, though Ray's more up to date on it. That terrible thing with the children, Iberia?"

"Liberia," I said.

"Three of the people we were studying witnessed that. It was hard on them."

"Hard on everybody. The children, especially."

"Monsters," Belda said, looking up. "You know I'm not political, and I'm not maternal, either. But what could have been in their minds, to think that something so terrible could help their cause?"

"It's not just a warrior mentality," Amelia said. "Doing that to your own people."

"Most of the Ngumi thinks we did it," Marty said, "and just manipulated things to make it look like they did ... as you say, no one would *do* that to their own people. That's proof enough right there."

"You think it was all a cynical plan?" Amelia said. "I can't imagine."

"No, the word we have—this is confidential and unsupported—is that it was one lunatic officer and a few followers. They're all disposed of now, and Ngumi Psychops, such as they are, are doing a lot of smoke and mirrors, proving that for some reason *we* would want to destroy a school full of innocent children, to make a point. To show how ruthless the Ngumi are, when of course everyone knows they're the army of and for the people."

"And they're buying it?" I asked.

"A lot of Central and South America is. You haven't been watching the news?"

"Off and on. What was the thing with Amnesty International?"

"Oh, the army let one of their lawyers jack into any string he wanted, on condition of confidentiality. He could testify that everyone was genuinely surprised by the atrocity, most people horrified. That's pretty much gotten us off the hook in Europe, and even Africa and Asia. Didn't make the news down south."

Asher and Reza came in together. "Hey, welcome back, you two. Run off and get married?"

"Ran off," Amelia said quickly, "but to work. We've been up in Washington."

"Government business?" Asher said.

"No. But it will be, after the weekend."

"Can we wheedle it out of you? Or is it too technical?"

"Not technical, not the most important part." She turned to Marty. "Is Ray coming?"

"No; he had a family thing."

"Okay. Let's get our drinks. Julian and I have a story to tell."

Once the waiter had delivered the wine and coffee and whiskey and disappeared, Amelia started the tale, the threat of absolute intergalactic doom. I added a few details here and there. Nobody interrupted.

Then there was a long pause. There had probably not been that many consecutive seconds of silence in all the years this group had been getting together.

Asher cleared his throat. "Of course the jury's not in yet. Literally."

"That's true," Amelia said. "But the fact that Julian and Peter got the same results—down to eight significant figures!—using two different starting points and two independent methods . . . well, I'm not worried about the jury. I'm just worried about the politics of shutting down such a huge project. And a little worried about where I'll be working next year. Next week."

"Ah," Belda said. "You've done a good job with the trees. Surely you've thought about the forest as well."

"That it's a weapon?" I said, and Belda nodded

slowly. "Yes. It's the ultimate doomsday weapon. It has to be dismantled."

"But the forest is bigger than that," Belda said, and sipped her coffee. "Suppose you don't just dismantle it—you destroy it without a trace. You go through the literature and erase every line that relates to the Jupiter Project. And then you have government goons go out and kill everyone who's ever heard of it. What happens then?"

"You tell me," I said. "You're going to."

"The obvious. In ten years, or a hundred, or a million, somebody else will come up with the idea. And they'll be squashed, too. But then in another ten or a million years, somebody else will come up with it. Sooner or later, somebody will threaten to use it. Or not even threaten. Just do it. Because they hate the world enough they want everything to die."

There was another long silence. "Well," I said, "that solves one mystery. People wonder where physical law comes from. I mean, supposedly, all the laws governing matter and energy had to be created with the pinprick that began the Diaspora. It seems impossible, or unnecessary."

"So if Belda's right," Amelia said, "physical law was all in place. Twenty billion years ago, someone pushed the 'reset' button."

"And some billions of years before that," Belda said, "someone had done it before. The universe only lasts long enough to evolve creatures like us." She pointed a V of bony fingers at Amelia and me. "People like you two."

Well, it didn't really solve the first-cause mystery; sooner or later there had to be an actual first time.

"I wonder," Reza said. "Surely in all the millions of galaxies there are other races who've made this discovery. Thousands or millions of times. They evidently have all been psychologically incapable of doing it, destroying us all.''

''Evolved beyond it,'' Asher said. ''A pity we haven't.'' He swirled the ice in his whiskey. ''If Hitler had had the button in his bunker . . . or Caligula, Genghis Khan . . .''

''Hitler only missed the boat by a century,'' Reza said. ''I guess we haven't evolved past the possibility of producing another one.''

''And won't,'' Belda said. ''Aggression's a survival characteristic. It put us at the top of the food chain.''

''Cooperation did,'' Amelia corrected. ''Aggression doesn't work against a saber-toothed tiger.''

''A combination, I'll grant you,'' Belda said.

''Cooperation and aggression,'' Marty said. ''So a soldierboy platoon is the ultimate expression of human superiority over the beasts.''

''You couldn't tell that by some of them,'' I said. ''Some of them seem to have devolved.''

''But allow me to keep this on track.'' Marty steepled his fingers. ''Think of it this way. The race against time has begun. Sometime within the next ten or a million years, we have to direct human evolution away from aggressive behavior. In theory, it's not impossible. We've directed the evolution of many other species.''

''Some in one generation,'' Amelia said. ''There's a zoo full of them down the road.''

''Delightful place,'' Belda said.

''We could do it in one generation,'' Marty said quietly. ''Less.'' The others all looked at him.

''Julian,'' he said, ''why don't mechanics stay in soldierboys for more than nine days?''

I shrugged. ''Fatigue. Stay in too long and you get sloppy.''

''That's what they tell you. That's what they tell everybody. They think it's the truth.'' He looked around uneasily. They were the only people in the room, but he lowered his voice. "This is secret. Very secret. If Julian were going back to his platoon, I couldn't say it, because then too many people would know. But I can trust everyone here."

"With a military secret?" Reza said.

"Not even the military knows. Ray and I have kept this from them, and it hasn't been easy.

"Up in North Dakota there's a convalescent home with sixteen inmates. There's nothing really wrong with them. They stay there because they know they have to."

"People you and Ray worked on?" I asked.

"Exactly. More than twenty years ago. They're middle-aged now, and know they'll probably have to spend the rest of their lives in seclusion."

"What the hell did you *do* to them?" Reza said.

"Eight of them stayed jacked into soldierboys for three weeks. The other eight for sixteen days."

"That's all?" I said.

"That's all."

"It drove them crazy?" Amelia asked.

Belda laughed, a rare sound, not happy. "I'll bet not. I'll bet it drove them sane."

"Belda's close," Marty said. "She has this annoying way of being able to read your mind without benefit of electricity.

"What happens is that after a couple of weeks in the soldierboy, you paradoxically can't be a soldier anymore."

"You can't kill?" I said.

"You can't even hurt anybody on purpose, except to save your own life. Or other lives. It permanently changes your way of thinking, of feeling; even after you unjack. You've been inside other people too long, shared their identity. Hurting another person would be as painful as hurting yourself."

"Not pure pacifists, though," Reza said. "Not if they can kill in self-defense."

"It varies from individual to individual. Some would rather die than kill, even in self-defense."

"Is that what happens to people like Candi?" I asked.

"Not really. People like her are chosen for empathy, for gentleness. You would expect being jacked to enhance those qualities in them."

"You just used random people in the experiment?" Reza asked.

He nodded. "The first one was random paid volunteers, off-duty soldiers. But not the second group." He leaned forward. "Half the second group were Special Forces assassins. The other half were civilians who had been convicted of murder."

"And they all became ... civilized?" Amelia said.

"The verb we use is 'humanized,' " Marty said.

"If a hunter/killer platoon stayed jacked for two weeks," I said, "they'd turn into pussycats?"

"So we assume. This was done before hunter/killers, of course; before soldierboys were used in combat."

Asher had been following this quietly. "It seems to me absurd to assume that the military hasn't duplicated your experiment. Then figured out a way around this inconvenient aberration, pacifism. Humanization."

"Not impossible, Asher, but unlikely. I'm jacked, one-way, with hundreds of military people, from private to general. If anyone was involved in an experiment, or had even heard a rumor of one, I would know."

"Not if everyone in authority was also jacked one-way. And the experimental subjects isolated, like yours, or disposed of."

That was worth a moment of silence. Would military scientists have inconvenient subjects killed?

"I'll admit the possibility," Marty said, "but it's remote. Ray and I coordinate all the military research on soldierboys. For someone to get a project approved, funded, and implemented without our being aware . . .

possible. But it's *pòssible* to flip a coin and come up
heads a hundred times in a row."

"Interesting that you bring up numbers, Marty," Reza
said. He'd been scribbling on a napkin. "Take a best-
case scenario, where you have everyone agreeing to become humanized, and lining up to get jacked.

"First of all, one out of ten or twelve dies or goes
crazy. I'm already trying to figure ways to get out of
it."

"Well, we don't know—"

"Let me go on just a second. If it's one out of twelve,
you're killing six hundred million people to ensure that
the rest of them won't kill anybody. You're already
making Hitler look like an amateur, by two orders of
magnitude."

"There's more, I'm sure," Marty said.

"There is. What do we have, six thousand soldierboys? Say we build a hundred thousand. Everybody has
to spend two weeks jacked—and that's *after* they spend
five days getting their brains drilled out and recovering.
Call it twenty days per person. Assuming seven billion
survive the surgery, that's seven thousand people per
machine. It sounds like a hundred forty thousand days
to me. That's almost four hundred years. Then we all
live happily ever after—the ones who live at all."

"Let me see that." Reza handed the napkin to Marty.
He traced the column of figures with his finger. "One
thing that's not in here is the fact that you don't need a
whole soldierboy. Just the basic brain-to-brain wiring,
and IV drips for nourishment. We could set up a million
stations, not a hundred thousand. *Ten* million. That re-
duces the time scale to four years."

"But not the half-billion deaths," Belda said. "It's
academic to me, since I only plan on living a few more
years. But it does seem a high price to ask."

Asher pushed the button for the waiter. "This didn't
come off the top of your head, Marty. How long have

you been thinking about it, twenty years?"

"Something like that," he admitted, and shrugged. "You don't really need the death of the universe. We've been on a slippery slope since Hiroshima. Since World War One, actually."

"A secret pacifist working for the military?" Belda said.

"Not secret. The army tolerates theoretical pacifism— look at Julian—so long as it doesn't interfere with work. Most of the generals I know would call themselves pacifists."

The waiter shambled in and took the order. When he left, I said, "Marty's got a point. It's not just the Jupiter Project. There are plenty of lines of research that could ultimately lead to the planet being sterilized, or destroyed. Even if the rest of the universe is unaffected."

"You're already jacked," Reza said, and finished his wine. "You don't get a vote."

"What about people like me?" Amelia said. "Who try to be jacked and fail? Maybe you can put us in a nice concentration camp, where we can't hurt anybody."

Asher laughed. "Come on, Blaze. This is just a thought experiment. Marty's not seriously proposing—"

Marty slapped the table with his palm. "Damn it, Asher! I've never been more serious in my life."

"Then you're crazy. It's never going to happen."

Marty turned to Amelia. "In the past, it's never been imperative that any one person *be* jacked. If it became an effort on the order of your Jupiter Project—the Manhattan Project—all the work that's been begging to be done would *be* done!" To Reza: "The same with your half-billion dead. This isn't something that would have to be implemented overnight. A lot of cautious, controlled research, refinement of techniques, and the casualty rate would dwindle, maybe to zero."

"Then to put it in the least kind terms," Asher said,

"you're accusing the army of murder. Granted, that's what they're supposed to do, but it's supposed to be people on the other side." Marty looked quizzical. "I mean, if you have thought all along that jacking installation could be made safe, why hasn't the army held off on making new mechanics until it *is* safe?"

"It's not the army who's a murderer, you're saying. It's me. Researchers like me and Ray."

"Oh, don't get dramatic. I'm sure you've done your best. But I've always felt the human cost of the program was way too high."

"I agree," Marty said, "and it's not just the one-in-twelve installation casualties. Mechanics have an unacceptably high death rate from stroke and heart attack." He looked away from me. "And suicide, during their enlistment or after."

"The death rate for soldiers is high," I said. "That's not news. But it's part of the argument: get rid of soldiering as an occupation.

"Suppose we *could* develop a way that jacking was a hundred percent successful, with absolutely no casualties. There's still no way you could get everyone to do it. I can just see the Ngumi lining up to have their heads drilled by a bunch of Alliance demon-scientists! Hell, you couldn't even convert our own military. Once the generals found out what you were doing, you'd be history. You'd be *compost*!"

"Maybe so. Maybe so." The waiter was bringing our drinks. Marty looked at me and stroked his chin. "You feel up to jacking?"

"I suppose."

"Free at ten tomorrow?"

"Yeah, until two."

"Come by my place. I need your input."

"You guys are going to hook up together and change the world?" Amelia said. "Save the universe?"

Marty laughed. "That's not exactly what I had in mind." But it was, exactly.

julian had to bicycle a mile through much-needed rain to get to Marty's lab, so he didn't arrive in too festive a mood.

Marty found him a towel, and a lab coat against the airco chill. They sat on a couple of straight-back chairs by the test bed, which was literally two beds, equipped with full-face helmets. There was a nice view of the sodden campus, ten stories down.

"I gave my assistants the Saturday off," Marty said, "and routed all my incoming calls to my home office. We won't be disturbed."

"At doing what?" Julian said. "What do you have in mind?"

"I won't know for sure until we're linked. But I'd just as soon keep it between ourselves, for the time being." He pointed to the data console on the other side of the room. "If one of my assistants was here, she could patch in one-way and eavesdrop."

Julian got up and inspected the test bed. "Where's the interrupt button?"

"You don't need one. You want out, just think 'quit' and the link is broken." Julian looked doubtful. "It's new. I'm not surprised you haven't seen it before."

"Otherwise, you're in control."

"Nominally. I control the sensorium, but that's trivial for conversation. I'll change it to whatever you want."

"One-way?"

"We can start out one-way and go limited two-way, 'stream of conversation,' on mutual consent." As Julian knew, Marty couldn't jack deeply with anyone; he'd had the ability removed for security reasons. "Nothing like you and your platoon. We can't really read each other's minds. Just communicate more quickly and clearly.''

"Okay." Julian hiked himself up on the bed and let out a long breath. "Let's get on with it." They both lay down and worked their necks into the soft collars, slipped the plastic sleeves off the water tubes and moved their heads around until the jacks clicked. Then the front half hinged shut over their faces.

An hour later the masks sighed open. Julian's face was slick with sweat.

Marty sat up, looking refreshed. "Am I wrong?"

"I don't think so. But I'd better go to North Dakota anyhow."

"It's nice this time of year. Dry."

it wasn't raining when I left Marty's lab, but that turned out to be temporary. I saw a squall line coming at me down the street, but was providentially right by the Student Center. I locked up the bike and got through the doors just as the storm hit.

There's a bright and noisy coffee place under the dome on the top of the building. That felt right. I'd spent too long cooped up in two skulls, contemplating skullduggery.

It was crowded for a Saturday, I guess because of the weather. It took me ten minutes to get through the line and negotiate a cup of coffee and a roll, and then there was no place to sit. But the inside of the dome had a ledge at the proper height for parking against.

I reviewed what I'd taken from Marty's brain:

The 10 percent casualty figure for jacking didn't tell the whole story. The raw figures were that 7.5 percent die, 2.3 percent are mentally disabled, 2.5 percent are slightly impaired, and 2 percent wind up like Amelia, unharmed but not jacked.

But the classified part is that more than half of the

deaths are draftees who were slated to be mechanics, killed by the complexity of the soldierboy interface. Many of the others are due to undertrained surgeons and bad operating conditions in Mexico and Central America. On the large scale Marty was talking about, you wouldn't use human surgeons at all, except for oversight. Automated brain surgery, Jesus. But Marty claimed it was a couple of orders of magnitude simpler when you didn't have to wire into a soldierboy.

And even if it were ten percent death, the alternative is one hundred percent, chasing life all the way out to Hubble's Wall.

Still, how do you get normal people to do it? Civilians who do it fit pretty narrow profiles: empaths, thrillseekers; the chronically lonely and the sexually ambiguous. A lot of people who are in Amelia's position: someone they love is jacked, and they want to be there.

The basic strategy is, first, you don't give it away. One thing we've learned from the Universal Welfare State is that people devalue things they don't pay for. It would cost a month of entertainment credits—but as a matter of fact, you'd be spending most of that month unconscious, anyhow.

And the empowerment factor will become compelling after a very few years: people who aren't humanized will be less successful in the world. Maybe less happy, too, though that's harder to demonstrate.

Another little problem was what to do with people like Amelia? They couldn't be jacked, and so they couldn't be humanized. They would be handicapped and angry—and able to do violence. Two percent of six billion is 120 million people. One wolf for every forty-nine sheep is another way of looking at it. Marty suggested that initially we relocate all of them onto islands, asking all the humanized islanders to emigrate.

Anybody could live comfortably anywhere, once we use the nanoforges to make other nanoforges and give them out freely to everyone, Ngumi or Alliance.

But the first order of business was to humanize the soldierboys and their leaders. That meant infiltrating Building 31 and isolating the high command for a couple of weeks. Marty had a plan for that, the War College in Washington ordering a simulation exercise that required isolation.

I was to be a "mole." Marty had had my records modified, so that I'd just had an understandable episode of nervous exhaustion. "Sergeant Class is fit for duty, but it is recommended that Portobello take advantage of his education and experience, and transfer him to the command cadre." Prior to that, he would do some selective memory transfer and storage: I would temporarily forget the suicide attempt, the takeover plot, and the apocalyptic results of the Jupiter Project. I would just go in and be myself.

My old platoon, as part of another "experiment," would stay jacked long enough to become humanized, and I could be inside Building 31 to open the door for them when they came in to replace the security platoon.

The generals would be treated well. Marty would have temporary attachment orders cut for a neurosurgeon and her anesthesiologist from a base in Panama; together they have a phenomenal success rate of ninety-eight percent in jack installation.

Today, Building 31; tomorrow, the world. We could work outward from Portobello, and downward from Marty's Pentagon contact, and quickly have all of the armed forces humanized. The war would end, incidentally. But the larger battle would just be beginning.

I stared out at the campus through the blurring sheets of water while I ate the sweet crab-apple roll. Then I leaned back against the glass and surveyed the coffee shop, coming back down to earth.

Most of these people were only ten or twelve years younger than me. It seemed impossible, an unbridgeable

chasm. But maybe I was never quite in that world—
chatter, giggle, flirt—even when I *was* their age. I had
my head in a book or a console all the time. The girls
I had sex with back then were in the same voluntarily
cloistered minority, glad to share quick relief and get
back to the books. I'd had terrible earthshaking loves
before college, like everybody, but after I was eighteen
or nineteen I settled for sex, and in that era there was
plenty of it. Now the pendulum was swinging back to
the conservatism of Amelia's generation.

Would that all change, if Marty had his way—if *we*
had our way? There's no intimacy like being jacked, and
a lot of the intensity of teenaged sex was fueled by a
curiosity that jacking would satisfy in the first minute.
It remains interesting to share experiences and thoughts
with the opposite sex, but the overall gestalt of being
male or female is just there, and is familiar a few
minutes after you make contact. I have physical memories of childbirth and miscarriage, menstruation and
breasts getting in the way. It bothers Amelia that I share
cramps and PMS with my platoon; that all the women
have been embarrassed by involuntary erections, have
ejaculated, know how the scrotum limits the ways you
sit and walk and cross your legs.

Amelia got a taste of that, a whisper, in the two
minutes or less we had in Mexico. Maybe part of our
problem now was rooted in her frustration at having had
just a glimpse. We'd only had sex a couple of times
since the abortive attempt the night after I saw her with
Peter. The night after I jackfucked with Zoë, to be fair.
And there was so much happening, the end of the universe and all, that we hadn't had time or inclination to
work on our own problems.

The place smelled kind of like a gym crossed with a
wet dog, with an overlay of coffee, but the boys and
girls didn't seem to notice. Searching, preening, display-

ing—a lot more outright primate behavior than they revealed in a physics class.

Watching all that casual mating ritual simmering, I felt a little sad and old, and wondered whether Amelia and I would ever completely reconcile. It was partly that I couldn't get the picture of her and Peter out of my mind. But I had to admit that part of it was Zoë, and all her tribe. We'd all felt kind of sorry for Ralph, his endless harrying after jills. But we'd also felt his ecstasy, which had never diminished.

I shocked myself by wondering whether I could live like that, and in the same instant shocked myself again by admitting I could. Relationships emotionally limited, temporarily passionate. And then back to real life for awhile, until the next one.

The undeniable lure of that extra dimension—feeling her feeling you, thoughts and sensations twining together—in my heart I'd built a wall around that, labeled it "Carolyn," and shut the door. But now I had to admit that it had been pretty impressive just with a stranger; however skilled and sympathetic, still a stranger, with no pretending about love.

No pretending: that was true in more than one way. Marty was right. Something like love was there automatically. Sex aside, for several minutes she and I had been closer, in terms of knowing, than some normal couple who'd been together fifty years. It does start to fade as soon as you unjack, and a few days later, it's the memory of a memory. Until you jack again, and it slams back. So if you kept it going for two weeks, it would change you forever? I could believe that.

I left Marty without discussing a timetable, which was literally an unspoken agreement. We wanted time to sort through each other's thoughts.

I also didn't discuss how he was able to have military medical records altered and have pretty high-ranking officers shuffled around at will. We hadn't been jacked deeply enough for that information to come through. There was an image of one man, a longtime friend. I wished I didn't even know that much.

I wanted to postpone any action, anyhow, until I had jacked with the humanized people in North Dakota. I didn't really doubt Marty's veracity, but I wondered about his judgment. When you're jacked with someone, "wishful thinking" has a whole new meaning. Wish hard enough and you can drag other people along with you.

julian watched the rain for about twenty minutes and decided it was not going to let up, so he splashed on home through it. Of course, it stopped when he was half a block from the apartment.

He locked the bike up in the basement and sprayed the chain and gears with oil. Amelia's bike was there, but that didn't mean she was home.

She was sound asleep. Julian made enough noise getting his suitcase to wake her.

"Julian?" She sat up and rubbed her eyes. "How did it go with—" She saw the suitcase. "Going somewhere?"

"North Dakota, for a couple of days."

She shook her head. "Why on earth . . . oh, Marty's freaks."

"I want to jack with them and check for myself. They may be freaks, but we may all be joining them."

"Not all," she said quietly.

He opened his mouth and shut it, and picked out three pairs of socks in the dim light. "I'll be back in plenty of time for the Tuesday class."

"Be getting a lot of calls Monday. The *Journal* doesn't come out till Wednesday, but they'll be calling everybody."

"Just stack 'em up. I'll tap in from North Dakota."

Getting to that state was going to be harder then he thought. He found three military flights that would zig-zag him to the water-filled crater Seaside, but when he tried to reserve space he was informed by the computer that he no longer had a "combat" flag, and so would have to fly standby. It predicted that he had about a fifteen percent chance of making all three flights. Getting back on Tuesday would be even more difficult.

He called Marty, who told him he'd see what could be done, and called back one minute later. "Give it another try."

This time he got all six flights booked with no comment. The "C" for combat had been restored to his serial number.

Julian carried his armload and the suitcase into the living room to pack. Amelia followed him, shrugging into a nightgown.

"I might be going to Washington," she said. "Peter's coming back from the Caribbean so that he can do a press conference tomorrow."

"That's a change of heart. I thought he'd gone down there to avoid publicity." He looked up at her. "Or is he coming back mainly to see you?"

"He didn't exactly say."

"But he *is* paying for the ticket, right? You don't have enough credit left this month."

"Of course he is." She folded her arms on her chest. "I'm his coresearcher. You'd be welcome there, too."

"I'm sure. Better that I investigate this aspect of the problem, though." He finished packing the small suitcase and looked around the room. He stepped over to an end table and picked up two magazines. "If I asked you not to go, would you stay here?"

"You would never ask me that."

"That's not much of an answer."

She sat down on the sofa. "All right. If you asked me

not to go, we would fight. And I would win."

"So is that why I don't ask you?"

"I don't know, Julian." She raised her voice a little. "Unlike some people, I can't *read minds*!"

He set the magazines inside the suitcase and carefully sealed it shut, thumbprinting the lock. "I really don't mind if you go," he said quietly. "This is something we have to get through, one way or another." He sat down next to her, not touching.

"One way or another," she repeated.

"Just promise me that you won't stay permanently."

"What?"

"Those of us who can read minds can also tell the future," he said. "By next week, half the people involved in the Jupiter Project will be sending out resumés. I'm only asking that if he offers you a position, don't just say yes."

"All right. I'll tell him I have to discuss it with you. Fair enough?"

"That's all I ask." He took her hand and brushed his lips across her fingers. "Don't rush into anything."

"How about . . . I don't rush and you don't rush."

"What?"

"Pick up the phone. Get a later flight to North Dakota." She rubbed the top of his thigh. "You're not going out that door until I convince you that you're the only one I love."

He hesitated and then picked up the phone. She knelt on the floor and started unbuckling his belt. "Talk fast."

the last leg of my flight was from Chicago, but it overshot Seaside by a few miles so we could get a glimpse of the Inland Sea. "Sea" is a little grandiose; it's only half again as big as the Great Salt Lake. But it's impressive, a perfect blue circle sketched inside with white lines of wakes from pleasure craft.

The place I was headed was only six miles from the airport. Taxis cost entertainment credits but bikes were free, so I checked one out and pedaled there. It was hot and dusty, but the exercise was welcome after being stuck in airplanes and airports all morning.

It was a fifty-year-old building style, all mirror glass and steel frame. A sign on the frizzled lawn said ST. BARTHOLOMEW'S HOME.

A man in his sixties, wearing a priest's collar with everyday clothes, answered the door and let me in.

The foyer was a white box devoid of ornament, except for a crucifix on one wall facing a holo of Jesus on the other. Uninviting institutional couch and chairs with inspirational literature on the table between them. We went through double doors into an equally plain hall.

Father Mendez was Hispanic, his hair still black, his lined dark face scored with two long old scars. He looked frightful, but his calm voice and easy smile dispelled that.

"Forgive us for not coming out to greet you. We don't have a car and we don't go out much. It helps maintain our image of being harmless old loonies."

"Dr. Larrin said your cover story contained a grain of truth."

"Yes, we're poor addled survivors of the first experiments with the soldierboy. People tend to shy away from us when we do go out."

"You're not an actual priest, then."

"In fact I am, or rather, was. I was defrocked after being convicted of murder." He stopped at a plain door that had a card with my name on it, and pushed it open. "Rape and murder. This is your room. Come on down to the atrium at the end of the hall when you've freshened up."

The room itself wasn't too monkish, an oriental carpet

on the floor, modern suspension bed contrasting with an antique rolltop desk and chair. There was a small refrigerator with soft drinks and beer, and bottles of wine and water on a sideboard with glasses. I had a glass of water and then one of wine while I took off my uniform and carefully smoothed and folded it for the return trip. Then a quick shower and more comfortable clothes, and I went off in search of the atrium.

The corridor was featureless wall along the left; on the right were doors like mine, with more permanent nameplates. A frosted-glass door at the end opened automatically as I reached for it.

I stopped dead. The atrium was a cool pine forest. Cedar smell and the bright sound of a creek tumbling somewhere. I looked up and, yes, there was a skylight; I hadn't somehow been jacked and transferred to somebody's memory.

I walked down a pebbled path and stood for a moment on the plank bridge over a swift shallow stream. I heard laughter up ahead and followed the faint smell of coffee around a curve into a small clearing.

A dozen or so people in their fifties and sixties stood and sat around. There was rustic wooden furniture, various designs arranged in no particular order. Mendez separated himself from a small conversational group and strode over to me.

"We usually gather here for an hour or so before dinner," he said. "Can I get you a drink?"

"Coffee smells good." He led me to a table with samovars of coffee and tea and various bottles. There was beer and wine in a tub of ice. Nothing homemade and nothing cheap; a lot of it imported.

I gestured at the cluster of Armagnacs, single-malts, añejos. "What, you have a printing press grinding out ration cards?"

He smiled and shook his head, filling two cups. "Nothing so legal." He set my cup down by the milk and sugar. "Marty said we could trust you enough to jack, so you'll know eventually." He studied my face. "We have our own nanoforge."

"Sure, you do."

"The Lord's mansion has many rooms," he said, "including a huge basement, in this case. We can go down and look at it later on."

"You're not kidding?"

He shook his head and sipped coffee. "No. It's an old machine, small, slow, and inefficient. An early prototype that was supposedly dismantled for parts."

"You're not afraid of making another big crater?"

"Not at all. Come sit over here." There was a picnic table with two pairs of black-box jacks. "Save a little time here." He handed me a green jack and took a red one. "One-way transfer."

I plugged in and then he did, and clicked a switch on and off.

I unjacked and looked at him, speechless. In one second, my entire world view was changed.

The Dakota explosion had been rigged. The nanoforge had been tested extensively in secret, and was safe. The Alliance coalition that developed it wanted to close off potentially successful lines of research. So after a few carefully composed papers—top-secret, but compromised—they cleared out North Dakota and Montana and supposedly tried to make a huge diamond out of a few kilos of carbon.

But the nanoforge wasn't even there. Just a huge quantity of deuterium and tritium, and an igniter. The giant H-bomb was buried, and shaped in such a way as to minimize pollution, while melting out a nice round glassy lake bed, large enough to be a good argument against trying to make your own nanoforge out of this and that.

"How do you know? Can you be sure it's true?"

His brow furrowed. "Maybe . . . maybe it is just a

story. Impossible to check by asking. The man who brought it into the chain, Julio Negroni, died a couple of weeks into the experiment, and the man he got it from, a cellmate in Raiford, was executed long ago.''

"The cellmate was a scientist?"

"So he said. Murdered his wife and children in cold blood. Should be easy enough to check the news records, I guess around '22 or '23."

"Yeah. I can do that tonight." I went back to the serving table and poured a splash of rum into the coffee. It was too good a rum to waste that way, but desperate times call for desperate measures. I remember thinking that phrase. I didn't yet know quite how desperate the times were.

"Cheers." Mendez raised his cup as I sat back down. I tipped mine toward him.

A short woman with long flowing gray hair came over with a handset. "Dr. Class?" I nodded and took it. "It's a Dr. Harding."

"My mate," I explained to Mendez. "Just checking to make sure I got here."

Her face on the handset was the size of my thumbnail, but I could see she was clearly upset. "Julian—there's something going on."

"Something *new*?" I tried to make that sound like a joke, but could hear the shakiness in my voice.

"The *Journal* jury rejected the paper."

"Jesus. On what grounds?"

"The editor says they 'decline to discuss it' with anyone but Peter."

"So what does Peter—"

"He's not *home*!" A tiny hand fluttered up to knead her forehead. "He wasn't on the flight. The cottage in St. Thomas says he checked out last night. But somewhere between the cottage and the airport he . . . I don't know . . ."

"Have you checked with the police on the island?"

"No . . . no; that's the next step, of course. I'm panicking. I just wanted to, you know, hoped he had talked to you?"

"Do you want me to call them? You could—"

"No, I'll do it. And the airlines, too; double-check. I'll get back to you."

"Okay. Love you."

"Love you." She switched off.

Mendez had gone off to refresh his coffee. "What about this jury? Is she in trouble?"

"We both are. But it's an academic jury, the kind that decides whether a paper gets published."

"Sounds like you have a lot tied up in this paper. Both of you."

"Both of us and everybody else in the world." I picked up the red plug. "This is automatically one-way?"

"Right." He jacked in and then I did.

I wasn't as good at transmitting as he was, even though I was jacked ten days a month. It had been the same with Marty the day before: if you're used to two-way, you wait for feedback cues that never come. So with a lot of blind alleys and backtracking, it took about ten minutes to get everything across.

For some time he just looked at me, or maybe he was looking inward. "There is no question in your own mind. It's doom."

"That's right."

"Of course I have no way to evaluate your logic, this pseudo-operator theory. I take it that the technique itself is not universally accepted."

"True. But Peter got the same result independently."

He nodded slowly. "That's why Marty sounded so strange when he told me you were coming. He used some stilted language like 'vitally important.' He didn't want to say too much, but he wanted to warn me." He leaned forward. "So we're walking along Occam's razor now. The simplest explanation of these events is that you and Peter and Amelia were wrong. The world, the universe, is not going to end because of the Jupiter Project."

"True, but—"

"Let me carry this along for a moment. From *your* point of view, the simplest explanation is that somebody in a position of power wants your warning to be suppressed."

"That's right."

"Allow me the assumption that nobody on this jury would profit from the destruction of the universe. Then why, in God's name, would anyone who thought your argument had merit want to suppress it?"

"You were a Jesuit?"

"Franciscan. We run a close second in being pains in the ass."

"Well . . . I don't know any of the people on the review board, so I can only speculate about their motivations. Of course they don't want the universe to go belly-up. But they might well want to put a lid on it long enough to adjust their own careers—assuming all of them are involved in the Jupiter Project. If our conclusions are accepted, there are going to be a lot of scientists and engineers looking for work."

"Scientists would be that venal? I'm shocked."

"Sure. Or it could be a personal thing against Peter. He probably has more enemies than friends."

"Can you find out who was on the jury?"

"I couldn't; it was anonymous. Maybe Peter could wheedle it out of someone."

"And what do you make of his disappearance? Isn't it possible he saw some fatal flaw in the argument and decided to drop out of sight?"

"Not impossible."

"You hope something bad happened to him."

"Wow. It's almost as if you could read my mind." I

sipped some coffee, now unpleasantly cool. "How much did I let slip there?"

He shrugged. "Not a lot."

"You'll know everything minutes after we jack two-way. I'm curious."

"You don't mask very well. But then you haven't had much practice."

"So what did you get?"

"Green-eyed monster. Sexual jealousy. One specific image, an embarrassing one."

"Embarrassing for you?"

He tilted his head to about ten degrees of irony. "Of course not. I was speaking conventionally." He laughed. "Sorry. I didn't mean to be patronizing. I don't suppose anything just physical would embarrass you, either."

"No. The other part is still hanging there, though. Unresolved."

"She's not jacked."

"No. She tried and it didn't take."

"Wasn't long ago?"

"Couple of months. May twentieth."

"And this, um, episode was after that?"

"Yeah. It's complicated."

He took the cue. "Let's go back to ground zero. What I got from you—assuming that you're right about the Jupiter Project—is that you and Marty, but Marty more than you, believe that we have to rid the world of war and aggression *right now*. Or the game is up."

"That's what Marty would say." I stood up. "Get some fresh coffee. You want something?"

"Splash of that rum. You're not as certain?"

"No . . . yes and no." I concentrated on the drinks. "Let me read your mind, for a change. You think that there's no need for haste, once the Jupiter Project's deactivated."

"You think otherwise?"

"I don't know." I set the drinks down and Mendez

touched his and nodded. "When I jacked with Marty I got a sense of urgency that was completely personal. He wants to see the thing well in process before he dies."

"He's not that old."

"No, sixty-some. But he's been obsessed with this since you guys were made; maybe before. And he knows it will take a while to get going." I searched for words; logician's words. "Marty's feelings aside, there's an objective rationale for urgency; the black-and-white one of scale: anything else we do or don't do is trivial if there's the slightest chance that this could come to pass."

He sniffed the rum. "The destruction of everything."

"That's right."

"Maybe you're too close to it, though," he said. "I mean, you're talking about a huge project here. It's not something that a Hitler or a Borgia could cook up in his backyard."

"In their own times, no. Now they could," I said. "You of all people should see how."

"Me of all people?"

"You've got a nanoforge in your basement. When you want it to make something, what do you do?"

"Ask it. We tell it what we want and it goes into its catalogue and tells us what raw materials we have to come up with."

"You can't ask it to make a duplicate of itself, though."

"They say no, it would melt down if you did. I'm not inclined to try."

"But that's just part of the programming, right? In theory, you could short-circuit it."

"Ah." He nodded slowly. "I see where you're heading."

"That's right. If you could get around that injunction, you could say, in effect, 'Re-create the Jupiter Project for me,' and if it had access to the raw materials, and the information, it could do it."

"As an extension of one person's will."

"That's right."

"My God." He drank the rum and set the glass down hard. "My God."

"Everything," I said. "A trillion galaxies disappear if one maniac says the right sequence of words."

"Marty has a lot of faith in the monsters he created," Mendez said, "to let us share this knowledge."

"Faith or desperation. Guess I got a mixture of both from him."

"You hungry?"

"What?"

"You want dinner now, or should we all jack first?"

"That's what I'm hungry for. Let's do it."

He stood up and brought his hands together in two explosive claps. "Big room," he shouted. "Marc, you stay out and keep watch." We followed everyone to a double door on the other side of the atrium. I wondered what I was getting myself into.

julian was used to being ten people at once, but it was stressful and confusing at times, even with people you had grown close to. He didn't really know what to expect, linking with fifteen men and women he'd never met, who had been jacked together for twenty years. That would be alien territory even without Marty's pacifistic transformation. Julian had used his horizontal liaison to weakly link with other platoons, and it was always like breaking in on a family discussion.

Eight of these had been mechanics, at least, or protomechanics. He was more nervous about the others, the assassins and murderers. More curious about them, too.

Maybe they could teach him something about living with memories.

The "big room" held a ring-shaped table surrounding

a holo pit. "Most of us get together here for the news,"
Mendez said. "Movies, concerts, plays. Fun to have all
the different points of view."

Julian wasn't sure about that. He'd mediated too many
firestorms in his platoon, where one person came up with
a strong opinion that divided the ten into two bickering
camps. It took about a second to start, and sometimes
an hour to sort out.

The walls were dark mahogany and the table and its
chairs were fine-grained spruce. A slight whisper of lin-
seed oil and furniture polish. In the pit, an image of a
forest clearing, dappled sunlight on wildflowers.

There were twenty seats. Mendez offered Julian a
chair and sat down next to him. "You might want to
plug in first," he said, "let people come in one at a time
and introduce themselves."

"Sure." Julian realized this had all been rehearsed.
He stared at the wildflowers and plugged himself in.

Mendez was the first one, waving a silent *hello*. The
link was strange, powerful in a way he'd never come
close to experiencing. It was startling, like seeing the sea
for the first time—and it was like a sea in a literal way;
Mendez's consciousness floated in a seemingly endless
expanse of shared memory and thought. And he was
comfortable with it the way a fish is comfortable with
the sea, moving through its invisibility.

Julian tried to communicate his reaction to Mendez,
along with a sense of rising panic; he wasn't sure
whether he could manage two such universes, let alone
fifteen. Mendez said it actually gets easier with more,
and then Cameron plugged in to prove it.

Cameron was an older man, who had been a professional soldier for eleven years when he volunteered for
the project. He had gone to a sniper school in Georgia,
and trained for long-distance murder with a variety of
weapons. Mostly he had used the Mauser Fernschiesser,
which could target people around a corner or even over

the horizon. He had fifty-two kills, and separate grief for each of them, and a single large pang for the humanity he had lost with the first shot. He also remembered the exhilaration the kills had given him, at the time. He had fought in Colombia and Guatemala, and automatically made a connection with Julian's jungle days, absorbing and integrating them almost instantly.

Mendez was still there, too, and Julian was aware of his immediate connection with Cameron, casually sorting through what the soldier had taken from his new contact. That part was not so alien, except for the speed and completeness of it. And Julian could understand why the totality could become more clear as more people joined: all the information was already there, but parts of it were better focused now that Cameron's point of view had combined with Mendez's.

Now Tyler. She was one of the murderers, too, having remorselessly killed three people in one year for money, to support a drug habit. That was just before cash became obsolete in the States; she had been captured in a routine check when she tried to emigrate to a country that had both paper pesos and designer drugs. Her crimes were older than Julian was, and although she didn't deny legal or moral responsibility for them, they literally had been done by a different person. The DD doper who lured three pushers into bed and killed them there, as a favor for their boss, was just a vivid melodramatic memory, like a movie you saw a few hours ago. For the peaceful part of her day, Tyler was part of the Twenty, as they still called themselves in their minds, even though four had died; other times she worked as an arbitrageur, bartering and buying commodities in dozens of different countries, Alliance and Ngumi. With their own nanoforge, the Twenty could survive without wealth—but then if the machine asked for a cup of praseodymium, it was nice to have a few million rupees close to hand, so Tyler could buy it without having to go through a lot of tiresome paperwork.

The others came in more rapidly, or seemed to, once Julian got over the initial strangeness.

As each of the fifteen presented himself or herself, another part of the vast, but now not endless, structure became clear. When they all had logged in, the ocean was more like an inland sea, huge and complex, but thoroughly mapped and navigable.

And they sailed together for what seemed like hours, in a voyage of mutual exploration. The only one they had ever jacked with outside the Twenty was Marty, who was a sort of godfather figure, remote because he only jacked one-way with them now.

Julian was a vast treasure of quotidian detail. They were hungry for his impressions of New York, Washington, Dallas—every place in the country had been drastically changed by the social and technological revolution, the Universal Welfare State, that the nanoforge had wrought. Not to mention the endless Ngumi War.

The nine who had been soldiers were fascinated with what the soldierboy had become. In the pilot program they had been taken from, the primitive machines were little more than stick men with one laser finger. They could walk around and sit or lie down, and open a door if the latch was simple. They all knew from the news what the current machines were capable of doing, and in fact three of them were warboys, after a fashion. They couldn't go to the conventions, but they followed units and jacked into soldierboy crystals and strings. It was nothing like being jacked two-way with an actual mechanic, though.

Julian was embarrassed by their enthusiasm but could share their amused feedback at his embarrassment. He was familiar enough with that from his platoon.

A lot of it became more and more familiar-feeling as he grew used to the scale of it. It wasn't only that the

Twenty had been together so long; they had also been *around* a long time. At thirty-two, Julian was the oldest in his platoon by several years; all together, they had less than three hundred years of experience. The aggregate age of the Twenty was well over a thousand, a lot of that time spent in mutual contemplation.

They weren't exactly a "group mind," but they were a lot closer to that state than Julian's platoon. They never argued, except for amusement. They were gentle and content. They were humane . . . but were they quite human?

This was the question that had been in the back of Julian's mind from the time Marty first described the Twenty: maybe war is an inevitable product of human nature. Maybe to get rid of war, we have to become something other than human.

The others picked up on this worry and said no, we're still human in all the ways that count. Human nature does change, and the fact that we've developed tools to direct that change *is* quintessentially human. And it must be a nearly universal concomitant to technological growth everywhere in the universe; otherwise, there would *be* no universe. Unless we're the only technological intelligence in the universe, Julian pointed out; so far there's no evidence to the contrary. Maybe our own existence is evidence that we're the first creatures to evolve far enough to hit the reset button. Someone does have to be first.

But maybe the first is always the last.

They caught the hopefulness that Julian was protecting with pessimism. You're much more idealistic than us, Tyler pointed out. Most of us have killed, but none of us was driven to attempt suicide by remorse over the act.

Of course there were a lot of other factors, which Julian didn't have to explain. He was cushioned by wisdom and forgiveness—and suddenly had to get out!

He pulled the plug and was surrounded but alone, fifteen people staring down at the wildflowers. Staring into their collective soul.

He checked his watch and was shocked. Only twelve minutes had actually passed during all those seeming hours.

One by one they unjacked. Mendez kneaded his face and grimaced. "You felt outnumbered."

"That's part of it . . . out-gunned. All of you are so good at this, it's automatic. I felt, I don't know, out of control."

"We weren't manipulating you."

Julian shook his head. "I know. You were being very careful that way. But I felt like I was being absorbed anyhow. By . . . by my own willingness. I don't know how long I could stay jacked with you before *becoming* one of you."

"And that would be such a bad thing?" Ellie Frazer said. She was the youngest, almost Amelia's age, beautiful hair prematurely white.

"Not for me, I think. Not for me personally." Julian studied her quiet beauty and knew, along with everyone else, exactly how desperately she desired him. "But I can't do it yet. The next stage of this project involves going back to Portobello with a set of false memories, infiltrating the command cadre. I can't be as . . . obviously different as you are."

"We know that," she said. "But you could still spend a lot more time with us—"

"Ellie," Mendez said gently, "turn off the goddamned pheromones. Julian knows what's best for him."

"I don't, actually. Who would? Nobody's ever done anything like this before."

"You have to be cautious," Ellie said in a way that was reassuring and infuriating: we know exactly what you think, and though you're wrong, we'll go along with it.

Marc Lobell, the chess master and wife murderer who had stayed out of the circle to answer the phone, ran pounding over the little bridges and skidded to a stop in front of them.

"A guy in uniform," he said, panting. "Here to see Sergeant Class."

"Who is it?" Julian said.

"A doctor," he said. "Colonel Zamat Jefferson."

mendez, in all the authority of his own black uniform, came along with me to meet Jefferson. He stood up slowly when we walked into the shabby foyer, setting down a *Reader's Digest* half his age.

"Father Mendez; Colonel Jefferson," I said. "You went to some trouble to find me."

"No," he said, "it was some trouble to *get* here, but the computer tracked you down in a few seconds."

"To Fargo."

"I knew you'd take a bicycle. There was only one place to do that at the airport, and you left them an address."

"You pulled rank."

"Not on civilians. I showed them my ID and said I was your doctor. Which is not false."

"I'm okay now. You can go."

He laughed. "Wrong on both counts. Can we sit?"

"We have a place," Mendez said. "Follow me."

"What is 'a place'?" Jefferson said.

"A place where we can sit." They looked at each other for a moment and Jefferson nodded.

Two doors down the corridor, we turned into an unmarked room. It had a mahogany conference table with overstuffed chairs and an autobar. "Something to drink?"

Jefferson and I wanted water and wine; Mendez asked

for apple juice. The bar wheelie brought our orders while
we were sitting down.

"Is there some way we can help each other?" Mendez
said, folding his hands on his small paunch.

"There are some things Sergeant Class might shed
some light on." He stared at me for one second. "I
suddenly made full colonel and had orders cut for Fort
Powell. Nobody in Brigade knew anything about it; the
orders came from Washington, some 'Medical Personnel
Redistribution Group.' "

"This was a bad thing?" Mendez said.

"No. I was gratified. I've never been happy with the
Texas and Portobello posting, and this move took me
back to the area where I grew up.

"I'm still in the middle of moving, settling in. But I
was going through my appointment calendar yesterday,
and your name came up. I was scheduled to jack with
you and see how well the antidepressants are working."

"They're working fine. Are you traveling thousands
of miles to check up on all your old patients?"

"Of course not. But I punched up your file out of
curiosity, almost automatically—and what do you
know? There's no record of your having contemplated
suicide. And it seems you have new orders cut, too. Au-
thorized by the same major general in Washington who
cut *my* orders. But you're not part of the 'Medical Personnel Redistribution Group'; you're in a training program for assimilation into command structure. A soldier
who wanted to commit suicide because he killed someone. That's interesting.

"And so I trace you down to here. A rest home for
old soldiers who aren't so old, and some of whom aren't
soldiers."

"So you want to lose your colonelcy," Mendez said,
"and go back to Texas? To Portobello?"

"Not at all. I'll risk telling you this: I didn't go
through channels. I don't want to rock the boat." He

pointed at me. "But I have a patient here, and a mystery I'd like to solve."

"The patient's fine," I said. "The mystery is something that you don't want to be involved in."

There was a long, thick silence. "People know where I am."

"We don't mean to threaten you, or frighten you," Mendez said. "But there's no way you have the clearance to be told about this. Julian can't let you jack with him, for that reason."

"I have top-secret clearance."

"I know." Mendez leaned forward and said quietly: "Your ex-wife's name is Eudora and you have two children—Pash, who's in medical school in Ohio, and Roger, who's in a New Orleans dance company. You were born on 5 March 1990 and your blood type is O-Negative. Do you want to know your dog's name?"

"You're not threatening me with this."

"I'm trying to communicate with you."

"But you're not even in the military. Nobody here is, except Sergeant Class."

"That should tell you something. You have top-secret clearance and yet my identity is concealed from you."

The colonel shook his head. He leaned back and drank some wine. "There's been time enough for somebody to find out these things about me. I can't decide whether you're some kind of super-spook or just one of the best bullshit artists I've ever come across."

"If I were bluffing, I'd threaten you now. But you know that, and that's why you said what you just said."

"And so you threaten me by making no threat."

Mendez laughed. "Takes one to know one. I will admit to being a psychiatrist."

"But you're not in the AMA database."

"Not anymore."

"Priest and psychiatrist is an odd combination. I don't

suppose the Catholic Church has any record of you, either.''

''That's harder to control. It would be cooperative of you not to check.''

''I don't have any reason to cooperate with you. If you're not going to shoot me or throw me in a dungeon.''

''Dungeon's too much paperwork,'' Mendez said. ''Julian, you've jacked with him. What do you think?''

I remembered a thread from the common mind session. ''He's completely sincere about doctor-patient confidentiality.''

''Thank you.''

''So if you left the room, he and I could talk patient-to-doctor. But there's a catch.''

''There is indeed,'' Mendez said. He remembered the thread as well. ''A trade you might not want to make.''

''What's that?''

''Brain surgery,'' Mendez said.

''You could be told what we're doing here,'' I said, ''but we'd have to make it so that no one could learn it from you.''

''Memory erasure,'' Jefferson said.

''That wouldn't be enough,'' Mendez said. ''We'd have to erase the memory of not only this trip and everything associated with it, but also your memories of treating Julian and people who knew him. That's too extensive.''

''What we'd have to do,'' I said, ''is take out your jack and fry all the neural connections. Would you be willing to give that up forever, to be let in on a secret?''

''The jack is essential to my profession,'' he said. ''And I'm used to it, would feel incomplete without it. For the secret of the universe, maybe. Not for the secret of St. Bartholomew's Home.''

Someone knocked on the door and Mendez said to

come in. It was Marc Lobell, holding a clipboard over his chest.

"May I have a word with you, Father Mendez?"

When Mendez left, Jefferson leaned over toward me. "You're here of your own free will?" he said. "No one's coerced you?"

"No one."

"Thoughts of suicide?"

"Nothing could be farther from my mind." The possibility was still back there, but I wanted to see how this turned out. If the universe ceased to exist, it would take me with it anyhow.

I suspected that that would be the attitude of someone resigned to suicide, and that realization may have shown on my face.

"But something's bothering you," Jefferson said.

"When did you last meet someone with nothing bothering him?"

Mendez came through the door alone, carrying the clipboard. A lock on the door clicked behind him.

"Interesting." He asked the bar for a cup of coffee and sat down. "You've taken a month's leave, Doctor."

"Sure, moving."

"People expect you back in what, a day or two?"

"Soon."

"What people? You're not married or living with anyone."

"Friends. Colleagues."

"Sure." He handed the clipboard to Jefferson.

He glanced at the top sheet and the one under it. "You can't do this. *How* could you do this?" I couldn't read what was on either sheet, but they were some sort of signed orders.

"Obviously, I can. As to how," he shrugged. "Faith can move mountains."

"What is it?"

"I'm TDY'ed here for three weeks. Vacation canceled. What the hell is going on?"

"We had to make a decision while you were still in the building. You've been invited to join our little project here."

"I decline the invitation." He tossed the clipboard down and stood up. "Let me out of here."

"Once we've had a chance to talk, you'll be free to stay or go." He opened a box inlaid in the table's surface and unreeled a red jack and a green one. "One-way."

"*No* way! You can't force me to jack with you."

"Actually, that's true." He gave me a significant look. "I couldn't do anything of the sort."

"I could," I said, and pulled the knife out of my pocket. I pushed the button and the blade flicked out and then began to hum and glow.

"Are you threatening me with a *weapon*? Sergeant?"

"No, I'm not. Colonel." I raised the blade to my neck and looked at my watch. "If you aren't jacked in thirty seconds, you'll have to watch me cut my own throat."

He swallowed hard. "You're bluffing."

"No. I'm not." My hand started to tremble. "But I suppose you've lost patients before."

"What is so goddamned important about this thing?"

"Jack and find out." I didn't look at him. "Fifteen seconds."

"He will, you know," Mendez said. "I've jacked with him. His death will be your fault."

He shook his head and walked back to the table. "I'm not sure of that. But you seem to have me trapped." He sat down and slid the jack in.

I turned off the knife. I think I was bluffing.

Watching people who are jacked is about as interesting as watching people sleep. There was nothing to read in the room, but there was a notepad and stylus, so I wrote a letter to Amelia, outlining what had been going

on. After about ten minutes, they started to nod regularly, so I finished the letter quickly, encrypted it and
sent it.

Jefferson unjacked and buried his face in his hands.
Mendez unjacked and stared at him.

"It's a lot to assimilate all at once," he said. "But I
really didn't know where to stop."

"You did right," Jefferson said, muffled. "I had to
have it all." He sat back and exhaled. "Have to link
with the Twenty now, of course."

"You're on our side?" I said.

"Sides. I don't think you have a snowball's chance.
But yes, I want to be part of it."

"He's more committed than you are," Mendez said.

"Committed but not convinced?"

"Julian," Jefferson said, "with all due respect for
your years as a mechanic, and all the suffering you've
gone through for what you've seen . . . for having killed
that boy . . . it may be that I know more about war and
its evil than you do. Secondhand knowledge, admittedly." He scraped sweat off his forehead with the blade
of his hand. "But the fourteen years I've spent trying to
put soldiers' lives back together make me a pretty good
recruit for this army."

I wasn't really surprised at that. A patient doesn't get
too much unguarded feedback from his therapist—it's
like a one-way jack with a few controlled thoughts and
feelings seeping back—but I knew how much he hated
the killing, and what the killing did to the killers.

amelia shut down her machine for the day and
was stacking papers, ready to go home, long bath and a
nap, when a short bald man tapped on her office door.
"Professor Harding?"

"What can I do for you?"

"Cooperate." He handed her an unsealed plain envelope. "My name is Harold Ingram, Major Harold Ingram. I'm an attorney for the army's Office of Technology Assessment."

She unfolded three pages of fine print. "So would you care to tell me in plain English what this is all about?"

"Oh, it's very simple. A paper that you co-authored for the *Astrophysical Journal* was found to contain material germane to weapons research."

"Wait. That paper never got past peer review. It was rejected. How could your office hear of it?"

"I honestly don't know. I'm not on the technical end."

She scanned the pages. " 'Cease and desist'? A subpoena?"

"Yes. In a nutshell, we need all of your records pertaining to this research, and a statement that you have destroyed all duplicates, and a promise that you will discontinue the project until you hear from us."

She looked at him and then back at the document. "This is a joke, right?"

"I assure you it is not."

"Major . . . this is not some sort of *gun* we're designing. It's an abstraction."

"I don't know anything about that."

"How on God's green earth do you think you can stop me from *thinking* about something?"

"That's not my business. I just need the records and the statement."

"Did you get them from my co-author? I'm really just a hired hand, called in to verify some particle physics."

"I understand that he's been taken care of."

She sat down and put the three pages on the desk in front of her. "You can go. I have to study these and consult with my department head."

"Your department head is in full cooperation with us."

"I don't believe that. Professor Hayes?"

"No. It was J. MacDonald Roman who signed—"

"*Macro?* He's not even in the loop."

"He hires and fires people like you. He's about to fire you, if you aren't cooperative." He was completely still, and didn't blink. It was his big line.

"I have to talk to Hayes. I have to see what my boss—"

"It would be better if you just signed both documents," he said mildly, theatrically, "and then I could come by tomorrow for the records."

"My *records*," she said, "cover the spectrum from meaningless to redundant. What does my collaborator have to say about all this?"

"I wouldn't know. I believe that was the Caribbean branch."

"He disappeared in the Caribbean. You don't suppose your department killed him."

"What?"

"Sorry. The army doesn't kill people." She got up. "You can stay here or come along. I'm going to copy these pages."

"It would be better if you didn't copy them."

"It would be lunacy if I didn't."

He stayed in her office, probably to snoop around. She walked past the copy room and took the elevator down to the first floor. She stuffed the papers into her purse and jumped into the lead cab at the stand across the street. "Airport," she said, and considered her diminishing options.

All of her travel to and from D.C. had been on Peter's open account, so she had plenty of credits to get to North Dakota. But did she want to leave a trail pointing directly to Julian? She would call him from the airport public phone.

But wait; think. She couldn't just get on a plane and sneak off to North Dakota. Her name would be on the

passenger list, and somebody would be waiting for her
when she got off the plane. "Change destination," she
said. "Amtrak station." The cab's voice verified the
change and it made a U-turn.

Not many people traveled long distances by train,
mostly people phobic about heights or just determined
to do things the hard way. Or people who wanted to go
someplace without leaving a document trail. You bought
train tickets by machine, with the same kind of anonymous entertainment chits you used for cabs. (Bureau-
crats and moralists would love to have had the clumsy
system replaced with plastic, like the old cash cards, but
voters would just as soon not have the government know
what they were doing when, and with whom. The individual coupons made barter and hoarding simple, too.)

Amelia's timing was perfect; she ran for the 6:00 Dallas shuttle and it pulled out just as she sat down.

She turned on the screen on the back of the seat in
front of her and asked for a map. If she touched two
cities, the screen would show departure and arrival
times. She jotted down a list; she could go from Dallas
to Oklahoma City to Kansas City to Omaha to Seaside
in about eight hours.

"Who you runnin' from, honey?" An old woman
with white hair in short spikes was sitting next to her.
"Some man?"

"Sure am," she said. "A real bastard."

The old woman nodded and pursed her lips. "Best
you get some good food to carry while you in Dallas.
You don' wanna be livin' on the crap they serve in that
lounge car."

"Thank you. I'll do that." The woman went back to
her soap opera and Amelia punched through the Amtrak
magazine, *See America!* Not much she wanted to see.

She pretended to nap the half hour to Dallas. Then
she said good-bye to the spike-coiffed lady and dove
into the crowd. She had more than an hour before the

train to Kansas City, so she bought a change of clothing—a Cowboys sweatshirt and loose black exercise
pants—and some wrapped sandwiches and wine. Then
she called the North Dakota number Julian had left her.

"Jury change its mind?" he asked.

"More interesting than that." She told him about Harold Ingram and the threatening paperwork.

"And no word from Peter?"

"No. But Ingram knew that he was in the Caribbean.
That's when I decided I had to run."

"Well, the army's tracked me down, too. Just a second." He left the screen and came back. "No, it's just
Dr. Jefferson, and nobody knows he's here. He's pretty
much joined us." The phone camera tracked him as he
sat down. "This Ingram didn't mention me?"

"No, your name's not on the paper."

"But it's only a matter of time. Even not connecting
me with the paper, they know that we live together and
will find out I'm a mechanic. They'll be here in a few
hours. Do you have to change trains anywhere?"

"Yes." She checked her sheet. "The last one is Omaha.
I'm supposed to get there just before midnight . . . eleven
forty-six Central Time."

"Okay. I can get there by then."

"But then what?"

"I don't know. I'll talk it over with the Twenty."

"The twenty whats?"

"Marty's bunch. Explain later."

She went to the machine and, after a moment's hesitation, just bought a ticket as far as Omaha. No need to
guide them any farther, if she was being followed.

Another calculated risk: two of the phones had data
jacks. She waited until a couple of minutes before the
train was going to leave, and called her own database.
She downloaded a copy of the *Astrophysical Journal*
article into her purse notebook. Then she instructed the
database to send copies to everyone in her address book

with *PHYS or *ASTR in their ID lines. That would be about fifty people, more than half of them involved with the Jupiter Project in some way. Would any of them read a twenty-page draft that was mostly pseudo-operator math, with no introduction, no context?

She herself, she realized, would look at the first line and dump it.

Amelia's reading on the train was less technical, but severely limited, since she couldn't identify herself to access any copyrighted material. The train had its own magazine on-screen, and courtesy images of *USA Today* and some travel magazines that were just ads and puffery. She spent a lot of time looking out the window at some of America's least appealing urban areas. The farmland that flowed by in the dusk between cities was peaceful, and she dozed. The seat woke her up as they pulled into Omaha. But it wasn't Julian waiting for her.

Harold Ingram stood on the platform, looking smug. "It's wartime, Professor Harding. The government is everywhere."

"If you tapped a public phone without a warrant—"

"Not necessary. There are hidden cameras in all train and bus stations. If you are wanted by the federal government, the cameras look for you."

"I haven't committed any crime."

"I don't mean 'wanted' in the sense of a wanted criminal. Just desired. Your government desires you. So it found you. Come with me, now."

Amelia looked around. Running was out of the question, with robot guards and at least one human policeman watching the area.

But then she saw Julian, in uniform, half hidden behind a column. He touched a finger to his lips.

"I'll go with you," she said. "But this is against my will, and we're going to wind up in court."

"I certainly hope so," the major said, leading her toward the terminal. "My natural habitat." They passed

Julian and she could hear him fall into step behind them.

They passed through the terminal and walked toward the lead cab in line outside.

"Where are we going?"

"First flight back to Houston." He opened the cab door and helped her in, not too gently.

"Major Ingram," Julian said.

One foot in the cab, he half-turned. "Sergeant?"

"Your flight's been canceled." He had a small black pistol in his hand. It fired almost inaudibly, and as Ingram slumped, Julian caught him and appeared to be helping him into the cab. "1236 Grand Street," he said, feeding it a chit from Ingram's book. He pocketed the book and closed the door. "Surface roads, please."

"It's good to see you," she said, trying to sound neutral. "We know someone in Omaha?"

"We know someone parked on Grand Street."

The cab worked its zigzag way across town, Julian watching behind for a tail. It would have been obvious in the sparse traffic.

When they turned onto Grand Street he looked ahead. "The black Lincoln in the next block. Double-park next to it and we'll get out there."

"If I am ticketed for double-parking, you will be liable, Major Ingram."

"Understood." They pulled up next to a big black limousine with North Dakota "clergy" plates and opaque windows. Julian got out of the cab and hauled Ingram into the back seat of the Lincoln. It looked like a soldier assisting a drunken comrade.

Amelia followed them. In the front seat was the driver, who was a rough-looking gray-haired man with a priest's collar, and Marty Larrin.

"Marty!"

"To the rescue. Is that the guy who served you the papers?" Amelia nodded. As the car started, Marty held out his hand to Julian. "Let me see his ID."

He handed over a long wallet. "Blaze, meet Father Mendez, late of the Franciscan order and Raiford Maximum Security Prison." He flipped through the wallet as he talked, holding it up to a small dashboard light.

"Dr. Harding, I presume." Mendez held a hand up in greeting while he steered with the other one, the automobile under manual control. In the next block a chime sounded and Mendez let go of the wheel and said, "Home."

"This is annoying," Marty said, and switched on the overhead light. "Check his pockets and see if he has a copy of his orders." He held up the wallet and scrutinized a photo of the man with a German shepherd. "Nice dog. No family pictures."

"No wedding ring," Amelia said. "Is that important?"

"Simplify things. Is he jacked?"

Amelia felt the back of his head while Julian rifled his pockets. "Wig." She lifted the back of it with a painful ripping sound. "Yes, he is."

"Good. No orders?"

"No. Flight manifest, though, for him and up to three others, 'two prisoners plus security.'"

"When and where?"

"Open ticket to Washington. Priority 00."

"Real high or real low?" Amelia asked.

"The highest. I think you might not be our only mole, Julian. We need one in Washington."

"*This* guy?" Julian said.

"After he's been jacked with the Twenty for a couple of weeks. It'll be an interesting test of the process's effectiveness." They didn't know how extreme a test it would be.

we hadn't brought handcuffs or anything, so

when he started to stir halfway to St. Bart's, I gave him another pop with the trank gun. Searching for his papers, I'd found an AK 101, a small Russian flechette pistol that's a favorite of assassins everywhere—no inconvenient metal. So I didn't want to sit in the back seat and chat with him, even with his gun safe in the glove compartment. He probably knew some way to kill me with his pinky.

It turns out I was close. When we got him to St. Bart—tying him to a chair before administering the antitrank—and jacked him one-way with Marty, we found out he was a "special operator" for Military Intelligence, assigned to the Office of Technology Assessment. But there was little else there, other than memories of his childhood and youth, and an encyclopedic knowledge of mayhem. He hadn't been treated to the selective memory transfer, or destruction, that Marty had said I would need for my own mole burrowing. It was just a strong hypnotic injunction, which wouldn't hold up for long, after he was jacked two-way with the Twenty.

Until then, all he and we knew was what room in the Pentagon he was to report to. He was to find Amelia and bring her back—or kill her and himself if it came to a desperate situation. All he knew about her was that she and another scientist had discovered a weapon so powerful that it could win the war for the Ngumi if it fell into the wrong hands.

That was an odd way of characterizing it. We used the metaphor "pressing the button," but of course for the Jupiter Project to proceed to its final cataclysmic stage, you needed a team of scientists, doing a sequence of complicated actions in the proper order.

The process *could* be automated, in theory, after the first careful walk-through. But then once you'd done it, there would be no one left to automate it.

So someone on the *Astrophysical Journal* jury was linked to the military establishment—no surprise. But then was the jury's rejection because of pressure from above, or had they actually found an error in our work?

One part of me wanted to think, well, if they actually had disproved our theory, there would be no reason to go after Amelia, and presumably Peter. But maybe Intelligence thought it would be prudent to get rid of them anyhow. There's a war on, they keep saying.

There were four of us in the plain conference room, besides the jacked couple: Amelia and me, Mendez, and Megan Orr, the doctor who checked out Ingram and administered the antitrank. It was three in the morning, but we were pretty wide awake.

Marty unjacked himself and then pulled the plug out of Ingram's head. "Well?" he said.

"It's a lot to assimilate," Ingram said, and looked down at his bound arms. "I could think better if you untied me."

"Is he safe?" I asked Marty.

"You're still armed?"

I held up the trank pistol. "More or less."

"We could untie him. Under some circumstances he might make trouble, but not in a locked room, observed, under armed guard."

"I don't know," Amelia said. "Maybe you ought to wait until he's had the sweetness-and-light treatment. He seems like a dangerous character."

"We can deal with him," Mendez said.

"It's important to talk with him while he's just had interrogational contact," Marty said. "He knows the facts of the matter, but he hasn't been engaged at a deep emotional level."

"I suppose," Amelia said. Marty untied him and sat back.

"Thank you," Ingram said, rubbing his forearms.

"What I'd like to know first is—"

What happened next was so quick that I couldn't have

described it until after I saw the record from the over-head camera.

Ingram shifted his chair slightly, as if half-turning to-ward Marty as he spoke. Actually, he was just getting leverage and clearance.

In a sudden move worthy of an Olympic gymnast, he twisted out of the chair and up, clipping Marty on the chin with his toe, and then making a complete spin half-way down the table to where I was sitting, the pistol in my hand but not aimed. I got off one wild shot and then he slammed into my chest with both feet, breaking two ribs. He snatched the gun out of midair and shoulder-rolled off the table, landing feet-first with a balletic spin that ended with his foot catching me in the throat as I fell. It was probably intended to kick my brains out, but nobody's perfect.

I couldn't see much from my vantage point on the floor, but I heard Marty say "Won't work," and then I passed out.

I woke up back in my chair, with Megan Orr with-drawing a hypodermic gun from my bare forearm. A man I recognized but couldn't name was doing the same to Amelia—Lobell, Marc Lobell, the only one of the Twenty I hadn't jacked with.

It was as if we'd gone back a few minutes in time and had been given a chance to start over. Everybody was back in their original positions; Ingram safely tied up again. But my chest hurt with every breath and I wasn't sure I could talk.

"Meg," I croaked. "Dr. Orr?" She turned around. "Can I see you when this is over? I think he broke a rib or two."

"You want to come with me now?"

I shook my head, which hurt my throat. "Want to hear what the bastard has to say."

Marc was standing at the open door. "Give me half a minute to get situated."

"Okay." Megan went over to Ingram, the only one not awake now, and waited.

"Observation room next door," Mendez said. "Marc watches what's going on and can flood the room with knockout gas in seconds. It's a necessary precaution, dealing with outsiders."

"You really can't do violence, then," Amelia said.

"*I* can," I said. "Mind if I kick him a few times before you revive him?"

"We can defend ourselves, actually. I can't imagine initiating violence." Mendez gestured at me. "But Julian presents a familiar paradox—if he *were* to attack this man, there's not much I could do."

"What if he attacked one of the Twenty?" Marty asked.

"You know the answer to that. It would be self-defense, then. He'd be attacking me."

"Should I go ahead?" Megan asked. Mendez nodded and she gave Ingram his shot.

He came to, instinctively pulling at his bonds, jerking twice, and then he settled back. "Quick anesthetic, whatever it was." He looked at me. "I could have killed you, you know."

"Bullshit. You did your best."

"You better hope you never find out what my best is."

"Gentlemen," Mendez said, "we'll agree that you two are the most dangerous people in this room—"

"Not by a long shot," Ingram said. "The rest of you are the most dangerous people under one roof in the whole world. Maybe in all of history."

"We've considered that viewpoint," Marty said.

"Well, consider it some more. You're going to make the human race extinct in a couple of generations. You're monsters. Like creatures from another planet, bent on our destruction."

Marty smiled broadly. "That's a metaphor I hadn't

thought of. But all we're really bent on destroying is the race's capability for self-destruction.''

"Even if that could work, and I'm not convinced it could, what good is it if we wind up being something other than men?''

"Half of us aren't men to begin with,'' Megan said quietly.

"You know what I mean.''

"I think you meant just what you said.''

"How much does he know,'' I asked, "about why this is urgent?''

"No details,'' Marty said.

" 'The ultimate weapon,' whatever that is. We've been surviving ultimate weapons since 1945.''

"Earlier,'' Mendez said. "The airplane, the tank, nerve gas. But this one's a little more dangerous. A little more ultimate.''

"And you're behind it,'' he said, looking at Amelia with an odd, avid expression. "But all these other people, this 'Twenty,' know about it.''

"I don't know how much they know,'' she said. "I haven't jacked with them.''

"But *you* will, soon enough,'' Mendez said to him. "Then it will all become clear.''

"It's a federal offense to jack someone against his will.''

"Really. I don't suppose they'd be amused about our drugging someone and kidnapping him, either. Then tying him up for interrogation.''

"You can untie me. I see that physical resistance is futile.''

"I think not,'' Marty said. "You're just a little too fast, too good.''

"I won't answer any questions, tied up.''

"Oh, I think you will, one way or another. Megan?''

She held up the hypo gun and turned a dial on the side two clicks. "Just give the word, Marty.''

"Tazlet F-3," Megan said, smiling.

"Now that's *really* illegal."

"Oh my. They'll just have to cut our bodies down and hang us again."

"That's not funny." Obvious strain in the man's voice.

"I think he knows about the side effects," Megan said. "They last a long time. Great for weight loss." She stepped toward him and he shrank back.

"All right. I'll talk."

"He'll lie," I said.

"Maybe," Marty said. "But we'll find out the next time we jack. You said we were the most dangerous people in the world. Going to make the human race extinct. Would you care to amplify that statement?"

"That's if you succeed, which I don't think is likely. You'll convert a large fraction of *us*, from the top down, and then the Ngumi, or whoever, will step in and take over. End of experiment."

"We'll be converting the Ngumi, too."

"Not many and not fast enough. Their leadership is too fragmented. If you converted all the South American goomies, the African ones would step in and eat them up."

Kind of a racist image, I thought, but kept it to my cannibal self.

"But if we do succeed," Mendez said, "you think that would be even worse?"

"Of course! Lose a war, you can rise up and fight again. Lose the ability to fight . . ."

"But there would be no one *to* fight," Megan said.

"Nonsense. This thing can't work on everybody. You have one tenth of one percent unaffected, they'll arm themselves and take over. And you'll just give them the key to the city and do whatever they say."

"It's not that simplistic," Mendez said. "We can defend ourselves without killing."

"What, the way you've defended yourself against me? Gas everybody and tie them up?"

"I'm sure we'll work out strategies well ahead of time. After all, we'll have plenty of minds like yours at our disposal."

"You're actually a soldier," he said to me, "and you go along with this foolishness?"

"I didn't ask to be a soldier. And I can't imagine a peace as foolish as this war we're in."

He shook his head. "Well, they've gotten to you. Your opinion doesn't count."

"In fact," Marty said, "he's on our side naturally. He hasn't gone through the process. Neither have I."

"Then the more fools you both are. Get rid of competition and you're just not human anymore."

"There's competition here," Mendez said. "Even physical. Ellie and Megan play vicious handball. Most of us are slowed down by age, but we compete mentally in ways you couldn't even comprehend."

"I'm jacked. I've done that—lightning chess and three-dimensional go. Even you must know it's not the same."

"No, it's *not* the same. You've been jacked, but not long enough to even understand the rules we play by."

"I'm talking about *stakes,* not rules! War is terrible and cruel, but so is life. Other games are just games. War is for real."

"You're a throwback, Ingram," I said. "You want to smear yourself with woad and go bash people's brains out."

"What I am is a man. I don't know what the hell you are, other than a coward and a traitor."

I can't pretend he didn't get to me. One part of me sincerely wanted to get him alone and beat him to a pulp. Which is exactly what *he* wanted; I'm sure he could have stuffed my foot up my ass and pulled it out through my throat.

"Excuse me," Marty said, and tapped his right earring to pick up a message. After a few moments, he shook his head. "His orders come from too high. I can't find out when they expect him back."

"If I'm not back in two—"

"Oh, shut up." He gestured to Megan. "Knock him out. The sooner we get him jacked, the better."

"You don't have to knock me out."

"We have to go to the other side of the building. I'd rather carry you than trust you."

Megan clicked the gun to another setting and popped him. He stared defiantly for a few seconds and then slumped. Marty reached to untie him. "Wait a half minute," Megan said. "He might be bluffing."

"That's not the same stuff as this?" I said, holding up the pistol.

"No, he's had plenty of that in one day. This doesn't work as fast, but it doesn't take as much out of you." She reached over and pinched his earlobe, hard. He didn't react. "Okay."

Marty untied the left arm and it jerked halfway to his throat and fell back limp. The lips twitched, eyes still shut. "Tough guy." He hesitated, then untied the other bonds.

I got up to help him carry, but winced with the pain in my chest. "You sit down," Megan said. "Don't lift a pencil until I get a look at you."

Everybody else hustled out with Ingram, leaving Amelia and me alone.

"Let me look at that," she said, and unbuttoned my shirt. There was a red area at the bottom of my rib cage that was already starting to turn bruise-tan, on its way to purple. She didn't touch it. "He could have killed you."

"Both of us. How does it feel to be wanted, dead or alive?"

"Sickening. He can't be the only one."

"I should have foreseen it," I said. "I should know how the military mind works—being part of one, after all."

She stroked my arm gently. "We were just worried about the other scientists' reactions. Funny, in a way. If I thought about outside reaction at all, I assumed people would just accept our authority and be glad we had caught the problem in time."

"I think most people would, even military. But the wrong department heard about it first."

"Spooks." She grimaced. "Domestic spies reading journals?"

"Now that we know they exist, their existence seems almost inevitable. All they have to do is have a machine routinely search for key words in the synopses of papers submitted for peer review in the physical sciences and some engineering. If something looks like it has a military application, they investigate and pull strings."

"And have the authors *killed*?"

"Drafted, probably. Let them do their work with a uniform on. In our case, your case, it called for drastic measures, since the weapon was so powerful it couldn't be used."

"So they just picked up a phone and had orders cut for someone to come kill me, and another one to kill Peter?" She whistled at the autobar and asked it for wine.

"Well, Marty got from him that his primary order was to bring you back. Peter's probably in a room like this somewhere in Washington, shot full of Tazlet F-3, verifying what they already know."

"If that's the case, though, they'll know about you. Make it sort of hard for you to sneak into Portobello as a mole."

The wine came and we tasted it and looked at each other, thinking the same thing: I was only going to be safe if Peter had died before he could tell them about me.

Marty and Mendez came in and sat down next to us, Marty kneading his forehead. "We're going to have to move fast now; move everything up. What part of the cycle is your platoon in?"

"They've been jacked for two days. In the soldier-boys for one." I thought. "They're probably still in Portobello, training. Breaking in the new platoon leader with exercises in Pedroville."

"Okay. The first thing I have to do is see whether my pet general can have their training period extended—five or six days ought to be plenty. You're sure that phone line's secure?"

"Absolutely," Mendez said. "Otherwise we'd all be in uniform or in institutions, including you."

"That gives us about two weeks. Plenty of time. I can do the memory modification on Julian in two or three days. Have orders cut for him to be waiting for the platoon in Building 31."

"But we're not sure whether he should go there," Amelia said. "If the people who sent Ingram after me got ahold of Peter and made him talk, then they know Julian collaborated on the math. The next time he reports for duty they'll grab him."

I squeezed her hand. "I suppose it's a risk I'll have to take. You can fix it so that they won't be able to learn about this place from me."

Marty nodded, thoughtful. "That part's pretty routine, tailoring your memory. But it does put us in a bind . . . we have to erase the memory of your having worked on the Problem, in order for you to get back into Portobello. But if they grab you because of Peter and find a hole there, instead of a memory, they'll know you've been tampered with."

"Could you link it with the suicide attempt?" I asked. "Jefferson was proposing to erase those memories anyhow. Couldn't you make it look like that's what had been done?''

"Maybe. Just maybe . . . may I?" Marty poured some wine into a plastic cup. He offered it to Mendez, and he shook his head. "It's not an *additive* process, unfortunately—I can take away memories, but I can't substitute false ones." He sipped. "It's a possibility, though. With Jefferson on our side. It wouldn't be hard to have him supposedly erase too much, so that it covered the week you were working up in Washington."

"This is looking more and more fragile," Amelia said. "I mean, I know almost nothing about being jacked—but if these powers that be tapped into you or Mendez or Jefferson, wouldn't the whole thing come tumbling down?"

"What we need is a suicide pill," I said. "Speaking of suicide."

"I couldn't ask people to do that. I'm not sure that *I* would do it."

"Not even to save the universe?" I meant that to be sarcastic, but it came out a simple statement.

Marty turned a little pale. "You're right, of course. I have to at least provide it as an option. For all of us."

Mendez spoke up. "This is not so dramatic. But we're overlooking an obvious way of buying time: we could move. Two hundred miles north and we're in a neutral country. They'd think twice before sending an assassin into Canada."

We all considered that. "I don't know," Marty said. "The Canadian government wouldn't have any reason to protect us. Some agency would come up with an extradition request and we'd be in Washington the next day, in chains."

"Mexico," I said. "The problem with Canada is it's not corrupt enough. Take the nanoforge down to Mexico and you can buy absolute secrecy."

"That's right!" Marty said. "And in Mexico there

are plenty of clinics where we can set up jacks and do memory modification.''

"But how do you propose getting the nanoforge there?'' Mendez said. "It weighs more than a tonne, not even counting all those vats and buckets and jars of raw materials it feeds on.''

"Use the machine to make a truck?'' I said.

"I don't think so. It can't make anything bigger than seventy-nine centimeters across. In theory, we could make a truck, but it would be in hundreds of pieces, sections. You'd need a couple of master mechanics and a big metalworking shop, to put it together.''

"Why couldn't we steal one?'' Amelia said in a small voice. "The army has lots of trucks. Your pet general can change official records and have people promoted and transferred. Surely he can have a truck sent around.''

"I suspect it's harder to move physical objects than information,'' Marty said. "Worth a try, though. Anybody know how to drive?''

We all looked at each other. "Four of the Twenty do,'' Mendez said. "I've never driven a truck, but it can't be that much different.''

"Maggie Cameron used to be a chauffeur,'' I recalled from jacking with them. "She's driven in Mexico. Ricci learned to drive in the army; drove army trucks.''

Marty stood up, moving a little slowly. "Take me to that secure line, Emilio. We'll see what the general can do.''

There was a quick light rap on the door and Unity Han opened it, breathless. "You should know. As soon as we jacked with him two-way, we found out . . . the man Peter, he's dead. Killed out of hand, for what he knew.''

Amelia bit a knuckle and looked at me. One tear.

"Dr. Harding . . .'' She hesitated. "You were going

to die, too. As soon as Ingram was sure your records had been destroyed."

Marty shook his head. "This isn't the Office of Technology Assessment."

"It's not Army Intelligence, either," Unity said. "Ingram is one of a cell of Enders. There are thousands of them, scattered all through the government."

"Jesus," I said. "And now they know that we can make their prophecy come true."

what ingram revealed was that he personally knew only three other members of the Hammer of God. Two of them were fellow employees of the Office of Technology Assessment—a civilian secretary who worked in Ingram's office in Chicago, and his fellow officer, who had gone to St. Thomas to kill Peter Blankenship. The third was a man he knew only as Ezekiel, who showed up once or twice a year with orders. Ezekiel claimed that the Hammer of God had thousands of people scattered throughout government and commerce, mostly in the military and police forces.

Ingram had assassinated four men and two women, all but one of them military people (one had been the husband of the scientist he was sent to kill). They were always far from Chicago, and most of the crimes had passed muster as death from natural causes. In one, he raped the victim and mutilated her body in a specific way, following orders, so the death would appear to have been one of a chain of serial killings.

He felt good about all of them. Dangerous sinners he had sent to Hell. But he had especially liked the mutilation, the intensity of it, and he kept hoping Ezekiel would bring him another order for one.

He'd had the jack installed three years before. His fellow Enders wouldn't have approved of it, and neither

did he approve of the hedonistic ways they were normally used. He only used his at the jack chapels and
sometimes the snuff shows, which also qualified as a
kind of religious experience for him.

One of the people he'd killed was an off-duty mechanic, a stabilizer like Candi. It made Julian wonder
about the men, maybe Enders, who had raped Arly and
left her for dead. And the Ender with the knife, outside
the convenience store. Were they just crazy, or part of
an organized effort? Or were they both?

the next morning i jacked with the bastard for an
hour, which was more than fifty-nine minutes too long.
He made Scoville look like a choirboy.

I had to get away. Amelia and I found bathing suits
and pedaled to the beach. In the men's changing room
two men watched me in a strangely hostile way. I supposed black people are rare up here. Or maybe bicyclists.

We didn't do much swimming; the water was too
salty, with a greasy metallic taste, and surprisingly cold.
For some reason, it smelled like cured ham. We waded
out and dried off, shivering, and walked for a while on
the odd beach.

The white sand wasn't native, obviously. We'd come
in pedaling over the actual crater surface, which was a
kind of dark umber glass. The sand felt too powdery
underfoot, and made a squeaking sound.

It seemed really strange compared to the Texas
beaches where we'd vacationed, Padre Island and Mat-
agorda. No seabirds, shells, crabs. Just a big round ar-
tifact full of alkaline water. A lake created by a
simpleminded god, Amelia said.

"I know where he could find a couple of thousand
followers," I said.

"I dreamed about him," she said. "I dreamed he had

gotten me, like the one you talked about.''

I hesitated. ''Do you want to talk about it?'' He had opened the victim from navel to womb, and then made a cross-slash through the middle of the abdomen, as a kind of decoration after cutting her throat.

She made a brushing-away gesture. ''The reality's more frightening than the dream. If it's at all like his picture of it.''

''Yeah.'' We'd discussed the possibility that there were only a few of them; maybe only four deluded conspirators. But he seemed to be able to draw on an awful lot of resources—information, money, and ration credits, as well as gadgets like the AK 101. Marty was going to talk to his general this morning.

''It's scary that their situation is the opposite of ours. We could locate and interrogate a thousand of them and never find anyone involved in the actual planning. But if they jack with any one of you, they know everything.''

I nodded. ''So we have to move fast.''

''Move, period. Once they track him or Jefferson up here, we're dead.'' She stopped walking. ''Let's sit here. Just sit quietly for a few minutes. It might be our last chance.''

She crossed ankles and drifted into a kind of lotus position. I sat down less gracefully. We held hands and watched morning mist burn off the dead gray water.

marty passed on what Ingram had revealed about the Hammer of God to the general. He said it sounded fantastic, but he would make cautious inquiries.

He also found for them two decommissioned vehicles, delivered that afternoon: a heavy-duty panel truck and a school bus. They turned the conspicuous army green into a churchly powder blue, and lettered "St. Bartholo-mew's Home" on both vehicles.

Moving the nanoforge was no picnic. The crew that had delivered it long ago had used two heavy dollies, a ramp, and a winch to get it into the basement. They used the machine to improvise duplicates, jacked it up onto the dollies and, after widening three doors, managed to get it into the garage in one backbreaking day. Then at night they snuck it out and winched it into the panel truck.

Meanwhile, they were modifying the school bus so that Ingram and Jefferson could stay jacked continuously, which meant taking out seats and putting in beds, along with equipment to keep them fed and watered and emptied. They would stay continually jacked to two of the Twenty, or Julian, working in staggered four-hour shifts.

Julian and Amelia were working as unskilled labor, tearing out the last four rows of seats in the bus and improvising a solid frame for the beds, sweating and swatting mosquitoes under the harsh light, when Mendez clomped into the bus, rolling up his sleeves: "Julian, I'll take over here. The Twenty need you to jack with them."

"Gladly." Julian got up and stretched, both shoulders crackling. "What's up? Ingram have a heart attack, I hope?"

"No, they need some practical input about Portobello. One-way jack, for safety's sake."

Amelia watched Julian go. "I'm afraid for him."

"I'm afraid for us all." He took a small bottle from his pants pocket, opened it, and shook out a capsule. He handed it to her, his hand quivering a little.

She looked at the silver oval. "The poison."

"Marty says it's almost instantaneous, and irreversible. An enzyme that goes straight to the brain."

"It feels like glass."

"Some kind of plastic. We're supposed to bite down on it."

"What if you swallow it?"

"It takes longer. The idea is—"

"I know what the idea is." She put it in her blouse pocket and buttoned it. "So what did the Twenty want to know about Portobello?"

"Panama City, actually. The POW camp and the Portobello connection to it, if any."

"What are they going to do with thousands of hostile prisoners?"

"Turn them into allies. Jack them all together for two weeks and humanize them."

"And let them *go*?"

"Oh, no." Mendez smiled and looked back toward the house. "Even behind bars, they won't be prisoners anymore."

i unjacked and stared down into the wildflowers for a minute, sort of wishing it had been two-way; sort of not. Then I stood up, stumbled, and went back to where Marty was sitting at one of the picnic tables. Incongruously, he was slicing lemons. He had a large plastic bag of them and three pitchers, and a manual juicer.

"So what do you think?"

"You're making lemonade."

"My specialty." Each of the pitchers had a measured amount of sugar in the bottom. When he sliced a lemon, he would take a thin slice out of the middle and throw it on the sugar. Then squeeze the juice out of both halves. It looked like six lemons per pitcher.

"I don't know," I said. "It's an audacious plan. I have a couple of misgivings."

"Okay."

"You want to jack?" I nodded toward the table with the one-way box.

"No. Give me the surface first. In your own words, so to speak."

I sat down across from him and rolled a lemon between my palms. "Thousands of people. All from a foreign culture. The process works, but you've only tried it on twenty Americans—twenty *white* Americans."

"There's no reason to think it might be culture-bound."

"That's what they say themselves. But there's no evidence to the contrary, either. Suppose you wind up with three thousand raving lunatics?"

"Not likely. That's good conservative science—we ought to do a small-scale test first—but we can't afford to. We're not doing science now—we're doing politics."

"Beyond politics," I said. "There's no word for what we're doing."

"Social engineering?"

I had to laugh. "I wouldn't say that around an engineer. It's like mechanical engineering with a crowbar and sledgehammer."

He concentrated on a lemon. "You do still agree that it has to be done."

"Something has to be done. A couple of days ago, we were still considering options. Now we're on some kind of slippery ramp; can't slow down, can't go back."

"True, but we didn't do it voluntarily, remember. Jefferson put us on the edge of the ramp, and Ingram pushed us over."

"Yeah. My mother likes to say, 'Do something, even if it's wrong.' I guess we're in that mode."

He set down the knife and looked at me. "Actually not. Not quite. We do have the option of just plain going public."

"About the Jupiter Project?"

"About the whole thing. In all likelihood, the government's going to discover what we're doing and squash us. We could take that opportunity away from them by going public."

Odd that I hadn't even considered that. "But we wouldn't get anything close to a hundred percent compliance. Less than half, you figured. And then we're in Ingram's nightmare, a minority of lambs surrounded by wolves."

"Worse than that," he said cheerfully. "Who controls the media? Before the first volunteer could sign up, the government would have us painted as ogres bent on world domination. Mind controllers. We'd be hunted down and lynched."

He finished with the lemons and poured equal amounts of juice into each pitcher. "Understand that I've been thinking about this for twenty years. There's no way around the central conundrum: to humanize someone, we have to install a jack; but once you're jacked two-way, you can't keep a secret.

"If we had all the time in the world, we could do it like the Enders' cell system. Elaborate memory modification for everybody who's not at the very top, so that nobody could reveal my identity or yours. But memory modification takes training, equipment, time.

"This idea of humanizing the POWs is partly a way of undermining the government's case against us, ahead of time. It's presented initially as a way of keeping the prisoners in line—but then we let the news media 'discover' that something more profound has happened to them. Heartless killers transformed into saints."

"Meanwhile, we're doing the same thing to all the mechanics. One cycle at a time."

"That's right," he said. "Forty-five days. If it works."

The arithmetic was clear enough. There were six thousand soldierboys, each serviced by three cycles. Fifteen days each, and after forty-five days you had eighteen thousand people on our side, plus the thousand or two who run the flyboys and waterboys, who would be going through the process.

What Marty's pet general was going to do, or try, was to declare a worldwide Psychops effort that required certain platoons to stay on duty for a week or a few weeks extra.

It only took five extra days to "turn" a mechanic, but then you couldn't just send him home. The change in behavior would be obvious, and the first time one was jacked, the secret would be out. Fortunately, once the mechanics *were* jacked, they'd understand the necessity for isolation, so keeping them on base wouldn't be a problem. (Except for feeding and housing all those extra people, which Marty's general would incorporate into the exercise. Never hurt a soldier to bivouac for a week or two.)

Meanwhile, the publicity over the miraculous "conversion" of the POWs would be priming the public to accept the next step.

The ultimate bloodless coup: pacifists taking over the army, and the army taking over the government. And then the people—radical idea!—taking over the government themselves.

"But the whole thing hinges on this mystery man, or woman," I said. "Someone who can shuffle medical records around, have a few people reassigned, okay. Appropriate a truck and a bus. That's nothing like setting up a global Psychops exercise. One that's actually a takeover of the military."

He nodded quietly.

"Aren't you going to put water in the lemonade?"

"Not until morning. That's the secret." He folded his arms. "As to the big secret, his identity, you're perilously close to solving it."

"The president?" He laughed. "Secretary of defense? Chairman of the Joint Chiefs of Staff?"

"You could figure it out with what you know, given a table of organization. Which is a problem. We're extremely vulnerable between now and the time your memory has been tailored."

I shrugged. "The Twenty told me about the suicide pills."

He carefully uncapped a brown vial and shook three hard pills into my hand. "Bite down on one and you'll be brain-dead in a few seconds. For you and me it ought to be in a glass tooth."

"In a tooth?"

"Old spy myth. But if they take you or me alive, and get a jack into us, the general's dead meat, and the whole thing is over."

"But you're one-way."

He nodded. "With me, it would take a little torture. With you . . . well, you might as well just know his name."

"Senator Dietz? The pope?"

He took my arm and started to lead me back to the bus. "It's Major General Stanton Roser, the Assistant Secretary for Force Management and Personnel. He was one of the Twenty who supposedly died, but with a different name and face. Now he has a disconnected jack, but otherwise he's well-connected indeed."

"None of the Twenty knows?"

He shook his head. "And they won't find out from me. Nor from you, now. You don't jack with anybody until we get to Mexico and tailor your memory."

their drive down to Mexico was too interesting. The fuel cells in the truck lost power so fast they had to be recharged every two hours. Before they got out of

South Dakota they decided to pull over for half a day and rewire the vehicle so it was powered directly by the nanoforge's warm fusion generator.

Then the bus broke down, the transmission turning to mush. It was essentially an airtight cylinder of powdered iron stiffened by a magnetic field. Two of the Twenty, Hanover and Lamb, had worked on cars, and together they figured out that the problem was in the shifting program—when the torque demand reached a certain threshold, the field switched off for a moment to shift to a lower gear; when it went below another threshold, it would shift up. But the program had gone haywire, and was trying to shift a hundred times a second, so the iron powder cylinder wasn't rigid long enough to transmit much power. After they figured out the nature of the problem, it was easy to fix, since the shifting parameters could be set manually. They had to reset them every ten or fifteen minutes, because the bus wasn't really designed for so heavy a load, and kept overcompensating. But they did lurch south a thousand miles a day, making plans.

Before they got into Texas, Marty had made arrangements of a shady nature with Dr. Spencer, who owned the Guadalajara clinic where Amelia had been operated on. He didn't reveal that he had a nanoforge, but he did say he had limited, but unsupervised, *access* to one, and he could make the doctor anything, within reason, that the thing could make in six hours. As proof, 2200 carats' worth, he sent along a one-pound diamond paperweight with Spencer's name lasered into the top facet.

In exchange for the six machine hours, Dr. Spencer shuffled his appointments and personnel so that Marty's people could have a wing to themselves, and the use of several technicians, for a week. Extensions to be discussed.

A week was all that Marty would need, to tailor Julian's memories and complete the humanization of his two captives.

Getting through the border into Mexico was easy, a simple financial transaction. Getting back the same way would be almost impossible; the guards on the American side were slow and efficient and difficult to bribe, being robots. But they wouldn't be driving back, unless things absolutely fell apart. They planned to be flying to Washington aboard a military aircraft—preferably not as prisoners.

It took another day to drive to Guadalajara; two hours crawling through the sprawl of Guadalajara itself. All the streets that were not under repair seemed not to have *been* repaired since the twentieth century. They finally found the clinic, though, and left the bus and truck in its undergound lot, guarded by an old man with a submachine gun. Mendez stayed with the truck and kept an eye on the guard.

Spencer had everything prepared, including the rental of a nearby guest house, la Florida, for the busload. No questions, except to verify their needs. Marty had Jefferson and Ingram installed in the clinic, along with a couple of the Twenty.

They began setting up the Portobello phase from la Florida. Assuming the local phones weren't secure, they had a scrambled military line bounced off a satellite and routed through General Roser.

It was easy enough to get Julian assigned to Building 31 as a kind of middle-management trainee, since he was no longer a factor in the company's strategic plans. But the other part of it—a request to extend his platoon's time in the soldierboys an additional week—was turned down at the battalion level, with the terse explanation that the "boys" had already gone through too much stress the past couple of cycles.

That was true enough. They had had three weeks, unjacked, to dwell on the Liberia disaster, and some had

not been in good soldierly shape when they came back.
Then there was the new stress of retraining with Eileen
Zakim, Julian's replacement. For nine days they would
be confined to Portobello—"Pedroville"—doing the
same maneuvers over and over, until their performance
with Eileen was close enough to what it had been with
Julian.

(It would turn out that Eileen did have one pleasant
surprise. She had expected resentment, that the new platoon leader had come from outside, rather than being
promoted from the ranks. It was quite the opposite: they
all had known Julian's job intimately, and none of them
wanted it.)

It was fortunate, but not exactly unusual, that the colonel who brusquely turned down the extension request
had himself a request for change of assignment in the
works. Many of the officers in Building 31 would rather
be assigned someplace with more action, or with less;
this colonel suddenly had orders delivered that sent him
to a relief compound in Botswana, a totally pacified
place where the Alliance presence was considered a god-
send.

The colonel who replaced him came from Washington, from General Stanton Roser's Office of Force Management and Personnel. After he'd settled in for a few
days, reviewing his predecessor's policies and actions,
he quietly reversed the one affecting Julian's old platoon. They would stay jacked until 25 July, as part of a
long-standing OFMP study. On the 25th, they'd be
brought in for testing and evaluation.

Brought in to Building 31.

Roser's OFMP couldn't directly affect what went on
in the huge Canal Zone POW camp; that was managed
by a short company from Army Intelligence, which had
a platoon of soldierboys attached to it.

The challenge was somehow to have all the POWs
jacked together for two weeks without any of the sol-

dierboys or Intelligence officers, one of whom was also jacked, eavesdropping.

To this end they conjured up a colonelcy for Harold McLaughlin, the only one of the Twenty who had both army experience and fluency in Spanish. He had orders cut to go to the Zone to monitor an experiment in extended "pacification" of the POWs. His uniforms and papers were waiting for him in Guadalajara.

One night in Texas, Marty had called all the Saturday Night Special people and asked, in an enigmatic and guarded way, whether they would like to come down to Guadalajara, to share some vacation time with him and Julian and Blaze: "Everyone has been under so much stress." It was partly to benefit from their varied and objective viewpoints, but also to get them across the border before the wrong people showed up asking questions. All of them but Belda said they were able to come; even Ray, who had just spent a couple of weeks in Guadalajara, having a few decades' worth of fat vacuumed out of his body.

So who should be first to show up at la Florida but Belda, after all, hobbling in with a cane and an overloaded human porter. Marty was in the entrance hall, and for a moment just stared.

"I thought it over and decided to take the train down. Convince me it wasn't a big mistake." She nodded at the porter. "Tell this nice boy where to put my things."

"Uh . . . *habitación dieciocho*. Room 18. Up the stairs. You speak English?"

"Enough," he said, and staggered up the stairs with the four bags.

"I know Asher's coming in this afternoon," she said. It was not quite twelve. "What about the others? I thought I might rest until the festivities begin."

"Good. Good idea. Everyone should be in by six or seven. We have a buffet set up for eight."

"I'll be there. Get some sleep yourself. You look terrible." She pulled herself up the stairs with cane and banister.

Marty looked as bad as she said, having just spent hours jacked with McLaughlin going over all the ins and outs, every possible thing that could go wrong with the POW aspect of "the caper," as McLaughlin called it. He'd be on his own most of the time.

There would be no problem as long as orders were followed, since the orders called for all of the POWs to be isolated for two weeks. Most of the Americans didn't like jacking with them anyhow.

After two weeks, starting right after Julian's platoon moved in on Building 31, McLaughlin would take a walk and disappear, leaving the POWs' humanization an irreversible fact of life. Then they would be connected with Portobello and prepare for the next stage.

Marty flopped down on the unmade bed in his small room and stared at the ceiling. It was stucco, and the crusted swirls of it made fantastic patterns in the shifting light that threaded across the room from the top of the shutters that cut off the view of the street; light reflected from the windshields and glittering canopies of the cars that crawled by in the street below, noisily unaware that their old world was about to die. If everything went right. Marty stared at the shifting shadows and catalogued all the things that could go wrong. And then their old world would die, literally.

How could they keep the plan secret, against all odds? If only the humanization didn't take so long. But there was no way around it.

Or so he thought.

i'd been looking forward to seeing the Saturday Night Special crowd again, and there couldn't have been a more welcome setting for the reunion, as tired as we were of road food. The dining table at la Florida was a crowded landscape of delights: a platter of jumbled sausages and another of roasted chickens, split and steaming; a huge salmon lying open on a plank; three colors of rice and bright bowls of potatoes and corn and beans; stacks of bread and tortillas. Bowls of salsa, chopped peppers, and guacamole. Reza was loading a plate when I came in; we exchanged greetings in silly gringo Spanish and I followed his example.

We'd just collapsed in overstuffed chairs, plates balanced on laps, when the others came downstairs in a group, led by Marty. It was a mob, a dozen of the Twenty as well as five from our crowd. I gave up my chair to Belda and filled a small plate to her specifications, saying hello to everyone, and eventually found a piece of floor in a corner with Amelia and Reza, who had also given up his early advantage to a white-haired woman, Ellie.

Reza poured us each a cup of red wine from an unlabeled jug. "Let me see your ID, soldier." He shook his head, drank half the cup and refilled it. "I'm emigrating," he said.

"Better bring lots of money," Amelia said. There were no jobs for Nortes in Mexico.

"You guys really have your own personal nanoforge?"

"Boy, security is tight around here," I said.

He shrugged. "I sort of heard Marty tell Ray about it. Stolen?"

"No, an antique." I told him as much of the story as I could. It was frustrating; everything I knew about its history came from being jacked with the Twenty, and there was no way to communicate all the nuance and complexity of its shadowy story. Like reading just the face level of a hypertext.

"So technically, it's not stolen. It does belong to you."

"Well, it's not legal for private citizens to own warm fusion plants, let alone the nanogenesis modules—but St. Bartholomew's was chartered by the army in a grant that hid all kinds of spooky classifed things. I guess the records got scrambled, and we're sort of caretaking the old machine until someone like the Smithsonian shows up for it."

"Good of you." He attacked a quarter-chicken. "Would I be wrong in assuming that Marty didn't summon us down here for our sage advice?"

"He'll ask your advice," Amelia said. "He asks for mine all the time." She rolled her eyes.

Reza dipped a chicken leg in jalapeños. "But basically, he's covering his rear. His rear flank."

"And protecting you," I said. "As far as we know, nobody's after Marty yet. But they're certainly after Blaze, for this ultimate weapon she knows all about."

"They killed Peter," she murmured.

Reza looked blank and then shook his head sharply. "Your coworker. Who did?"

"The one who came after me said he was from the army's 'Office of Technology Assessment.' " She shook her head. "He was and he wasn't."

"Spooks?"

"Worse than that," I said. I explained about the Hammer of God.

"So why not just go public?" he said. "You didn't plan for it to stay secret."

"We will," I said, "but the later, the better. Ideally, not until we have all the mechanics converted. Not just Portobello, but everywhere."

"Which will take a month and a half," Amelia said, "if everything goes according to plan. I can imagine how likely *that* is going to be."

"You won't even get to that stage," Reza said. "All those people able to read minds? I'd bet you a month's alcohol ration it'll blow up in your face before you get the first platoon converted.''

"No bet," I said. "As little as I need your ration. The only chance we have is to stay a little ahead of the game. Try to be ready for disaster when it strikes."

A stranger sat down with us and I realized it was Ray, the three quarters of him that was left after cosmetic surgery. "I jacked with Marty." He laughed. "God, what a screwball plan. Go away for a couple of weeks and everybody goes crazy."

"Some are born crazy," Amelia said. "Some achieve craziness. We had craziness thrust upon us."

"Bet that's a quote," Ray said, and crunched down on a carrot. He had a plate full of raw vegetables. "True enough, though. One person dead and how many of us to follow? To take on the unlikely task of improving human nature."

"If you want out," I said, "it better be now."

Ray set his plate down and helped himself to some wine. "No way. I've worked with jacks as long as Marty. We've been playing with this idea longer than you've been playing with girls." He glanced at Amelia and smiled and looked down at his plate.

Marty rescued him by dinging a spoon on a water glass. "We have a vast range of experience and expertise here, and won't often all be together in one room. I think it would be smart this first time, though, to limit ourselves to getting our timetable and other information straight—things the jacked people all know in detail, but the rest of us only in bits and pieces."

"Let's take it backward," Ray said. "We conquer the world. What's the step just before that?"

Marty stoked his chin. "September first."

"Labor Day?"

"It's also Armed Forces Day. The one day in the year when we can have a thousand soldierboys marching down the streets of Washington. Peacefully."

"One of the few days," I added, "when most of the politicians are also in Washington. And more or less in one place, at the parade."

"A lot of what happens before, just before that, is control of the news. 'Spin,' they used to call it.

"Two weeks before, we will have finished humanizing the entire POW compound down in Panama City. It's going to be a miracle—all those unruly, hostile captives transformed into a forgiving, cooperative nation, eager to use their newfound harmony to end the war."

"I see where this is going," Reza said. "We'll never get away with it."

"Okay," Marty said. "Where are we going?"

"You get everybody excited about turning these nasty goomie soldiers into angels, and then you whip aside the magic curtain and say, 'Ta-da! We've done the same thing to all *our* soldiers. By the way, we're taking over Washington.' "

"Not quite that subtle." Marty rolled up a tortilla with a strange mixture of beans, shredded cheese, and olives. "By the time the public learns about it, it will be 'Oh, by the way, we've taken over Congress and the Pentagon. Stay out of our way while we work this out.' " He bit into the tortilla and shrugged at Reza.

"Six weeks from now," Reza said.

"Six eventful weeks," Amelia said. "Just before I left Texas, I sent the rationale for the doomsday scenario to about fifty scientists—everyone in my address book tagged as a physicist or astronomer."

"That's funny," Asher said. "I wouldn't have gotten it, since I'd be in your book as 'math' or 'old fart.' But you'd think some colleague would have mentioned it by now. How long's it been?"

"Monday," Amelia said.

"Four days." Asher filled a mug with coffee and steaming milk. "Have you contacted any of them?"

"Of course not. I haven't dared to pick up a phone or log on."

"Nothing in the news," Reza said. "Aren't any of your fifty publicity-hungry?"

"Maybe it was intercepted," I said.

Amelia shook her head. "It was from a public phone, a data jack in the Dallas train station; maybe a microsecond download."

"So why hasn't anybody reacted?" Reza said.

She kept shaking her head. "We've been so . . . so busy. I should have . . ." She set down her plate and fished through her purse for a phone.

"You're not—" Marty said.

"I'm not calling anybody." She punched a sequence of numbers from memory. "But I never checked the echo of that call! I just assumed everybody got . . . oh, shit." She turned the handset around. It showed a random jumble of numbers and letters. "The bastard got to my database and scrambled it. In the forty-five minutes it took for me to get to Dallas and make the call."

"It's worse than that, I'm afraid," Mendez said. "I've jacked with him for hour after hour. He didn't do it; didn't think of it."

"Jesus," I said into the silence. "Could it have been someone in our department? Someone who could decrypt your files and cream them?" She'd been keying through the text. "Look at this." There was nothing but gibberish until the last word:

"$G_iO_iD_iS_iW_iI_iL_iL$."

it takes time for information to percolate up through a cell system. By the time Amelia found evidence that the Hammer of God had scrambled her files, there was still one day left before the very highest echelon knew that God had given them a way to bring on the Last Day: all they had to do was keep anybody from interfering with the Jupiter Project.

They were not dumb, and they knew a thing or two about spin themselves. They leaked the "news" that there were lunatic-fringe conservatives who wanted to convince you that the Jupiter Project was a tool of Satan; that continuing it could precipitate the end of the world. The End of the Universe! Could anything be more ridiculous? A harmless project that, now that it was set in motion, cost nobody anything, and might give us real information as to how the universe began. No wonder those religious kooks wanted it suppressed! It might prove that God didn't exist!

What it proved, of course, was that God did exist, and was calling us home.

The Ender who had decrypted and destroyed Amelia's files was none other than Macro, her titular boss, and he was glad beyond words to see that his part in the plan was crystallizing.

Macro's involvement did help the other Plan—Marty's rather than God's—in that he deflected attention from the disappearance of Amelia and Julian. He had set up Ingram to get rid of Amelia, and assumed he had taken care of the black boyfriend at the same time, good riddance to both of them. He had forged letters of resignation from both, in case anyone came looking. He'd assigned their teaching duties to people who were too grateful to be curious, and there was already so much rumor brewing about them that he didn't bother to manufacture a cover story. Young black man and older white woman. They probably pulled up stakes and went to Mexico.

fortunately, i still had the rough draft of the paper on my own notebook. Amelia and I could clean it up and send a delayed broadcast after we left Guadalajara. Ellie Morgan, who had been a journalist before committing murder, volunteered to write a simplified version for general release, and one with everything but equations for a popular science magazine. That would be a pretty short article.

The staff removed all the plates, empty or piled with bones, and brought back plates of cookies and fruit. I couldn't look at another calorie, but Reza attacked both.

"Since Reza has his mouth full," Asher said, "let me be devil's advocate for a change.

"Suppose all it took to become humanized was a simple pill. The government demonstrates how it's going to make life better for everyone—or even that life will end if everyone doesn't take it—and they supply the pills to everybody. Pass a law saying it's life imprisonment if you don't take the pill. How many would manage not to take it anyhow?"

"Millions," Marty said. "Nobody trusts the government."

"And instead of a pill, you're talking about a complex surgical procedure that only works ninety-some percent of the time and when it doesn't work, it usually kills or stupefies the victim. You'll have people running for the hills."

"We've been through this," Marty said.

"I know. I got the argument when we were jacked. You don't provide it for free—you charge for it and make it a symbol of status and individual empowerment. How many Enders do you think you're going to get that way? And what about the people who already have status and power? They're going to say, 'Oh, good, now everybody else can be like me'?"

"The fact is," Mendez said, "it does give you power. When I'm linked with the Twenty, I understand five languages; I have twelve degrees; I've lived over a thousand years."

"The status part will be propaganda at first," Marty said. "But when people look around and see that virtually everything of interest is being done by the humanized, we won't have to sell the idea."

"I'm worried about the Hammer of God," Amelia said. "We're not likely to convert many of them, and some of them like to serve God by murdering the godless."

I agreed. "Even if we convert a few like Ingram, the nature of the cell system would keep it from spreading."

"They're notoriously antijack anyhow," Asher said. "Enders in general, I mean. And arguments about status and power aren't going to move them."

"Spiritual arguments might," Ellie Morgan said. She looked kind of saintly herself, all in white with long flowing white hair. "Those of us who are believers find our belief strengthened, and broadened."

I wondered about that. I'd felt her belief, jacked, and was attracted by the comfort and peace she derived from it. But she'd instantly accepted my atheism as "another path," which didn't sound much like any Ender I'd met. The hour I'd spent linked with Ingram and two others, Ingram had used the power of the jack to visualize imaginative hells for the three of us, all involving anal rape and slow mutilation.

It would be interesting to jack with him after he'd been humanized, and play those hells back for his entertainment. I suppose he'd forgive himself.

"That's an angle we ought to map out," Marty said. "Using religion—not your kind, Ellie, but organized religion. We'll automatically have people like the Cyber-Baptists and Omnia on our side. But if we could be endorsed by some mainstream religion, we could have a big bloc that not only preached our gospel, but demonstrated its effectiveness." He picked up a cookie and inspected it. "I've been concentrating so much on the military aspects that I've neglected other concentrations of power. Religion, education.''

Belda tapped her cane on the floor. ''I don't think deans and professors are going to see the appeal of gaining knowledge without working through their institutions. Mr. Mendez, you plug into your friends and speak five languages. I only speak four, none of them that well, and it took a large piece of my youth, sitting and memorizing, to learn three of those four. Pedagogues are jealous of the time and energy they invest in gaining knowledge. You offer it to people like a sugar pill.''

''But no, it's not like that at all,'' Mendez said earnestly. ''I only understand things in Japanese or Catalan when one of the others is thinking with that language. I don't keep it.''

''It's like when Julian joined us,'' Ellie said. ''The Twenty never had a physical scientist before. When he was linked with us, we understood his love for physics, and any of us could use his knowledge directly—but only if we knew enough, anyhow, to ask the right questions. We couldn't suddenly do calculus. No more than we understand Japanese grammar when we're linked with Wu.''

Megan nodded. ''It's sharing information, not transferring it. I'm a doctor, which may not be a huge intellectual accomplishment, but it does take years of study and practice. When we're all jacked together and someone complains of a physical problem, all the others can follow my logic in diagnosis and prescribing, while it's happening, but they couldn't have come up with it on their own, even though we've been jacked together off and on for twenty years.''

''The experience might even motivate someone to study medicine, or physics,'' Marty said, ''and it certainly would help a student, to have instant intimate contact with a doctor or a physicist. But you still have to unplug and hit the books, if you want to actually have the knowledge.''

''Or never unplug at all,'' Belda said. ''Just unplug to eat or sleep or go to the toilet. That's really attractive. Billions of zombies who are temporarily expert in medicine and physics and Japanese. For all of their so-called waking hours.''

''It'll have to be regulated,'' I said, ''the way it is now. People will spend a couple of weeks jacked, to humanize them. But after that . . .''

The front door opened so hard it banged against the wall, and three large policemen strode in with submachine guns. An unarmed policeman, smaller, followed them.

''—I have a warrant for Dr. Marty Larrin,'' he said in Spanish.

''—What is the warrant for?'' I asked. ''—What is the charge?''

''—I am not paid to answer to negros. Which of you is Dr. Larrin?''

''I am,'' I said in English. ''You can answer to me.''

He gave me a look I hadn't seen in years, not even in Texas. ''—Be silent, negro. One of you white men is Dr. Larrin.''

''What is the warrant about?'' Marty asked, in English.

''Are you Professor Larrin?''

''I am and I have certain rights. Of which you are aware.''

''You do not have the right to kidnap people.''

''Is this person I supposedly kidnapped a Mexican citizen?''

''You know he is not. He's a representative of the government of the United States.''

Marty laughed. ''Then I suggest you send around some other representative of the government of the

United States." He turned his back on the guns. "Where were we?"

"To kidnap is against Mexican law." He was turning red in the face, like a cartoon cop. "No matter who kidnaps who."

Marty picked up a phone handset and turned around. "This is an internal matter between two branches of the United States government." He walked up to the man, holding the phone like a weapon, and switched to Spanish. "—You are a bug between two heavy rocks. Do you want me to make the phone call that crushes you?"

The cop rocked back but then held his ground. "I don't know anything about that," he said in English. "A warrant is a simple matter. You must come with me."

"Bullshit." Marty touched one number and unreeled a jack connector from the side of the handset. He clicked it onto the back of his head.

"I demand to know who you are contacting!" Marty just stared at him, slightly wall-eyed. "¡Cabo!" He gestured, and one of the men put the muzzle of his submachine gun under Marty's chin.

Marty reached back slowly and unjacked. He ignored the gun and looked down into the little man's face. His voice was shaky but firm. "In two minutes you may call your commander, Julio Casteñada. He will explain in detail the terrible mistake you almost made, in all innocence. Or you might decide to just go back to the barracks. And not further disturb Comandante Casteñada."

They locked eyes for a long second. The cop jerked his chin sideways and the private withdrew his gun. Without another word, the four of them filed out.

Marty eased the door shut behind them. "That was expensive," he said. "I jacked with Dr. Spencer and he jacked with someone in the police. We paid this Casteñada three thousand dollars to lose the warrant.

"In the long run, money isn't important, because we can make anything and sell it. But here and now, we don't have a 'long run.' Just one emergency after another."

"Unless somebody finds out you have a nanoforge," Reza said. "Then it won't be a few cops with guns."

"These people didn't look us up in the phone book," Asher said. "It had to be someone in your Dr. Spencer's office."

"You're right, of course," Marty said. "So at the very least, they do know we have access to a nanoforge. But Spencer thinks it's a government connection I'm not able to talk about. That's what these police will be told."

"It stinks, Marty," I said. "It stinks on ice. Sooner or later, they'll have a tank at the door, making demands. How long are we here?"

He flipped open his notebook and pushed a button. "Depends on Ingram, actually. He should be humanized in six to eight days. You and I are going to be in Portobello on the twenty-second, regardless."

Seven days. "But we don't have a contingency plan. If the government or the Mafia puts two and two together."

"Our 'contingency plan' is to think on our feet. So far, so good."

"At the very least, we ought to split up," Asher said. "Our being in one place makes it too easy for them."

Amelia put a hand on my arm. "Pair up and scatter. Each pair with one person who knows Spanish."

"And do it now," Belda said. "Whoever sent those boys with guns has his own contingency plan."

Marty nodded slowly. "I'll stay here. Everybody else call as soon as you find a place. Who speaks enough Spanish to take care of rooms and meals?" More than half of us; it took less than a minute to sort up into pairs. Marty opened a thick wallet and put a stack of currency on the table. "Make sure each of you has at least five hundred pesos."

"Those of us who are up to it ought to take the subway," I said. "An army of cabs would be pretty conspicuous, and traceable."

Amelia and I got our bags, not yet unpacked, and were the first ones out the door. The subway was a kilometer away. I offered to take her suitcase, but she said that would be too conspicuously un-Mexican. She should take mine, and walk two paces behind me.

"At least we'll get a little breathing space to work on the paper. None of this will mean anything if the Jupiter Project is still going September fourteenth."

"I spent a little time on it this morning." She sighed. "Wish we had Peter."

"Never thought I'd say it . . . but me, too."

they would soon find out, along with the rest of the world, that Peter was still alive. But he was in no shape to help with the paper.

Police in St. Thomas arrested a middle-aged man wandering through the market at dawn. Dirty and unshaven, dressed only in underwear, at first they thought he was drunk. When the desk sergeant questioned him, though, she found that he was sober but confused. Monumentally confused: he thought the year was 2004 and he was twenty years old.

On the back of his skull, a jack connection so fresh it was crusted with blood. Someone had invaded his mind and stolen the last forty years.

What was taken from his mind corroborated the text of the article, of course. Within a few days, the glorious truth had spread to all of the upper echelons of the Hammer of God: God's plan was going to be fulfilled, appropriately enough, by the godless actions of scientists.

Only a few people knew about the glorious End and Beginning that God would give them on September 14.

One of the paper's authors was safe, most of his brain in a black box somewhere. The academics who had juried the paper had all been taken care of, by accident or "disease." One author was still missing, along with the agent who had been sent to kill her.

The assumption was that they were both dead, since she hadn't surfaced to warn the world. Evidently the authors had been uncertain how much time they had before the process became irreversible.

The most powerful member of the Hammer of God was General Mark Blaisdell, the undersecretary of the Defense Advanced Research Projects Agency. Not too surprisingly, he knew his arch-rival, Marty's General Roser, in a casual social way; they took meals at the same Pentagon dining room—"officers' mess," technically, if you can apply the term to a place with mahogany paneling and a white-clad server for each two "messers."

Blaisdell and Roser did not like each other, though both hid it well enough to occasionally play tennis or billiards together. When Roser once invited him to a poker game, Blaisdell coldly said, "I have never once played cards."

What he did like to play was God.

Through a series of three or four intermediaries, he supervised most of the murder and torture that was regrettably necessary to hasten God's plans. He used an illegal jack facility in Cuba, where Peter had been taken to have his memory stripped. It was Blaisdell who reluctantly decided to let the scientist live, while the five jurors were succumbing to their accidents and diseases. Those five scientists lived all over the world, and there wasn't much to immediately link their deaths and disabilities—two of them were in comas, and would sleep through the end of the world—but if Peter showed up dead as well, it could make trouble. He was moderately famous, and there were probably dozens of people who knew the identities of the five jurors and the fact that they had turned down his paper. An investigation might lead to a re-evaluation of the paper, and the fact that Blaisdell's agency had mandated its refusal might attract unwanted scrutiny to other activities.

He tried to keep his religious beliefs to himself, but he knew there were people—like Roser—who knew he was very conservative, and might suspect, given a whisper of fact or rumor, that he was an Ender. The army wouldn't demote him for that, but they could make him the highest-ranking supply clerk in the world.

And if they found out about the Hammer of God, he'd be executed for treason. He would personally prefer that, of course, to demotion. But the secret had been sealed for years, and he would be the last one to give it away. Marty's group was not the only one with pills.

Blaisdell came home from the Pentagon and put on sport coveralls and went to an evening soccer game in Alexandria. At the hot dog stand he talked to the next woman in line, and as they walked back toward the bleachers, he said their agent Ingram had gone to the Omaha train station the evening of July 11th, to pick up and eliminate a scientist, Blaze Harding. Agent and scientist left the station together—security cameras confirmed that—but then both had disappeared. Find them and kill Harding. Kill Ingram if he does anything that makes you think he's on the wrong side.

Blaisdell returned to his seat. The woman went to the ladies' room and disposed of her hot dog, and then went home to her weapons.

Her first weapon was an illegal FBI infoworm, threading undetected through municipal transportation records. She found out that a third party shared the cab with the agent and his supposed victim; they had stopped the cab on Grand Street, no particular address. The original order had been for 1236 Grand, but they'd stopped early, a verbal cancel.

She went back to the security tapes and saw that the two had been followed by a large black man in uniform. She didn't yet know that there was a connection between the scientist and the black mechanic. She assumed he was a backup for Ingram; Blaisdell hadn't mentioned it, but maybe it was an arrangement Ingram had made on his own.

So Ingram probably had a car waiting, to drive his victim out into the country to dispose of her.

The next stage depended on luck. The Iridium system that provided global communication by way of a fleet of low-flying satellites had been quietly co-opted by the government after the start of the Ngumi War; all of the satellites had been replaced by dual-function ones: they still took care of phone service, but each one also spied continuously on the strip of land it passed over. Had one of them passed over Omaha, over Grand Street, just before midnight on the 11th?

She wasn't military, but she had access to Iridium pictures through Blaisdell's office. After a few minutes of sorting, she had an image of the cab leaving and the black mechanic getting into the back seat of a long black limousine. The next shot was a low angle that showed the limousine's license plate: "North Dakota 101 Clergy." In less than a minute, she had it traced to St. Bartholomew's.

That was strange enough, but her course was clear. She already had a bag packed with a business suit and a frilly dress, two changes of underwear, and a knife and a gun made completely of plastic. There was also a jar of vitamins with enough poison to murder a small town. In less than an hour she was in the air, headed for the crater city Seaside and its mysterious monastery. St. Bartholomew's had some military connection, but General Blaisdell didn't have high enough clearance to find out what it was. It occurred to her that she might be getting in over her head. She prayed for guidance, and God told her in his stern fatherly voice that she was doing the right thing. Stay your course and don't fear dying. Dying is just coming home.

She knew Ingram; he was a third of her cell—and she knew how much better he was at mayhem. She had killed more than twenty sinners in service to the Lord, but always at a distance or protected by extremely close contact. God had gifted her with great sexual attractiveness, and she used it as a weapon, allowing sinners in between her legs while she reached under the pillow for the crystal knife. Men who don't close their eyes when they ejaculate will close their eyes a moment later. If she was on her back with the man above her, she would embrace him with her left arm and then drive the dagger into his kidney. He would straighten up in tetanic shock, his penis trying to ejaculate again, and she could sweep the razor-keen blade across his throat. When he sagged, she would make sure both carotid arteries were severed.

Sitting in the plane, she put her knees together and squeezed, remembering how the last dying thrust felt. It probably didn't hurt the man too much, it was over so fast, and he faced an eternity of torment anyhow. She had never done it to anyone who had taken Jesus as his Savior. Instead of being washed in the Blood of the Lamb, they drowned in their own. Atheists and adulterers, they deserved even worse.

Once a man had almost escaped, a pervert she had allowed to engage her from behind. She'd had to half-turn and stab him in the heart, but she didn't have full force or good aim, and the point of the knife broke off in his breastbone. She dropped the knife and he ran for the door, and might have run naked and bleeding into the hotel corridor, but she had double-locked it, and while he was struggling with the combination of latches, she retrieved the knife and reached around him and

slashed open his abdomen. He was a gross fat man, and
an incredible mess spilled out. He made a lot of noise
dying, while she knelt helplessly sick in the bathroom,
but the hotel was evidently well soundproofed. She left
by way of window and fire escape, and the morning
news said that the man, a well-connected city commis-
sioner, had died at home, peacefully, in his sleep. His
wife and children had been full of praise for him. A
godless swine too fat to engage a woman normally. He
had even pretended to pray before they had sex, currying
favor because of her crucifix, and then expected her to
use her mouth to make him ready. It was while she was
doing that, that she had savored the image of splitting
him open. But her hate hadn't prepared her for the mul-
ticolored jumble of gore.

Well, this one would be clean. She had killed women
twice before, each one a merciful pistol shot to the head.
She would do that and then escape or not. She hoped
she wouldn't have to kill Ingram, a stern but nice man
who had never looked at her with lust. He was still a
man, though, and it was possible that this redheaded professor had led him astray.

It was after midnight by the time she got to Seaside.
She got a room at the hotel closest to St. Bartholomew's,
slightly more than a kilometer away, and walked over
to take a look.

The place was completely dark and silent. Not surprising for a monastery, she supposed, so she went back
to the hotel and slept for a few hours.

One minute after 8:00, she phoned the place, and got
an answering machine. The same at 8:30.

She put on her weapons and walked over and rang
the doorbell at 9:00. No response. She walked completely around the building and saw no sign of life. The
lawn needed mowing.

She noted several places she could break in, come

nightfall, and went back to the hotel to do some electronic snooping.

She found no reference to St. Bartholomew's in any database of religious activity, other than acknowledgment of its existence and location. It was founded the year after the nanoforge cataclysm that formed the Inland Sea.

It was doubtless a cover organization for something, and that something was somehow connected with the military—in Washington, when she'd typed in the name, working under Blaisdell's aegis, she'd gotten a message that "need-to-know" documents would have to be processed through Force Management and Personnel. That was pretty spooky, since Blaisdell had unquestioned access to top-secret material in any part of the military establishment.

So the people in that monastery were either very powerful or very subtle. Maybe both. And Ingram was evidently part of them.

The obvious conclusion would be that they were part of the Hammer of God. But then Blaisdell would know about their activities.

Or would he? It was a large organization, with linkages so complex and well-protected that it was possible even the man in charge could have lost track of an important part. So she should be ready to go in shooting, but also ready to tiptoe away quietly. God would guide her.

She spent a couple of hours assembling an Iridium mosaic of snapshots of the place since the 11th. There were no pictures of the black limousine, which was not too surprising, since the monastery had a large garage and there were never any vehicles parked outside.

Then she saw the army truck and bus appear, and watched them reappear as blue church vehicles, and leave.

It would take a long time, and a lot of luck, to trace

them through the Interstate system. Fortunately, the powder blue was an unusual color. But before she settled into that mind-numbing chore, she decided to go check the monastery for clues.

She put on her business suit over the weapons and assembled the ID package and pocket litter that identified her as an FBI agent from Washington. She wouldn't get past a retinal scan at a police station, but she didn't foresee going into any police station alive.

Again, no response from the doorbell. It took her only a couple of seconds to pick the lock, but it was deadbolted. She took out the pistol and blew the deadbolt off, and the door swung open.

She hurried in with the gun drawn and shouted "F.B.I.!" at the dusty waiting room. She went into the main corridor and started a hasty search, hoping to get through and out before the police arrived. She figured, accurately, that it was possible the folks at St. Bart's didn't have a burglar alarm because they didn't want any police showing up suddenly, but she didn't want to count on that.

The rooms off the corridor were disappointing—two meeting rooms and individual dormitory rooms or cells.

The atrium stopped her, though, with the towering trees and active brook. A trash container had six empty Dom Pérignon bottles. Off the atrium, a large circular conference room built around a huge hologram plate. She found the controls and turned it on to the peaceful woodland scene.

At first she didn't recognize the electronic modules at each seat—and then it dawned on her that this was a place where two dozen sinners could jack together!

She'd never heard of anything like that outside of the military. Maybe that was the military connection, though: a top-secret soldierboy experiment. The office of Force Management and Personnel might indeed be behind it.

That made her hesitant about proceeding. Blaisdell was her spiritual superior as well as her cell leader, and she would normally follow his orders without question. But it seemed increasingly obvious that there could be aspects to this he was unaware of. She would go back to the hotel and try to set up a secure line to him.

She turned off the hologram and tried to return to the atrium. The door was locked.

The room spoke up: "Your presence here is illegal. Is there any way you would care to explain it?" The voice was Mendez's; he was viewing her from Guadalajara.

"I'm Agent Audrey Simone from the Federal Bureau of Investigation. We have reason to believe—"

"Do you have a warrant to search this establishment?"

"It's on file with the local authorities."

"You forgot to bring a copy when you broke in, though."

"I don't have to explain myself to you. Show yourself. Open this door."

"No, I think you'd better tell me the name of your supervisor and the location of your branch. Once I verify that you are who you say you are, we can discuss your lack of a warrant."

With her left hand she pulled out her wallet and turned in a circle, displaying the badge. "Things will go a lot easier for you if—" She was interrupted by the invisible man's laugh.

"Put the fake badge away and shoot your way out. The police should have arrived by now; you can explain about your warrant to them."

She had to shoot off both hinges as well as the three bolts on this door. She ran across the brook and found that the door out of the atrium was now similarly secured. She reloaded, automatically counting the number of remaining air cartridges, and tried to open this one with three shots. It took her four more.

i was watching her on the screen from behind Mendez. She was finally able to push the door down with her shoulder. He pushed two buttons and switched to the corridor camera. She went pounding down the corridor in a dead run, the pistol held out in front of her with both hands.

"Does that look like an FBI agent going out to reason with the local cops?"

"Maybe you should have actually called them."

He shook his head. "Unnecessary bloodshed. You didn't recognize her?"

"Afraid not." Mendez had called me when she shot down the front door, on the off chance that I might recognize her from Portobello.

Before she went out the front door, she slipped the pistol into a belly holster, and buttoned just the top button of her suit, so it was like a cape, concealing without restraining. Then she walked casually out the door.

"Pretty smooth," I said. "She might not be official. She could have been hired by anyone."

"Or she could be a Hammer of God nutcase. They had Blaze tracked as far as the train station in Omaha." He switched to an outside camera.

"Ingram had a lot of government authority, as well as being a nut. I guess she might, too."

"I was sure the government lost her in Omaha. If anyone had followed the limo, St. Bart's would have had company long before now."

She stepped out and looked around, her face revealing nothing, and started up the sidewalk toward town like a tourist on a morning constitutional, neither slow nor hurried. The camera had a wide-angle lens; she dwindled away pretty fast.

"So should we check the hotels and try to find out who she is?" I asked.

"Maybe not. Even if we got a name, it might not do us any good. And we don't want anyone to make a connection between St. Bart's and Guadalajara."

I gestured at the screen. "No one can track that signal to here?"

"Not the pictures. It's an Iridium service. I decrypt them passively from anywhere in the world." He turned off the screen. "You going to the unveiling?" Today was the day Jefferson and Ingram were to have finished the humanization process.

"Blaze wondered whether I ought to. My feelings about Ingram are still pretty Neanderthal."

"I can't imagine. He only tried to murder your woman and then you as well."

"Not to mention insulting my manhood and attempting to destroy the universe. But I'm due in the Clinic this afternoon anyhow, to get my memory fucked with. Might as well see Wonder Boy in action."

"Give me a report. I'm going to stay by the screen for the next day or two, in case 'Agent Simone' tries another visit."

Of course I wouldn't be able to give him a report, because the encounter with Ingram was related to all the stuff I was having erased, or at least so I assumed—I wouldn't be able to remember his assault on Amelia without recalling what she had done to attract his attention. "Good luck. You might check with Marty—his general might have some way to access FBI personnel records."

"Good idea." He stood up. "Cup of coffee?"

"No, thanks. Spend the rest of the morning with Blaze. We don't know who I'm going to be tomorrow."

"Frightening prospect. But Marty swears it's totally reversible."

"That's true." But Marty was going ahead with the plan even though it meant the risk of a billion or more dying or losing their sanity. Maybe my losing or keeping my memories didn't rank too high on his list of priorities.

the woman who called herself Audrey Simone, whose cell name was Gavrila, would never go back to the monastery. She had learned enough there.

It took her more than a day to put together a mosaic of Iridium pictures of the two blue vehicles making their way from North Dakota to Guadalajara. By God's grace the last picture was perfect timing: the truck had disappeared and the bus was signaling for a left turn into an underground parking garage. She used a grid to find the address and was not surprised when it turned out to be a clinic for installing jacks. That Godless practice was at the heart of everything, obviously.

General Blaisdell arranged transportation to Guadalajara for her, but she had to wait six hours for an express package to arrive. There was no sporting goods store in North Dakota where she could replace the ammunition she'd used up opening doors—Magnum-load dum-dum bullets that wouldn't set off airport detectors. She didn't want to run out of them, if she had to fight her way to the redheaded scientist. And perhaps Ingram.

ingram and jefferson sat together in hospital blues. They were in straight-backed chairs of expensive teak or mahogany. I didn't notice the unusual wood first, though. I noticed that Jefferson sat with a serene, relaxed expression that reminded me of the Twenty. Ingram's expression was literally unreadable, and both of his wrists were handcuffed to the chair arms.

There was a semicircle of twenty chairs facing them in the featureless white round room. It was an operating theater, with glowing walls for the display of X-ray or positron transparencies.

Amelia and I took the last empty chairs. "What's with Ingram?" I said. "It didn't take?"

"He just shut down," Jefferson said. "When he realized he couldn't resist the process, he went into a kind of catatonia. He didn't come out of it when we unjacked him."

"Maybe he's bluffing," Amelia said, probably remembering the conference room at St. Bart's. "Waiting for an opportunity to strike."

"That's why he's handcuffed," Marty said. "He's a wild card now."

"He's just not there," Jefferson said. "I've jacked with more people than everybody in this room put together, and nothing like this has ever happened. You can't unjack yourself mentally, but that's what it felt like. Like he decided to pull the plug."

"Not exactly a selling point for humanization," I said to Marty. "It works on everyone but psychopaths?"

"That's the word they used to describe me," Ellie said, saintly and serene. "And it was accurate." She had murdered her husband and children, with gasoline. "But the process worked with me, and still works after all these years. Without it, I know I would have gone crazy; stayed crazy."

"The term 'psychopath' covers a lot of territory," Jefferson said. "Ingram is intensely moral, even though he's repeatedly done things that all of us would call immoral; outrageously so."

"When I was jacked with him," I said, "he reacted to my outrage with a kind of imperturbable condescension. I was a hopeless case who couldn't understand the rightness of the things he had done. That was the first day.''

''We wore him down a little over the next couple of days,'' Jefferson said. ''By not disapproving; by trying to understand.''

''How can you 'understand' someone who can follow an order to rape a woman and then mutilate her in a specific way? He left her tied up and gagged, to bleed to death. He's not even human.''

''But he *is* human,'' Jefferson said, ''and however bizarre his behavior is, it's still human behavior. I think that's what shut him down—we refused to see him as some sort of avenging angel. Just a profoundly sick man we were trying to help. He could take your condemnation and laugh at it. He couldn't take Ellie's Christian charity and lovingkindness. Or, for that matter, my own professional detachment.''

''He should be dead by now,'' Dr. Orr said. ''He hasn't taken any food or water since the third day. We've kept him on IVs.''

''A waste of glucose,'' I said.

''You know better.'' Marty waved fingers in front of Ingram's face and he didn't blink. ''We have to find out why this happened, and how common it's going to be.''

''Not common,'' Mendez said. ''I was with him before, during, and after his retreat into wherever he is now. From the first, it was like jacking with some kind of alien, or animal.''

''I'll go along with that,'' I said.

''But nevertheless very analytical,'' Jefferson said. ''Studying us intently from the very first.''

''Studying what we knew about jacking,'' Ellie said. ''He wasn't that interested in anybody as a person. But he had only jacked before in a limited, commercial way, and he was hungry to absorb our experience.''

Jefferson nodded. ''He had this vivid fantasy that he

extrapolated from the jack joints. He wanted to be jacked with someone and kill him.''

''Or her,'' Amelia said, ''like me, or that poor woman he raped and cut up.''

''The fantasy was always a male,'' Ellie said. ''He doesn't see women as worthy opponents. And he doesn't have much of a sex drive—when he raped that woman, his penis was just another weapon.''

''An extension of his self, like all of his weapons,'' Jefferson said. ''He's more obsessive about weapons than any soldier I ever jacked with.''

''He missed his calling. I know some guys he'd get along with fine.''

''I don't doubt it,'' Marty said. ''Which makes him that much more important to study. Some people in hunter/killer platoons have similar personality traits. We have to find a way to keep this from happening.''

Good riddance, I didn't say. ''So you won't be coming with me tomorrow? Stay here?''

''No, I'm still going to Portobello. Dr. Jefferson's going to work on Ingram. See whether he can walk him back with a combination of drugs and therapy.''

''I don't know whether to wish you luck. I really prefer him this way.'' Maybe it was just my imagination, but I thought the bastard showed a glimmer of expression at that. Maybe we should send Marty down to Portobello alone, and leave me up here to taunt him out of catatonia.

julian and marty missed by only a few minutes sharing the Guadalajara airport with the woman who had come down to kill Amelia. They got on a military flight to Portobello while she took a taxi from the airport to the hotel across the street from the Clinic. Jefferson was staying there, no coincidence, and so were two of the

Twenty—Ellie and the old soldier Cameron.

Jefferson and Cameron were dawdling over breakfast in the hotel cantina when she walked in to get a cup of coffee to take back to her room.

They both looked at her automatically, as men will when a beautiful woman makes an entrance, but Cameron kept staring.

Jefferson laughed and put on the accent of a popular comedian. "Jim . . . you don't stop puttin' eye tracks on her, she's gonna come over and smack you one." The two men had become friends, having worked their way up from the same beginning, the lower-class black suburbs of Los Angeles.

He turned around with a careful expression and said quietly, "Zam, she might more'n smack me. Kill me just for practice."

"What?"

"Bet she's killed more people than I have. She has that sniper look: everyone's a potential target."

"She does hold herself like a soldier." He slid a glance over to her and back. "Or a certain kind of patient. Obsessive-compulsive."

"How 'bout let's not ask her over to join us?"

"Good idea."

But when they left the cantina a few minutes later, they ran into her again. She was trying to deal with the night clerk, a frightened teenaged girl whose English was not good. Gavrila's Spanish was worse.

Jefferson walked over to the rescue. "—Can I be of some assistance?" he asked in Spanish.

"You're American," Gavrila said. "Will you ask her if she's seen this woman?" It was a picture of Blaze Harding.

"—You know what she's asking," he said to the clerk.

"Sí, claro." The woman opened both her hands. "—I

have seen the woman; she has been in here for meals a few times. But she doesn't stay here.''

"She says she's not sure," Jefferson translated. "Most Americans look pretty much the same to her."

"Have *you* seen her?" Gavrila asked.

Jefferson studied the photograph. "Can't say as I have. Jim?" Cameron stepped over. "You seen this woman?"

"I don't think so. A lot of Amricans coming and going.''

"You're here at the Clinic?"

"Consulting." Jefferson realized he'd hesitated a moment too long. "Is she a patient?"

"I don't know. I just know she's here."

"What do you want her for?" Cameron asked.

"Just a few questions. Government business."

"Well, we'll keep an eye out. You're . . . ?"

"Francine Gaines. Room 126. I'd surely appreciate any help you could give me."

"Sure." They watched her walk away. "Is this deep shit," Cameron whispered, "or just meters of excrement?"

"We have to get a picture of her," Jefferson said, "and send it on to Marty's general. If the army's after Blaze, he can probably get rid of her."

"But you don't think she's army."

"Do you?"

He hesitated. "I don't know. When she looked at you, and when she looked at me, she looked first at the middle of the chest and then between the eyes. Targeting. I wouldn't make any sudden movements around her."

"If she's army, she's a hunter/killer."

"We didn't have that term when I was in the service. But it takes one to know one, and I know she's killed a lot of people."

"A female Ingram."

"She might be even more dangerous than Ingram. Ingram rather looks like what he is. She looks like . . ."

"Yeah." Jefferson looked at the elevator door that
had just been graced by her presence. "She sure does."
He shook his head. "Let's get a picture and get it over
to the Clinic for when Mendez checks in." He was down
in Mexico City, scrounging raw materials for the nanoforge. "He had some crazy woman break into St.
Bart's."

"No resemblance," Cameron said. "She was ugly
and had frizzy red hair."

Actually, she'd had a wig and a pressure mask.

we walked right into Building 31, no trouble. To
their computer, Marty was a brigadier general who had
spent most of his career in academic posts. I was sort of
my old self.

Or not. The memory modification was seamless, but
I think if I had jacked with anyone in my old platoon
(which should have been done as a security measure; we
were just lucky) they would have known immediately
that there was something wrong. I was too healthy. They
had all sensed my problem and, in a way you can't put
into words, had always "been there"; had always helped
me get from one day to the next. It would be as obvious
as an old friend showing up without the limp he'd had
all his life.

Lieutenant Newton Thurman, who was given the task
of finding me a place to be useful, was an oddity: he
had started out as a mechanic but developed a kind of
allergy to being jacked—it gave him intense headaches
that were no fun for him or for anybody jacked with
him. I wondered at the time why they would put him in
Building 31 rather than just retiring him, and it was clear
that he wondered the same thing. He'd only been there
a couple of weeks. In retrospect, it's obvious that he was

planted as part of the overall plan. And what a mistake!

The staff in Building 31 was top-heavy in terms of rank: eight generals and twelve colonels, twenty majors and captains, and twenty-four lieutenants. That's sixty-four officers, giving orders to fifty NCOs and privates. Ten of those were just guards, too, and not really in the chain of command, unless something happened.

My memory of those four days, before I had my actual personality restored, is vague and confused. I was slotted into a time-consuming but unchallenging make-work position, essentially verifying the computer's decisions about resource allocation—how many eggs or bullets to go where. Surprise, I never found a mistake.

Among my other unchallenging duties was the one, as it turned out, that everything else was a smoke screen for: the "guard sitrep-log," or situation report log. Every hour I jacked in with the guard mechanics and asked for a "sitrep." I had a form with boxes to check, according to what they reported each hour. All I had ever done was check the box that said "sitrep negative": nothing's happening.

It was typical bureaucratic make-work. If anything of interest did happen, a red light would go on on my console, telling me to jack in with the guards. I could fill out a form *then*.

But I hadn't given any thought to the obvious: they needed someone inside the building who could check on the actual *identities* of the mechanics running the guard soldierboys.

I was sitting there on the fourth day, about one minute before sitrep time, and the red light suddenly started blinking. My heart gave a little stutter and I jacked in.

It wasn't the usual Sergeant Sykes. It was Karen, and four other people from my old platoon.

What the hell? She gave me a quick gestalt: *Trust us; you had to undergo memory modification so we could Trojan-horse our way in here* and then a broad outline of the plan and the incredible Jupiter Project development.

I acknowledged a numb kind of affirmative, unjacked, and checked the "sitrep negative" box.

No wonder I had been so damned confused. The phone buzzed and I thumbed it.

It was Marty, in hospital greens with a neutral expression. "I have you down for a little brain surgery at 1400. You want to come down and prep when your shift's over?"

"Best offer I've had all day."

it was more than just a bloodless coup—it was a silent, invisible coup. The connection between a mechanic and his or her soldierboy is only an electronic signal, and there are emergency mechanisms in place to switch connections. It would only take a few minutes after something like the Portobello massacre, where every mechanic was disabled, to patch in a new platoon from a few hundred or a thousand miles away. (The actual limit was about thirty-five hundred miles, far enough for the speed of light to be a slight delaying factor.)

What Marty had done was set things up so that at the push of a button all five guard mechanics in the basement of Building 31 would be switched off from their soldierboys, and simultaneously, control of the machines would be switched over to five members of Julian's platoon, with Julian being the only person in Building 31 in a position to notice.

The most aggressive thing they did, immediately after taking over, was to pass on an "order" from Captain Perry, the guard commander, to the five shoe guards, that they had to report immediately to room 2H for an emergency inoculation. They went in and sat down and a pretty nurse gave them each a shot. Then she stood quietly behind them and they all fell asleep.

The rooms 1H through 6H were the hospital wing, and it was going to be busy.

At first, Marty and Megan Orr could be doing all the jack installations. The only bedridden patient in H wing, a lieutenant with bronchitis, was transferred to the base hospital when the order came down from the Pentagon to isolate Building 31. The doctor who normally came around every morning couldn't have access.

Two new doctors came in, though, the afternoon after the morning coup. They were Tanya Sidgwick and Charles Dyer, the jack team from Panama who had a ninety-eight percent success rate. They were mystified over their orders to come to Portobello, but sort of looked forward to the vacation—they'd been installing jacks in POWs at the rate of ten or twelve a day, too fast for comfort or safety.

The first thing they did after settling into their quarters was to go down to the H wing and see what was happening. Marty got them comfortable on a pair of beds and said they had to jack with a patient. Then he plugged them into the Twenty, and they instantly realized just what kind of a vacation they were in for.

But after a few minutes of deep communication with the Twenty, they were converts—in fact, they were a lot more sanguine about the plan than most of the original planners were. That simplified the timing, because it wasn't necessary to humanize Sidgwick and Dyer before putting them on the team.

They had sixty-four officers to deal with, and only twenty-eight of them were already jacked; only two of the eight generals. Twenty of the fifty NCOs and privates were jacked.

The first order of business was to get the ones who were already jacked into bed and plugged in with the Twenty. They lugged fifteen beds into the H wing from the Bachelor Officer Quarters. That gave forty spaces in H; for the other nine, they could install jack interfaces in their rooms.

But the first order of business for Marty and Megan Orr was to restore Julian's lost memories. Or try.

There was nothing complicated about it. Once Julian was under, the procedure was totally automated and only took forty-five minutes. It was also totally safe, in terms of the patient's physical and mental health. Julian knew that.

What he didn't know was that it only worked about three quarters of the time. About one in four patients lost something.

Julian lost a world.

i felt refreshed and elated when I woke up. I could remember the mind-numbed state I'd been in for the past four days, and could also remember all the detail that had been taken away from me—odd to feel happiness at being able to remember a suicide attempt and the imminent danger of the world coming to an end—but in my case it was a matter of providing actual *reasons* for the sense of unease that had pervaded my world.

I was sitting on the edge of the bed, looking at a silly Norman Rockwell print of soldiers reporting for duty, remembering furiously, when Marty walked in looking grim.

"Something's wrong," I said.

He nodded. From a black box on the bed table he unreeled two jack cables and handed one to me, wordlessly.

We plugged in and I opened up, and there was nothing. I checked the jack connection and it was secure. "Are you getting anything?"

"No. I didn't in post-op either." He fed his cable back in, and then mine.

"What is it?"

"Sometimes people permanently lose the memories we removed—"

"But I've got it all back! I'm certain!"

"—and sometimes they lose the ability to jack."

I felt cold sweat prickling on my palms and forehead and under my arms. "It's temporary?"

"No. No more than it is with Blaze. It's what happened to General Roser."

"You knew." The sick feeling of loss was turning into rage. I stood up and towered over him.

"I told you you might lose . . . something."

"But you meant *memory*. I was willing to give up *memory*!"

"That's an advantage to jacking one-way, Julian. Two-way, you can't lie by omission. If you had asked me, 'Could I lose the power to jack?' I would have told you. Fortunately, you didn't ask."

"You're an MD, Marty. How does the first part of that oath go?"

" 'Do no harm.' But I was a lot of things before I got that piece of paper. A lot of things afterward."

"Maybe you better get out of here before you start explaining."

He stood his ground. "You're a soldier in a war. Now you're a casualty. But the part of you that died—*only* a part—died to shield your unit, to get it safely into position."

Rather than hit him, I sat back down on the bed, out of range. "You sound like a goddamned warboy. A warboy for peace."

"Maybe so. You must know how badly I feel about this. I knew I was betraying your trust."

"Yeah, well, I feel pretty bad about it, too. Why don't you just leave?"

"I'd rather stay and talk to you."

"I think I have it figured out. Go on. You have dozens of people to operate on. Before the world has the slightest chance of being saved."

"You do still believe that."

"I haven't had time to think about it, but yes, if the stuff you put back in my mind about the Jupiter Project is true, and if the Hammer of God is real, then something has to be done. You're doing something."

"You're all right about it?"

"That's like being 'all right' about losing an arm. I'm fine. I'll learn to shave with the other hand."

"I don't want to leave you like this."

"Like *what*? Just get out of my sight. I can think about it without your help."

He looked at his watch. "They *are* waiting for me. I have Colonel Owens on the table."

I waved him away. "So go do it. I'll be all right."

He looked at me for a moment and then got up and left without a word.

I fished around in my breast pocket. The pill was still there.

back in guadalajara that morning, Jefferson had warned Blaze to stay out of sight. That was no problem; she was holed up with Ellie Morgan several blocks away, working on the various versions of the paper that would warn the world about the Jupiter Project.

Then Jefferson and Cameron sat for a few hours in the cantina, a small camera on the table between them, watching the elevator doors.

They almost missed her. When she came back down, her silky blond hair was tucked under a wig of black ringlets. She was dressed conservatively and had toned her visible skin to a typical Mexican olive hue. But she hadn't disguised her perfect figure or the way she walked.

Jefferson froze in mid-conversation and surreptitiously slid the camera around with his forefinger.

They had both idly watched her exit the elevator. "What?" Cameron whispered.

"That's her. Made up like a Mexican."

Cameron craned around in time to see her glide through the revolving door. "Good God, you're right."

Jefferson took the camera upstairs and called Ray, who, along with Mendez, was coordinating things in Marty's absence.

Ray was at the Clinic. He downloaded the pictures of her and studied them. "No problem. We'll keep an eye out for her."

Less than a minute later, she walked into the Clinic. The metal detectors didn't catch either of her weapons.

But she didn't pull out a picture of Amelia and ask whether anyone had seen her; Gavrila knew that Amelia had been in this building, and assumed it was enemy territory.

She told the receptionist she wanted to talk about a jack installation, but she refused to talk to anyone but the top man.

"Dr. Spencer's in surgery," she said. "It will be at least two hours, maybe three. There are plenty of other people—"

"I'll wait." Gavrila sat down on a couch with a clear view of the entrance.

In another room, Dr. Spencer joined Ray looking at a monitor watching the woman watching the entrance.

"They say she's dangerous," Ray said; "some sort of spy or assassin. She's looking for Blaze."

"I don't want any trouble with your government."

"Did I say she was government? If she was official, wouldn't she produce credentials?"

"Not if she was an assassin."

"The government doesn't *have* assassins!"

"Oh, really. Do you also believe in your Santa Claus?"

"I mean, no, not for *us*. There's a crackpot religious group that's after Marty and his people. She's either one of them or she was hired by them." He explained about her suspicious activity at the hotel.

Spencer stared at her image. "I believe you are correct. I have studied thousands of faces. Hers is Scandinavian, not Mexican. She probably has dyed her blond hair—or no, she's wearing a wig. But what do you expect me to do about her?"

"I don't suppose you could just lock her up and throw away the key."

"Please. This is not the United States."

"Well . . . I want to talk to her. But she may be really dangerous."

"She has no knife or gun. That would have registered as she walked through the door."

"Hm. Don't suppose I could borrow a guy with a gun to watch over her while we talked?"

"As I said—"

" 'This is not the United States.' What about that old *hombre* downstairs with the machine gun?"

"He does not work for me. He works for the garage. How dangerous could this woman be, if she has no weapon?"

"More dangerous than me. My education was sadly neglected in the mayhem category. Do you at least have a room where I could talk to her and have somebody watching, in case she decides to tear off my head and beat me to death with it?"

"That's not difficult. Take her to room 1." He aimed a remote and clicked. The screen showed an interview room. "It's a special room for *seguridad*. Take her in there and I will watch. For ten or fifteen minutes; then I will ask someone else to watch.

"These *ultimodiadores*—you call them Enders—is that what this is all about?"

"There's a relation."

"But they are harmless. Silly people, and what, blaspheming? But harmless, except to their own souls."

"Not these, Dr. Spencer. If we could jack, you'd understand how scared I am of her." For Spencer's protection, no one who knew the whole plan could jack with him two-way. He accepted the condition as typical American paranoia.

"I have a male nurse who is very fat . . . no, very large—and who knows, who grasps, a black belt in karate. He will be watching along with me."

"No. By the time he got down the stairs, she could kill me."

Spencer nodded and thought. "I'll put him in the room next door, with a beeper." He held up the remote and pushed a button. "Like now. This will call him."

Ray excused himself and went to the bathroom, where he was unable to do anything but catalogue his weapons: a key ring and a Swiss Army knife. Back in the observation room he met Lalo, who had arms the size of Ray's thighs. He spoke no English and moved with the nervous delicacy of a man who knows how easily things break. They walked downstairs together. Lalo slipped into room 2, and Ray went into the lobby.

"Madame?" She looked up at him, targeting. "I'm Dr. Spencer. And you?"

"Jane Smith. Can we go someplace and talk?"

He led her to room 1, which was larger than it had seemed in the camera. He motioned her to the couch and pulled over a chair. He straddled it, the chair back a protective shield between them.

"How may I help you?"

"You have a patient named Blaze Harding. Professor Blaze Harding. It is absolutely imperative that I speak to her."

"In the first place, we don't give out the names of our clients. In the second place, our clients don't always give us their real names. Ms. Smith."

"Who are you, really?"

"What?"

"My sources said Dr. Spencer was Mexican. I never met a Mexican with a Boston accent."

"I assure you that I am—"

"No." She reached into her waistband and pulled out a pistol apparently made of glass. "I don't have time for this." Her face became grim, set; totally mad. "You are going to quietly take me from room to room until we find Professor Harding."

Ray paused. "And if she's not here?"

"Then we'll go to a quiet place where I will cut your fingers off, one by one, until you tell me where she is."

Lalo eased the door open and swung in with a large black pistol coming up to aim. She gave him an annoyed look and shot him once in the eye. The glass pistol was almost completely silent.

He dropped the gun and fell to one knee, both hands over his face. He began a girlish keening but her second shot sheared off the top of his head. He toppled forward silently in a flood of blood and brain and cerebrospinal fluid.

Her tone of voice was unchanged: earnest and flat. "You see, the only way you're going to live to see the night is to cooperate with me."

Ray was struck dumb, staring at the corpse.

"Get up. Let's go."

"I . . . I don't think she's here."

"Then where—" She was interrupted by the rattling sound of metal shutters rolling down over the door and window.

Ray heard a faint hissing sound, and remembered Marty's story about the interrogation room at St. Bart's. Maybe they had the same architect.

She evidently didn't hear it—too many hours on the firing range—but she looked around and did see the television camera, like a stub of pencil pointed at them from an upper corner of the room. She jerked him around to face the camera and put the pistol to his head. "You have three seconds to open that door, or I kill him. Two."

"Señora Smith!" A voice came from everywhere. "To open that door, it requires a, *el gato* . . . a jack. It will take two minutes, or three."

"You have two minutes." She looked at her watch. "Starting now."

Ray slumped and suddenly collapsed, rolling out on his back. His head hit the floor with a solid whack.

She made a disgusted noise. "Coward." Then a few seconds later, she herself staggered, and then sat down hard on the floor. Wavering, she held the pistol with both hands and shot Ray in the chest four times.

my place in the BOQ had two rooms—a bedroom and an "office," a gray cubicle with just enough room for a cooler, two hard chairs, and a small table in front of a simple comm console.

On the table, a glass of wine and my last meal: a gray pill. I had a yellow legal tablet and a pen, but couldn't think of anything to say that wasn't obvious.

The phone rang. I let it go three times, and said hello.

It was Jefferson—my psychiatric nemesis, come to save me in the eleventh hour. The instant he hangs up, I resolved, I'm taking the pill.

But like the room and the pill, Jefferson was gray, more gray than black. I hadn't seen anybody that color since my mother had called to tell me Aunt Franci had died. "What's wrong?" I said.

"Ray's dead. He was killed by an assassin they sent after Blaze."

" 'They'? The Hammer of God?" The wavering silver bar at the top of the screen meant the encryption was working; we could say anything.

"We assume she's one of them. Spencer's drilling her out now for a jack."

"How do you know she was after Amelia?"

"She had her picture; was nosing around the hotel here—Julian, she killed Ray just for the hell of it, after she'd killed another man. She walked right through the security screen at the clinic, with a gun and a knife of some plastic. We're scared shitless that she's not here alone."

"God. They tracked us to Mexico?"

"Can you get up here? Blaze needs your protection— we *all* need you!"

I actually felt my jaw drop. "You need *me* to come up and be a soldier?" All those professional snipers and convicted murderers.

spencer unplugged his jack and walked to the window. He raised the blinds and squinted at the rising sun, yawning. He turned to the woman who was bound to a wheelchair with locked restraints.

"Señora," he said, "you are crazy nuts."

Jefferson had unjacked a minute before. "That would be my professional opinion, too."

"What you've done is completely illegal and immoral," she said. "Violating a person's soul."

"Gavrila," Jefferson said, "if you have a soul, I couldn't find it in there."

She jerked at her bonds and the wheelchair rocked toward him.

"She does have a point, though," he said to Spencer.

"We can't very well turn her over to the police."

"I will, as you Americans say, keep her under observation indefinitely. Once she's well, she's free to go." He scratched the stubble on his chin. "At least until the middle of September. You believe that, too?"

"I can't do the math. But Julian and Blaze can, and they don't have any doubts."

"It's the Hammer of God coming down," Gavrila said. "Nothing you can do will stop it."

"Oh, shut up. Can we put her someplace?"

"I have what you would call a 'rubber room.' No lunatic has ever escaped from it." He went to the intercom and arranged for a man named Luis to take her there.

He sat down and looked at her. "Poor Lalo; poor Ray. They didn't suspect what a monster you were."

"Of course not. Men just see me as a receptacle for their lust. Why should they fear a *cunt*?"

"You're going to find out a lot about that," Jefferson said.

"Go ahead and threaten me. I'm not afraid of rape."

"This is more intimate than rape. We're going to introduce you to some friends. If you do have a soul, they'll find it."

She didn't say anything. She knew what he meant; she knew about the Twenty from being jacked with him. For the first time, she looked a little frightened.

There was a knock on the door, but it wasn't Luis. "Julian," Jefferson said, and gestured. "Here she is."

Julian studied her. "She's the same woman we saw in the monitor at St. Bart's? Hard to believe." She was staring at him with an odd expression. "What?"

"She recognizes you," Jefferson said. "When Ingram tried to kidnap Blaze off the train, you followed them. She thought you were with Ingram."

Julian walked over to her. "Take a good look. you to dream about me."

"I'm so frightened," she said.

"You came here to kill my lover, and instead killed an old friend. And another man. They say you didn't blink." He reached slowly toward her. She tried to dodge, but he grabbed her throat.

"Julian . . ."

"Oh, don't worry." The wheels on the chair were locked. He pushed slowly on her throat and she tipped back. He held her at the balance point. "You're going to find everyone here so nice. They just want to help you." He let go, and the wheelchair fell over with a jarring crash. She grunted.

"I'm not one of them, though." He got down on his hands and knees, his face directly over hers. "I'm not nice, and I don't want to help you."

"That's not going to work with her, Julian."

"It's not for her. It's for me." She tried to spit at him, but missed. He stood up and casually flipped the wheelchair into an upright position.

"This isn't like you."

"*I'm* not like me. Marty didn't say anything about my losing the ability to *jack*!"

"You didn't know that could happen with the memory manipulation?"

"No. Because I didn't *ask*."

Jefferson nodded. "That's why you and I haven't been scheduled together lately. You might have asked me about it."

Luis came into the room and they didn't say anything while Spencer instructed him and he rolled Gavrila out.

"I think it's more sinister than that, more manipulative," Julian said. "I think Marty needed somebody who'd been a mechanic, knows soldiering, but is immune to being humanized." He gestured with a thumb at Spencer. "He knows everything now?"

"e essentials."

"ink Marty wants me this way in case there's a

need for violence. Just like you—when you called me to come protect Blaze, you implied the same.''

"Well, it's just that—"

"And you're right, too! I'm so fucking mad that I could kill someone. Isn't that crazy?"

"Julian . . ."

"Oh, you don't use the word 'crazy.'" He lowered his voice. "But it's odd, isn't it? I've sort of come full circle."

"That could be temporary, too. You have every right to be angry."

Julian sat down and clasped his hands together, as if to restrain them. "What did you learn from her? Are there other assassins in town, headed here?"

"The only other one she actually knew was Ingram. We do know the name of the man above her, though, and he must be close to the top. It's a General Blaisdell. He's also the one who ordered the suppression of your paper and had Blaze's partner killed."

"He's in Washington?"

"The Pentagon. He's the undersecretary of the Defense Advanced Research Projects Agency—DARPA."

Julian almost laughed. "DARPA kills research all the time. I've never heard of them killing a *researcher* before."

"He knows she came to Guadalajara, and that she was coming to a jack clinic, but that's all."

"How many clinics are there?"

"One hundred thirty-eight," Spencer said. "And when Professor Harding had her work done here, the only connections to her real name are my own office records and the . . . what did you call the thing you signed?"

"Power of attorney."

"Yes, that's buried in a law office's files, and even so, there shouldn't be anything connecting it with this clinic."

"I wouldn't get too complacent," Julian said. "If Blaisdell wants to, he can find us the same way she did. We left some kind of a trail. The Mexican police could probably place us in Guadalajara—maybe even right here—and they could be bribed pretty easily. Begging your pardon, Dr. Spencer."

He shrugged. *"Es verdad."*

"So we suspect anyone who comes through that door. But what about Amelia, Blaze—is she nearby?"

"Maybe a quarter of a mile," Jefferson said. "I'll take you there."

"No. They might be following either of us. Let's not double their odds. Just write down the name of the place. I'll take two cabs."

"Do you want to surprise her?"

"What does that mean? She's staying with someone?"

"No, no. Yeah, but it's Ellie Morgan. Nothing to get all bothered about."

"Who's *bothered*? It was just a question."

"All I meant was, should I call and say you're coming?"

"Sorry. I'm in a state. Go ahead and give her a ... wait, no. The phone might be tapped."

"Not possible," Spencer said.

"Humor me?" He looked at the address Jefferson had written down. "Good. I'll take a cab to the *mercado*. Lose myself in the crowd and then dive into the subway."

"Your caution verges on paranoia," Spencer said.

"Verges? I'm well over the edge, actually. Wouldn't you be paranoid if one of your best friends just ripped out half your life—and some Pentagon general is sending assassins down after your lover?"

"It's like they say," Jefferson said. "Just because you're paranoid doesn't mean there isn't someone after you."

having said i was going to the market, instead I took a cab out to T-town and then the subway back into the city. No such thing as being too careful.

I slipped from a side street into the courtyard of Amelia's motel. Ellie Morgan answered the door.

"She's asleep," she said in a half-whisper, "but I know she'd want to be woken up." They had adjoining rooms. I went through and she eased the door closed behind me.

Amelia was warm and soft from sleep and smelled of lavender from the bath salts she liked.

"Marty told me what happened," she said. "It must be horrible, like losing one of your senses."

I couldn't answer that. I just held her close for a moment longer.

"You know about the woman and . . . and Ray," she stammered.

"I've been there. I spoke to her."

"The doctor was going to jack her."

"They did that, a high-risk speed installation. She's Hammer of God, same cell as Ingram." I told her about the general in the Pentagon. "I don't think you're safe here. Nowhere in Guadalajara. She traced us from St. Bart's right to the clinic door, through low-orbit spy satellites."

"Our country uses satellites to spy on its own people?"

"Well, the satellites go all around the world. They just don't bother to turn them off over the U.S." There was a coffee machine set into the wall. I kept talking while I set it up. "I don't think this Blaisdell knows exactly where we are. Otherwise we probably would have had a SWAT team instead of a lone assassin, or at least a team backing her up."

"Did the satellites actually see us as individuals, or just the bus?"

"The bus and the truck."

"So I could walk out of here and go to the train station, and just slip away to some random part of Mexico."

"I don't know. She had a picture of you, so we have to assume that Blaisdell can give a copy to the next hit man. They might be able to bribe someone, and you'd have every policeman in Mexico looking for you."

"Nice to feel wanted."

"Maybe you should come back to Portobello with me. Hole up in Building 31 until it's safe. Marty can have orders cut for you, probably with a couple of hours' notice."

"That's good." She stretched and yawned. "I just have a few hours to go on this proof. I'd like to have you go over it; then we can send it out through an airport phone just before we leave."

"Good. It'll be a relief to do some physics for a change."

Amelia had written a good concise argument. I added a long footnote about the appropriateness of pseudo-operator theory in this regime.

I also read Ellie's version for the popular press. To me it seemed unconvincing—no math—but I supposed it would be best to bow to her expertise and keep my mouth shut. Ellie had intuited my unease, though, and had remarked that not using mathematics was like writing about religion without mentioning God, but editors believed that ninety percent of their readers would quit at the first equation.

I had called Marty. He was in surgery, but an assistant called back and said that orders would be waiting for Amelia at the gate. He also passed along the unsurprising news that Lieutenant Thurman was not going to be among the humanized. We'd hoped that the peaceful mental environment, being jacked with people from my converted platoon, would eliminate the stress that was causing his migraines. But no, they just came on later and stronger. So like me, he'd have to sit this one out. Unlike me, he was virtually under house arrest, since the few minutes he did spend jacked were enough for him to learn far too much.

I looked forward to talking to him, since we were no longer bureaucrat-and-flunky. We suddenly had a lot in common, involuntary ex-mechanics.

I also suddenly had a lot more in common with Amelia. If there was any advantage in my losing the ability to be jacked, that was it: it erased the main barrier between us. Cripples together, from my point of view, but together nonetheless.

It felt so good working with her, just being in the same room with her, it was hard for me to believe that the day before, I'd been ready to take the pill.

Well, I wasn't "me" anymore. I supposed I could put off finding out who I was until after September 14. By then, it might be immaterial—*I* might be immaterial! A plasma, anyhow.

While Amelia was packing her small bag, I called the airport for the flight number, and verified that they had pay phones with long-distance data links. But then I realized that if Amelia had orders waiting down in Portobello, we could probably deadhead down in a military flight. I called D'Orso Field and, sure enough, Amelia was "Captain Blaze Harding." There was a flight leaving in ninety minutes, a cargo flyboy with plenty of room if we didn't mind sitting on benches.

"I don't know," Amelia said. "Since I outrank you, I should get to sit on your lap."

The cab made good time. Amelia uploaded twelve copies of the proof, along with personal messages, to trusted friends, and then posted copies on the public domain physics and math nets. She put Ellie's version on both popular science and general news, and then we ran for the flyboy.

rushing off to the air base, rather than waiting in the motel for the next commercial flight, probably saved their lives.

A half hour after they left, Ellie answered a knock on the door to Amelia's adjoining room. Through the peephole, she saw a Mexican maid, apron and broom, pretty with long black hair in ringlets.

She opened the door. "I don't speak Spanish—" The end of the broom handle plunged into her solar plexus and she staggered backwards, crashing to the floor in a ball.

"Neither do I, Satan." The woman lifted her easily and threw her into a chair. "Don't make a sound or I'll kill you." She pulled a roll of duct tape out of the apron pocket and wound it around the woman's wrists, and then wound a tight loop twice around her chest and the chair back. She tore off a small piece and smoothed it over Ellie's mouth.

She shrugged off the apron. Ellie gasped through her nose when she saw the hospital blues underneath, streaked with blood.

"Clothes." She ripped off the blood-stained pyjamas. She pivoted, tense muscular voluptuousness, and saw Ellie's suitcase through the open double door. "Ah."

She walked through the door and came back with jeans and a cotton shirt. "They're a little baggy, but they'll do." She folded them neatly on the end of the bed and peeled away enough of the tape so that Ellie could speak.

"You're not getting dressed," Ellie said, "because you don't want to get blood on your clothes. My blood on my clothes."

"Maybe I want to excite you. I think you're a lesbian, living here alone with Blaze Harding."

"Sure."

"Where is she?"

"I don't know."

"Of course you do. Do I have to hurt you?"

"I'm not telling you anything." Her voice shook and she swallowed. "You're going to kill me no matter what."

"Why do you think that?"

"Because I can identify you."

She smiled indulgently. "I just killed two guards and escaped from the high-security area of your clinic. A thousand police know what I look like. I can let you live." She bent to the floor in a gymnast's sweep and took a glittering scalpel from the apron pocket.

"You know what this is?"

Ellie nodded and swallowed.

"Now, I solemnly swear that I will not kill you if you answer my questions truthfully."

"Do you swear to God?"

"No, that's blasphemy." She hefted the scalpel and stared at it. "In fact, though, I won't even kill you if you tell me lies. I'll just hurt you so badly that you'll beg for death. But, instead, just before I leave, I'll cut out your tongue so you can't tell them anything about me. And then cut off your hands so you can't write. I'll tourniquet them with this tape, of course. I want you to have a long life of regret."

Urine dripped on the floor and Ellie started sobbing. Gavrila smoothed the tape back over her mouth.

"Did your mother ever say '*I'll* give you something to cry about'?" She stabbed down hard and pinned Ellie's left hand to the chair.

Ellie stopped sobbing and stared dully at the handle of the scalpel and the rivulet of blood.

Gavrila rocked the blade slightly and eased it out. The flow of blood increased, but she gently folded a Kleenex over it and taped it in place. "Now if I let you talk, will you just answer questions? Not cry out?" She nodded her head listlessly and Gavrila peeled back half the tape.

"They went to the airport."

"They? Her and her black friend?"

"Yes. They're going back to Texas. To Houston."

"Oh. That's a lie." She positioned the scalpel over the back of Ellie's other hand, and raised her fist like a hammer.

"Panama!" she said in a hoarse shout. "Portobello. Don't . . . please don't—"

"Flight number?"

"I don't know. I heard him writing it down"—she pointed with her head—"over by the phone there."

She walked over and picked up a piece of paper. " 'Aeromexico 249.' I guess they were in such a hurry they left it."

"They were in a hurry."

Gavrila nodded. "I suppose I should be, too." She came back and looked at her victim thoughtfully. "I won't do all those terrible things to you, even though you lied." She smoothed the tape over Ellie's mouth and took another small piece and pinched her nose shut with it. Ellie began kicking wildly and jerking her head back and forth, but Gavrila managed to make a couple of tight turns of tape around her head, fixing the two small pieces in place and cutting off any possibility of air. In her struggles, Ellie tipped the chair over. Gavrila bought her back upright with an effortless lift, as Julian had done with her a couple of hours earlier. Then she dressed slowly, watching the pagan's eyes as she died.

there was a message waiting for us in my BOQ office, flashing on the console screen, that Gavrila had overcome her guard and escaped.

Well, there was no way she could get to us inside the base, locked inside a building isolated by Pentagon decree. Amelia was worried that the woman might find out where she had been living, so she called Ellie. There was no answer. She left a message, warning about Gavrila and advising her to move to some random place across town.

Marty's schedule said he was in surgery and wouldn't be free until 1900—five hours. There was some cheese and beer in the cooler. We had a slow snack and then collapsed into bed. It was narrow for two people, but we were so exhausted that anything horizontal would do. She fell asleep with her head on my shoulder, for the first time in a long time.

I woke up groggily to the console pinging. It didn't wake Amelia, but I did, in my clumsy efforts to extricate myself. My left arm was asleep, a cold tingling log, and I had romantically left a spot of drool on her cheek.

She rubbed at that and opened her eyes to slits. "Phone?"

"Go back to sleep. I'll tell you if it's anything." I walked into the office, beating my left arm against my side. I snagged a ginger ale from the cooler—the favorite drink of whoever had lived there previously, and sat down to the console:

Marty will meet you and Blaze at 1915 in the mess hall. Bring this.

Name	Rank	Implant	Humanization: Begin/ Complete	Name	Rank	Implant	Humanization: Begin/ Complete
Tames	PFC	—	26J/9A	Sutton	1LT	28J/1	29J/12
Reynolds	PFC	—	"	Whipple	1LT	29J/2	30J/13
Benyo	PFC	—	"	Daniel	1LT	29J/2	30J/13
Jewel	TCH	—	"	Suggs	1LT	29J/2	30J/13
Monez	5SGT	—	"	Johnson B.	1LT	29J/2	30J/13
				Hazeltine	1LT	29J/2	30J/13
Foster	2GEN	—	"	Maxberry	1LT	29J/2	30J/13
Pagel	1GEN	—	"	Lanardson	1LT	29J/2	30J/13
Fox	CNL	—	"	Dare	2LT	29J/2	30J/13

Name	Rank	Implant	Humanization: Begin/Complete
Lyman	CNL	—	•
MCcnnell	CNL	—	•
Lorenz	LCNL	—	•
Mealy	LCNL	—	•
Swim	LCNL	—	•
Barbea	MAJ	—	•
Barnes	MAJ	—	•
Costello	MAJ	—	•
Dick	MAJ	—	•
Donahue	MAJ	—	•
Evans	MAJ	—	•
Ho	MAJ	—	•
Washington	MAJ	—	•
Griffen	1LT	—	•
Hyde	1LT	—	•
Lake	1LT	—	•
Neumann	1LT	—	•
Phan	1LT	—	•
Steinberg	1LT	—	•
Check	2LT	—	•
Thurman	2LT	(X)	(X)
Friedman	2LT	—	•
Steinman	2LT		•
Thomson	2LT	—	•
Troxler	2LT	—	•
Spoa	3GEN	27J/2	28J/11A
Pew	2GEN	27J/2	28J/11A
Bowden	1GEN	28J/2	29J/12A
Nguyen	1GEN	28J/2	29J/12A
Hoffher	1GEN	29J/2	30J/13A
Kummer	CNL	27J/1	28J/11A
Loftus	CNL	2J/1	28J/11A
Owens	CNL	27J/1	28J/11A
Snyder	LCNL	27J/1	28J/11A
Stallings	LCNL	27J/1	28J/11A
Tomy	LCNL	27J/2	28J/11A
Allan	MAJ	27J/2	28J/11A
Blackney	MAJ	27J/2	28J/11A
Bobo	MAJ	27J/2	28J/11A
DeHenning	MAJ	28J/2	29J/12A
Edwards	MAJ	28J/2	29J/12A

Name	Rank	Implant	Humanization: Begin/Complete
Butwell	2LT	29J/1	30J/13
Lavallec	2LT	29J/1	30J/13
Kelly	2LT	29J/1	30J/13
Gilpatrick	9SGT	27J/2	28J/11
Miller	7SGT	27J/2	28J/11
Holloway	7SGT	27J/1	28J/11
Garrison	7SGT	29J/1	30J/13
McLaughlin	6SGT	29J/1	30J/13
Rowe	6SGT	3J/1	31J/13
Hughes	6SGT	30J/1	31J/13
Smith, R.	5SGT	30J/1	31J/13
Duffy	5SGT	30J/1	31J/13
Ching	5SGT	30J/1	31J/13
Schauer	TCH	30J/2	31J/13
Williams	TCH	30J/2	31J/13
Perkins	TCH	30J/2	31J/13
Hunt	TCH	30J/2	31J/13
Taral	TCH	30J/2	31J/13
Kanzer	PFC	30J/2	31J/13
Pincay	PFC	30J/2	31J/13
Hyde	PFC	30J/2	31J/13
Blinken	PFC	31J/1	01A/14
Merrill	PFC	31J/1	01A/14
Ramsden	PFC	31J/1	01A/14
Yalowitz	PVT	31J/1	01A/14
Santos	PVT	31J/1	01A/14
Merci	PVT	31J/2	01A/14
Kantor	PVT	31J/2	01A/14
Walleri	PVT	31J/2	01A/14
Scanlan	PVT	31J/2	01A/14
Pomoroy	PVT	31J/2	01A/14
De Berry	PVT	31J/2	01A/14
Pesk	PVT	31J/2	01A/14
Gilbertson	9SGT	—	26J/09
Tasille	7SGT	—	•
Flynn	7SGT	—	•
Mintner	6SGT	—	•
Raymond	6SGT	—	•
Goldsmith	5SGT	—	•
Sweeney	5SGT	—	•
Lyons	5SGT	—	•
Cavan	5SGT	—	•

Ford	MAJ	28J/2	29J/12A	West	TCH	—	.
Lynch	MAJ	28J/2	29J/12A	Lubhausel	TCH	—	.
Majors	MAJ	28J/2	29J/12A	Chin	TCH	—	.
Nestor	MAJ	28J/1	29J/12A	Yarrow	TCH	—	.
Perry	MAJ	28J/1	29J/12A	Spender	PVT	—	.
Roxy	MAJ	28J/1	29J/12A	Warren	PVT	—	.
Van Horn	MAJ	28J/1	29J/12A				

The size of the roster was familiar, a listing of the entire complement of Building 31, minus me. I'd probably seen it a hundred times a day in my old job.

The order of the listing was odd, since it had nothing to do with people's functions (I'd normally seen it as a duty roster), but it only took a minute to figure it out. The first five names were the mechanic guards whose soldierboys my platoon had taken over. Then a list of all the jacked officers, who had been jacked together since 26 July, presumably not all in one big group.

Likewise, the end of the roster was all of the jacked noncoms and privates, besides the guards. They also had been jacked together since day before yesterday. They would all theoretically come out of it on the 9th of August, cured of war.

In between those two groups, a list of the sixty-some who had spent all their lives up to now under the handicap of normality. The four doctors had been drilling since yesterday. It looked like team 1 was doing about five a day, and team 2—presumably the hotshots from the Canal Zone—were doing eight.

I heard Amelia moving in the bedroom, changing out of the clothes she'd slept in. She came out combing her hair and wearing a dress, a red-and-black Mexican thing I'd never seen.

"I didn't know you brought a dress."

"Dr. Spencer gave it to me; said he bought it for his wife, but it didn't fit her."

"Likely story."

She looked over my shoulder. "Lot of people."

"They're doing about a dozen a day, with two teams. I wonder whether they're sleeping at all."

"Well, they're eating." She checked her watch. "How far away is that mess hall?"

"Couple minutes."

"Why don't you change your shirt and shave?"

"For Marty?"

"For me." She plucked at my shoulder. "Shoo. I want to call Ellie again."

I scraped a quick shave and found a shirt that had one day's wear.

"Still no answer," Amelia said from the other room. "There's no one at the motel desk, either."

"You want to check with the Clinic? Or Jefferson's motel room?"

She shook her head and pushed the PR button. "After dinner. She's probably out." A copy of the roster drifted out of the slot; Amelia caught it, folded it, and put it in her purse. "Let's go find Marty."

the mess hall was small but, to Amelia's surprise, not totally automated. There were machines for some standard simple food, but also an actual food station with an actual cook, who Julian recognized.

"Lieutenant Thurman?"

"Julian. Still can't tolerate jacking, so I volunteered to step in for Sergeant Duffy. Don't get your hopes up, though; I can only cook four or five things." He looked at Amelia. "You would be . . . Amelia?"

"Blaze," Julian said, and introduced them. "Were you jacked with them for any length of time?"

"If you mean 'Are you in on it,' yes, I got the general idea. You did the math?" he asked Amelia.

"No, I did the particles; just tagged along behind Julian and Peter on the math."

He started tossing two salads.

"Peter, the cosmology guy," he said. "I saw about him on the news yesterday."

"Yesterday?" Julian said.

"You didn't hear? They found him wandering around dazed on some island." Thurman told them all he remembered about the news item.

"But he doesn't recall anything about the paper?" Amelia said.

"I guess not. Not if he thinks it's the year 2000. You think he can get it back?"

"Only if the people who took out the memory saved it," Julian said, "and that doesn't sound likely. Sounds like a pretty crude job."

"At least he's still alive," Amelia said.

"Not much good to us," Julian said, and caught a look from Amelia. "Sorry. True, though."

Thurman gave them their salads and started a couple of hamburgers. Marty came in and asked for the same.

They went to the end of a long empty table. Marty slumped into the chair and unpeeled a speedie from behind his ear. "Better sleep a few hours."

"How long you been on your feet?"

He looked at his watch without focusing on it. "I don't want to know. We're just about through with the colonels. Two Team's just up from a nap; they'll do Tomy and the topkick, what's his name?"

"Gilpatrick," Julian said. "He could use a little humanizing."

Thurman brought over Marty's salad. "That was a mess up in Guadalajara," he said. "The news came in from Jefferson just before I left the Twenty." Most of the communication between Guadalajara and Portobello was via jack circuit rather than conventional phone—you got through more information in less time, and everyone who was jacked would know sooner or later, anyhow.

"It was sloppy," Julian said. "They should have been more careful with that woman."

"That's for sure." Thurman went back to his hamburgers. Neither of them knew they were talking about two different incidents; they'd tried Thurman on the jack twice; he'd been in contact when the news came in about the killing rampage that ended in Ellie's murder.

"What woman?" Marty said between bites.

Julian and Amelia looked at each other. "You don't know about Gavrila. About Ray."

"Nothing. Is Ray in trouble?"

Julian took a breath and let it out. "He's dead, Marty."

Marty dropped his fork. "Ray?"

"Gavrila's a Hammer of God assassin who was sent down to kill Blaze. She smuggled a gun into an interrogation room and shot him."

"Ray?" he repeated. They'd been friends since graduate school. He was still and pale. "What will I tell his wife?" He shook his head. "I was best man."

"I don't know," Julian said. "You can't just say 'He gave his life for peace,' though it's true, in a way."

"It's also true that I dragged him away from his safe, comfortable office and put him in the way of a lunatic murderer."

Amelia took his hand in both of hers. "Don't worry about it now. Nothing you can do will change anything."

He stared at her blankly. "She's not expecting him back until the fourteenth. So maybe the universe will make it all irrelevant by exploding."

"More likely," Julian said, "he'll wind up just one in a long list of casualties. You might as well wait and announce them all after the shitstorm. After the bloodless revolution."

Thurman came over quietly and served them their hamburgers. He'd overheard enough to realize that they didn't yet know about Ellie's murder, and perhaps the fact that Gavrila was loose.

He decided not to tell them. They would know soon enough. There might be something in the delay that he could turn to his advantage.

Because he wasn't going to just stand around and let these lunatics wreck the military. He had to stop them, and he knew exactly where to go.

Through the migraine haze that kept him from communing with these misdirected idealists, some real information did bleed through. Like the identity of General Blaisdell, and his powerful position.

Blaisdell had the power to neutralize Building 31 with a phone call. Thurman had to get to him, and soon. "Gavrila" might do as a code word.

when we got back to our billet, there was a message on the console for Amelia, not me, to call Jefferson immediately on the secure line. He was in his own motel room in Guadalajara, eating dinner. He was wearing a handgun in a shoulder holster, a dart-thrower.

He stared out of the screen. "Sit down, Blaze." She eased herself slowly into the chair in front of the console. "I don't know how secure Building 31 is supposed to be. I don't think it's secure enough.

"Gavrila escaped. She's left a trail of bodies leading to you. She killed two people at the Clinic, and one of them she apparently had tortured into giving up your address."

"No . . . oh, no!"

Jefferson nodded. "She got there right after you left. We don't know what Ellie might have told her before she died."

That may have hit me harder than it did her. Amelia had lived with Ellie, but I had lived *inside* her.

She turned pale and spoke almost without moving her lips. "Tortured her."

"Yes. And went straight to the airport and took the next flight to Portobello. She's somewhere in the city now. You have to assume she knows exactly where you are."

"She couldn't get in here," I said.

"Tell me about it, Julian. She couldn't get *out* of here, either."

"Yeah, all right. Are you set up to jack?"

He gave me a cautious doctor look. "With you?"

"Of course not. With my platoon. They're standing guard here, and could use a description of the bitch."

"Of course. Sorry."

"You tell them everything you know, and then we'll go to Candi for a debriefing."

"All right . . . just remember Gavrila's been jacked with me two-way—"

"What? That was smart."

"We thought she'd be in a straitjacket for the duration. It was the only way to get anything from her, and we got a lot. But you have to assume she'll retain a lot of what she got from Spencer and me."

"She didn't retain my address," Amelia said.

Jefferson shook his head. "I didn't know it, and neither did Spencer, in case. But she knows the broad outline of the Plan."

"Damn. She'll have passed it on."

"Not yet. She has a superior in Washington, but she won't have talked to him yet. She idolizes him, and combining that with her rigid fanaticism . . . I don't think she'll call until she can say 'Mission accomplished.' "

"So we don't just stay away from her. We catch her and make sure she doesn't talk."

"Nail her into a room."

"Or a box," I said.

He nodded and broke the circuit.

"Kill her?" Amelia said.

"Won't be necessary. Just turn her over to the medicos and she'll sleep past D day." Probably true, I thought, but pretty soon Amelia and I were going to be the only people in this building physically *able* to kill.

what candi told them was frightening. Not only was Gavrila vicious and well trained and motivated by love and fear of God and His avatar, General Blaisdell— but it would be easier for her to get into Building 31 than Julian would have supposed. Its main defenses were against military attack and mob assault. It didn't even have a burglar alarm.

Of course she first would have to get onto the base. They sent descriptions of her in the two modes they knew of, and copies of her fingerprints and retina scans, to the gate, with strict detention orders—"armed and dangerous."

There were no security cameras in the Guadalajara airport, but there were plenty at Portobello. No one who looked like her had gotten off any of the six flights arriving from Mexico that afternoon and evening, but that could just mean a third disguise. There were a few women her size and shape. Their descriptions also went to the gate.

In fact, as Jefferson might have predicted, in her paranoia Gavrila bought a ticket to Portobello, but didn't use it. Instead, she flew to the Canal Zone disguised as a man. She went down to the waterfront and found a drunken soldier who resembled her, and killed him for his papers and uniform. She left most of the body in a hotel room, first cutting off the hands and head, wrapping them well, and mailing them at the cheapest rate to a fictitious address in Bolivia. She took the monorail

to Portobello and was inside the base an hour before
they started looking for her.

She didn't have her plastic gun and knife, of course;
she'd even left behind the scalpel she'd used on Ellie.
There were thousands of weapons inside the base, but
all were locked up and accounted for, except for a few
guards and MPs with pistols. Killing an MP sounded
like a bad way to get a weapon. She went down to the
armory and loitered for a while, inspecting it while ap-
pearing to read the notices on the bulletin board, then
waiting in line for a few minutes and rushing off as if
she'd forgotten something.

She went outside the building and then re-entered
through a back door. From the floor plan she'd memo-
rized, she went straight to ROUTINE MAINTENANCE.
There was a duty roster posted; she went to an adjacent
room and called the specialist on maintenance duty, and
told him a Major Feldman wanted to see him at the desk.
He left the room unlocked, and Gavrila slipped in.

She had perhaps ninety seconds. Find something le-
thal that looked like it worked and wouldn't be missed
immediately.

There was a jumbled pile of M-31s, mud-spattered but
otherwise in good shape. Probably used in an exercise—
by officers, who wouldn't be expected to clean them
afterward. She picked one and wrapped it in a green
towel, along with a cassette of exploding darts and a
bayonet. Poison darts would have been better, quieter,
but there weren't any in the open stock.

She slipped outside undetected. This didn't appear to
be the kind of base where a soldier could casually carry
a light assault weapon around, so she kept the M-31
wrapped up. She put the sheathed bayonet inside her
belt, under her shirt.

The binding that compressed her breasts was uncomfortable, but she left it on in case it would buy her an
extra second or two of surprise. The uniform was loose,

and she looked like a slightly chubby man, short with a barrel chest. She walked carefully.

Building 31 looked no different from the ones that surrounded it, except for a low electrified fence and a sentry box. She walked by the box in the dusk, fighting the temptation to rush the shoe guard and shoot her way in. She could do some real damage with the forty rounds in the cassette, but she knew from Jefferson that there would be soldierboy guards on duty. The black man Julian's platoon. Julian Class.

Dr. Jefferson hadn't known anything about the building's floor plan, though, which was what she needed now. If she knew where Harding was, she could create a diversion for the soldierboys as far as possible from her quarry, and then go after her. But the building was too large to just go in cold and hope to find her while the soldierboys were occupied for a few minutes.

They would be expecting her, too, of course. She didn't look at Building 31 as she walked by. They certainly knew about the torture-murders. Was there any way she could use that knowledge against them? Make them careless through fear?

Whatever action she took, it would have to be within the building. Otherwise, outside forces would deal with it, while Harding was protected by the soldierboys.

She stopped dead and then forced herself to move on. That was it! Create a diversion outside, but be inside when they find out about it. Follow the soldierboys to her prey.

Then she would need God's help. The soldierboys would be swift, though probably pacified, if the humanizing scheme had worked. She had to kill Harding before they restrained her.

But she was all confidence. The Lord had gotten her this far; He would not fail her now. Even the woman's name, Blaze, was demonic, as well as her mission. Everything was right.

She turned the corner and said a quiet prayer. A child was playing alone on the sidewalk. A gift from the Lord.

we were lying in bed talking when the console chimed its phone signal. It was Marty.

He was weary but smiling. "They called me out of surgery," he said. "Good news, for a change, from Washington. They did a segment on your theory on the *Harold Burley Hour* tonight."

"Supporting it?" Amelia said.

"Evidently. I just saw a minute of it; back to work. It should be linked to your data queue by now. Take a look." He punched off and we found the program immediately.

It started out with an optical of a galaxy exploding dramatically, sound effects and all. Then the profile of Burley, serious as usual, faded in, looking down on the cataclysm.

"Could this be us, only a month from now? Controversy rages in the highest scientific circles. And not only scientists have questions. The police do, too."

A still picture of Peter, bedraggled and forlorn, naked from the waist up, holding up a number for the police camera. "This is Peter Blankenship, who for two decades has been one of the most highly regarded cosmologists in the world.

"Today he doesn't even know the right number of planets in the Solar System. He thinks he's living in the year 2004—and is confused to be a twenty-year-old man in a sixty-four-year-old body.

"Someone jacked him and extracted all his past, back to that year. Why? What did he know? Here is Simone Mallot, head of the FBI's Forensic Neuropathology Unit." A woman in a white coat, with a jumble of gleaming equipment behind her. "Dr. Mallot, what can you tell us about the level of surgical technique used on this man?''

''The person who did this belongs in jail,'' she said. ''Subtle equipment was used, or misused; microscopic AI-directed investigation shows that they initially tried to erase specific, fairly recent, memories. But they failed repeatedly, and finally erased one huge block with a surge of power. It was the murder of a personality and, we know now, the destruction of a great mind.''

Beside me, Amelia sighed, almost a sob, but leaned forward, studying the console intently.

Burley peered directly out of the screen. ''Peter Blankenship did know something—or at least believed something, that profoundly affects you and me. He believed that unless we take action to stop it, the world will come to an end on September fourteenth.''

There was a picture of the Multiple Mirror Array on the far side of the Moon, irrelevant to anything, tracking ponderously. Then a time-lapse shot of Jupiter rotating. ''The Jupiter Project, the largest, most complex scientific experiment ever conducted. Peter Blankenship had calculations that showed it had to be stopped. But then he disappeared, and came back in no shape to testify about anything scientific.

''But his assistant, Professor Blaze Harding''—an inset of Amelia lecturing—''suspected foul play and herself disappeared. From a hiding place in Mexico she sent dozens of copies of Blankenship's theory, and the high hard mathematics behind it, to scientists all over the world. Opinions are divided.''

Back in his studio, Burley faced two men, one of them familiar.

''God, not Macro!'' Amelia said.

''I have with me tonight Professors Lloyd Doherty and Mac Roman. Dr. Doherty's a longtime associate of Peter Blankenship. Dr. Roman is the dean of sciences at the University of Texas, where Professor Harding works and teaches.''

''Teaching isn't work?'' I said, and she shushed me.

Macro settled back with a familiar self-satisfied expression. ''Professor Harding has been under a great deal of strain recently, including a love affair with one of her students as well as one with Peter Blankenship.''

''Stick to the science, Macro,'' Doherty said. ''You've read the paper. What do you think of it?''

''Why, it's . . . it's utterly fantastic. Ridiculous.''

''Tell me why.''

''Lloyd, the audience could never understand the mathematics involved. But the idea is absurd on the face of it. That the physical conditions that obtain inside something smaller than a BB could bring about the end of the universe.''

''People once said it was absurd to think that a tiny germ could bring about the death of a human being.''

''That's a false analogy.'' His ruddy face got darker.

''No, it's precise. But I agree with you about it not destroying the universe.''

Macro gestured at Burley and the camera. ''Well, then.''

Doherty continued. ''It would only destroy the Solar System, perhaps the Galaxy. A relatively small corner of the universe.''

''But it *would* destroy the Earth,'' Burley said.

''In less than an hour, yes.'' The camera came in close on him. ''There's no doubt about that.''

''But there *is*!'' Macro said, off camera.

Doherty gave him a weary look. ''Even if the doubt were reasonable, and it is not, what sort of odds would be acceptable? A fifty-fifty chance? Ten percent? One chance in a hundred that everyone would die?''

''Science doesn't work like that. Things aren't ten percent true.''

''And people aren't ten percent *dead*, either.'' Doherty turned to Burley. "The problem I found isn't with the first few minutes or even millenniums of the prediction. I just think they've made an error extrapolating into intergalactic space."

"Do tell," Burley said.

"Ultimately, the result would just be twice as much matter; twice as many galaxies. There's room for them."

"If one part of the theory is wrong—" Macro began.

"*Further*more," Doherty contined, "it looks as if this *has* happened before, in other galaxies. It actually clears up some anomalies here and there."

"Getting back to Earth," Burley said, "or at least to this solar system. How big a job would it be to stop the Jupiter Project? The largest experiment ever set up?"

"Nothing to it, in terms of science. Just one radio signal from JPL. Getting people to send a signal that will end their careers in science, that would normally be hard. But *everybody's* career ends September fourteenth, if they don't."

"It's still irresponsible nonsense," Macro said. "Bad science, sensationalism."

"You have about ten days to prove that, Mac. A long line is forming behind that button."

Close-up on Burley, shaking his head. "They can't turn it off too soon for me." The console went dead.

We laughed and hugged and split a ginger ale in celebration. But then the screen chimed and turned itself on without my hitting the answer button.

It was the face of Eileen Zakim, my new platoon leader. "Julian, we have a real situation. Are you armed?"

"No—well, yes. There's a pistol here." But it had been left behind, like the ginger ale; I hadn't checked to see if it was loaded. "What's up?"

"That crazy bitch Gavrila is here. Maybe inside. She killed a little girl out front in order to distract the shoe guard at the gate."

"Good grief! We don't have a soldierboy out front?"

"We do, but she patrols. Gavrila waited until the soldierboy was on the opposite side of the compound. The way we've reconstructed it, she slashed up the child and threw her, dying, up against the sentry box door. When the shoe opened the door, she cut his throat and then dragged him across the box and used his handprint to open the inner door."

I had the pistol out and threw the dead bolt on the door. "Reconstructed? You don't know for sure?"

"No way to tell; the inner door isn't monitored. But she did drag him back into the box, and if she's military, she knows how the handprint locks work."

I checked the pistol's magazine. Eight packs of tumblers. Each pack held 144 razor-sharp tumblers—each actually a folded, scored piece of metal that shatters into 144 pieces when you pull the trigger. They come out in a hail of fury that can chew off an arm or a leg.

"Now that she's in the compound—"

"We don't know that for sure."

"If she is, though, are there any more handprint locks? Any monitored entrances?"

"The main entrance is monitored. No handprints; just mechanical locks. My people are checking every door."

I winced a little at "my" people. "Okay. We're secure here. Keep us posted."

"Will do." The console went dark.

We both looked at the door. "Maybe she doesn't have anything that can get through that," Amelia said. "She used a knife on the child and guard."

I shook my head. "I think she did that for her own amusement."

gavrila huddled in a cabinet under a laundry sink, waiting, the M-31 cradled, ready to fire, and the guard's assault rifle digging into her ribs. She had come in through a service door that was open to the night air, and locked it behind her.

While she watched through a crack, her patience and foresight were rewarded. A soldierboy slipped silently up to the door, checked the lock, and moved on.

After one minute, she got out and stretched. She had to either find out where the woman was staying or find some way to destroy the whole building. But fast. She was ridiculously outnumbered, and in gaining the advantage of terror she had sacrificed the possibility of surprise.

There was a beat-up keyboard and console, gray plastic turning white with some kind of soap film, built into the wall. She went over to it and pushed a random letter, and it turned itself on. She typed in "directory" and was rewarded with a list of personnel. Blaze Harding wasn't there, but Julian Class was, at 8-1841. That looked like a phone number, rather than a room number.

Guessing, she rolled a pointer over to his name and clicked on it. That gave her 241, more useful. It was a two-story building.

A sudden loud rattling startled her. She spun around, pointing both weapons, but it was just an unattended washing machine that had been dormant while she was hidden.

She ignored the freight elevator and shouldered though a heavy FIRE EXIT door that opened on a dusty staircase. There didn't seem to be any security cameras. She climbed quickly and quietly up to the second floor.

She thought for a moment and left one of the weapons by the door on the landing. She only needed one for the kill. Besides, she'd be retreating fast, and might want an element of surprise. They would know she had the guard's assault rifle, but probably didn't know about the M-31 yet.

Opening the door a crack, she could see that the odd-numbered rooms were across from her, numbers increasing to the right. She closed her eyes for a deep breath and a silent prayer, and then burst through the door in a dead run, assuming there were cameras and soldierboys in her near future.

There were neither. She stopped at 241, took a fraction of a second to note the CLASS nameplate, leveled the assault rifle, and fired a silenced burst at the lock.

The door didn't open. She aimed six inches higher and this time blew out the dead bolt. The door opened a couple of inches and she kicked it the rest of the way.

Julian was standing there, in the shadow, holding the pistol straight out with both hands. She spun away instinctively as he fired, and the burst of razors that would have beheaded her instead just tore out a piece of her left shoulder. She fired two random blasts into the darkness—trusting God to guide them not to him, but to the white scientist she was there to punish—and leaped back out of the way of his second shot. Then she sprinted back to the stairwell and just got through the door as his third shot redecorated the hall.

There was a soldierboy waiting there, hulking huge at the top of the stairs. She knew from picking Jefferson's mind that the mechanic controlling it probably had been brainwashed so it couldn't kill her. She emptied the rest of the magazine into the thing's eyes.

The black man was shouting for her to throw out her weapon and come out with her hands up. All right. He was probably the only thing between her and the scientist.

She toed the door open, ignoring the soldierboy groping blindly behind her, and threw out the useless assault rifle. "Now come out slowly," the man said.

She took one moment to visualize her move while she eased back the arming lever of the M-31. Shoulder-roll across the corridor and then a continuous sweeping burst in his direction. She leaped.

It was all wrong. He got her before she hit the ground, an ungodly pain in her belly. She saw her own death happening, a thick spray of blood and entrails as her shoulder hit the floor and she tried to complete the roll but just slid. She managed to get up on her knees and elbows, and something slimy fell out of her body. She fell over facing him, and through a darkening haze raised the weapon toward him. He said something and the world ended.

i shouted "drop it!" but she ignored me, and the second shot disintegrated her head and shoulders. I fired again, reflexively, blowing apart the M-31 and the hand that was aiming it, and turning her chest into a bright red cavity. Behind me, Amelia made a choking sound and ran to the bathroom to vomit.

I had to stare. She didn't even look human, from the waist up; just a messy montage of butchered meat and rags. The rest of her was unaffected. For some reason I held up my hand to block out the gore and was a little horrified to see that her lower body was in a relaxed, casually seductive pose.

A soldierboy slowly pushed the door open. The sensory apparatuses were a chewed-up mess. "Julian?" it said in Candi's voice. "I can't see. Are you all right?"

"I'm okay, Candi. I think it's over. Backup coming?"

"Claude. He's downstairs."

"I'll be in the room." I walked back through the door on automatic pilot. I'd almost meant it when I said I was okay. I just turned a human being into a pile of steaming meat, hey, all in a day's work.

Amelia had left the water running after washing her face. She hadn't quite made it to the toilet, and was trying to clean up the mess with a towel. I set down the pistol and helped her to her feet. "You lie down, honey. I'll take care of this."

She was weeping. She nodded into my shoulder and let me guide her to the bed.

After I cleaned it up and threw the towels into the recycler, I sat on the end of the bed and tried to think. But I couldn't get past the horrible sight of the woman bursting open three times, each time I pulled the trigger.

When she silently threw the rifle out, for some reason I knew she would come through the door shooting. I had a sight picture and the trigger halfway pulled when she leaped out into the corridor.

I'd heard a pattering sound, which must have been her silenced weapon blinding Candi. And then when she threw it out without hesitation, I guess I assumed it was empty and she had another weapon.

But the way I felt as I eased down on the trigger and waited for her to show herself . . . I had never felt that way in the soldierboy. Ready.

I really wanted her to come out and die. I really wanted to kill her.

Had I changed that much in a few weeks? Or was it actually change? The boy was a different case, an "industrial accident" that I didn't completely cause, and if I could bring him back, I would.

I wouldn't bring Gavrila back except to kill her again.

For some reason I remembered my mother, and her rage when President Brenner was assassinated. I was four. She hadn't liked Brenner at all, I learned later, and that made it worse, as if she had some complicity in the crime. As if the murder were some kind of wish fulfillment.

But that wasn't close to the personal hate I felt for Gavrila—besides, she was almost not human. It was like disposing of a vampire. A vampire who was single-mindedly stalking the woman you loved.

Amelia was quiet now. "I'm sorry you saw that. It was pretty awful."

She nodded, face still buried in the pillow. "At least it's over. That part's over."

I rubbed her back and murmured agreement. We didn't know how Gavrila—like the vampire—was going to return from her grave to kill again.

in the guadalajara airport, Gavrila had written a short note to General Blaisdell and put it in an envelope with his home address. She put that in another envelope, addressed to her brother, with instructions to send it on unread if Gavrila didn't call by tomorrow morning.

This is what it said: *If you haven't heard from me by now, I'm dead. The man in charge of the group that killed me is MG Stanton Roser, the most dangerous man in America. An eye for an eye?*

Gavrila.

After she had sent that one, she realized it wasn't enough, and on the plane she scribbled another two pages, trying to set down everything she could remember from the minutes when she'd been able to see into Jefferson's mind. Luck was on the other side for that one, though. She dropped it in a mailbox in the Canal Zone and it was automatically routed through Army Intelligence, where a bored tech sergeant read part of it and recycled it as crank mail.

But she hadn't been the only one on the wrong side who had been exposed to the Plan. Lieutenant Thurman heard of Gavrila's death a few minutes after it happened, and put two and two together, and changed into his dress uniform and slipped out into the night. He got by the sentry box with no problem. The shoe who had been pressed into service to replace the one Gavrila had murdered was just this side of catatonic. He passed Thurman through with a rigid salute.

He didn't have any money for a commercial flight, so he had to gamble on using the military. If the wrong person asked for his travel orders, or if he had to go through a retinal scan for security, that would be it— not just AWOL, but fleeing from administrative detention.

A combination of luck and bluff and planning worked, though. He got off the base just by getting aboard a supply chopper that was returning to the Canal Zone. He knew that the CZ had been in bureaucratic chaos for months, ever since it had seceded from Panama and become a U.S. Territory. The Air Force base there was not exactly overseas and not exactly stateside, either. He wait-listed himself on a flight to Washington, misspelling his name, and a half hour later flashed his picture ID and rushed aboard.

He arrived at Andrews Air Force Base at dawn, had a big free breakfast at the Transient Officers' Mess, and then loitered around until nine-thirty. Then he called General Blaisdell.

Lieutenant's bars don't move you through the Pentagon's switchboards very fast. He told two civilians, two sergeants, and a fellow lieutenant that he had a personal message for General Blaisdell. Finally, he wound up with a bird colonel who was his administrative assistant.

She was an attractive woman a few years older than Thurman. She eyed him suspiciously. "You're calling from Andrews," she said, "but my board says you're stationed in Portobello."

"That's right. I'm on compassionate leave."

"Hold your orders up to the lens."

"They aren't here." He shrugged. "My luggage went missing."

"You *packed* your orders?"

"By mistake."

"That could be an expensive mistake, lieutenant. What is this message for the general?"

"With all due respect, colonel, it's very personal."

"If it's that personal, you'd better put it in a letter and mail it to his home. I pass on everything that goes through this office."

"Please. Just tell him it's from his sister—"

"The general doesn't have a sister."

"His sister *Gavrila*," he pressed on. "She's in trouble."

Her head jerked up suddenly and she spoke beyond the screen. "Yes, sir. Immediately." She pushed a button and her face was replaced by the green DARPA sigil. A shimmering encryption bar appeared over it, and then it dissolved to the general's face. He looked kind, grandfatherly.

"Do you have security on your end?"

"No, sir. It's a public phone. But there's no one around."

He nodded. "You spoke with Gavrila?"

"Indirectly, sir." He looked around. "She was captured and had a jack installed. I jacked briefly with her captors. She's dead, sir."

He didn't change expression. "Did she complete her assignment?"

"If that was to get rid of the scientist, no, sir. She was killed in the attempt."

While they were talking, the general made two unobtrusive hand gestures, recognition signals for Enders and for Hammer of God. Of course Thurman didn't respond to either one. "Sir, there's a huge conspiracy—"

"I know, son. Let's continue this conversation face-to-face. I'll send my car down for you. You'll be paged when it arrives."

"Yes, sir," he said to a blank screen.

Thurman drank coffee for most of an hour, looking at the paper without actually reading it. Then he was paged and told that the general's limousine was waiting for him in the arrivals area.

He went there and was surprised to see that the limo had a human driver, a small young female tech sergeant in dress greens. She opened the back door for him. The windows were opaque mirrors.

The seats were deep and soft but covered with uncomfortable plastic. The driver didn't say a word to him, but did turn on some music, soft-drift jazz. She didn't drive, either, other than pushing a button. She read from an old-fashioned paper Bible and ignored the numbing monotony of the huge gray Grossman modules that housed a tenth of a million people each. Thurman was kind of fascinated by them. Who would live that way voluntarily? Of course most of them were probably government draftees, just marking time until their term of service was up.

They traveled alongside a river, in a greenbelt, for several miles, and then went spiraling up an entrance ramp to a broad highway that led to the Pentagon, which was actually two pentagons—the smaller historical building nested inside the one where most of the work was actually done. He could only see the whole structure for a few seconds, and then the car banked down a long arc of concrete toward its home.

The limousine came to a stop outside a loading bay, identified only by the flaking yellow letters BLKRDE21. The driver put her Bible down and got out and opened Thurman's door. "Please follow me, sir."

They went through an automatic door straight into an elevator, whose walls were an infinite regression of mirrors. The driver put her hand on a touchplate and said "General Blaisdell."

The elevator crawled for about a minute, while Thurman studied a million Thurmans going off in four directions, and tried not to stare at the various attractive angles of his escort. A Bible-thumper, not his type. Nice butt, though.

The doors opened to a silent and spare reception room. The sergeant went behind the desk and turned on a console. "Tell the general that Lieutenant Thurman is here." There was a whisper and she nodded. "Come with me, sir."

The next room was more like a major general's office. Wood paneling, actual paintings on the walls, a pic window that displayed Mount Kilimanjaro. One wall of awards and citations and holos of the general with four presidents.

The old gentleman rose gracefully from behind his acre of uncluttered desk. He was obviously athletic and had a twinkle in his eye.

"Lieutenant, please sit over here." He indicated one of a pair of leather-upholstered easy chairs. He looked at the sergeant. "And bring in Mr. Carew."

Thurman sat uneasily, "Sir, I'm not sure how many people ought to—"

"Oh, Mr. Carew's a civilian, but we can trust him. He's an information specialist. He'll jack with you and save us all kinds of time."

Thurman had a premonitory migraine glow. "Sir, is that absolutely necessary? Jacking—"

"Oh yes, yes. The man's a jack witness in the federal court system. He's a marvel, a real marvel."

The marvel came in without speaking. He looked like a wax replica of himself. Formal tunic and string tie.

"Him," he said, and the general nodded. He sat down in the other chair and pulled two jack cables from a box on the table between him and Thurman.

Thurman opened his mouth to explain, but then just plugged in. Carew followed suit.

Thurman stiffened and his eyes rolled back. Carew stared at him with interest and started breathing hard, sweat dotting his forehead.

After a few minutes he unplugged, and Thurman sagged into relieved unconsciousness. "That was hard on him,'' Carew said, ''but I have a great deal of interesting information.''

''Have it all?'' the general said.

''All we need and more.''

Thurman started to cough and slowly levered himself into a normal sitting position. He clamped his forehead with one hand and massaged a temple with the other. ''Sir . . . could I ask for a Pain-go?''

''Certainly . . . sergeant?'' She went out and returned with a glass of water and a pill.

He gulped it down gratefully. ''Now . . . sir. What do we do next?''

''The next thing *you* do, son, is get some rest. The sergeant will take you to a hotel.''

''Sir, I don't have a ration book, or any money. It's all back in Portobello; I was under detention.''

''Don't worry. We'll take care of everything.''

''Thank you, sir.'' The headache was retreating, but he had to close his eyes at the mirrored elevator car, or face the prospect of watching himself puke a thousand times at once.

The limousine hadn't moved. He slid gratefully onto the soft slick plastic.

The driver closed his door and got in the front. ''This hotel,'' he asked her, ''are we going all the way downtown?''

''No,'' she said, and started the engine. ''Arlington.'' She turned and raised a silenced .22 automatic and shot him once in the left eye. He clawed for the door handle and she leaned over and shot him again, point-blank in the temple. She made a face at the mess and pushed the button that directed the car to the cemetery.

marty dropped his bombshell by bringing a friend to breakfast. We were eating out of the machines,

as usual for the morning meal, when Marty walked in
with someone whom I didn't at first recognize. He
smiled, though, and I remembered the diamond set into
his front tooth.

"Private Benyo?" He was one of the mechanic
guards replaced by my old platoon.

"In the flesh, sarge." He shook hands with Amelia
and introduced himself, then sat down and poured a cup
of coffee.

"So what's the story?" I asked. "It didn't take?"

"Nope." He grinned again. "What it didn't take was
two weeks."

"What?"

"It doesn't take two weeks," Marty said. "Benyo is
humanized, and so are all the others."

"I don't get it."

"Your stabilizer, Candi, was in the loop. That's what
did it! It only takes about two days, if you're jacked
with somebody who's already humanized."

"But . . . then why did it take the whole two weeks
with Jefferson?"

Marty laughed. "It *didn't*! He was one of them after
a couple of days, but people didn't recognize it, since
he was the first—and he was ninety percent there from
the beginning. Everybody, Jefferson included, was concentrating on Ingram, not him."

"But then you take a guy like me," Benyo said,
"who hates the idea from the very start—and wasn't
exactly a sweetheart to begin with—hell, *everybody*
could tell when *I* converted."

"And you *are* converted?" Amelia said. He got a
serious look and nodded in jerks. "You don't feel re-
sentful about . . . losing the man you used to be?"

"It's hard to explain. What I am now *is* the man I
used to be. But more me than I used to be, get it?" He
made a helpless gesture with both hands. "What I mean

is I never in a million years could've found out who I really was, even though it was there all the time. I needed the others to show me."

She smiled and shook her head. "It sounds like a religious conversion."

"It is, sort of," I said. "It literally was, with Ellie." I shouldn't have said that; she started to cloud up. I put my hand on hers.

For a moment everyone was silent. "So," Amelia said. "What does this do to the timetable?"

"If we'd known before the thing started, it would've sped it up considerably—and of course it will do that in the long run, when we're out to change the world.

"Right now the limiting factor is the surgery schedule. We plan to finish the last set of implants on the thirty-first. So by the third of August, we should have a building-full of converts, general to private."

"What about the POWs?" I asked. "McLaughlin didn't convert them in two days, did he?"

"Again, if we'd only known. He was never jacked with them for more than a few hours at a time. It would be good to know whether it does work with thousands of people at once."

"How do you know it's one or the other?" Amelia said. "Two weeks if they're all just 'normal' people; two days if one of the elect is with them all the time. You don't know anything about intermediate states."

"That's right." He rubbed his eyes and grimaced. "And no time to experiment. There's some fascinating science to be done, but as we said up at St. Bart's, we're not doing science quite yet." His phone pinged. "Just a second."

He touched his earring and listened, staring. "Okay . . . I'll get back to you. Yes." He shook his head.

"Trouble?" I asked.

"Could be nothing; could be disaster. We've lost our cook."

That took me a moment. "Thurman's gone AWOL?"

"Yep. He cruised right past the guard last night, right after you . . . after Gavrila died."

"No idea where he went?"

"He could be anywhere in the world. Could be downtown living it up. You jacked with him, Benyo?"

"Huh-uh. But Monez did, and I'm with Monez all the time. So I got a little. Not much, you know, his headaches."

"Do you have any secondhand impression of him?"

"Just a guy." He rubbed his chin. "I guess he was a little more army than most. I mean he kind of liked the idea."

"He didn't much like *our* idea, then."

"I don't know. I'd guess not."

Marty looked at his watch. "I'm due in surgery in twenty minutes. Be doing jacks until one. Julian, you want to track him down?"

"Do what I can."

"Benyo, you jack with Monez and whoever else was with Thurman. We have to know how much he knows."

"Sure." He stood up. "I think he's down by the game room."

We watched him go. "At least he couldn't have known who the general was."

"Not Roser," Marty said. "But he might have gotten the name of Gavrila's boss, Blaisdell, through one of the people in Guadalajara. That's what I want to find out." He checked his watch again. "Call Benyo about it in an hour or so. And check all the flights to Washington."

"Do what I can, Marty. Once he's out of Porto, hell, there must be ten thousand ways to get to Washington."

"Yeah, right. Maybe we should just wait and see whether we hear from Blaisdell."

We were about to.

blaisdell spent a few minutes talking to Carew—
the actual "download" of information from the jack session would take several hours' patient interrogation under hypnosis, by machine, but he did learn that there were a couple of days unaccounted for, between the time Gavrila was jacked in Guadalajara and her death more than a thousand miles away. What did she learn that sent her to Portobello?

He stayed in the office until he got the coded message from his driver that matters had been disposed of, and then he drove himself home—an eccentricity that sometimes was useful.

He lived alone, with robot servants and soldierboy guards, in a mansion on the Potomac less than a half hour's drive from the Pentagon. An eighteenth-century home with original exposed timbers and a wooden floor buckled with age, it was consistent with his image of himself—a man destined from birth, privileged birth, to change the history of the world.

And now his destiny was to end it.

He poured his daily ounce of whiskey into a crystal snifter and sat down to the mail. When he turned on the console, before the index came up, a blinker told him he had paper mail waiting.

Odd. He asked the wheelie to fetch it, and it brought back a single letter, no return address, postmarked from Kansas City that morning. It was interesting, considering the intimacy of some aspects of their relationship, that he didn't recognize Gavrila's handwriting on the envelope.

He read the short message twice and then burned it. Stanton Roser the most dangerous man in America? How unlikely, and how convenient: they had a golf date Saturday morning at the Bethesda Country Club. Golf could be a dangerous game.

He bypassed his mail and opened up the line to his computer at work. "Good evening, general," it said in a carefully modulated sexless voice.

"List for me every project rated 'secret' or above that has been initiated in the past month—no, eight weeks—by the Office of Force Management and Personnel. Delete any that have no connection to General Stanton Roser."

There were only three projects on the list; he was surprised at how little of Roser's work was classified. But one of those "projects" was essentially a file of miscellaneous classified actions, with 248 entries. He tabled that one and looked at the other two, separated because they were Top Top Secret.

They were apparently unrelated, except that both projects had been initiated the same day, and—aha!—both were in Panama. One was a pacification experiment on the detainees in a POW camp; the other, a management evaluation scheme at Fort Howell in Portobello.

Why hadn't Gavrila given more details? Damn the woman's flair for the dramatic.

When had she gone to Panama? That was easy enough to check. "Show me all the DARPA travel voucher requests for the past two days."

Interesting. She had bought a ticket to Portobello under a female code name and one to the Canal Zone under a male code name. Which flight did she actually take? The note had been on Aeromexico stationery, but that was no help; both flights used that carrier.

Well, which identity had she used in Guadalajara? The computer said that neither code name had flown into the city in the past two weeks, but it was a good assumption that she wouldn't have gone through the inconvenience of masquerading as a male while she was tracking down that woman. Therefore it was likely that she did cross-dress to elude detection on the flight down.

Why Panama, why the Canal Zone, why the connection with mousy old Stanton? Why didn't she just come back to the States, after the damned woman's theory about the Jupiter Project was splashed all over the news?

Well, he knew the answer to the last one. Gavrila watched the news so seldom she probably didn't even know who was president. As if the country *had* an actual president nowadays.

Of course, the Canal Zone could have been a feint. She could get to Portobello from there in minutes. But why would she want to go to either place?

Roser was the key. Roser was protecting the scientist by hiding her in one of those two bases. "Give me a list of noncombat deaths of Americans in Panama over the past twenty-four hours."

All right: there were two at Fort Howell, a male private who was "KILODNC"—killed in the line of duty, noncombat—and an unidentified female, homicide. Details available, no surprise, on a need-to-know basis from the Office of Force Management and Personnel.

He touched the KILODNC, which was not restricted, and found that the man had been murdered while standing guard at the central administration building. That must have been Gavrila's work.

A soft chime and a picture of the interrogator, Carew, appeared in the corner of the screen. He touched it and a hundred-thousand-word hypertext report appeared. He sighed and decided to have a second ounce of whiskey, in coffee.

we were going to be a little crowded in Building 31. The people in Guadalajara were too vulnerable; there was no telling how many nutcases like Gavrila might be available to Blaisdell. So our administrative experiment suddenly needed a couple of dozen civilian consultants, the Saturday Night Special crowd and the Twenty. Alvarez stayed behind with the nanoforge, but everybody else got away within twenty-four hours.

I wasn't sure it was a good idea—after all, Gavrila had killed almost as many people here as she had in Guadalajara. But the guards were *really* on guard now; three soldierboys patrolling instead of one.

It did simplify the humanization schedule. We had been set up to use the Twenty one at a time, by way of the secure phone line at the Guadalajara clinic. Once they were physically inside Building 31, we could use them four at a time, in rotation.

I wasn't looking forward to the Twenty arriving so much as I was the others—my old friends who now shared with me an inability to read minds. Everybody who was jacked was completely caught up in this huge project, in which Amelia and I were reduced to the status of retarded helpers. It was good to be around people with a few ordinary, noncosmic problems. People who had time for my *own* ordinary problems. Like becoming a murderer for a second time. No matter how much she deserved it, and had brought it on herself, it was still my finger on the trigger, my head full of the indelible image of her last horrifying moments.

I didn't want to bring it up with Amelia, not now, maybe not for a long time.

Reza and I were sitting out on the lawn at night, trying to pick out a few stars hidden in the glare and haze from the city.

"It couldn't possibly have bothered you as much as the boy," he said. "If anybody ever had it coming to them, she did."

"Oh, hell," I said, and opened a second beer. "At a visceral level, it doesn't make any difference who they were or what they did. The kid just got a red spot on his chest and fell over dead. Gavrila, I sprayed her guts and brains and fucking *arms* all over the corridor."

"And you keep thinking about it."

"Can't help it." The beer was still cool. "Every time my stomach growls or I get a little pain down there, I can see her bursting open. Knowing I have the same stuff inside."

"But it's not as if you've never seen it before."

"Never *caused* seeing it before. Big difference."

There was an awkward silence. Reza ran a fingertip around the rim of his wineglass, but it just hissed. "So are you going to try it again?"

I almost said *Try what again?* but Reza knew me better than that. "I don't think so. Who ever knows? Until you die of something else, you can always kill yourself."

"Hey, I never thought of it quite that way. Thanks."

"Thought you needed cheering up."

"Yeah, right." He licked his finger and tried the glass again, with no result. "Hey, is this an army-issue wineglass? How you guys expect to win a war without decent glassware?"

"We learn to rough it."

"So are you taking medicine?"

"Antidepressants, yeah. I don't think I'm going to do it."

I was startled to realize I hadn't thought about suicide all day, until Reza brought it up. "Things have to get better."

I spilled my beer hitting the dirt. Then the sound registered with Reza—machine-gun fire—and he joined me on the ground.

the defense advanced research Projects Agency does not have any combat troops. But Blaisdell *was* a major general, and among his secret coreligionists was Philip Cramer, the vice president of the United States.

Cramer's primacy on the National Security Council, especially in light of the absence of oversight from the most feckless president since Andrew Johnson, allowed him to grant Blaisdell authority for two outrageous actions. One was the temporary military occupation of the Jet Propulsion Laboratories in Pasadena, essentially preventing anybody from pushing the button that would end the Jupiter Project. The other was an "expeditionary force" under his control in Panama, a country with which the United States was not at war. While the senators and justices blustered and postured over these two blatantly illegal actions, the soldiers involved locked and loaded and went forth to follow orders.

The JPL action was trivially easy. A convoy pulled up at three A.M. and chased out all the night workers, and then locked the place up tight. Lawyers rejoiced, as did America's persistent antimilitary minority. Some scientists felt the celebration was premature. If the soldiers stayed in place for a couple of weeks, constitutional issues would become irrelevant.

Attacking an actual army base was not so simple. A brigadier general filed a battle order and died seconds later, personally disposed of by General Blaisdell. It sent a hunter/killer platoon, along with a support company, on a short hop from Colón to Portobello, supposedly to put down an insurrection by traitorous American troops. For security reasons, they of course were forbidden to contact the Portobello base, and they knew very little other than the fact that the insurrection was limited to the central command building. They were to take control of it and await orders.

The major in charge sent back a query as to why, if the insurrection was so limited, they hadn't given the assignment to a company that was already on the base. There was no answer, the general being dead, so the major had to assume that all of the base was potentially hostile. The map showed that Building 31 was conveniently close to the water, so he improvised an amphibious attack: the soldierboys waded into the water at a deserted beach north of the base, and walked underwater for a few miles.

Moving through water so close to the shore, they eluded submarine defenses, a deficiency the major recorded for his eventual report.

i could hardly believe what I was seeing: soldierboy versus soldierboy. Two of the machines had come up out of the water and were crouching on the beach, blasting away at two of the guard soldierboys. The other guard machine was hanging back around the corner of the building, ready to join in but keeping an eye on the front.

Nobody had noticed us, evidently. I shook Reza's shoulder to get his attention—he was transfixed by the pyrotechnics of the duel—and whispered, "Stay down! Follow me!"

We low-crawled to a line of shrubs and then ran crouched over to the building's front door. The shoe guard down by the gate saw us and fired a warning shot—or a badly aimed one—over our heads. I yelled "Arrowhead!" at him, the day's password, and it evidently worked. He shouldn't have been looking in our direction anyway, but I could lecture him on that some other time.

We piled through the narrow door together like a pair of slapstick comics and confronted a blind soldierboy, the one Gavrila had damaged. We hadn't sent it out for repair because we didn't want to anwer questions, and four soldierboys seemed like plenty. Before we found ourselves in the middle of a war.

"Password," somebody yelled. I said "Arrowhead"

and Reza, helpfully, said "Arrowsmith," a movie I missed. Close enough, though. The woman who was kneeling behind the reception desk, acting as eyes for the soldierboy, waved us on.

We crouched down next to her. I was out of uniform. "I'm Sergeant Class. Who's in charge?"

"God, I don't know. Sutton, maybe. She's the one who told me to come down here and spot for the thing." There were two loud explosions out back. "Do you know what the hell's going on?"

"We're being attacked by friendlies, is all I know. That, or the enemy has finally gotten soldierboys."

Whatever was happening, I realized that the attackers had to move fast. Even if there weren't any other soldierboys in the base, we should have flyboys any minute.

She was thinking along the same lines. "Where are the flyboys? They should be scrambled by now."

That's right; they were always on duty, always plugged in. Was it possible they had been taken over? Or had orders not to interfere?

There wasn't anything like an "operations room" in Building 31, since they never actually directed battles from there. The sergeant said that Lieutenant Sutton was in the mess hall, so we headed there. A windowless basement room, it was probably as safe as anywhere, if the soldierboys started to take the building apart.

Sutton was sitting at a table with Colonel Lyman and Lieutenant Phan, who were both jacked. Marty and General Pagel, both jacked, were at another table, with Top, Chief Master Sergeant Gilpatrick, anxiously fidgeting. There were a couple of dozen shoes and unjacked mechanics crouched around with weapons, waiting. I spotted Amelia with a crowd of civilians underneath a heavy metal serving table and waved.

Pagel unjacked and handed the cable to Top, who plugged in. "What's going on, sir?" I asked.

Surprisingly, he recognized me. "I can't tell much,

Sergeant Class. They're Alliance troops, but we can't make contact. It's like they came from Mars. And we can't raise Battalion or Brigade.

"Mr. Larrin—Marty—is trying to subvert their command structure, the way he did here, through Washington. We have ten mechanics waiting on-line, though not in cages."

"So they could take control, but not do anything fancy."

"Walk around, use simple weapons. Maybe all they have to do is make the soldierboys just stand there, or lie down. Anything but attack."

"Our flyboy and waterboy communications have been cut off, apparently right at this building." He pointed at the other table. "Lieutenant Phan's trying to patch through."

There was another explosion, powerful enough to rattle dishes. "You'd think someone would notice."

"Well, everybody knows the compound's isolated for a top-secret simulation exercise. All this commotion could be special training effects."

"Until they actually vaporize us," I said.

"If they'd intended to destroy the building, they could have done that in the first second of the engagement."

Top unplugged. "Shit. Pardon me, sir." There was a huge crash upstairs. "We're dead meat. Four soldierboys against ten, we never had a chance."

"Had?" I said.

Marty unjacked. "They got all four. They're inside."

A glossy black soldierboy clomped up to the mess hall door, bristling with weapons. It could kill us all in an instant. I didn't move a muscle, except for an eyelid twitching uncontrollably.

Its contralto voice was loud enough to hurt the ears. "If you follow orders there is no reason for anyone to be hurt. Everyone with weapons, place them on the floor. Everyone move to the wall opposite me, leaving your hands visible." I backed up with my hands in the air.

The general stood up a little too fast, and both laser and machine-gun barrels swiveled to target him. "I'm Brigadier General Pagel, the ranking officer here—"

"Yes. Your identity is verified."

"You know you are going to be court-martialed for this? That you'll spend the rest of your life—"

"Sir, begging your pardon, but I am under orders to disregard the rank of anyone in this building. My orders come from a major general, who I understand will be here eventually. I respectfully suggest you wait to discuss it with him."

"So are you going to shoot me if I don't go to that wall with my hands up?"

"No, sir. I'll fill the room with vomiting agent and not kill anyone unless they touch a weapon."

Top turned pale. "Sir . . ."

"All right, Top. I've had a sniff of it myself." The general sulked back to the wall with his hands in his pockets.

Two more soldierboys rolled up behind her, along with a couple of dozen people from other floors, and I heard the faint sound of a cargo helicopter apporaching; then a small flyboy. They both landed on the roof and went silent.

"Is that your general?" Pagel said.

"I wouldn't know, sir." After a minute a bunch of shoes came in, ten and then another dozen. They were wearing camouflage coveralls with head nets, no insignia or unit markings. That could make you nervous. They stacked their own weapons in the hall outside, and gathered armloads from the floor.

One of them stepped out of his coveralls and tossed away the head covering. He was bald except for a few strands of white hair. He looked kindly in spite of his major general's uniform.

He stepped up to General Pagel and they exchanged salutes. "I want to speak to Dr. Marty Larrin."

"General Blaisdell, I presume," Marty said.

He walked over to him and smiled. "We have to speak, of course."

"Of course. Maybe we can convert one another."

He looked around and stared at me. "You're the black physicist. The murderer." I nodded. Then he pointed at Amelia. "And Dr. Harding. I want all of you to come with me."

On his way out, he tapped the first soldierboy. "Come along for my protection," he said, smiling. "Let's go talk in Dr. Harding's office."

"I don't really have an office," she said, "just a room." She seemed to be straining not to look at me. "Room 241."

We did have a weapon there. Did she think I could outdraw a soldierboy? Excuse me, general; let me open this drawer and see what I find. Oops, fried Julian.

But it might be the only chance we'd have at him.

The soldierboy was too big for all of us to fit in the freight elevator, so we walked up the stairs. Blaisdell led at a quick pace. Marty got a little winded.

The general was obviously disappointed that room 241 wasn't full of test tubes and blackboards. He consoled himself with a ginger ale from the cooler.

"I suppose you're curious about my plan," he said.

"Not really," Marty said. "It's a fantasy. No way you can prevent the inevitable."

He laughed, quiet amusement rather than a madman's cackle. "I have JPL."

"Oh, come on."

"It's true. Presidential order. There are no scientists there tonight. Just my loyal troops."

"All of them Hammer of God?" I asked.

"All the leaders," he said. "The others are just a cordon, to keep the world of unbelievers away."

"You seem like a normal person," Amelia said, lying through her teeth. "Why would you want all this beautiful world to end?"

"You don't really think I'm normal, Dr. Harding, but you're wrong. You atheists in your ivory towers, you don't have any idea how real people feel. How perfect this is."

"Killing everything," I said.

"You're worse than she is. This is not death; it's *rebirth*. God has used you scientists as tools, so He can cleanse everything and start over."

It did make a crazy kind of sense. "You're nuts," I said.

The soldierboy swiveled to face me. "Julian," it said in a deep voice, "I'm Claude." There was an uncertain tremor to his movements that said he wasn't in a cage, warmed up, but was operating the soldierboy from a remote jack.

"What's going on here?" Blaisdell said.

"The transfer algorithm worked," Marty said. "Your people aren't in control of the soldierboys. Ours are."

"I know that's not possible," he said. "The safeguards—"

Marty laughed. "That's right. The safeguards against transfer of control are profoundly complex and powerful. I should know. I put them there."

Blaisdell looked at the soldierboy. "Soldier. Leave this room."

"Don't, Claude," Marty said. "We may need you."

It stayed put, rocking slightly. "That was a direct order from a major general," Blaisdell said.

"I know who you are, sir."

Blaisdell made a leap for the door, surprisingly fast. The soldierboy reached to grab his arm but punched him down instead. He shoved him back into the room.

He stood up slowly and brushed himself off. "So you're one of these humanized ones."

"That's right, sir."

"You think that gives you the right to disregard orders from your superiors?"

"No, sir. But my orders include assessing your actions, and orders, as those of a man who is mentally ill, and not responsible."

"I can still have you *shot*!"

"I suppose you could, sir, if you could find me."

"Oh, I know where you people are. The mechanics' cages for this building's guards are in the basement, in the northeast corner." He pinched his earring. "Major Lejeune. Come in." He pinched it again. "Come in."

"Nothing gets out of this room but static, sir, except on my frequency."

"Claude," I said, "why don't you just go ahead and kill him?"

"You know I can't do that, Julian."

"You could kill him to save your own life."

"Yes, but his threat to find my cage is not realistic. In fact, my body is not there."

"But look. He's proposing to kill not only you, but everybody else in the world. In the universe."

"Shut up, sergeant," Blaisdell snarled.

"You couldn't have a more clear-cut case of self-defense if he was standing with a gun at your head."

The soldierboy was silent for a long moment, weapons at its side. The laser came up partway and fell back. "I can't, Julian. Even though I don't disagree with you, I can't kill him in cold blood."

"Suppose I ask you to leave the room," I said. "Go stand in the corridor. Could you do that?"

"Of course." It staggered outside, taking off a piece of the doorjamb with its shoulder.

"Amelia . . . Marty . . . please go out there, too." I pulled open the top drawer of the bureau. The tumbler pistol had two rounds left. I took it out.

Amelia saw the gun and started to stammer something.

"Just go outside for minute." Marty put his arm
around her and they stepped awkwardly, crabwise,
through the door.

Blaisdell stood up straight. "So. I take it you're not
one of them. The humanized."

"Actually, I'm partway there. At least I understand
them."

"Yet you'd kill a man for his religious beliefs."

"I'd kill my own dog if it had rabies." I clicked the
safety off.

"What kind of devil are you?"

The aiming laser spot danced on the center of his
chest. "I'm finding out." I squeezed the trigger.

the soldierboy didn't interfere when Julian fired
and almost literally blew Blaisdell into two pieces. Part
of the body knocked over a lamp and the room was in
darkness except for the light from the corridor. Julian
stood rigid, listening to the wet sounds of the corpse
settling.

The soldierboy glided in behind him. "Let me have
the gun, Julian."

"No. It's of no use to you."

"I'm afraid for you, old friend. Give me the
weapon."

Julian turned in the half-light. "Oh. I see." He stuck
the pistol in his belt. "Don't worry, Claude. I'm okay
with that."

"Sure?"

"Sure enough. Pills, maybe. Guns, no." He walked
around the soldierboy and into the hall. "Marty. How
many people do we have who aren't humanized?"

It took Marty a minute to find the composure to answer. "Well, a lot of them are partway. Everyone who's recovered from surgery is either humanized or hooked up.

"So how many haven't been operated on? How many people in this building can *fight*?"

"Maybe twenty-five, thirty. Most over in E Wing. The ones who aren't under guard downstairs."

"Let's go there. Find as many weapons as we can."

Claude came up behind him. "We had lots of NLIs in the old soldierboys"—the somewhat pacifistic weapons of nonlethal intent—"and some of them must still be intact."

"Get them, then. Meet us over at E Wing."

"Let's take the fire escape," Amelia said. "We can sneak around to E without going through the lobby."

"Good. Do we have all the soldierboys?" They started toward the fire escape.

"Four," Claude said. "But the other six are harmless, immobilized."

"Do the enemy shoes know yet?"

"Not yet."

"Well, we can capitalize on that. Where's Eileen?"

"Down in the mess hall. She's trying to figure out a way to disarm the shoes without anybody getting hurt."

"Yeah, good luck." Julian opened the window and looked out cautiously. Nobody in sight. But then, down the hall, the elevator pinged.

"Everybody look away and cover your ears," Claude said. When the elevator door opened, he launched a concussion grenade down the hall.

The flash and bang blinded and deafened the shoes who had been sent to check on Blaisdell. They started shooting at random. Claude stepped between the firing and the window. "Better move," he said unnecessarily. Julian was pushing Amelia through the window in an ungentlemanly way, and Marty was about to crawl over both of them.

They pounded down the metal steps and sprinted toward the ell of E Wing. Claude fired scary bursts that just missed them, alternating machine gun and laser, that chewed up and scorched the ground to their left and right in the darkness.

The people in E Wing had already armed themselves as much as possible—there was a storage room with a rack of six M-31s and a box of grenades—and had improvised a defensive position by piling up mattresses in a shoulder-high semicircle at the end of the main corridor. Their lookout, fortunately, recognized Julian, so when they burst through the front door they weren't mowed down by the distinctly unhumanized, and completely terrified, group behind the mattresses.

Julian outlined the situation for them. Claude said that two of the soldierboys had gone outside to check on the remains of our original soldierboys, the ones with weapons of nonlethal intent. The current crop of soldierboys were peaceful types, but it's hard to express your pacifism with grenades and lasers. Tear gas and vomiting agent didn't kill, but it was less dangerous just to put people to sleep and collect their weapons.

As long as the enemy shoes stayed inside, that was a possibility. Unfortunately, Building 31 wasn't set up the way the Guadalajara clinic and St. Bart's were, where you could maneuver people into the right room and push a button and knock them out. But two of the original soldierboys had been carrying crowd-control canisters of Sweet Dreams, which was a combination knockout gas and euphoriant—you put them to sleep and they wake up laughing.

Both of those machines, though, were wreckage strewn along about a hundred meters of beach. The two searchers sorted through the scattered junk pile and did come up with three intact gas canisters. But they were all identical modules; there was no way to tell whether they would make you sleep or cry or puke. With a normal cage hookup, the mechanics could have let out a little gas and smelled it, but they couldn't smell anything with the remote.

They didn't have a lot of time to work on the problem, either. Blaisdell had covered his tracks well, so they weren't getting any long-distance calls from the Pentagon, but there was plenty of curiosity in Portobello itself. For a training exercise, aspects of it were profoundly real; two civilians had been injured by stray rounds. Most of the city was huddled in cellars. Four squad cars of police ringed the entrance to the base, with eight nervous officers hiding behind their cars shouting, in English and Spanish, at a soldierboy guard that didn't respond. They couldn't know it was empty.

"Be back in a minute." The soldierboy controlled by Claude went rigid as its operator rotated to check out the six immobilized ones. When he got to the one at the front gate, he fired a few laser bursts at the tires of the squad cars, which made nice explosions.

He inhabited one in the mess hall for a few minutes while Eileen expedited a solution to the lady-and-the-tiger canister problem. She took three "prisoners" (choosing among officers she didn't care for) and marched them down to the beach.

It turned out that they did have one each of each variety: one colonel fell asleep blissfully and another was blinded by tears. A general got to practice his projectile vomiting technique.

Claude rotated back to E Wing when Eileen's soldierboy walked into the mess hall with a gas canister under its arm. "I think we're almost out of danger," he said. "Anybody know where we can find a few hundred yards of rope?"

i did know where some rope was stashed, clothesline in the laundry room, I guess in case all the dryers broke down at the same time. (Thanks to my exalted former position in Building 31, I may have been the *only* person who knew about the rope, or where you could find three dusty cans of twelve-year-old peanut butter.)

We waited a half hour for fans to blow out the residual Sweet Dreams, and then went into the mess hall to sort through friends and foe, disarming and tying up Blaisdell's troops. All men, it turned out, all built like fullbacks.

There was enough of the Sweet Dreams hanging around to give you a little buzz, relaxing and uninhibiting. We stacked Blaisdell's commandos in pairs, face to face, assuming and hoping they would wake up in a homophobic panic. (A side effect of Sweet Dreams for males is profound tumescence.)

One of the shoes had a bandolier of tumbler ammunition. I took it outside and sat on the steps, my head clearing as I shoved the rounds into the weapon's side port. There was a faint glow to the east. The sun was about to rise on a most interesting day. Maybe my last.

Amelia came out and sat down next to me silently. She stroked my arm.

"How are you doing?" I asked.

"I'm not a morning person." She took my hand and kissed it. "It must be hell on you."

"I took my pills." I jammed the last round in and hefted it. "I killed a major general in cold blood. The army's going to hang me."

"It was as you told Claude," she said. "Self-defense. Defending the whole world. The man was the worst kind of traitor imaginable."

"Save it for the court martial." She leaned against me, crying softly. I put the gun down and held her. "I don't know what the hell's going to happen now. I don't think Marty does, either."

A stranger came running toward us, his hands in the

air. I picked up the weapon and pointed it in his direction. "This facility is closed to unauthorized personnel."

He stopped about twenty feet away, his hands still in the air. "Sergeant Billy Reitz, sir, motor pool. What on earth is going on?"

"How did you get in here?"

"I just ran by the soldierboy; nothing happened. What *is* all this craziness?"

"As I said—"

"I don't mean in there!" He gestured wildly. "I mean *out here*!"

Amelia and I looked out past the compound's fence. In the dim dawn light stood thousands of silent people, stark naked.

the fewer than twenty individuals who comprised the Twenty were able to solve interesting and subtle problems with their combined experience and intelligence. They'd had this enhanced ability from the first instant they were humanized.

The thousands of POWs in the Canal Zone were a much larger entity, which only had two problems to work on: How do we get out of here? and What then?

Getting out was so easy as to be almost trivial. Most of the labor in the camp was done by POWs; together, they knew more about how it actually ran than did the soldiers and computers that ran it. Taking over the computers was simple, a matter of properly timing a simulated medical emergency in order to get the right woman (whom they knew to be kindhearted) to leave her desk for a crucial minute.

This was at two in the morning. By two-thirty, all the soldiers had been awakened at gunpoint and marched to a maximum-security compound. They gave up without a shot being fired, which was not surprising, given that they faced thousands of apparently angry armed enemy prisoners. They couldn't know that the enemy were not really angry, and constitutionally unable to pull the trigger.

None of the POWs knew how to operate a soldierboy, but they could turn them off from Command and Control, and leave them immobile while they pried the mechanics out of their cages, and took them down to join the shoes in prison. They left them plenty of prison food and water, and then went on to the next step.

They could have simply escaped and dispersed. But then the war would go on, the war that had turned their peaceful, prosperous country into a strangled battlefield.

They had to go to the enemy. They had to offer themselves.

There were regular freight shipments between Portobello and CZ via monorail. They left their weapons behind, along with a few people who could speak perfect American English (to maintain for a few hours the illusion of a functioning POW camp), and crowded into a few freight cars manifested as fresh fruit and vegetables.

As the cars pulled in to the commissary station, they all undressed, so as to present themselves as totally unarmed and vulnerable—and also to confuse the Americans, who were strange about nudity.

Several of their number had been sent to the camp from Portobello, so when the doors opened and they stepped in unison into the shocked floodlights, they knew exactly where to go.

Building 31.

i watched the soldierboy at the guard box teeter for a second and then swivel, taking in the magnitude of the phenomenon.

"What the hell is going on?" Claude's voice boomed out. "*¿Qué pasa?*"

A wrinkled old man shuffled forward, holding a portable jack transfer box. A shoe rushed up behind him, raising an M-31 butt-first.

"Stop!" Claude said, but it was too late. The buttplate smacked into the old man's skull with a cracking sound, and he skidded forward to lie at the soldierboy's feet, unconscious or dead.

It was a scene the whole world would see the next day, and nothing Marty could have orchestrated would have had such an effect.

The POWs turned to look at the shoe with expressions of quiet pity, forgiveness. The huge soldierboy knelt down and carefully scooped up the frail body, cradling him, and looked down at the shoe. "He was just an old man, for Christ's sake," he said quietly.

And then a girl of about twelve picked the box up off the ground and pulled out one cable and offered it wordlessly to the soldierboy. It went down on one knee and accepted it, awkwardly plugging it in while not letting go of the old man. The girl plugged the other jack into her own skull.

The sun comes up fast in Portobello, and for the couple of minutes that tableau lasted, thousands of still people and one machine in thoughtful communion, the street began to glow, gold and rose.

Two shoes in hospital whites came up with a stretcher. Claude unjacked and gently lowered the body into their care. "—This is Juan José de Cordoba," he said in Spanish. "—Remember his name. The first casualty of the last war."

He took the little girl's hand and they walked toward the entrance.

they did call it The Last War, perhaps too optimistically, and there were tens of thousands more casualties. But Marty had predicted the course of it and the outcome pretty accurately.

The POWs, who collectively called themselves Los Liberados, "the Freed," actually absorbed Marty and his group, and led the way to peace.

They started out with an impressive display of intellectual force. They deduced from first principles the nature of the signal that would turn off the Jupiter Project, and used a small radio telescope in Costa Rica to bleep the signal out there—saving the world, as an opening move in an enterprise that resembled a game as much as a war. A game whose goal was to discover its own rules.

A lot that happened over the next two years was difficult for we merely normal people to understand. In a way, the conflict ultimately would be almost Darwinian, one ecological niche contested by two different species. Actually, we were subspecies, *Homo sapiens sapiens* and *Homo sapiens pacificans,* because we could interbreed. And there never was any doubt that *pacificans* was going to win in the long run.

When they began to isolate us "normals," who would be the subnormals in less than a generation, Marty asked me to be the chief liaison for the ones in the Americas, who would be populating Cuba, Puerto Rico, and British Columbia. I said no, but eventually gave in to wheedling. There were only twenty-three normals in the world who had once had the experience of jacking with the humanized. So we would be a valuable resource to the other normals who were filling up Tasmania, Taiwan, Sri Lanka, Zanzibar, and so on. I supposed eventually we would be called "islanders." And the humanized would take over our former name.

Two years of chaos stubbornly resisting the new order. It all sort of crystallized that first day, though, after Claude had taken the little girl in to jack completely two-way with her brothers and sisters in Building 31.

It was about noon. Amelia and I were dog-tired, but unwilling, almost unable, to sleep. I certainly was never going to sleep in that room again, though an orderly had come by and discreetly told me that it had been "tidied up." With buckets and scrub brushes and a body bag or two.

A woman had come by with baskets of bread and hard-boiled eggs. We spread a sheet of newspaper on the steps and assembled lunch, slicing the eggs onto the bread.

A middle-aged woman came up smiling. I didn't recognize her at first. "Sergeant Class? Julian?"

"*Buenos días,*" I said.

"I owe you everything," she said, her voice shaking with emotion.

Then it clicked, her voice and face. "Mayor Madero."

She nodded. "A few months ago, you saved me from killing myself, aboard that helicopter. I went to la Zona and was *conectada,* and now I live; more than live. Because of your compassion and swiftness.

"All the time I was changing, these past two weeks, I was hoping you would still be alive so that we could, as you say, *jack* together." She smiled. "Your funny language.

"And then I come here and find out that you live but have been blinded. But I have been with those who knew you and loved you when you could see into each other's hearts."

She took my hand and looked at Amelia and offered her other hand. "Amelia . . . we also have touched for one instant."

So the three of us held hands in a triangle, a silent circle. Three people who almost threw away their lives, for love, for anger, for grief.

"You . . . you," she said. "*No hay palabras.* There

are no words for this.'' She let go of our hands and walked toward the beach, wiping her eyes in the brightness.

We sat and watched Madero for some time, our bread and eggs drying in the sun, her hand clenched tight in mine.

Alone, together. The way it always used to be.

ALSO FROM

Hugo and Nebula award–winning author

JOE HALDEMAN

MARSBOUND

After training for a year and preparing to leave on a six-month journey through space, young Carmen Dula and her family embark on the adventure of a lifetime—they're going to Mars.

But on the Red Planet, things don't seem so different from Earth. That is until a simple accident leads Carmen to the edge of death—and she is saved by an angel.

An angel with too many arms and legs, a head that looks like a potato gone bad, and a message for the newly arrived human inhabitants of Mars:

We were here first...

M265T0810

A SEPARATE WAR
AND OTHER STORIES

36 Years of Award-Winning Stories from

JOE HALDEMAN

Winner of the Hugo, Nebula, and John W. Campbell Awards

"If there was a Fort Knox for the science fiction writers who really matter, we'd have to lock Haldeman up there."
—Stephen King

"Haldeman has long been one of our most aware, comprehensive, and necessary writers. He speaks from a place deep within the collective psyche and, more importantly, his own. His mastery is informed with a survivor's hard-won wisdom."
—Peter Straub

"Haldeman trips through history wearing alien goggles but his message is all about human nature."
—*Entertainment Weekly*

penguin.com

THE ULTIMATE WRITERS OF SCIENCE FICTION

John Barnes	Jack McDevitt
William C. Dietz	Alastair Reynolds
Simon R. Green	Allen Steele
Joe Haldeman	S. M. Stirling
Robert Heinlein	Charles Stross
Frank Herbert	Harry Turtledove
E. E. Knight	John Varley

penguin.com/scififantasy